Elfriede Jelinek was born in the Austrian alpine resort of Mürzzuschlag and grew up in Vienna, where she attended the famous Music Conservatory. The leading Austrian writer of her generation, her other works include *Wonderful, Wonderful Times*, *Women as Lovers*, and *Lust* (all published by Serpent's Tail), as well as plays and essays. In 1986 she was awarded the Heinrich Böll prize for her contribution to German language literature, and in 1998 she received the prestigious Georg Büchner Prize for the entirety of her work. In 2004, she was awarded the Nobel Prize for Literature.

THE
PIANO TEACHER

ELFRIEDE JELINEK

Translated by Joachim Neugroschel

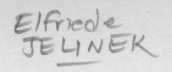

Elfriede
JELINEK

Library of Congress Catalog Card Number: 99-63596

A complete catalogue record for this book can be obtained from the British Library on request

The right of Elfriede Jelinek to be identified as the author of this work has been asserted by her in accordance with the Copyright, Designs and Patents Act 1988

Copyright © 1983 by Rowohlt Verlag GmbH
Translation copyright © 1988 by Wheatland Corporation

Originally published in German as *Die Klavierspielerin* by Rowohlt Verlag, Reinbek

First published in English by Weidenfeld & Nicolson, New York, 1988

First published in this 5-star edition in 1999

First published in 1989 by Serpent's Tail,
4 Blackstock Mews, London N4 2BT
Website: www.serpentstail.com

Printed in Great Britain by Mackays of Chatham

10 9 8 7 6

I

THE PIANO TEACHER, Erika Kohut, bursts like a whirlwind into the apartment she shares with her mother. Mama likes calling Erika her little whirlwind, for the child can be an absolute speed demon. She is trying to escape her mother. Erika is in her late thirties. Her mother is old enough to be her grandmother. The baby was born after long and difficult years of marriage. Her father promptly left, passing the torch to his daughter. Erika entered, her father exited. Eventually, Erika learned how to move swiftly. She had to. Now she bursts into the apartment like a swarm of autumn leaves, hoping to get to her room without being seen. But her mother looms before her, confronts her. She puts Erika against the wall, under interrogation—inquisitor and executioner in one, unanimously recognized as Mother by the State and by the Family. She investigates: Why has Erika come home so late? Erika dismissed her last student three hours ago, after heaping him with scorn. You must think I won't find out where you've been, Erika. A child should own up to her mother without being asked. But Mother never believes her because Erika tends to lie. Mother is waiting. She starts counting to three.

By the count of two, Erika offers an answer that deviates sharply from the truth. Her briefcase, filled with musical scores, is wrenched from her hands—and Mother instantly finds the bitter answer to all questions. Four volumes of Beethoven sonatas indignantly share cramped quarters with an obviously brand-new dress. Mother rails against the purchase. The dress, pierced by a hook, was so seductive at the shop, so soft and colorful. Now it lies there, a droopy rag, pierced by Mother's glare. The money was earmarked for their savings account. Now it's been spent prematurely. The dress could have been visible at any time as an entry in the bank book—if you didn't mind going to the linen closet, where the bank book peeks out from behind a pile of sheets. But today, the bank book went on an outing, a sum was withdrawn, and the result can now be seen. Erika should put this dress on whenever they wonder where the nice money went. Mother screams: You've squandered your future! We could have had a new apartment someday, but you couldn't wait. All you've got now is a rag, and it'll soon be out of fashion. Mother wants everything "someday." She wants nothing right now—except the child. And she always wants to know where she can reach the child in an emergency, in case Mama is about to have a heart attack. Mother wants to save now in order to enjoy someday. And then Erika goes and buys a dress, of all things! Something more fleeting than a dab of mayonnaise on a sardine sandwich. This dress will soon be totally out of fashion—not even next year, but next month. Money never goes out of fashion.

They are saving to buy a large condominium. The cramped apartment they now rent is so ancient, you might as well just abandon it. When they decide on the condominium, they will

be allowed to specify where to put the closets and partitions.
You see, an entirely new construction system is being used.
Every aspect is custom-designed, according to your precise
wishes. You pay your money and you get your choice. Mother,
who has only a tiny pension, gets her choice and Erika pays.
In the brand-new, state-of-the-art condominium, mother and
daughter will each have her own realm, Erika here, Mother
there, both realms neatly divided. However, they will have a
common living room to meet in. If they wish. But of course
they do, because they belong together. Even here, in this dump,
which is slowly falling to pieces, Erika already has her own
realm, her own roost, which she rules and is ruled in. It is only
a provisional realm; Mother can walk in at any time. There is
no lock on Erika's door. A child has no secrets from her mother.

Erika's living space consists of her own small room, where
she can do as she pleases. No one may interfere: this room is
her property. Mother's realm is the rest of the apartment: the
housewife, being in charge of everything, keeps house everywhere, and Erika enjoys the fruits of her mother's labor. Erika
has never had to do housework, because dustrags and cleansers
ruin a pianist's hands. During Mother's rare breathers, she
occasionally worries about her vast and varied holdings. You
can't always tell where everything is. Just where is Erika, that
fidgety property? Where is she wandering? Is she alone or with
someone else? Erika is such a live wire, such a mercurial thing.
Why, she may be running around at this very moment, up to
no good. Yet every day, the daughter punctually shows up
where she belongs: at home. Mother worries a lot, for the first
thing a proprietor learns, and painfully at that, is: Trust is fine,
but control is better. Her greatest anxiety is to keep her property immovable, tie it down so it won't run away. That's why
they have the TV set, which prefabricates, packages, and home-
delivers lovely images, lovely actions. So Erika is almost always

at home. If not, her mother knows where she's flitting about. Now and then, Erika may attend an evening concert, but she does so less and less. Instead, she sits at her piano, pounding away at her long-discarded career as a concert pianist. Or else she's an evil spirit, haunting some rehearsal with her students. Her mother can ring her up there in an emergency. Or else Erika enjoys performing with congenial colleagues, exuberantly playing chamber music. Her mother can telephone her at such times too. Erika pulls against apron strings, she repeatedly begs her mother not to telephone. But Mother ignores her pleas, for she alone dictates the shalts and shalt-nots. Mother also controls the general demand for her daughter, so that ultimately fewer and fewer people wish to see Erika, or even speak to her. Erika's vocation is her avocation: the celestial power known as music. Music fills her time completely. Her time has no room for anything else. Nothing offers so much pleasure as a magnificent performance by the finest virtuosi.

Erika visits a café once a month, but her mother knows which café, and she can ring her up there too. Mother makes generous use of this privilege, this homemade structure of security and intimacy.

❑

Time around Erika is slowly turning into a plaster cast. It crumbles the instant her mother strikes it. At such moments, Erika sits there, with remnants of time's brace around her thin neck. Mother has called her up, making her a laughingstock, and Erika is forced to admit: I have to go home now. Home. If ever you run into Erika on the street, she is usually on her way home.

Mother says: Erika suits me just fine the way she is. Nothing more will come of her. She's so gifted, she could have easily become a nationally renowned pianist—if only she'd left everything to me, her mother. But Erika ignored her mother's wishes, and sometimes yielded to other influences. Self-centered male love threatened to interfere with her studies. Superficial things like makeup and clothes reared their ugly heads. And her career ended before it ever got underway. Still, you need some kind of security: the position of piano teacher at the Vienna Conservatory. And she didn't even have to pay her dues by teaching at one of the neighborhood music schools, where so many people grind away their young lives, turning dusty gray, hunchbacked—a swiftly passing throng, barely noticed by the principal.

❑

But that vanity of hers, that wretched vanity. Erika's vanity is a major problem for her mother, driving thorns into her flesh. Erika's vanity is the only thing Erika should learn to do without. Better now than later. For in old age, which is just around the corner, vanity is a heavy load to bear. And old age is enough of a burden as it is. Oh, that Erika! Were the great musicians vain? They weren't. The only thing Erika should give up is her vanity. If necessary, Mother can smooth out the rough edges, so there won't be anything abrasive in Erika's character.

That's why Mother tries to twist the new dress out of Erika's convulsed fingers. But these fingers are too well trained. Let go, Mother snaps, hand it over! You've got to be punished for caring so much about trivial things. Life has punished you by ignoring you, and now your mother will punish you in the same way, ignoring you, even though you dress up and paint your face like a clown. Hand it over!

Erika dashes to the closet. Her dark suspicion has been confirmed several times in the past. Today, something else is missing: the dark-gray autumn ensemble. What's happened?

Whenever Erika realizes something is missing, she instantly knows whom to blame: the only possible culprit. You bitch, you bitch! Erika furiously yells at the superior authority. She grabs her mother's dark-blond hair with its gray roots. A beautician is expensive. So once a month, Erika colors her mother's hair with a brush and dye. Now, Erika yanks at the hair that she herself beautified. She pulls it furiously. Her mother weeps. When Erika stops pulling, her hands are filled with tufts of hair. She gazes at them, dumbfounded. Chemicals have already broken the resistance of this hair, which nature did not make all that strong in the first place. Erika doesn't know what to do with the discolored dark-blond tufts. She goes into the kitchen and throws them into the garbage can.

Mother, with less hair on her head, stands crying in the living room, where her Erika often gives private concerts. She is the very best performer ever to play in the living room, because no one else ever performs here. Mother's trembling hands still clutch the new dress. If she wants to resell it, she'll have to hurry. This design, with poppies as big as cabbages, can be worn for only one year—then never again. Mother's head hurts in the places where hair is now missing.

The daughter comes back, upset, weeping. She curses her mother, calls her a vicious bitch, but hopes Mother will make up with her right away. Kiss and make up. Mother swears that Erika's hand will drop off because she hit her mother and tore out her hair. Erika sobs louder and louder. She's sorry. After all, her mama works her fingers to the bone for her. As a rule, Erika instantly regrets anything she does to her, for she loves her, Mama's known her since infancy. Eventually Erika relents, as expected; she bawls bitterly. Mama is willing, all too willing, to give in; she cannot be truly angry at her daughter. Let me fix some coffee and we'll drink it together. During the coffee break, Erika feels even sorrier for her mother, and the final vestiges of her anger vanish in the cake. She examines the bare spots on her mother's head. But she doesn't know what to say, just as she didn't know what to do with the tufts of hair. She sheds a few more tears, for good measure, because Mother is old and won't live forever; and because Erika's youth is gone. Or, more generally, because all things pass and few ever return.

Mother now explains why a pretty girl never has to get gussied up. Erika confirms it. She has so many things hanging in her closet. But why bother? She never wears any of them. Her clothes hang there uselessly, decorating the closet. Mother can't always prevent Erika from buying something, but she can dictate what Erika puts on. Mother is an absolute ruler. She decides what Erika will wear outside the house. You are not going out in that getup, Mother dictates, fearing what will happen if Erika enters strange homes with strange men in them. Erika has resolved never to wear her clothes. It is a mother's duty to help a child make up her mind and to prevent wrong decisions. By not encouraging injuries, a mother avoids having to close wounds later on. Erika's mother prefers inflicting injuries herself, then supervising the therapy.

Their conversation becomes more and more vitriolic: Mother and daughter spray acid at students who do better than Erika or threaten to do so. You shouldn't give them free rein, you don't need to. You should stop them. But you let them get away with murder! You're not smart enough, Erika. If a teacher puts her mind to it, none of her students will succeed. No young woman will emerge from her classroom and pursue a career against Erika's wishes. You didn't make it—why should others reach the top? And from *your* musical stable to boot?

Erika, still sniveling, takes the poor dress into her arms. Mute and miserable, she hangs it in the closet, among the other dresses, pantsuits, skirts, coats, and ensembles. She never wears any of them. They are merely supposed to wait here until she comes home in the evening. Then, after laying them out, she drapes them in front of her body and gazes at herself in the mirror. For these clothes belong to her! Mother can take them away and sell them, but she cannot wear them herself, for Mother, alas, is too fat for these narrow sheaths. They do not fit her. These things are all Erika's. They are hers. Hers. The dress does not yet realize that its career has just been interrupted. It has been put away unused, and it will never be put on. Erika only wants to own it and look at it. Look at it from afar. She doesn't even want to try it on. It's enough for her to hold up this poem of cloth and colors and move it gracefully. As if a spring breeze were wafting it. Erika tried the dress on in the boutique, and now she will never slip into it again. Erika has already forgotten the brief, fleeting spell it cast on her in the shop. Now she has one more corpse in her wardrobe, but it is *her* property.

At night, when everyone else is asleep, Erika remains awake and alone, while the other half of this twosome (they are chained together by ties of blood) sleeps like a baby, dreaming up new methods of torture. Sometimes, very seldom, Erika gets up, opens the closet door, and caresses the witnesses to her secret desires. Actually, these desires are not all that secret; they shriek out their prices, they yell: Why did Erika go to all that trouble anyway? The colors shriek along, in a chorus of mixed voices. Where can you wear something like that without being hauled off by the police? (Normally, Erika wears only a skirt and a sweater or, in summer, a blouse.) Sometimes Mother wakes with a start, and she instinctively knows: Erika's looking at her clothes again. That vain piece of baggage! Mother is certain, for the closet doors do not squeak just to amuse the closet.

Worst of all, these purchases keep the new apartment beyond reach forever, and Erika is always in danger of falling, tumbling, into love. Suddenly they would have a cuckoo egg, a male in their nest. Tomorrow, at breakfast, Erika can expect a severe dressing-down for her frivolity. Why, Mother could have died yesterday from injuries done to her hair, from the shock. Erika will be given a deadline for the next installment on the apartment; she'll simply have to give more private lessons.

The only item missing from her dismal wardrobe is, fortunately, a wedding gown. Mother does not wish to become a mother-in-law. She prefers remaining a normal mother; she is quite content with her status.

But today is today. Time to sleep! That's what Mother, in her matrimonial bed, demands. But Erika is still rotating in front of her mirror. Mother's orders smash into her back like hatchets. Erika quickly touches a fetchingly flowery cocktail dress, barely grazing its hem. These flowers have never breathed fresh air, nor have they ever experienced water. The dress, as Erika assures her mother, comes from a first-class fashion house in the heart of Vienna. Its quality and workmanship will make it a joy forever. It fits Erika like a glove (not too much junk food!). The instant she saw the dress, Erika had a vision: I can wear it for years, and it will always be at the height of fashion. It will never sink from that height by even a hair's breadth. This argument is wasted on her mother. Mama should do some careful soul-searching. Didn't she wear a similar dress when she was young? But she denies it on principle. Nonetheless, Erika concludes that this purchase makes sense. The dress will never be out of date; Erika will still be able to wear it in twenty years.

Fashions change quickly. The dress remains unworn, although in perfect shape. But no one asks to see it. Its prime is past, ignored, and it will never come again—or at best in twenty years.

◻

Some students rebel against their piano teacher. But their parents force them to practice art, and so Professor Kohut can likewise use force. Most of the keyboard pounders, however, are well-behaved and interested in the art they are supposedly mastering. They care about it even when it is performed by others, whether at a music society or in a concert hall. The students compare, weigh, measure, count. Many foreigners come to Erika, more and more each year. Vienna, the city of music! Only the things that have proven their worth will continue to do so in this city. Its buttons are bursting from the fat white paunch of culture, which, like any drowned corpse that is not fished from the water, bloats up more and more.

The closet receives the new dress. One more! Mother doesn't like seeing Erika leave the apartment. Her dress is too flashy, it doesn't suit the child. Mother says there has to be a limit. Erika doesn't know what she means. There's a time and a place for everything, that's what Mother means.

Mother points out that Erika is not just a face in the crowd: She's one in a million. Mother never stops making that point. Erika says that she, Erika, is an individualist. She claims she cannot submit to anyone or anything. She has a hard time just fitting in. Someone like Erika comes along only once, and then never again. If something is especially irreplaceable, it is called Erika. If there's one thing she hates, it's standardization in any shape, for example a school reform that ignores individual qualities. Erika will not be lumped with other people, no matter how congenial they may be. She would instantly stick out. She is simply who she is. She is herself, and there's nothing she can do about it. If Mother can't see bad influences, she can at least sense them. More than anything, she wants to prevent Erika from being thoroughly reshaped by a man. For Erika is an individual, although full of contradictions. These contradictions force Erika to protest vigorously against any kind of standardization. Erika is a sharply defined individual, a personality. She stands alone against the broad mass of her students, one against all, and she turns the wheel of the ship of art. No thumbnail sketch could do her justice. When a student asks her what her goal is, she says, "Humanity," thus summing up Beethoven's *Heiligenstadt Testament* for her pupils—and squeezing in next to the hero of music, on his pedestal.

Erika gets to the heart of artistic and individual considerations: She could never submit to a man after submitting to her mother for so many years. Mother is against Erika's marrying later on, because "my daughter could never fit in or submit anywhere." That's the way she is. She's no sapling anymore. She's unyielding. So she shouldn't marry. If neither spouse can yield, then a marriage is doomed. Just be yourself, Mother tells Erika. After all, Mother made Erika what she is. You still aren't married, Fräulein Erika? the dairy woman asks, and so does the butcher. You know I can never find a man I like, Erika replies.

Erika comes from a family of signposts that stand all alone in the countryside. There are few of them. The members of her family breed sparingly and sluggishly, which is how they deal with life in general. Erika did not see the light of day until the twentieth year of her parents' marriage—a marriage that drove her father up the wall and behind the walls of an asylum, where he posed no danger to the world.

Maintaining noble silence, Erika buys a stick of butter. She's still got her mom, she don't need no Tom. No sooner does this family get a new member than he is rejected and ejected. They make a clean break with him as soon as he proves useless and worthless. Mother taps the family members with a mallet, separating them, each in turn. She sorts and rejects. She tests and ejects. In this way, there'll be no parasites, who always want to take things that you want to keep. We'll just keep to ourselves, won't we, Erika? We don't need anyone else.

Time passes, and we pass the time. They are enclosed together in a bell jar: Erika, her fine protective hulls, her mama. The jar can be lifted only if an outsider grabs the glass knob on top and pulls it up. Erika is an insect encased in amber, timeless, ageless. She has no history, and she doesn't make a fuss. This insect has long since lost its ability to creep and crawl. Erika is baked inside the cake pan of eternity. She joyfully shares this eternity with her beloved composers, but she certainly can't hold a candle to them when it comes to being loved. Erika struggles for a tiny place within eyeshot of the great musical creators. This place is fought for tooth and nail; all Vienna would like to put up a tiny shack here. Erika stakes off her lot, a reward for her competence, and begins digging the foundation pit. She has earned her place fair and square, by studying and interpreting! After all, performance is form, too. The performer always spices the soup of his playing with something of his own, something personal. He drips his heart's blood into it. The interpreter has his modest goal: to play well. He must, however, submit to the creator of the work, says Erika. She willingly admits that this is a problem for her. She simply cannot submit. Still, Erika has one goal in common with all the other interpreters: to be better than the rest!

❑

SHE is pulled into streetcars by the weight of musical instruments, which dangle from her body, in front and behind, along with the stuffed briefcases. An encumbered butterfly. The creature feels it has dormant strength for which music does not suffice. The creature clenches its fist around the handles of violins, violas, flutes. It likes to make negative use of its energy, although it does have a choice. Mother offers the selection: a broad spectrum of teats on the udder of the cow known as music.

SHE bangs into people's backs and fronts with her stringed instruments and wind instruments and her heavy musical scores. Her weapons bounce off these people, whose fat is like a rubber buffer. Sometimes, if the whim strikes her, she holds an instrument and a briefcase in one hand while insidiously thrusting her other fist into someone's winter coat, rain cape, or loden jacket. She is blaspheming the Austrian national costume, which tries to ingratiate itself with her, grinning from all its staghorn buttons. Emulating a kamikaze pilot, she uses herself as a weapon. Then again, with the narrow end of the instrument (sometimes the violin, sometimes the heavier viola), she beats into a cluster of work-smeared people. If the trolley is mobbed, say around six in the evening, she can injure a lot of people just by swinging around. There's no room to take a real swing. SHE is the exception to the norm that surrounds her so repulsively. And her mother likes explaining to her very meticulously that she is an exception, for she is Mother's only child, and has to stick to the straight and narrow. Every day, the streetcar shows her the people she never wants to become. SHE plows through the gray flood of passengers with or without tickets, those who have just gotten in and those who are about to leave, those who have gotten nothing where they were and who have nothing to expect where they are going. They are anything but chic. Some get out before they have even sat down properly.

If mass anger orders her to get out, even if she is still far from home, her own anger, concentrated in her fist, yields obediently, and she actually gets out—but only to wait patiently

for the next trolley, which is as certain to come as the amen
at the end of a prayer. These are chains that never break. Then,
all fueled up, she mounts a new assault. Bristling with instruments, she arduously staggers into the mobs of homebound
workers, detonating among them like a fragmentation bomb.
If need be, she hides her true feelings and says, "Pardon me,
I'm getting off here." The approval is unanimous. She should
leave the clean public vehicle at once! It's not meant for people
like her! Paying passengers shouldn't let people get away with
things like this.

They look at the music student and imagine that music has
raised her spirits; but the only thing that's raised is her fist.
Sometimes a gray young man with repulsive things in a thread-
bare haversack is unjustly accused, for he is a more likely
culprit. He'd better get out and go back to his friends before
he catches it from a powerful loden-sheathed arm.

The mass anger, which has, after all, paid its fare, is always
in the right for its three schillings and can prove it in case the
tickets are inspected. During a surprise inspection the mass
anger proudly shows its marked ticket and has the trolley car
all to itself. In this way, it saves itself weeks of unpleasant,
fearful purgatory, wondering whether an inspector might
come.

A lady, who feels pain as deeply as you do, suddenly shrieks.
Somebody's kicked her shin, that vital part on which her weight
partially rests. In this dangerous shoving and pushing, the
culprit, true to the principle of guilt, cannot be determined.
The crowd is battered with a barrage of oaths, curses, insults,
complaints, entreaties, accusations. The laments pour out of
mouths that vent their spleen over their owners' lives, the
charges are discharged upon other people. The passengers are
squeezed together like sardines, but they are not packed in oil.
They won't be anointed until later.

SHE furiously kicks a hard bone, which belongs to a man. One day, SHE is with a fellow student, a girl, who has two wonderful high heels that blaze as two eternal flames, and a new fur-lined coat in the latest style. The girl amiably asks Erika: What are you dragging around, what's it called? I meant this case here, and not your head up there. It's called a viola, SHE replies politely. A viooola? What a weird word, I've never heard it, lipstick-coated lips say in amusement. Someone carries something called a viooola, which doesn't serve any noticeable purpose. And everyone has to get out of the way because this viooola takes up so much space. SHE walks around with it in public, and no one catches her *in flagrante delicto*.

The people hanging heavily from the straps and those few lucky devils who can sit—they all crane their necks high out of their used-up torsos, but it's no use, they spot no one. There's no one they can gang up on for maltreating their legs with a hard object. "Someone stepped on my toes," and a deluge of foul language gushes from a mouth. Who did it? The First Viennese Trolley Court, infamous throughout the world, is in session in order to issue a warning and pass a sentence. In every war movie, there's always at least one person who volunteers, even if it's for a suicide mission. But this cowardly dog is hiding behind our patient backs. A whole batch of ratty workers, on the verge of retirement, with tool bags on their shoulders, shove and kick their way out of the trolley. They're deliberately walking to the next stop! When a ram disturbs the peace and quiet among all the sheep in the car, then you desperately need fresh air, and you find it outside. If you're going to chew out your wife at home, you have to have oxygen; otherwise you may not be up to chewing her out. Something with a vague color and shape starts swaying, slips along; someone screams as if stabbed. A thick, steamy mist of Viennese venom rolls across this public meadow. Someone even calls for an executioner because his evening has been ruined prematurely. My, but they're furious. Their evening relaxation, which should have begun twenty minutes ago, has not set in. Or else it has been abruptly cut off, like the colorfully printed package of the victim's life (with instructions), which he cannot put back on the shelf. (He cannot simply reach inconspicuously for a new, intact package; otherwise the salesgirl would have him arrested for shoplifting. Follow me quietly! But the door that leads, or seems to lead, into the manager's office is a phony door, and there are no announcements of weekly specials on the windows of the brand-new supermarket. There is nothing, absolutely nothing, only darkness. And the customer plunges into a bottomless pit.) Someone says in the officialese that is customary in public vehicles here: You are to vacate this trolley car without futher delay. A tuft of chamois hair grows rankly from a cranium; the man is disguised as a hunter.

SHE, however, bends in time, planning to try a new, nasty trick. First, SHE has to put down the bulky refuse of her instruments. They form a fence around her. She pretends to tie her shoelaces in order to prepare a noose for the next passenger. Almost casually, she viciously pinches the female calf to her left or her right (these women all look alike). A bruise awaits the victim. The disfigured passenger, a widow, shoots up, a bright, radiant, illuminated fountain at night—the fountain can at last be the focus of attention. The widow outlines her family connections tersely and precisely, and she ominously predicts that these connections (especially her dead husband) will wreak horrifying vengeance on her tormentor. She demands a policeman; but the police will not come, they cannot worry about everything.

The harmless expression of a musician is slipped over her face. SHE acts as if she were yielding to those mysterious powers of musical romanticism, powers moving to ever higher emotional peaks—she acts as if she could not be thinking about anything else in the world. The populace then speaks as if with one voice: It couldn't have been the girl with the machine gun. The populace is wrong again, as it is so often.

Occasionally, someone thinks harder and then eventually points to the true culprit: "You're the one!" SHE is asked what in the name of all that's holy she has to say for herself. SHE does not speak. The lead plug that her trainers have surgically inserted behind her soft palate prevents her from speaking, from unwittingly accusing herself. She does not defend herself. A few people pounce on a few others for accusing a deaf mute. But the voice of reason maintains that someone who plays the violin couldn't possibly be deaf. Perhaps she is only mute or perhaps she is taking the violin to someone else. Failing to reach an agreement, they give up their plan. Their minds are haunted by the thought of a glass of wine, which wipes out several pounds of other thoughts. The actual wine will demolish any remaining thoughts. This is the land of wines. This is the city of music. The girl peers into distant worlds of profound emotions, and her accuser can at best drown his sorrow in a glass of wine. So he falls silent under her gaze.

Shoving is beneath her dignity: The mob shoves, but not the violinist and violist. For the sake of these little trolley joys, she even puts up with coming home late—to find her mother standing there with a stopwatch and a warning. SHE endures such agonies, even though she has played all afternoon, focusing her mind, wielding her bow, and laughing at pupils who played worse than she. She wants to teach people how to be afraid, how to shudder. Such feelings run rampant through the playbills of Philharmonic Concerts.

A member of the Philharmonic audience reads the program notes and is prompted to tell someone else how profoundly his innermost being throbs with the pain of this music. He's read all about it. Beethoven's pain, Mozart's pain, Schumann's pain, Bruckner's pain, Wagner's pain. These pains are now his sole property, and he himself is the owner of the Pöschl Shoe Factory or Kotzler Construction Material Wholesalers. Beethoven manipulates the levers of fear, and these owners make their workers jump fearfully. There's also a Ph.D. here who's been intimate with pain for a long time. For the past ten years, she has been trying to fathom the ultimate secret of Mozart's Requiem. So far, she's gotten nowhere, for his opus is unfathomable. It is beyond our comprehension: The woman calls it the most brilliant work ever commissioned in the history of music. That is indisputable for her and for few other people. The Ph.D. is one of the chosen few who know that some things can never be fathomed, no matter how hard you try. What good are explanations? There is no possibility of explaining how such a work could ever have come into being. (The same holds true for certain poems, which should not be analyzed either.) A mysterious stranger in a coachman's black coat turned up and made the down payment for the Requiem. The Ph.D., and the others who have seen the Mozart movie, know that the mysterious stranger was—Death himself! By thinking this thought, she bites a hole in the flesh of one of the great geniuses and pushes her way inside. In rare cases, one grows along with the genius.

Ugly masses of people throng about HER uninterruptedly. People are always pushing their way into HER field of perception. The mob not only grabs hold of art without being entitled to do so, but it also enters the artist. It takes up residence inside the artist and smashes a few holes in the wall, windows to the outer world: The mob wants to see and be seen. With sweaty fingers, that cloddish mob is tapping out something that rightfully belongs to HER alone. Unasked, unbidden, they sing along with the cantilenas. Moistening their forefingers, they pursue

a theme, looking for the secondary theme, but failing to find
it. And so, nodding their heads, they are content to rediscover
and repeat the main theme. Recognizing it, they wag their
tails. For most of them, the principal charm of art is to recognize
something that they think they recognize. A wealth of sen-
sations overwhelms a butcher. He can't help it, even though
he is used to his bloody profession. He is paralyzed with astonishment. He sows not, he reaps not, he doesn't hear so well.
But if he goes to a public concert, people can see him. Next to
him, his better half; she wanted to come along.

SHE kicks the right heel of an old woman. SHE is able to
assign every phrase its preordained location. SHE alone can
take every sound and insert it in the right place, in its proper
niche. SHE packs the ignorance of these bleating lambs into
her own scorn, using it to punish them. Her body is one big
refrigerator, where Art is well stored.

HER instinct for cleanliness is astonishingly sensitive. Dirty
bodies form a resinous forest all around her. Not only the dirt
of bodies, but the grossest kinds of filth struggling out of arm-
pits and groins, the subtle urine stench of the old woman, the
nicotine gushing from the network of the old man's veins and
pores, those innumerable piles of lowest-quality food stewing
in the stomachs. Not only the faint wax stench of scurf and
scab, not only the stink of shit microtomes under the fingernails—a very, very faint odor, but the expert can sniff them
so easily, those residues left from burning colorless food, gray,
leathery delights (if they can be called delights). They torment
HER sense of smell, HER tastebuds. What upsets HER most
of all is the way these people dwell in one another, the way
they shamelessly take possession of one another. Each pushes
his way into other minds, into their innermost attention.

They have to be punished. By HER. And yet she can never
get rid of them. She shakes them, shreds them, like a dog

mauling its prey. And yet, unbidden, they rummage around in her, they observe HER innermost thoughts, and then they dare to say that they can't do anything with these thoughts, that they don't even like them. Why, they actually go so far as to say they don't like Webern or Schönberg.

Mother, without prior notice, unscrews the top of HER head, sticks her hand inside, self-assured, and then grubs and rummages about. Mother messes everything up and puts nothing back where it belongs. Making a quick choice, she plucks out a few things, scrutinizes them closely, and tosses them away. Then she rearranges a few others and scrubs them thoroughly with a brush, a sponge, and a dustrag. Next, she vigorously dries them off and screws them in again. The way you twist a knife into a meatgrinder.

An old woman has just gotten into the trolley, but she doesn't notify the conductor. She thinks she can keep her presence a secret. Actually, she got out of everything long ago, and she knows she did. Paying is too much trouble. She's already got her ticket to eternity in her handbag. The ticket must be valid in a streetcar, too.

Now some woman asks HER for directions, but SHE doesn't answer. SHE doesn't reply although SHE does know the way. The woman won't give up, she pokes her way through the entire car, pushing people aside so she can peer under seats and find her stop. She is a grim wanderer along forest paths, and she has a habit of using her skinny cane to tickle ant hills and arouse the ants from their contemplative lives. She makes the disturbed creatures spray acid. She is one of those people who leave no stone unturned, lest they find a snake underneath. Every clearing, no matter how small, is conscientiously combed for mushrooms or berries. That's the kind of people they are. They squeeze every last drop from every single artwork and explain it vociferously to everyone else. In parks, they use their handkerchiefs to dust a bench before sitting down. In restaurants, they polish the silverware with a napkin. They go through a relative's suit with a fine-tooth comb, hunting for hair, letters, grease spots.

And now this lady vociferously complains that no one can give her the information she needs. She says that no one *wants* to give it to her. This lady represents the ignorant majority, which does however possess one thing in abundance: It is raring for a fight. She'll challenge anyone if she has to.

She gets off at the very street the woman asked about, and as she steps out, she sneers at her.

The buffalo understands, and she is so angry that her pistons grind to a halt. A short time from now, she will describe these moments of her life to a friend while devouring sauerbraten with beans. She will prolong her life by the length of her story, even though time will wear on inexorably as she tells it, thus depriving her of the chance to have a new experience.

SHE peers back several times at the completely disoriented woman before setting off on the familiar road to her familiar home. SHE smirks at the woman, forgetting that a few minutes from now, SHE will feel the hot flame of her mother's blowtorch and SHE will be burned to a pile of ashes because SHE is late in getting home. No art can possibly comfort HER then, even though art is credited with many things, especially an ability to offer solace. Sometimes, of course, art creates the suffering in the first place.

❑

Erika, the meadow flower. That's how she got her name: *erica*. Her pregnant mother had visions of something timid and tender. Then, upon seeing the lump of clay that shot out of her body, she promptly began to mold it relentlessly in order to keep it pure and fine. Remove a bit here, a bit there. Every child instinctively heads toward dirt and filth unless you pull it back. Mother chose a career for Erika when her daughter was still young. It had to be an artistic profession, so she could squeeze money out of the arduously achieved perfection, while average types would stand around the artist, admiring her, applauding her. Now, Erika has at last been patted into perfection. Such a girl was not meant to do crude things, heavy manual labor, housework. She was destined, congenitally, for the subtleties of classical dance, song, music. A world-famous pianist—that is Mother's ideal. And to make sure the child finds her way through every entanglement, Mother sets up guideposts along the way, smacking Erika if she refuses to practice. Mother warns Erika about the envious horde that always tries to destroy other people's achievements—a horde made up almost entirely of men. Don't get distracted! Erika is never allowed to rest at any level she reaches, never allowed to catch her breath and lean on her icepick. For she has to keep climbing. To the next level. Forest animals come too close for comfort; they want to turn Erika into an animal. Competitors try to lure Erika to a cliff, pretending they'd like to show her the view. But how easily one can plunge down! Mother graphically describes the chasm, so her child will watch out. The peak offers international fame, which is never reached by most climbers. A cold wind blows up there, the artist is lonesome and admits his solitude. So long as Mother lives and continues planning Erika's future, there is only one possibility for the child: the top of the world.

Mama pushes from below, for she has both feet planted solidly on the ground. And soon Erika no longer stands on the inherited motherland, she is on someone else's back, someone she has ousted with her back-stabbing. What shaky ground! Erika stands on tiptoe, on her mother's shoulders. Her trained fingers clutch the peak, which, alas, soon turns out to be merely a crag; it only looks like the peak. Straining the muscles of her upper arm, Erika hoists and heaves herself up. Now, her nose is already over the edge, but all she sees is a new rock, steeper than the first. However, an ice factory of fame has a branch here, which keeps huge blocks in storage, thereby holding down its overhead. Erika, an adolescent, licks at one of the blocks and believes that a recital she gives is already the Chopin Competition. She believes that the peak is only a few inches away!

Mother taunts Erika for being too modest. You're always the last! Noble restraint is useless. One should always be at least in third place; anything less is garbage. That's what Mother says. She knows best; she wants only the best for her child. She won't let her stay out in the street: After all, she shouldn't get involved in athletic competitions and neglect practicing.

Erika doesn't like being conspicuous. She elegantly holds back (the offended mother-animal laments) and waits for others to achieve something for her. Mother, bitterly complaining that she has to do everything for the child herself, jubilantly plunges into the thick of the fray. Erika nobly puts herself last, and her efforts don't even bring her a couple of pennies for stockings or panties.

Mother nags away at friends and relatives (of whom there are very few, for she broke with them long ago; she wanted to keep Erika safe from their influence). Mother tells all these people that Erika is a genius. She says she keeps realizing it more and more clearly. Erika is truly a keyboard genius, but she has not been properly discovered as yet. Otherwise, she would have long since soared over the mountains, like a comet. Compared with that, the birth of Jesus was chickenshit.

The neighbors agree. They enjoy listening when the girl practices. It's like the radio, only you don't need to have a set. All you have to do is open the windows and perhaps the doors, the music comes in, spreading like poison gas into every nook and cranny. People indignant about the noise stop Erika whenever they run into her, and they ask her for peace and quiet. Mother tells Erika how enthusiastic the neighbors are about her outstanding mastery of the keyboard. Erika is carried along like a dribble of spit on a thin stream of maternal enthusiasm. Later on, she is surprised when a neighbor complains. Her mother never said anything about complaints!

Eventually, Erika outdoes her mother when it comes to sniffing at people. Who cares about those laymen, Mama. Their powers of judgment are crude, their sensibilities are unrefined; only the professionals count. Mother retorts: Do not make fun of praises from simple people. They listen to music with their hearts and enjoy it more than those who are spoiled, jaded, blasé. Mother knows nothing about music, but she forces her child into its yoke. A fair if vindictive rivalry develops between mother and daughter, for the child soon realizes that she has outgrown her mother with regard to music. The daughter is the mother's idol, and Mother demands only a tiny tribute: Erika's life. Mother wants to utilize the child's life herself.

Erika is not allowed to associate with ordinary people, but she is permitted to listen to their praises. Unfortunately, the experts do not praise Erika. A dilettantish, unmusical Fate has exalted other people. But it has passed Erika by, averting its face. After all, Fate wants to remain disinterested and not be taken in by an attractive mask. Erika is not pretty. Had she wanted to be pretty, her mother would have promptly ordered her to forget it. Erika stretches her arms out to Fate. But it's no use; Fate will not turn her into a pianist. Erika is hurled to the ground as sawdust. Erika does not understand what is happening to her, for she has been as good as the masters for a long time now.

Then, one day, at an important concert at the Academy of

Music, Erika fails totally. She fails in front of the friends and
relatives of her competitors and in front of her mother, who
sits there alone. Mother spent her last penny on the dress Erika
wears for this recital. Afterward, Mother slaps Erika's face, for
even musical laymen could read Erika's failure in her face if
not her hands. Furthermore, Erika did not choose a piece for
the broadly rolling masses. She decided on a Messiaen, against
her mother's urgent warning. This is no way for the child to
smuggle herself into the hearts of the masses, whom mother
and child have always despised: the mother because she has
always been merely a small, plain part of the masses; and the
child because she would never want to become a small, plain
part of the masses.

Erika reels from the podium, shamefaced. She is received
shamefully by her sole audience: Mother. Erika's teacher, who
used to be a famous pianist, vehemently scolds her for her lack
of concentration. A wonderful opportunity has been wasted,
and it knocks but once. Someday soon, Erika will be envied by
no one, idolized by no one.

What else can she do but become a teacher? A difficult step
for a master pianist, who is suddenly confronted with stammering freshmen and soulless seniors. Conservatories and acad-
emies, as well as private teachers, patiently accept a lot of
students who really belong on a garbage dump or, at best, a
soccer field. Many young people are still driven to art, as in
olden times. Most of them are driven by their parents, who
know nothing about art—only that it exists. And they're so
delighted that it exists! Of course, art turns many people away,
for there has to be a limit. The limits between the gifted and
the ungifted. Erika, as a teacher, is delighted to draw that limit.
Selecting and rejecting make up for a lot. After all, she was
once treated like a goat and separated from the sheep. Erika's
students are a coarsely diverse mixture, and none of them has

ever been really tested or tasted. One seldom finds a red rose among them. Occasionally, during the first year, Erika manages to wrest a Clementi sonata from one or two students, while others still grunt and root about in Czerny's elementary études. These students are then discarded after the intermediary examination, because they can't find the wheat and they can't find the chaff, even though their parents are firmly convinced that their children will soon feast on nectar and ambrosia.

Erika's mixed joys are the good advanced students, who make an effort. She can wrest all sorts of things from them: Schubert sonatas, Schumann's *Kreisleriana*, Beethoven sonatas, those high points in the life of a piano student. The work tool, a Bösendorfer, excretes an intricate blend. And next to it stands the teacher's Bösendorfer, which only Erika can play, unless two students are practicing a piece for two pianos.

After three years, the piano student has to enter the next level; to do so, he must pass an exam. Most of the work for this exam is assigned to Erika; she has to take the idling student engine and step on the gas, slam down hard in order to rev it up. Sometimes the engine doesn't really catch, it would rather be doing something else, something that has little to do with music—for instance, pouring melodious words into a girl's ear. Erika doesn't care for such behavior; she tries to stop it whenever she can. Often, before an exam, Erika sermonizes: Fluffing a note, she says, isn't as bad as rendering a piece in the wrong spirit, a spirit that does not do justice to it. She is preaching to deaf ears, which have been closed by fear. For many of her students, music means climbing from the depths of the working class to the heights of artistic cleanliness. Later on, they too will become piano teachers. They are afraid that when they play at the examination, their sweaty, fear-filled fingers, driven by a swifter pulse beat, will slip to the wrong keys. Erika can talk a blue streak about interpretation, but the only thing the students wish to do is play the piece correctly to the end.

Erika likes thinking about Walter Klemmer, a nice-looking blond boy, who lately has been the first to show up in the morning and the last to leave in the evening. A busy beaver, Erika must admit. He is a student at the Engineering Academy, where he is learning all about electricity and its beneficial features. Recently he has been listening to all the music students, from the first hesitant picking and pecking to the final crack of Chopin's Fantasy in F Minor, Op. 49. He seems to have a lot of time on his hands, which is rather unlikely for a student in the final phase of his studies. One day, Erika asks him whether he wouldn't rather practice Schönberg, instead of lounging around so unproductively. Doesn't he have any studying to do? No lectures, no drills, nothing? He says he's on his semester break, which hadn't occurred to Erika, although she teaches so many students. Vacation at the music academy doesn't coincide with vacation at the university. Strictly speaking, there are no holidays for art; art pursues you everywhere, and that's just fine with the artist.

Erika is surprised: How come you always show up here so early, Herr Klemmer? If a student is working on Schönberg's 33b, as you are, he can't possibly be interested in minor frivolities. So why do you listen to the others? The hardworking student lies. He says you can profit from anything and everything, no matter how little it may be. You can learn a lesson from just about anything, says this con man, who has nothing better to do. He claims he can get something from even the least of his brothers, so long as he remains curious and thirsty for knowledge. Except that you have to overcome those minor things in order to get further. A student can't stay with the losers, otherwise his superiors will interfere.

Besides, the young man likes listening to his teacher perform, even if it's just singsong, tralala, or the B major scale. Don't start flattering your old teacher, Herr Klemmer. But he replies that she's not old, and he's not "flattering" her. I really mean every word I say, it comes from the bottom of my heart! Sometimes this nice-looking boy asks for a favor, extra homework, he'd like to practice something extra, because he's overzealous. He gazes expectantly at his teacher, hoping for a hint, lying in wait for a pointer. His teacher, on her high horse, cuts the young man down to size when she sneers: You still don't know the Schönberg all that well. The student enjoys being in the hands of such a teacher, even when she looks down at him while holding the reins tightly.

That dashing young man seems to be in love with you, Mother says venomously, in a bad mood, when she happens to call for Erika at the conservatory. She wants to take a walk with Erika, two women, arm in arm, intricately interwoven. The weather plays its part as the women walk. There are a lot of things to see in the shop windows—elegant shoes, pocketbooks, hats, jewelry—but Erika should not see them under any circumstances. That is why Mother came to pick her up. Mother takes Erika on a circuitous route, telling her it's because of the beautiful weather. The parks are blossoming, the roses and tulips are blooming, and the flowers certainly don't buy their dresses. Mother talks to Erika about natural beauty, which doesn't require any artificial embellishment. Natural beauty is beautiful on its own, just like you, Erika. Why all the baubles?

The outskirts of the city beckon with warm calls of nature, with fresh hay in the stables. Mother heaves a sigh of relief, she pushes her daughter past the boutiques. Mother is delighted that this stroll has once again cost her no more than some shoe leather. Better to wear worn shoes than to polish the boots of some shop owner.

The population in this part of Vienna is rather long in the tooth. You see lots of old women. Luckily this one old woman, Mother Kohut, has managed to obtain a younger hanger-on, of whom she can be proud, and who will take care of her until death do them part. Only death can separate them, and death is marked as the destination on Erika's suitcase. Sometimes, a series of murders takes place in this area, a couple of old crones die in their lairs, which are chock full of waste paper. God only knows where their bankbooks are; but the cowardly murderer knows it too, he looked under the mattress. The jewelry, what little there was, is also gone. And the only son, a silverware salesman, gets nothing. Vienna's slums are a popular area for murder. It's never hard to figure out where one of those old women lives. Just about every building here has at least one—she's the laughingstock of the other tenants. And when a man knocks and says he's the meter reader, but presents no ID card, she lets him in anyway. They've been warned often enough, but still they open their hearts and doors, for they are lonesome. That's what old Frau Kohut tells Fräulein Kohut, trying to discourage her from ever leaving her mother alone.

The other inhabitants here are petty officials and placid clerks. There are few children. The chestnut trees are blooming and the trees in the Prater are blossoming. The grapes are turning green in the Vienna Woods. Unfortunately, the Kohut ladies have to abandon all hope of ever going there for a good look, since they don't own a car.

However, they often take the trolley to a carefully chosen last stop, where they get out with all the other passengers and cheerfully stride off. Mother and daughter, looking for all the world like Charley Frankenstein's Wild Aunts, carry rucksacks on their shoulders. Or rather: only the daughter carries a rucksack, which protects Mother's few belongings, concealing them from curious eyes. Brogue shoes with Solid Soles. Protection

against rain is not forgotten (just read *The Hiker's Guide*).
Forewarned is forearmed. Otherwise you'll be left out in the
cold.

The two women stride along, hale and hearty. They never
sing, because, knowing a thing or two about music, they don't
care to violate music by singing. This is like the days of Eich-
endorff, Mother chirps, the important thing is your spirit, your
attitude toward nature! Nature itself is secondary! The two
women have the proper spirit, for they are able to delight in
nature wherever they catch sight of it. If they stumble upon a
rippling brook, they instantly drink fresh water from it. Let's
hope no doe has pissed into it. If they come to a thick tree
trunk or dense underbrush, they can take a piss themselves,
and the nonpisser stands guard to ward off any impudent
peepers.

By taking their hike, the two Kohut women store up energy
for a new work week, in which Mother will have little to do,
and Erika's blood will be sucked out by her students. Every
evening, Mother asks the same question: Did they give you a
hard time? No, it was all right, the frustrated pianist replies;
she still has hope, but Mother plucks it apart in her long-winded
way. Mother complains about Erika's lack of ambition. The
child has been hearing these wrong notes for more than thirty
years now. Feigning hope, the daughter realizes that the only
thing she can look forward to is tenure: the title of professor,
which she already uses and which is conferred by the president
of Austria. In a simple festivity celebrating many years of
service. Someday—and it's not that far off—she'll retire. Vienna is generous with pensions, but official retirement hits an
artistic career like a bolt of lightning. If you're struck, you feel
it. The City of Vienna brutally terminates the transmission of
art from one generation to the next. The two woman talk about
how greatly they look forward to Erika's retirement! They have

all sorts of plans for the future. By then, the condominium
will be shipshape, and the mortgage paid off. They'll also have
a piece of country property to build on. A cottage, for the two
Kohut women and no one else. Plan ahead. It's better to be an
ant than a grasshopper. By then, Mother will be one hundred
years old, but still sprightly.

The foliage in the Vienna Woods, ignited by the sunshine,
blazes on the slope.

Here and there, spring flowers peek out; mother and daugh-
ter pick them and pack them away. Serves the flowers right.
Insolence has to be punished, Frau Kohut puts her foot down.
The flowers are just right for the round light-green vase from
Gmunden, isn't that so, Erika?

□

The adolescent girl lives in a sanctuary, where no one is
allowed to bother her. She is shielded from influences, and
never exposed to temptations. This hands-off policy applies
only to pleasure, not work. Mother and grandmother, the female brigade, stand guard, rifle in hand, to protect Erika against
the male hunter lurking outside. They may even have to give
the intruder a physical warning. The two elderly women, with
their dried, sealed vaginas, throw themselves in front of every
man, to keep him away from their fawn. The young female
should not be bothered by love or pleasure. The vaginal lips
of the two old women have turned into siliceous stone. Rattling
dryly, their snatches snap like the jaws of a dying stag beetle,
but catch nothing. So the two women hold on to the young
flesh of their daughter and granddaughter, slowly mangling it,
while their shells keep watch to make sure no one else comes
along and poisons the young blood. They've got spies for miles
around to keep an eye on the girl outside the house; these spies
come for a cup of coffee and cheerfully reveal everything to

the women in charge of bringing up the child. Their tongues
loosened by the homemade cake, the spies report what they
saw the precious child doing with a student down by the dam.
The child will not be released from her domestic precinct until
she turns over a new leaf and swears off that man.

Their farmhouse overlooks a valley, where the spies live,
and the spies are in the habit of gazing up at the house through
binoculars. They have no intention of putting their own house
in order first. Indeed, they completely neglect their house when
the vacationers finally come from the city, because it is summer
now. A brook trickles through a meadow. A large hazelnut
bush abruptly slices off any further view of the brook, which
flows invisibly into the meadow belonging to the next farmer.
To the left of the house, a mountain meadow climbs high,
ending in a forest, part of which is private property, and the
rest national. All around, dense pine forests hem in the view;
but you can still see what your neighbor is doing, and he can
see what you're doing. Cows trudge along the trail to the
pastures. In back, to the left, an open pile of charcoal; and to
the right a clearing, and a strawberry patch. Overhead, clouds,
birds, including hawks and buzzards.

The hawk mother and the buzzard grandmother order the
child, their charge, not to leave the eyrie. They cut off HER
life in thick slices, and the neighbors are already snipping away
at HER character. Every stratum in which life still stirs, if only
slightly, is declared rotten and slashed away. Too much strolling
is bad for your studies. Down there, at the weir, young men
are splashing around. SHE feels drawn to them. They laugh
loudly and duck under. SHE could shine there, among the
country bumpkins. She has been trained to shine. She has been
drilled, she has been taught that she is the sun, the center of
all orbits. She only has to stand still, and the satellites will
come and worship her. She knows she is better because that is

what she is always told. But it's better not to examine her assumption.

Reluctantly, the violin finally moves under her chin, heaved up by an unwilling arm. Outdoors, the sun is smiling, the water beckoning. The sun lures you into undressing in front of others, something the old ladies in the house have ordered her not to do. Her fingers press the painful steel strings down the fingerboard. Mozart's tormented spirit, moaning and choking, is forced out of the resonator. Mozart's spirit shrieks from an infernal abode because the violinist feels nothing, but she has to keep enticing the notes. Shrieking and groaning, the notes squirm out of the instrument. SHE does not need to fear criticism, so long as something can be heard, for the sounds indicate that the child has ascended the scale, to reach loftier spheres, while leaving her body down below as a dead frame. The daughter's physical remains, sloughed off in her ascent, are combed for any traces of male use and then thoroughly shaken. After completing the music, she can slip back into her mortal coils, which have been nicely dried and starched crisp and stiff. Her frame is now unfeeling, and no one has the right to feel it.

Mother makes a cutting remark: If SHE were left to her own devices, SHE would show more enthusiasm for some young man than for her piano-playing. The piano has to be tuned every year, for this raw Alpine climate quickly thwarts the finest tuning. The piano tuner arrives on the train from Vienna. He pants his way up the mountain, where some lunatics claim they've got a grand piano, three thousand feet above sea level! The tuner prophesizes that this instrument can be worked for another year or two; by then, rust and rot and mildew will have gobbled it up in unison. Mother makes sure the piano is kept properly tuned; and she also keeps twisting her daughter's vertebrae, unconcerned about the child's mood, worrying solely about her own influence on this stubborn, easily deformable, living instrument.

Mother insists on keeping the windows wide open when the child "plays a recital" (that sweet reward for practicing nicely). This way, the neighbors too can delight in the dulcet melodies. Mother and Grandmother, armed with binoculars, stand on their lofty vantage point, checking whether the nearby farmer's wife and all her kith and kin are sitting, quiet and disciplined, in front of the cottage, listening respectfully. The farmer's wife wants to sell milk, cottage cheese, butter, eggs, and vegetables, and so she has to sit and listen in front of her home. Grandmother finds it commendable that the old neighbor finally has time to fold her hands in her lap and listen to music. The farmer's wife has been waiting for this opportunity all her life. And the opportunity has come in her old age. How beautiful it is again! The summer vacationers likewise seem to be sitting there, listening to Brahms. Mother cheerily crows that they are getting genuinely fresh grade-A music, delivered along with their genuinely fresh grade-A milk, still warm from the cow. Today, Chopin, freshly implanted in the child, will be performed for the farmer's wife and her guests. Mother cautions the child to play nice and loud, for the neighbor is gradually going deaf. So the neighbors hear a new melody, which they have never heard before. They will get to hear it over and over, until they could recognize it in the dark. Let's open the door too, so they can hear better. The wave of classical music breaks through all the openings of the house and then pours down the slopes and into the valley. The neighbors will feel as if they were standing right next to the piano. All they have to do is open their mouths, and Chopin's warm milk will gush into their throats. And then later, Brahms, that musician of frustrated people, especially women.

She gathers all her energy, spreads her wings, and then

plunges forward, toward the keys, which zoom up to her like the earth toward a crashing plane. If she can't reach a note at first swoop, she simply leaves it out. Skipping notes, a subtle vendetta against her musically untrained torturers, gives her a tiny thrill of satisfaction. An omission is never noticed by a layman, but a wrong note will yank the vacationers out of their deck chairs. What's that coming down from up there? Every year they pay the farmer's wife high prices for rustic stillness, and now loud music is booming down from the hill.

The two venomous women, a pair of spiders, listen to their victim, whom they have sucked almost dry. In their dirndls with flowery aprons, they are more considerate of their clothes than of their prisoner's feelings. They bask in their own hubris: How modest the child will remain, even though she'll be enjoying international fame and fortune. For now they are holding back the child and grandchild, keeping her away from the world, so that someday she won't belong to Mama and Grandma anymore, she'll belong to the whole world. They tell the world to be patient, it will get the child eventually.

You've got a big audience again today! Just look: at least seven people in colorful lounge chairs. This is a test. But when Brahms is finally over, what are they forced to hear? It resounds, virtually an unrefined echo: a fit of roaring laughter from the gullets of the vacationers down there. What are they laughing at so mindlessly? How can they be so disrespectful? Mother and daughter, armed with milk cans, stride down into the valley on behalf of Brahms: a retaliatory raid for the laughter. The summer guests complain about the noise, the disruption of nature. Mother venomously retorts that Schubert's sonatas contain more forest hush than the forest itself. They simply don't understand. With country butter and the fruit of her womb, Mother, nose in air, sniffishly climbs back up the lonesome mountain. Her daughter walks proudly, holding the milk can. The two of them won't show up in public again until the next evening. The vacationers talk on and on about their hobby: country boozing.

SHE feels left out of everything because she *is* left out of everything. Others go farther, even climbing over her. She looks like such a minor obstruction. The hiker strides on, but she remains on the road, like a greasy sandwich wrapper, perhaps fluttering slightly in the breeze. The paper can't get very far, it rots away right there. The rotting takes years, monotonous years.

For a change of pace, her cousin comes for a visit, and he fills the house with his hustling, bustling life. Not only *his* life. He also brings along other lives, which he attracts the way light seduces flying insects. The cousin, a medical student, draws the young people here with his boastful vitality and athletic prowess. When he feels like it, he tells a medical joke; and he's known as quite a guy because he has a sense of humor. He looms like a rock from the foaming surge of country bumpkins, who want to imitate him in every way. Suddenly, life has entered the house, for a man always brings life into a house. Smiling indulgently but proudly, the women of the house gaze at the young man, who has to let off steam. They warn him only about female adders, who might try to trick him into marriage. This young man prefers letting off steam in public, he needs an audience, and he gets one. Even HER strict mother smiles. Eventually, the young man will have to go out into the hostile world, but the daughter must strive and strain with music.

The boy prefers wearing very skimpy bathing briefs, and he likes a girl to wear a teeny-weeny bikini, which has just come into fashion. With his friends, he uses a slide rule to measure what a girl has to offer him, and he makes fun of what she doesn't have to offer. He plays badminton with the country girls. He makes an effort to initiate them into this sport, which requires concentration more than anything else. He holds the girl's hand when she holds the racket, and she is embarrassed in her teeny-weeny bikini. She's a salesgirl, and she's saved up to buy her bikini. She'd like to marry a doctor, and she shows off her figure so the future physician knows what he's getting. He doesn't have to buy a pig in a poke. The boy's genitals are just barely squeezed into a pouch, which is attached to two strings; these strings run over his hips, and are knotted on each side, left and right. They're bound sloppily, he's not such a stickler. Sometimes the knots unravel, and the boy has to tie them again. It's a mini-swimsuit.

More than anything else, the young man enjoys showing off his latest wrestling moves, right here, on the mountain, where he can still reap admiration. He also knows a few complicated judo tricks. He often performs a new stunt. If a layman knows nothing about this sport, he won't be able to resist the move, he won't get out of the hold. Howling mirth pours from the mouths of the onlookers, and the loser cheerily joins in the laughter, trying to show that he's a good loser. The girls bounce around the boy like ripe fruits falling from a tree. The young athlete only has to pick them up and gulp them down. The girls screech and squeal, while observing themselves from the corners of their eyes as they try to get close to him. They slide down hills and giggle, they fly into gravel or thistles and screech. The young man stands over them, triumphant. He grabs a girl's wrists and squeezes and crushes. He uses a secret grip. It's hard to make out exactly what he's doing, but the guinea pig, overcome by his superior strength and a dirty trick, sinks to her knees, down to the guy's feet. Who could resist the young student? If he's in a really good mood, he allows the girl, who's crawling on the ground, to kiss his feet; otherwise, the guy won't let her up. His feet are kissed, and the willing victim hopes for more kisses, which will be sweeter, because they'll be given and gotten in secret.

The sunlight plays with their heads; water hurtles up from the small wading pools and flashes in the sun. SHE practices on her piano, ignoring the salvos of laughter that shoot up in fits and starts. HER mother has urgently told her to pay no attention. Mother stands on the steps of the porch, laughing. She laughs and holds a plate of cookies in her hand. Mother says you're only young once, but no one can hear her amid all the screeching.

SHE always has one ear attuned to the noise outside, the noise created by her cousin and the girls. SHE listens as he digs his healthy teeth into time, devouring it with gusto. SHE becomes more painfully aware of time with every passing second. Like clockwork, her fingers tick the seconds into the keys. The windows of her practice room are barred. The bars form a cross, which is held up to the wild rumpus outside, as if it were a vampire looking for blood to suck.

Now the young man jumps into the pond, he deserves to cool off a little. Fresh water has been let in, ice-cold well water. Only the valiant, who sit on top of the world, have the courage to jump in. Snorting and wheezing merrily like a whale, the guy surfaces again. SHE notices it without seeing it. Amid loud cheers, the freshly baked girlfriends of the future doctor quickly dive, squeezing into the tiny pond. What a splashing and thronging! They imitate everything he does, laughs Mother. She is lenient. The old grandmother, whom SHE shares with the cousin, comes hurrying over to watch the monkeyshines. The ancient grandma is also splashed, because the guy considers nothing sacrosanct, not even old age. But they laugh at the virile, lively grandson. Mother throws in a sensible comment: The boy should have first cooled the pit of his stomach very slowly. But in the end, she laughs louder than the others, in spite of herself. Her body shakes and jolts with laughter when the guy imitates a seal, so real, so lifelike. Mother shakes and jolts as if glass marbles were hurtling around inside her. Now the guy goes so far as to toss an old ball into the air and catch it on his nose. But even juggling has to be practiced. Everyone is twisting with laughter, bodies are quaking with laughter, tears are running. Someone yodels loudly, shouting with joy, the way people do in the mountains. It's almost lunchtime. Cool off now, rather than after lunch, when it would be dangerous.

The final note dies out, fades away. HER tendons relax. The alarm clock, which Mother set herself, has rung. SHE jumps up in the middle of the musical phrase and dashes out, full of complicated adolescent emotions, just to catch a final bit of the singing and prancing. SHE, his cousin, is duly welcomed. Did you have to practice so long again? Her mother should leave her alone, they're on vacation. Mother tells him not to be a bad influence on her child. The guy, who never smokes or drinks, digs his teeth into a sandwich. Even though lunch is almost ready, the women of the house cannot refuse their darling a bite to eat. Then the guy generously pours raspberry syrup (they picked the berries themselves) into a tall glass, fills the glass up with well water, and pours the drink down his throat. He has drawn new strength. Now he sensually smacks his flat hand on his muscular belly. He smacks other muscles too. Mother and Grandmother can talk about the guy's marvelous appetite for hours on end. They outdo one another with inventive culinary details, they argue all day long about what the guy would rather eat, veal cutlets or pork chops. Mother asks her nephew how his studies are going, and he replies that he'd like to forget about school for a while. He wants to be young, he wants to live it up. Someday he'll be able to say that his youth is long past.

The guy looks HER in the eye and tells her she ought to laugh a bit. Why is SHE so serious? He tells her to try exercise, that'll get HER to laugh, and generally it'll do her good. The cousin enjoys sports so much that he laughs out loud, and bits of the sandwich fly from his gaping mouth. He moans blissfully. He stretches pleasurably. He spins around like a top and throws himself into the grass, as if he were dead. But then he leaps up again, don't worry. Now it's time to cheer his little cousin up by showing her the patented wrestling hold. His cousin is delighted, his aunt annoyed.

SHE zooms downhill, so long. A one-way trip. She collapses along her longitudinal axis. Off we go, down we go. The trees, the small staircase with the wild rose hedge, the people shoot past her, vanishing from her field of vision. They're yanked upward. Her ribs are crushed, the guy's chest hair disappears over her head, the edge of his bathing suit shifts by, the strings on which his testicles are suspended come into view. Relentlessly, the small, red Mount Everest crops up, and underneath. A close-up: the long, fair, downy hairs on the upper thighs. Suddenly, the descent halts. Main floor. Somewhere in her back, her bones crack crudely, hinges grind: they were squeezed together too hard. And she's already kneeling. Hurray! The guy has once again succeeded in catching a girl unawares. She kneels before her vacationing cousin, one holiday child in front of the other. A thin varnish of tears shines on HER face as she peeks up into a mask of mirth, which is bursting at the seams. This good-for-nothing has really done it to her, and he's happy about his victory. She is pushed into the Alpine earth. Mother is shocked at how badly her child is treated by the local adolescents—this gifted daughter, who is usually admired by one and all.

The red genital pouch sways and dangles, it swings seductively before HER eyes. It belongs to a seducer, whom no one can resist. She leans her cheek against it for only a split second. She doesn't quite know what she's doing. She wants to feel it just once, she wants to graze that glittering Christmas-tree ornament with her lips, just this once. For one split second, SHE is the addressee of this package. SHE grazes it with her lips or was it her chin? It was unintentional. The guy doesn't realize he's triggered a landslide in his cousin. She peers and peers. The package has been arranged for her, like a slide under a microscope. Just let this moment linger, it's so good.

No one's noticed anything, they're all busy with lunch. The guy releases HER instantly and swings back one step. For propriety's sake, he'll do without the foot kiss that usually concludes the exercise. He sways back and forth to limber up a bit, hops embarrassedly into the air, and then dashes off in long leaps. The meadow swallows him up; the women summon him to lunch. The guy has flown away, he's jumped from the nest. He remains silent. Soon he'll vanish into thin air. A couple of buddies dash after him. Off they swoop. Mother mildly condemns him in absentia for his wildness: She's gone to so much trouble preparing lunch, and now she's left holding the bag.

The guy doesn't return until much later. Evening hush everywhere, only the nightingale warbling at the brook. They're playing cards on the veranda. Butterflies, half unconscious, circle the kerosene lamp. SHE is not attracted by a bright circle. SHE sits alone in her room, isolated from the crowd, which has forgotten her because she is such a lightweight. She jostles no one. From an intricate package, she carefully unwraps a razor blade. She always takes it everywhere. The blade smiles like a bridegroom at a bride. SHE gingerly tests the edge; it is razor-sharp. Then she presses the blade into the back of her hand several times, but not so deep as to injure tendons. It doesn't hurt at all. The metal slices her hand like butter. For

an instant, a slit gapes in the previously intact tissue; then the
arduously tamed blood rushes out from behind the barrier. She
makes a total of four cuts. That's enough, otherwise she'll bleed
to death. The razor blade is always wiped clean and then
wrapped up again. Bright red blood trickles and trails from the
wounds, sullying everything as it flows. It oozes, warm, silent,
and the sensation is not unpleasant. It's so liquid. It runs incessantly. It reddens everything. Four slits, oozing nonstop.
On the floor and on the bedding, the four tiny brooks unite
into a raging torrent. "Just keep following my tears, and the
brook will take you in." A small puddle forms. And the blood
keeps running. On and on. It runs and runs and runs and runs.

Erika, as always the well-groomed teacher, has no regrets
about leaving her musical headquarters today. Her inconspicuous departure is accompanied by blasting horns and trumpets
and the wail of a single violin; everything bursts through the
windows at the same time. Erika barely weighs on the outside
steps. Today, Mother isn't waiting. Erika instantly and resolutely heads in a direction that she has already taken several
times in the past. The way does not lead straight home. Perhaps
some splendid big, bad wolf is leaning against a rustic telegraph
pole, picking the remnants of his latest victim from his teeth.
Erika would like to place a milestone in her monotonous life
and invite the wolf with her gazes. She will spot him from far
away and catch the sound of skin being torn and flesh ripped.
By then, it will be late in the evening. The event will loom
from the fog of musical half-truths. Erika strides resolutely.

Chasms of streets open up, then close again because Erika
can't make up her mind to enter them. She simply stares
straight ahead when a man happens to wink at her. He isn't
the wolf, and her vagina doesn't flutter open; it clamps shut,

hard as steel. Erika jerks her head like a huge pigeon, to send the man packing. Terrified by the landslide he's triggered, he loses all desire to use or protect this woman. Erika sharpens her face arrogantly. Her nose, her mouth—everything becomes an arrow pointing in one direction; it plows through the area as if to say: Keep moving. A pack of teenagers makes a derogatory comment about Erika, the lady. They don't realize they are dealing with a professor, and they show no respect. Erika's pleated skirt with its checkered pattern covers her knees, not one millimeter too high or too low. She's also wearing a silk middy, which covers her torso precisely. Her briefcase is clamped under her arm as usual, tightly zipped up closed. Erika has closed everything about her that could be opened.

Let's take the trolley. It runs out into the working-class suburbs. Her monthly pass isn't valid on this line, so she has to buy a ticket. Normally, she doesn't travel here. These are areas you don't enter if you don't have to. Few of her students come from here. No music lasts longer here than the time it takes to play a number on a jukebox.

Small greasy spoons spit their light at the sidewalk. Groups of people argue in the islands of streetlights, for someone has said something wrong. Erika has to look at many unfamiliar things. Here and there, mopeds start up, rattling needle pricks into the air. Then they vanish quickly as if someone were waiting for them somewhere—in a rectory, where they're throwing a party, and where they want to get rid of the moped drivers immediately for disturbing the peace and quiet. Normally, two people sit on a feeble moped to use up the space. Not everyone can afford a moped. Tiny cars are usually packed to capacity out here. Often a great-grandmother sits inside a car, amid her relatives who take her for a pleasure spin to the graveyard.

Erika gets out and continues on foot. She looks neither left

nor right. Employees lock and bolt the doors of a supermarket.
In front, you can hear the final, gently throbbing engines of
housewife chitchat. A soprano overcomes a baritone: The
grapes were really moldy. The worst were at the bottom of the
plastic basket. That's why no one bought them today. All this
is spread out loudly and rattlingly in front of the others—a
garbage heap of complaints and anger. Behind the locked glass
doors, a cashier wrestles with her register. She simply can't
track down the mistake. A child on a scooter and another child
running alongside him, weeping and yammering that he'd like
to ride it, the other kid promised. The rider ignores the requests
of his less-privileged colleague. You don't see these scooters in
other neighborhoods anymore, Erika muses to herself. Once
she got one as a present and she was so happy. Unfortunately,
she couldn't ride it because the street kills children.

The head of a four-year-old is thrown back by a mother's
slap of hurricane strength. For a moment, the head rotates
helplessly, like a rolypoly that has lost its balance and is having
a hard time getting back on its feet. Eventually the child's head
is vertical again and back in its proper place. But now it emits
horrible sounds, whereupon the impatient mother promptly
knocks it out of plumb again. Now the child's head is marked
by invisible ink and ordained for a much worse fate. The mother
has heavy bags to struggle with, and she'd much rather see her
little girl vanish down a sewer. You see, in order to mistreat
her daughter, she has to keep putting down her bags, which
only adds to her drudgery. Yet the extra effort seems worth-
while. The child is learning the language of violence, though
not willingly. At school, she likewise picks up very little. She
knows a few words, the most necessary ones, even though you
can barely understand them among her sobs and tears.

Soon the woman and the noisy child are way behind Erika.
After all, they keep stopping! They can never keep up with the

swiftness of time. Erika, a caravan, marches on. This is a res-
idential neighborhood, but not a good one. Fathers, straggling
home late, lunge into building entrances, ready to pounce on
their families like dreadful hammers. The final car doors slam
shut, proud and self-assured, for these tiny autos can get away
with anything, they are the darlings of their families. Glittering
amiably, they remain behind at the curbside, while their owners
hurry to supper. Anyone without a home-sweet-home may
wish for one, but he'll never manage to build one, even with
the help of a generous mortgage. Anyone with a home around
here, of all places, would much rather spend most of his time
somewhere else. More and more men cross Erika's path. The
women, as if having heard a magic formula, have vanished into
the holes that are called "apartments" here. They do not venture outdoors alone at this time of night, unless accompanied
by family members—adults—to have a beer or visit a relative.
Their inconspicuous but so necessary activities are pervasive
everywhere. Kitchen odors. Sometimes the soft clattering of
pots and scratching of forks. The first early-evening sitcoms
seep bluishly from one window, then another, then many.
Sparkling crystals to adorn the gathering night. The building
fronts become flat backdrops, behind which there is probably
nothing: All these birds are of one feather. Only the TV sounds
are real, they are the actual events. All the people around here
experience the same things at the same time, except for some
loner, who switches to the educational channel. This individualist is informed about a eucharistic congress, provided with
facts and figures. Nowadays, if you want to be different, you
have to pay your dues.

You can hear bellowing Turkish vowels. A second voice instantly enters: a guttural Serbo-Croatian countertenor. Gangs
of men, on tenterhooks, small troops, hurrying here in dribs
and drabs, now turning left underneath the roaring elevated

train: A peep show has been set up under one of the viaduct arches. The space is exploited so efficiently, down to every last nook and cranny, no centimeter wasted. The Turks are, no doubt, vaguely familiar with the arch shape from their mosques. Maybe the whole thing recalls a harem. A viaduct arch, hollowed out and full of naked women. Each woman gets a chance, each in turn. A miniature Venusberg. Here comes Tannhäuser, he knocks with his staff. This arch is built of bricks, and so many men have gawked at so many beautiful women here. This little shop of whorers, in which naked women stretch and sprawl, fits precisely into the arch, hand in glove. The women spell one another. They rotate, according to some displeasure principle, through a whole chain of peepshows, so that steady customers can always get to see new flesh at specific intervals. Otherwise the regulars will stop coming. After all, they bring good money here and insert it, coin for coin, into an insatiably gaping slot. Just when things are getting hot, another coin has to go in. One hand inserts, the other senselessly pumps and dumps the virile strength. At home the man eats enough for three people, and here he heedlessly scatters his energy to the winds.

Every ten minutes, the Vienna Municipal Railroad thunders overhead. The train shakes the entire arch, but, unshakable, the girls keep turning. They've got the hang of it. You get used to the din. The coin goes in, the window goes up, and rosy flesh comes out—a miracle of technology. You mustn't touch this flesh; you couldn't, because of the wall. The outside window is covered with black paper. It is decorated with lovely yellow ornaments. A small mirror is inserted in the black paper, so you can look at yourself. Who knows why. Maybe so you can comb your hair afterward.

A small sex shop is attached to the peep show. There you can buy what you've been turned on to. No women, but, to make up for that lack, tiny nylon panties with many slits, in front and/or in back. At home, you can put them on your wife and then reach in, and your wife doesn't have to take them off. There's a matching tank top with two round holes. The woman sticks her breasts through these holes, and the rest of her torso is covered transparently. The tank top is lined with teensy frills and ruffles. You can choose between dark red and black. Black looks better on a blonde, red goes better with black hair.

You can also find books here, magazines, videocassettes, and 8mm movies in various stages of dustiness. These items don't move at all. The customers don't own VCRs or projectors. The hygienic rubbers with various kinds of ribbed surfaces sell a lot better; so do the inflatable women. First the customers look at the genuine article, then they buy the imitation. Unfortunately, the customer cannot take along the beautiful naked women in order to screw them royally in his protective little room. These women have never experienced anything profound, otherwise they wouldn't flaunt their bodies here. They'd come along nicely rather than just pretend to come. This is no work for a woman. A customer would gladly take any of them, it doesn't matter which, they're all alike. You can barely tell them apart; at most, by the color of their hair. The men, in contrast, have individual personalities: some men like one thing, some like something else. On the other hand, the horny bitch behind the window, beyond the barrier, has only one urgent desire: That asshole behind the glass window should keep jerking until his cock falls off. In this way, the man and the woman each get something, and the atmosphere is nice and relaxed. Everything has its price. You pay your money and you get your choice.

Erika's pocketbook, which she carries along with her music case, is stuffed with coins. Few women ever wander this way, but Erika likes getting her own way. That's the way she is. If many people do something, then she likes to do the exact opposite. If some people say go, Erika alone says stop, and she's proud of it. That's the only way she can get them to notice her. Now she wants to come here.

The Turkish and Yugoslav enclaves retreat at the approach of this creature from another world. All at once, they're practically helpless; but if they had their druthers, they'd rape any woman they could. They yell things at Erika that she doesn't understand, luckily. She keeps her head high. No one grabs at Erika, not even a drunk. Besides, an elderly man is watching. Is he the owner, the proprietor? The few Austrians hug the wall. No group bolsters their egos, and in addition, they have to graze past people whom they usually avoid. They make undesired physical contact, while the desired physical contact never comes. Unfortunately, male drives are powerful. These men don't have enough cash for a genuine wine spritzer, it's almost the end of the week. The natives trudge hesitantly along the viaduct wall. One arch before the big show, there's a ski shop, and one arch before that, a bicycle store. These places are asleep now, their interiors are pitch-black. But here, friendly lamplight shines out into the street, luring these bold moths, these creatures of the night. They want something for their money. Each client is rigorously separated from the next. Plywood booths are precisely custom-tailored to their needs. These booths are small and narrow, and their temporary inhabitants are little people. Besides, the smaller each booth, the more booths you can squeeze together. In this way, a relatively high number of men can find considerable relief within a relatively short period.

The clients take along their worries, but leave their precious semen. Cleaning women make sure the seeds don't sprout—even though each customer, if asked, would assure you how fertile he is. Usually, all the booths are occupied. This business is a treasure trove, a gold mine. The foreign workers patiently line up in little groups. They kill time by cracking jokes about women. The small space of the booth is directly proportional to the small space of their living quarters, which are sometimes only quarters of a room. They are used to cramped rooms, and they can even find privacy here between partitions. Only one man to a booth. Here, he is all alone with himself. The beautiful woman appears in the peephole as soon as he inserts his coin. The two one-room apartments with individual service for more demanding gentlemen are almost always empty. Few clients here are in a position to make special requests.

Erika, thoroughly a professor, enters the premises.

A hand hesitantly reaches out for her, but then shoots back. She does not walk into the employee section, she steps into the section for paying guests—the more important section. This woman wants to look at something that she could see far more cheaply in her mirror at home. The men voice their amazement: They have to pinch every penny they secretly spend here hunting women. The hunters peer through the peepholes, and their housekeeping money goes down the drain. Nothing can elude these men when they peer.

All Erika wants to do is watch. Here, in this booth, she becomes nothing. Nothing fits into Erika, but she, she fits exactly into this cell. Erika is a compact tool in human form. Nature seems to have left no apertures in her. Erika feels solid wood in the place where the carpenter made a hole in any genuine female. Erika's wood is spongy, decaying, lonesome wood in the timber forest, and the rot is spreading. Still, Erika struts around like a queen. Inside, she is decaying, but she glares discouragingly at the Turks. The Turks would like to arouse her to life, but they bounce off her haughtiness. Erika, every inch a queen, strides into the Venus grotto. The Turks utter no cordialities, and also no uncordialities. They simply let Erika go in with her briefcase full of scores. She can even pass to the head of the line, and no one protests. She's also wearing gloves. The man at the entrance bravely addresses her as "Ma'am." Please come in, he says, welcoming her into his parlor, where the small lamps glow tranquilly over boobs and cunts, chiseling out bushy triangles, for that's the first thing a man looks at, it's the law. A man looks at nothing, he looks at pure lack. After looking at this nothing, he looks at everything else.

Erika is personally assigned a deluxe booth. She doesn't have to wait, she's a lady. The others have to wait longer. She holds her money ready the way her left hand clutches a violin. In the daytime, she sometimes calculates how much peeping she can do for her saved coins. She saves them by eating less at her coffee breaks. Now, a blue spotlight sweeps across flesh. Even the colors are handpicked. Erika lifts up a tissue from the floor; it is encrusted with sperm. She holds it to her nose. She deeply inhales the aroma, the fruits of someone else's hard labor. She breathes and looks, using up a wee bit of her life. There are clubs where you can shoot pictures. Each client selects his model himself, according to his mood and taste. But Erika doesn't want to act, she only wants to look. She simply wants to sit there and look. Look hard. Erika, watching but not touching. Erika feels nothing, and has no chance to caress herself. Her mother sleeps next to her and guards Erika's hands. These hands are supposed to practice, not scoot under the blanket like ants and scurry over to the jam jar. Even when Erika cuts or pricks herself, she feels almost nothing. But when it comes to her eyes, she has reached an acme of sensitivity.

The booth smells of disinfectant. The cleaning women *are* women, but they don't look like women. They heedlessly dump the splashed sperm of these hunters into a filthy garbage can.

And now concrete-hard squooshed tissue is lying there again.
As far as Erika is concerned, the cleaning women can take a
break and relax their harried bones. They have to bend an
infinite number of times. Erika simply sits and peers. She
doesn't even remove her gloves, so she won't have to touch
anything in this smelly cell. Perhaps she keeps her gloves on
so no one can see her handcuffs. Curtain up for Erika, she can
be seen in the wings, pulling the wires. The whole show is put
on purely for her benefit! No deformed woman is ever hired
here. Good looks and a good figure are the basic requirements.
Each applicant has to undergo a thorough physical investigation: No proprietor buys a pig without poking her. Erika never
made it on the concert stage, and so other women make it in
her stead. They are evaluated according to the size of their
female curves. Erika keeps watching. A single sidelong glance—
and a couple of coins have gone the way of all flesh.

A black-haired woman assumes a creative pose so the on-
looker can look into her. She rotates on a sort of potter's wheel.
But who is spinning it? First she squeezes her thighs together,
you see nothing; but mouths fill with the heavy water of an-
ticipation. Then she slowly spreads her legs as she moves past
several peepholes. Sometimes, despite all efforts at equal time,
one window sees more than the other because the wheel keeps
rotating. The peep slits click nervously. Nothing ventured,
nothing gained. Venture once more, and maybe you'll gain
something more.

The surrounding crowd zealously rubs and massages, and is
simultaneously mixed by a gigantic but invisible dough-
kneading machine. Ten little pumps are churning away at top
capacity. Outside, some customers are secretly pre-milking a
bit, so they can spend less. Each man will have a woman to
keep him company.

In the neighboring cells, the thrusting, jerking pumps discharge their precious freight. Soon they fill up again, and a yearning must be satisfied again. If you're jammed, you'll be charged quite a bit until you've discharged. Especially if you're so busy looking that you forget to work your pump. That's why they often bring new women in, as a distraction. The jerk gawks but doesn't jerk.

Erika looks. The object of her peeping thrusts her hand between her thighs and shows her pleasure by forming a tiny O with her mouth. Delighted at being watched by so many eyes, she closes her own eyes, reopening them and rolling them up very high in her head. She raises her arms and massages her nipples, making them stand up straight. Then she sits down comfortably and splays her legs far apart. Now you can peer into the woman from a worm's-eye view. She toys playfully with her pubic hair. She licks her lips palpably, while now one sportsman, now another, cocks his rubber worm. Her entire face reveals how wonderful it would be if only she could be with you. But unfortunately, that's out of the question because of the overwhelming demand. This way, everybody, not just one man, can get something.

Erika watches very closely. Not in order to learn. Nothing stirs or moves within her. But she has to watch all the same. For her own pleasure. Whenever she feels like leaving, something above her energetically presses her well-groomed head back to the pane, and she has to keep looking. The turntable on which the beautiful woman is perched keeps revolving. Erika can't help it. She has to keep looking. She is off-limits to herself.

To her left and right, she hears joyful moans and howls. I personally can't go along with that, Erika Kohut replies, I expected more. Something spurts and splashes against the plywood wall. The walls are easy to clean, their surfaces are smooth. On her right, some gentleman has lovingly notched a few words into the wall, "Holy Mary goddamn slut," in correct

German. The men don't scrawl that many things here, they
have other fish to fry. Anyway, they're not all that good when
it comes to writing. They've only got one free hand, and usually
not even that. Besides, they have to keep inserting money.

A dragon lady with dyed red hair now thrusts her chubby
backside into view. For years now, cheap masseurs have been
working their fingers to the bone on her alleged cellulite. However, she shows the viewers more for their money. The right-
hand booths have already seen the front of the woman; now,
the left-hand booths get a look. Some men like to evaluate a
woman from the front, others from the back. The redhead
moves muscles that she normally uses to walk or sit. Today,
she's earning her living with them. She massages herself with
her right hand, which has blood-red claws. Her left hand
scratches around on her breasts. Her sharp artificial nails tug
at her nipple as if it were rubber, and then let it bounce back.
Her nipple seems alien to her body. The redhead is practiced
enough to know that the candidate is about to make it! Any
man who can't do it now will never do it again. Any man who's
alone now has only himself to blame. Like it or not, he's going
to remain alone for a long time.

Erika has reached her limit. You have to know when to stop.
That's really going too far, she says as so often before. She
stands up. Erika staked off her own limits long ago, securing
them with ironclad treaties. She surveys everything from a
high vantage point, which allows her to look far across the
countryside. Good visibility is required. But once again, Erika
does not care to look any farther. She leaves.

Her gaze alone suffices to push aside the waiting customers.
A man greedily takes her place. A road emerges through the
customers; Erika strides across and marches away. She walks
and walks quite mechanically, just as she previously looked and
looked. Anything Erika does, she does wholeheartedly. Do

nothing halfheartedly, her mother always demanded. Nothing vaguely. No artist tolerates anything incomplete or half-baked in his work. Sometimes a work is incomplete because the artist dies prematurely. Erika walks along. Nothing is torn, nothing is faded. Nothing is bleached out. She's achieved nothing.

At home, a mild reproach from her mother descends upon the warm incubator that the two of them inhabit. Hopefully, Erika didn't catch cold during her trip (she fibs about the destination). The daughter slips into a warm bathrobe. She and her mother eat a duck stuffed with chestnuts and other goodies. This is a banquet. The chestnuts are bursting through the seams of the duck; Mother has gilded the lily, as is her wont. The salt and pepper shakers are silver-plated, the silverware is pure silver. The child's got red cheeks today, Mother is delighted. Hopefully, the red cheeks aren't due to fever. Mother probes Erika's forehead with her lips. Erika gets a thermometer along with the dessert. Luckily, fever is crossed off as a possible cause. Erika is in the pink of health—a well-nourished fish in her mother's amniotic fluid.

❑

Icy streams of neon light roar through ice-cream parlors, through dance halls. Clusters of humming light dangle from whip-shaped lampposts over miniature golf courses. A flickering torrent of coldness. People HER age, enjoying the lovely peace and quiet of habit, loll around kidney-shaped tables. Tall glasses, containing long spoons, look like cool blossoms: brown, yellow, pink; chocolate, vanilla, raspberry. The colorful, steaming scoops are tinted an almost uniform gray by the ceiling lights. Glittering scoopers wait in containers of water, with threads of ice cream floating on the surface. In the casualness of fun, which doesn't have to keep proving itself, the young

silhouettes relax in front of their ice-cream towers. Tiny, gaudy
umbrellas stick out of the glasses, concealing the harsh detritus
of maraschino cherries, pineapple chunks, chocolate chips. The
loungers incessantly poke pieces of coldness into their own ice
caves, cold to cold; or else they heedlessly let the good stuff
melt, while telling one another things that are more important
than the icy delight.

SHE only has to glance at this scene, and HER face instantly
becomes disapproving. SHE considers her feelings unique when
she looks at a tree; she sees a wonderful universe in a pinecone.
Using a small mallet, she taps reality; she is a zealous dentist
of language. The tops of simple spruces turn into lonesome,
snowy peaks for her. The horizon is lacquered by a spectrum
of colors. Far in the distance, huge, unidentifiable airplanes
glide past, their gentle thunder barely audible. They are the
giants of music and the giants of poetry, wrapped in enormous
camouflage. Hundreds of thousands of bits of data flash through
HER well-trained mind. An insane, intoxicated mushroom of
smoke shoots up, and then, in an ash-gray act of vomiting,
slowly descends to the ground. A fine, gray dust quickly covers
all the apparatuses, all the test tubes and capillary tubes, all
the flasks and spiral condensers. HER room turns to solid rock.
Gray. Neither cold nor warm. In between. A pink nylon curtain
crackling at the window, not stirred by any puff of wind. The
interior furnished neatly. Untenanted. Unowned.

The piano keys begin to sing under fingers. The gigantic tail
of culture-refuse moves forward, softly rustling as it curls
around, closing into a tight circle, millimeter by millimeter.
Dirty tin cans, greasy plates with leftovers, filthy silverware,
moldy remnants of fruit and bread, shattered records, ripped,
crumpled paper. In other homes, hot steaming water hisses into
bathtubs. A girl mindlessly tries a new hairdo. Another girl

picks the right blouse for the right skirt. There are new, sharply pointed shoes here, to be worn for the first time. A telephone rings. Someone picks up. Someone laughs. Someone says something.

The garbage, an immense mass, lumbers along between HER and THE OTHERS. Someone gets a new permanent wave. Someone matches a new nail polish to a lipstick. Tinfoil twinkles in the sun. A sunbeam gets caught on the tine of a fork, on the edge of a knife. The fork is a fork. The knife is a knife. Ruffled by a gentle breeze, onion skins rise up, tissue paper rises up, sticky with sweet raspberry syrup. The decaying strata underneath, dusty and disintegrated, are an inner lining for the rotting cheese rinds and melon skins, for the glass shards and blackish cotton swabs, all facing the same doom.

And Mother yanks at HER guide ropes. Two hands zoom out and play the Brahms again, this time better. Brahms is very cold when he inherits the classics, but quite moving when he grieves or gushes. Mother, however, is never moved by Brahms.

A metal spoon is simply left in melting strawberry ice cream because a girl just has to say something, which another girl laughs at. The other girl rearranges the gigantic plastic barrette, shimmering like mother-of-pearl, in her upswept hairdo. Both girls are well versed in feminine movements! Femininity pours from their bodies like small, clean brooks. A plastic compact is opened; in the shine of the mirror, something is freshened in frosty pink, something is emphasized in black.

SHE is a weary dolphin, listlessly preparing to do her final trick. Wearily eyeing the ludicrously multicolored ball that the animal pushes on its snout—a movement that has become an old routine. The animal takes a deep breath and then makes the ball whirl like a top. In Buñuel's *An Andalusian Dog*, you see two concert grand pianos. Then the two donkeys, half-rotten, bloody heads suspended over the keyboards. Dead. Putrescent. Outside of everything. In a totally airless room.

A chain of false eyelashes is glued to natural lashes. Tears flow. An eyebrow is painted vehemently. The same eyebrow pencil makes a black dot on a mole right by the chin. The stem of a comb is inserted repeatedly into a very high topknot, in order to loosen the haystack. Then a clasp holds some hair fast again. Stockings are pulled up, a seam is straightened. A patent-leather pocketbook swings up and is carried away. Petticoats rustle under short taffeta skirts. The girls have paid, they leave.

A world opens up to HER, a world whose existence no one else even suspects. Legoland, Minimundus, a miniature world of red, blue, and white plastic tiles. The pustules with which the world can be joined together release an equally tiny world of music. HER left hand—rigid talons paralyzed in incurable awkwardness—scratches feebly on several keys. She wants to soar up to exotic spheres, which numb the senses, boggle the mind. She doesn't even make it to the gas station, for which there is a very precise model. SHE is nothing but a clumsy tool. Encumbered with a slow, heavy mind. Leaden dead weight. A hindrance! A gun turned against HERSELF, never to go off. A tin screw clamp.

Orchestras made up of nothing but some one hundred recorders begin to howl. Recorders of various sizes and types. Children's flesh is puffed into them. The notes are created by children's breath. No keyboard instruments are summoned. Cases for the recorders have been sewn by the mothers. The cases also contain small round brushes for cleaning the instruments. The bodies of the recorders are covered with the condensation of warm breath. The many notes are created by small children with the help of breath. No support is provided by any piano!

❑

The very private chamber concert for voluntary listeners takes place in an old patrician apartment on the Danube Canal; a Polish émigré family, which has lived in Vienna for four generations now, has opened up its two grand pianos and its rich collection of scores. Furthermore, in a place where other people keep their automobiles (close to the heart), these people have a collection of old instruments. They don't own a car, but they do own a few lovely Mozart violins and Mozart violas, as well as an exquisite viola d'amore, which hangs on the wall, constantly guarded by a family member when chamber music erupts in their home, and taken down only for purposes of study. Or in case of fire. These people love music, and want others exposed to it too. With loving patience; if necessary, by force. They wish to make music accessible to adolescents, for it's not much fun grazing in these meadows alone. Like boozers or junkies, they absolutely have to share their hobby with as many people as possible. Children are cunningly driven toward them. The fat little grandson, whom everyone knows, whose wet hair sticks to his head, who yells for help at the slightest occasion. The latchkey child, who stoutly resists, but has to submit in the end. No snacks are served during a recital. Nor can you nibble on the hallowed silence. No breadcrumbs, no grease spots on the upholstery, no red-wine stains on piano cover one or piano cover two, absolutely no chewing gum! The children are sieved for any garbage brought in from outside. The coarser children remain in the sieve, they will never achieve anything on their instruments.

This family is not going to any unnecessary expense; only music should operate here, by itself and of its own accord.

Music should beat its path into the hearts of the listeners here. After all, the family is spending next to nothing on itself. Erika has virtually subpoenaed all her piano students. The professor only has to wave her little finger. The children bring a proud mother, a proud father, or both, and these intact nuclear families fill the premises. The pupils know they would receive poor grades if they didn't show up. Death would be the sole excuse for abstaining from art. Other reasons are simply not understood by the professional art lover. Erika Kohut is brilliant.

As a curtain-raiser, Bach's second concerto for two pianos. The second piano is played by an old man, who, earlier in his life, once performed at Brahms Hall, on a single piano all to himself. Those times are past, but the oldest people here can still remember. The approaching reaper seems unable to prod this gentleman, whose name is Dr. Haberkorn, to repeat the marvels he, the reaper, once achieved with Mozart and Beethoven, as well as Schubert. And Schubert certainly didn't have much time. Before we begin, the old man, despite his age, greets Professor Erika Kohut, his partner at the second keyboard, by gallantly kissing her hand—a national custom.

Dear music lovers and guests. The guests dash to the table and smack their lips over the Baroque ragout. Pupils scrape their feet at the very start, their heads filled with evil desires, but lacking the courage to carry them out. They do not escape from this chicken coop of artistic devotion even though the laths are quite thin. Erika wears a silk blouse and a simple, floor-length black velvet chimney skirt. Barely shaking her head, she eyes some of her pupils with a glare that could cut glass (the very glare her mother hurled at her daughter's skull after Erika messed up her big concert). The two pupils were talking, thus disrupting the host's introduction. They will not be warned a second time. In the front row, next to the hostess, Erika's mother sits in a special armchair, feeding on a box of candy (she is the only one permitted to do so) and feasting on the attention enjoyed by her daughter.

The light is vehemently dimmed when a cushion is propped against the piano lamp. The cushion causes the players to be shrouded in a demonic red glow. Bach rushes by earnestly. The pupils are in their Sunday best, or what their parents consider their Sunday best. Moms and dads have crammed their offspring into this Polish vestibule so that the parents can have some peace and the children can learn some quiet. The Polish vestibule is decorated with a gigantic Art Nouveau mirror depicting a naked maiden with water lilies on which little boys stand still forever. Later, up in the music room, the children will sit in front and the adults in back, because they're above it all. The elder ones give the host and hostess a hand when it's time to make a younger colleague stop short.

Walter Klemmer hasn't missed a single evening here since sweet seventeen, when he started working a piano seriously and not just for fun. Here he receives inspirations for his own playing—cashlike incentives.

The Bach swirls into the presto movement, and Klemmer, with a spontaneous hunger, scrutinizes the back of his piano teacher, whose body is cut off by the stool. That is all he can see of her figure, all he can judge it by. He cannot make out her front part because a fat mother blocks his view. (His favorite seat is occupied today. During lessons, SHE always sits at the second piano.) The maternal frigate is flanked by a tiny lifeboat, her son, a beginner, wearing black trousers, a white shirt, and a red bow tie with white dots. The boy is already slouching in his seat, like a nauseated airplane passenger who only wants the plane to land. Art sends Erika gliding through higher air corridors, almost off into the ether. Walter Klemmer eyes her anxiously, because she is floating away from him. But he is not the only person to reach out to her involuntarily. Her mother likewise grabs the string of this kite known as Erika. Don't let go of the string! It already yanks away so violently that Mother has to stand on tiptoe. The wind howls fiercely around the kite as it always does at this high altitude.

During the final movement of the Bach, Herr Klemmer gets a red rosette on each cheek, left and right. He then holds a single red rose in his hand in order to present it afterward. He unselfishly admires Erika's technique, he admires the way her back moves to the beat, the way her head sways, judiciously weighing the nuances she produces. He sees the play of muscles in her upper arm, he is excited by the collision of flesh and motion. The flesh obeys an inner motion that has been triggered by the music, and Klemmer beseeches his teacher to obey him some day. He masturbates in his seat. One of his hands involuntarily twitches on the dreadful weapon of his genital. The student has a hard time controlling himself as he mentally gauges Erika's overall proportions. He compares her upper part with her lower part, which may be a tad too plump, but he basically enjoys that. He balances the upper part against the lower part. The upper part: just a tad too thin. The lower part: it has its plus. But Klemmer likes Erika's overall appearance. He personally finds that Fräulein Kohut is a delightful-looking woman. If, furthermore, she pushed up some of her lower excess, she would be quite attractive. The reverse process would also be possible, of course, but Klemmer wouldn't like that as much. If she planed away something below, her entire body would be quite harmonious. But then she'd be too thin again! It is this minor imperfection that makes Erika so accessible to, hence desirable for, the grown-up student. You can capture any woman if you exploit her awareness of her own physical inadequacies. Besides, this woman is growing visibly older, and he is still young. Klemmer has a second goal, along with music; and he now thinks it through. He is crazy about music. He is also secretly crazy about his music teacher. He is of the highly personal opinion that Fräulein Kohut is the very woman a young man desires as an overture to life. The young man starts out on a small scale and climbs rapidly. Everyone has to start sooner or later. Soon he will be able to leave the beginner's level behind him, just like a new driver, who first buys a small secondhand car, then replaces it with a new and bigger model as soon as he becomes an experienced driver.

Fräulein Erika consists purely of music, and she's not all that old. That's how her student evaluates his experimental model. Klemmer even starts out one level higher: no VW, but an Opel Cadet. Walter Klemmer, secretly in love, clamps his teeth into the vestige of one of his fingernails. His face is red all over, the rosettes have spread out, and his shoulder-length hair is dark blond. He is moderately stylish. He is moderately intelligent. There is nothing salient about him, there is nothing excessive. He's let his hair lengthen a bit, so as not to look too up-to-date, but also not too old-fashioned. He won't grow a beard, though he has often been tempted to do so. He has always managed to resist this temptation. Someday, he'd like to give his teacher a long kiss and feel up her body. He wants to confront her with his animal instincts. He wants to graze her firmly, almost accidentally, as if some clumsy oaf were pushing him against her. He will then press harder against her, but apologize. Eventually, he will press against her on purpose, perhaps rub against her firmly if she lets him. He will do what she tells him to do, he wants to profit from her, then apply his experiences to more serious loves later on. He would like to learn from a much older woman—you don't have to be that careful with her. He would like to learn how to deal with young girls, who won't put up with as much nonsense. Does this have anything to do with civilization? The young man must first stake off his borders; then he can cross them successfully. Soon, he will kiss his teacher until she almost suffocates. He will suck her all over, wherever he may. He will bite her wherever she lets him. Later on, he will consciously indulge in extreme intimacies. He will start with her hand and work his way up. He will teach her how to love, or at least accept, the body she has always negated. He will cautiously teach her everything she needs for love, but then he will turn to more rewarding goals and more difficult tasks in regard to the female enigma. The eternal enigma. Someday he will become her teacher. He doesn't like those dark-blue pleated skirts and shirtwaists she always wears, and with so little self-awareness to boot. Her clothes should be youthful and colorful. Colors! He will explain to her what he means in regard to colors. He will show her what it means to be truly young and particolored and to enjoy it properly. And when she knows how young she really is, he will leave her for a younger woman. I have a feeling that you despise your body and that you only value art, Professor Kohut, says Klemmer. You only value your urgent needs, but eating and sleeping aren't enough! Fräulein Kohut, you believe that your appearance is your enemy, and the only friend you have is music. Why, just look in the mirror, look at your reflection, you'll never find a better friend than yourself. So just make yourself a little pretty, Fräulein Kohut. If I may call you that.

Herr Klemmer would love to be friends with Erika. After all, this shapeless cadaver, this piano teacher, whose profession is as plain as the nose on her face, could still develop; for this flabby bag of tissue isn't too old at all. Why, she's relatively young, compared with her mother. This pathologically twisted joke of a creature, this rapturous idiot, clutching her ideals, living only spiritually, will be spun around by this young man: from otherworldly to worldly. She'll enjoy the delights of love, just wait! In the summer, and even in the spring, Walter Klemmer goes white-water canoeing. He even loops around gates.

He conquers his element. And he will likewise subjugate his teacher, Erika Kohut. One fine day, he'll even show her the structure of a canoe. Next, she'll have to learn how to keep it afloat. By then he'll be calling her by her first name: Erika! This bird will feel her wings growing; the man will see to it.

Some men like one thing; Herr Klemmer likes this.

Bach has come to rest. His run is finished. Both performers, the master and the mistress, rise from their stools and bow their heads. They are patient horses sticking their noses into the feedbags of everyday life, which has reawakened. They say they are bowing their heads to Bach's genius rather than to this meagerly applauding crowd, which understands nothing and is too stupid even to ask questions. Only Erika's mother claps till her hands hurt. She shouts, Bravo! Bravo! Her appreciation is supported by the smiling hostess.

The crowd, shanghaied from a dung heap and sporting such ugly colors, now scrutinizes Erika. They blink into the light. Someone has removed the cushion from the lamp, and the lamp can shine unhindered. So this is Erika's audience. If you didn't know that these are supposed to be human beings, you could scarcely believe your eyes. Erika is far superior to any of them, but they are already thronging about her, brushing against her, talking nonsense. She has bred this young audience in her own incubator. Using dishonest methods, such as coercion, extortion, intimidation, she ordered these youngsters to come here. The only one who isn't here under duress is probably Herr Klemmer, the hardworking student. The rest would rather be watching TV, playing Ping-Pong, reading a book, or doing something equally stupid. They all had to come. They seem to delight in their mediocrity! Yet they dare to tackle Mozart, Schubert! They take up room: fat islands floating in the amniotic fluid of the notes. They imbibe temporarily, but do not understand what they are drinking. After all, people with a

herd instinct hold mediocrity in high esteem. They praise it as
having great value. They believe they are strong because they
are the majority. The middling level has no terrors, no anxieties. They huddle together, indulging in the illusion of
warmth. If you're in the middle, then you're alone with nothing, and certainly not yourself. And how content they are with
that state of affairs! Nothing in their existence offers them any
reproaches and no one could reproach them for their existence.
And even Erika's reproaches that an interpretation is unsuccessful would simply bounce off this soft, patient wall. For
Erika, you see, is all alone on the other side, and instead of
being proud of her situation, she wreaks vengeance. Every three
months, she forces the others to pass through the gate, which
she holds open, so that these sheep can listen to her perform.
Running a gamut from self-complacency to boredom, they now
dash off, baaing, jostling, falling all over one another when
some unreasonable individual holds them up because he hung
his coat underneath, and now he can't find it. First, all of them
want to get in; then they all want to get out as fast as possible.
And always in unison. They imagine that the sooner they can
get to the other pasture, the pasture of music, the sooner they
can leave it. But now all of Brahms is coming, after a brief
intermission, ladies and gentlemen. Dear students. Today, Erika's exceptional status is not a failing, but an asset. For they
are all gaping and gawking at her even though they secretly
hate her.

Herr Klemmer, winding his way over to her, beams at her
with festive blue eyes. His two hands reach for her pianist
hand, and he says, Congratulations, adding that words fail him,
Professor. Erika's mama cuts in, emphatically prohibiting any
handshake. There is to be no sign of friendship because it could
twist the tendons and interfere with her playing. The hand
should remain in its natural position, if you please. Well, we

don't have to be all that particular for this third-class audience, do we, Herr Klemmer? One has to tyrannize them, one has to suppress them and oppress them, just to get through to them. One should use clubs on them! They want thrashings and a pile of passions that each composer should experience vicariously for them and carefully set down. They want shouts and shrieks, otherwise they would have to shout and shriek all the time. Out of boredom. The gray tones, the fine nuances, the delicate distinctions are beyond their grasp anyway. Yet in music, as in any realm of art, it is much easier juxtaposing harsh contrasts, brutal antitheses. But that's trash, nothing more! These lambs don't know it. They don't know anything. Erika takes hold of Klemmer's arm; this intimate gesture makes him tremble.. He can't be cold amid these healthy teenagers with their excellent circulation; these barbarians who have eaten their fill, in a country whose culture is ruled by barbarians. Just look at the newspapers: They're more barbaric than the things they report on. A man who meticulously slices up his wife and children and then stores them in the refrigerator in order to eat them later on is no more barbaric than the newspaper that runs the item. And then the papers call each other names. Klemmer, just imagine! And now I've got to say hello to Professor Vyoral, if you don't mind. I'll see you later, Herr Klemmer!

Mother grabs a light-blue angora jacket that she crocheted herself and drapes it over Erika's shoulders. The lubricant mustn't suddenly freeze in these joints, raising the frictional resistance. The little jacket is like a cozy over a teapot. Sometimes useful things like toilet-paper rollers have such homemade caskets on them, with colorful pom-poms. They decorate the rear windows of cars. Right in the center. Erika's pom-pom is her head, which looms proudly. She trips along on her high heels across the smooth ice of the inlaid floor (areas subject to great stress are protected today by cheap runners). Erika heads toward an older colleague in order to receive congratulations from expert lips. Mother gently pushes her forward. Mother has a hand on Erika's back, on her right shoulder blade, on the angora jacket.

Walter Klemmer still doesn't drink or smoke; nevertheless, he has astonishing amounts of energy. As if attached to her with suction cups, he trails behind his teacher, plowing his way through the clucking horde. He sticks to her. If she needs him, he'll be at hand. If she needs male protection. She only has to turn around and she'll bump right into him. He actually seeks this body check. The brief intermission is almost over. He inhales Erika's presence with flaring nostrils as if he were on a high Alpine meadow that one seldom visits, so one must therefore breathe deeply. In order to bring a lot of oxygen back to the city. He removes a stray hair from the sleeve of the light blue jacket, reaping thanks, oh, my. Erika's mother nebulously senses something, but she cannot help appreciating his good manners and sense of duty. His behavior contrasts sharply with everything that is customary and necessary nowadays between the sexes. Herr Klemmer is a young man for Erika's mother but a man of the old stamp.

Now for a small chat before we come to the final round. Klemmer wants to know why, and regrets that, such cultivated home recitals are gradually dying out. First the masters died, now their music is dying, because people only want to listen to pop, rock, and punk. Families like our host and hostess no longer exist. In earlier times, there were so many like them. Generations of laryngologists would satiate themselves on, if not wear themselves out with, Beethoven's late quartets. During the day, they painted sore throats; in the evening, they got their reward when they hobnobbed with Beethoven. Today, the academics do nothing but stamp their feet to the beat of

Bruckner's elephant trumpets and heap praises on that provincial tunesmith. Scorning Bruckner is a youthful peccadillo to which many people have succumbed, Herr Klemmer. One does not understand him until much later, believe me. Avoid fashionable judgments until you have a wider grasp, my dear colleague. Klemmer is happy to hear the word "colleague" from competent lips. He then launches into poignant jargon about Schubert's and Schumann's darkening descent into madness. He talks about their subtle shades and nuances, while using mothlike tints of gray in gray.

Next comes a Kohut/Klemmer duet, in venomous lemon-yellow, about the local concert business. Molto vivace. Their duet is well rehearsed. Neither musician has any part in this business. They are allowed to participate only as consumers, yet their qualifications are vastly superior! Still, they are nothing but listeners, deluding themselves about their knowledge. One part of this duet could have taken part: Erika. But it didn't come about.

Now the two of them delicately pass across the loose dust of intermediary tones, intermediary worlds, intermediary realms, for this is where the middle stratum feels at home. Schubert's descent into madness opens the dance—like the darkening, as Adorno describes it, in Schumann's Fantasy in C Major. It flows into the far distance, into nothingness, yet without wearing the apotheosis of conscious fading! It darkens without realizing it, indeed without referring to itself! The duettists grow silent for a moment in order to enjoy the things they have articulated in an inappropriate place. Each of them thinks he understands more than the other; one thinks so because of his youth, the other because of her maturity. They take turns outdoing each other's fury at the ignorant, the uncomprehending—many of whom are gathered right here. Just look at them, Professor! Just take a good look at them, Herr

Klemmer! The bond of scorn links the trainer and the trainee. The fading of Schubert's, of Schumann's, life-light is the extreme opposite of what the healthy masses mean when they call a tradition healthy and wallow in it luxuriantly. Health—how disgusting. Health is the transfiguration of status quo. The hacks who fill up the playbills for the Philharmonic Concerts are the most repulsive conformists. Just imagine: They make something like health the chief criterion of important music. Well, health always sides with the victors; the weak fall away. Yet these sauna-users and happy pissers deserve to fail. Beethoven, the master whom they consider so healthy—yet he was deaf, alas. And that profoundly healthy Brahms. Klemmer precariously tosses something in (and gets his ball into the basket): He has always thought of Bruckner as being very healthy. Klemmer is sharply rebuked. Erika modestly displays the wound inflicted on her by her personal experiences with the music business in Vienna and the provinces. Until she resigned herself. A sensitive person gets burned, like a delicate moth. And that, says Erika Kohut, is why these two extremely sick composers, Schumann and Schubert (they share the first syllable), are closest to my bruised heart. Not the Schumann whose thoughts have all fled him, but the Schumann just before that! A hair's breadth before that! He already has an inkling that his mind will flee, he suffers from his inkling, down to his finest veins, he takes leave of his conscious life as he enters the choirs of angels and demons, yet he clutches that conscious life one final time, even though he is no longer fully conscious of himself. He yearningly tries to catch the fading echoes, he mourns the loss of the most precious thing: himself. This is the phase in which one knows how great the loss of oneself is before one is utterly abandoned.

Erika, in gentle music, tells Klemmer that her father lost his mind and died in the Steinhof Asylum. That is why people have to be considerate of Erika, she has gone through so much. Amid all this splendid and resplendent health, Erika does not want to say any more, but she does drop a few hints. Hoping to flay some feelings out of Klemmer, she ruthlessly applies the chisel. Because of her suffering, this woman deserves every ounce of male interest she can squeeze out. The young man's interest is then harshly reawakened.

The intermission is over. Please be seated. Now come Brahms lieder, sung by a young soprano, a student. And then the recital ends. The Kohut/Haberkorn duo couldn't have been topped anyway. The applause is louder than before the intermission because everyone is relieved that the soirée is over. Even more bravos, not only from Erika's mama, but also from Erika's best pupil. The mother and the best pupil scrutinize each other from the corners of their eyes, both shout energetically and grow terribly suspicious. One wants something; the other does not care to give it up. The light is turned up full blast, so are the chandeliers, nothing is spared in this beautiful moment. The host has tears in his eyes. Erika has played Chopin as an encore, and the host thinks of Poland in the night, the land of his ancestors. The soprano and Erika, her charming accompanist, receive gigantic bouquets of flowers. Two mothers and a father appear, and they likewise present bouquets to the professor, who is helping their children. The gifted young vocalist gets only one bouquet. Erika's mother affably helps mummify the bouquets in tissue paper for the trip home. We only have to carry these gorgeous flowers to the trolley stop and then the trolley will take us comfortably almost to our door. You start by saving on a cab, and you end up with an apartment. Indispensable friends and helpers offer rides in their own cars, but Mother calls them all dispensable. Thanks but no thanks. We accept no favors, and we offer none.

Walter Klemmer strides over and helps his piano teacher

into her winter coat with the fox collar; he is quite familiar with her coat from all their lessons. It's got a belt and it's also got that sumptuous fur collar. He covers the mother in her black Persian-lamb-paw coat. He wants to continue the conversation, which had to be interrupted. He instantly says something about art and literature, in case Fräulein Kohut has bled out all her music after the triumph she has just celebrated. He latches on to her, digging his dentition into her. He helps her into her sleeves, he is even so bold as to pull her shoulder-length hair out of the collar and arrange it neatly upon the fur. He offers to accompany the two ladies to the trolley stop.

Mother senses something that can't yet be expressed. Erika has mixed feelings about any attention showered upon her. Let's hope it won't turn into hail the size of hen's eggs, the hailstones could strike holes in her! She too has been given a gigantic box of candy; Walter Klemmer has wrested it from her and is now carrying it. He is also holding an orange lily bouquet or something of the sort. Burdened with all kinds of things, not the least of which is music, the three of them (after cordially saying goodbye to our host and hostess) trudge to the trolley stop. The young people should walk ahead, Mama can't keep up with those young feet. Besides, Mama has a much better view from behind and can hear much better. Erika is already hesitating, because poor Mama has to slog along behind them, all alone. Usually, the two Kohut ladies enjoy walking arm in arm, discussing Erika's achievements and unabashedly praising them. But today, some young male upstart is replacing faithful old Mother, who, crumpled and neglected, has to bring up the rear. The apron strings tighten and pull Erika back. They pinch her because Mother has to walk behind her. The fact that she herself offered to do so only makes it worse. If Herr Klemmer weren't so seemingly indispensable, Erika could comfortably walk next to her mother. The two women could

ruminate about the recital and perhaps graze in the candy box.
A foretaste of the cozy, homey warmth awaiting them in their
parlor. Perhaps they can even catch the late show on TV. That
would be the nicest finale to such a musical day. And that
student keeps getting closer and closer to her. Can't he keep
his distance? It's embarrassing to feel a warm, steaming, youthful body next to you. This young man seems so dreadfully
intact and carefree that Erika panics. He doesn't intend to burden her with his health, does he? The twosomeness at home,
which no one else can share, appears threatened. Who else but
Mother could guarantee peace and quiet, order and security in
their own four walls? Every fiber in Erika's body longs for her
soft TV armchair behind a locked door. She has her customary
chair, Mother has her own, with a Persian pouf for her often-
swollen feet. Their domesticity goes awry because Klemmer
won't skedaddle. He doesn't intend to force his way into their
home, does he? Erika would much prefer to creep into her
mother and rock gently in the warm fluid of her womb. As
warm and moist outside as inside. She stiffens in front of her
mother when Klemmer gets too close for comfort.

Klemmer talks and talks. Erika remains silent. Her rare ex-
periments with the opposite sex flash through her mind, but
the memories aren't good. Nor was the reality any better. Once
it happened with a salesman who tried to pick her up in a café;
she finally gave in just to shut him up. The wretched collection
of white-skinned homebodies is completed by a young law
student and a young high school teacher. Since then, years
have passed and passed away. After a concert, two academics
had held up her coat sleeves like machine-gun barrels, thereby
disarming her: They had the more dangerous weapons. After
each of these experiences, Erika wanted to get back to her
mother as fast as possible. Mother didn't suspect a thing. In
this way, Erika grazed through two or three bachelor pads with

kitchenettes and sitz baths. Sour pastures for the gourmet of art.

At first, she enjoyed preening herself: a pianist, albeit temporarily not performing. None of these men had ever had a pianist sitting on his sofa. Each man instantly behaved like a gentleman, and the woman enjoyed a wide view, over and above the man. But when she's having sex, no woman remains grandiose. The young men soon took charming liberties, both indoors and outdoors. Car doors were no longer held open, fun was poked at clumsiness. The woman was then lied to, cheated on, tormented, and often not called. She was intentionally left up in the air about his intentions. One or two letters went unanswered. The woman waited and waited, in vain. And she did not ask why she was waiting, because she feared the answer more than the waiting. Meanwhile, the man began to deal with other women in another life.

Sex started those young men rolling with Erika, and then they stopped sex. They turned off the gas, leaving only a whiff. Erika tried to hold them with passion and pleasure. She pounded her fists on the swaying dead weight on top of her, she was so excited she couldn't help shrieking. Her nails pointedly scratched the back of each antagonist. She felt nothing. She simulated overwhelming pleasure so that the man would finally stop. The man did stop, but then he came another time. Erika felt nothing, she has always felt nothing. She is as unfeeling as a piece of tar paper in the rain.

Each gentleman soon left Erika, and now she doesn't care to have a gentleman. Only feeble charms emanate from a man, who makes very little effort anyway. Men do not go to any trouble for such an extraordinary woman as Erika. Yet they will never meet such a woman again. For this woman is unique. They will always regret it, but they leave anyway. They look at Erika, turn and depart. They make no effort to investigate her truly unique artistic qualities; they prefer to deal with their own mediocre knowledge and chances. This woman seems like too large a chunk for their dull little knives. They accept the fact that this woman will soon wither and wane. They lose no sleep over their realization. Erika is shrinking into a mummy, and they go about their dreary business as if a rare flower were not asking to be watered.

Unaware of such events, Herr Klemmer sways along, like a living bouquet of flowers, next to the younger Kohut; the older Kohut follows in his wake. He is so young. He doesn't realize how young he is. He risks a venerating, conspiratorial sidelong glance at his teacher. He shares the secret of understanding art with her. He is certain that the woman next to him is wondering, as he is, how to render the mother harmless. How can he invite Erika for a glass of wine so that the day might end on a festive note? Klemmer's thoughts go no further. His teacher is pure for him. See the mother home, take Erika out. Erika! He pronounces her name. She pretends she has misunderstood, and she quickens her pace, so we can advance, and so the young man won't have some bizarre whim. He should simply go away! There are so many streets he can vanish in. Once he's gone, she and her mother will gossip about the fact that this student has a secret crush on her. Are you going to watch the Fred Astaire movie tonight? Yes, indeed. I wouldn't miss it for the world. Now Herr Klemmer knows what to expect: nothing.

In the dark underpass of the elevated line, Klemmer makes a daredevil attempt, he briefly grabs at the professor's hand. Give me your hand, Erika. This hand can play the piano so marvelously. Now the hand coldly slips through his net and is gone. A puff of air arose, and then the air fell still again. Erika acts as if she hasn't noticed the attempt. First misfire. The hand got up its nerve only because Erika's mother was walking side by side with them for a brief distance. Mother has become a sidecar in order to supervise the front line of the young couple. There are no autos in the street now, and the sidewalk is narrow at this point. Erika perceives a danger and gets her foolhardy mother back on the sidewalk immediately. Klemmer's hand falls by the wayside.

Klemmer now sends his mouth on this zealous trip. His mouth, lacking the fine creases of age, opens and closes effortlessly. He wants to talk to Erika about a novel by Norman Mailer, whom Klemmer admires as a man and as an artist. Klemmer saw such and such in the book; perhaps Erika saw something entirely different? Erika hasn't read it, and the discussion seeps away. No exchange can ever come about in this way. Erika would trade anything for her lost youth, and Klemmer would like to trade his youth for experience. The young face of the young man shimmers softly under streetlights and illuminated store windows; next to him, the pianist shrivels, a piece of paper burning in a stove of lust. She doesn't have the nerve to look at him. Mother will certainly try to separate them if necessary. Erika is monosyllabic and uninterested, becoming more and more so the closer they get to the trolley stop. Mother prevents the transaction between the two young people by talking about the danger of a cold and by tempting fate with a detailed description of the symptoms. Erika agrees with her. One should be careful not to catch something now; tomorrow may be too late. Herr Klemmer makes a final desperate attempt to spread his wings. He blares about knowing a good way to prevent colds: You have to harden your body in advance. He recommends going to a sauna. He recommends a few good laps in a pool. He recommends sports in general and the most exciting kind, white-water canoeing, in particular. Now, in winter, the ice gets in the way, you have to make do with other sports for the time being. But soon it'll be spring, and that's the best time for white-water canoeing, because the rivers will be filled with melted snow and ice, and they'll pull everything along. Klemmer again recommends going to a sauna. He recommends long-distance running, cross-country running, fitness running in general. Erika isn't listening, but her eyes sweep over him; then, embarrassed, they instantly glide away. Almost unintentionally, she peers out from the prison of her aging body. She will not file away at the bars. Mother won't let her touch her bars. Klemmer won't go along with that, no matter what Erika says. This ardent warrior boldly gropes another step forward, a young bull, stamping around the fence. Is he trying to get to the cow, or does he merely want to get to a new meadow? Who can say? He recommends sports so you can have fun and generally develop a sense of your body, through your body. You wouldn't believe how much a person can enjoy his own body, Professor! Ask your body what it wants and it'll tell you. At first, your body may look plain and homely. But then, oh, boy! It comes alive, and the muscles develop. It stretches in fresh air. But it also knows its limits. And Klemmer can reap all these benefits from his favorite sport, white-water canoeing. A flimsy memory flashes through Erika's mind; she once saw something or other on TV: white-water canoers. They popped up in a weekend sports panorama, before the movie. The paddlers were wearing orange life vests and reinforced helmets. They were squeezed into tiny boats or similar contraptions, like baby pears in a bottle of liqueur. They frequently toppled into the water. Erika smiles. She briefly recalls one of the men, whom she loudly cheered, and then instantly forgets him. All that remains is a feeble desire, which she likewise instantly forgets. Well, we're almost there!

The words freeze in Herr Klemmer's mouth. He arduously mumbles something about skiing, the season's about to start. You don't have to go that far from the city to reach the finest slopes, almost any angle you like. Isn't that great? Why don't you come along sometime, Professor, young people belong together. We'll find friends my age there, and they'll take marvelous care of you, Professor. Mother terminates the conversation: We're not all that athletic. She has never watched any athletics from closer up than the boob tube. In winter, we'd much rather retreat with a good whodunnit. We generally prefer to retreat, you know, from anything whatsoever. We know what we're retreating from, and we'd rather not know where we're going. A person can break a leg.

Herr Klemmer says he can borrow his father's car almost anytime if he lets him know in advance. His hand burrows around in the darkness and reemerges completely empty.

Erika feels a growing repulsion. If only he were gone! And let him take his hand along with him. Go away! He is a terrible challenge hurled at her by life, and the only challenge she normally accepts is to perform an opus faithfully. At last, the trolley stop heaves into view, the Plexiglas shelter is illuminated reassuringly, as is the small bench inside. No mugger, no killer in sight, and the two women can deal with Klemmer easily. A lamp is shining. Two other people are waiting, a pair of women, unescorted, unprotected. This late at night, the trolleys run less frequently, and Klemmer, unfortunately, still won't leave. The killer may not be skulking around, but he might still show up, and they would then need Klemmer. Erika shudders; he should stop trying to get to her. Here comes the trolley! Soon she'll be able to discuss the whole business in detail with Mother, from a distance, once Herr Klemmer is gone. He has to leave; then he'll be a topic of thorough discussion. Not much more tickly than a feather on your skin. The trolley arrives and blithely carries off the Kohut ladies. Herr Klemmer waves, but the ladies are preoccupied with their purses and tickets.

❑

The child, whose talent is discussed for miles around, falls. She is dreadfully clumsy. She usually moves as if she were inside a sack, up to her neck, stumbling over objects, arms and legs flailing. SHE loudly complains that these tripwires have been placed in her path because other people are so inattentive. SHE herself is never to blame. Teachers who have observed it all greet and comfort the girl who trudges along under the exorbitant demands of music. On the one hand, SHE sacrifices all her free time to music; on the other hand, SHE makes herself ridiculous in other people's eyes. Despite their observations, the teachers feel a vague repulsion when they state that SHE is the only one who doesn't have just nonsense on HER mind after school. Nonsensical insults weigh upon HER mind, which she tries to unburden at home, with her mother. Racing off to the school, Mother complains loudly about the other pupils, who are trying to destroy her wonderful offspring. And then the concentrated fury of the others really strikes home. There is a vicious circle of complaints and more vehement causes for complaints. Metal crates full of empty milk bottles from the school lunchroom turn up in HER path, demanding an attention that they do not receive. All HER attention is secretly focused on the boys at school. From the extreme corners of her eyes, she steals glances at them, while her head, held high, flails in a totally different direction, taking no notice of these future men—or boys trying to practice manliness.

Obstacles lurk in the smelly classrooms. Every morning, they fill up with the sweat of each simple normal student who just manages to get by, while his parents hectically work their fingers to the bone, fiddling around on the switchboard of his mind, trying to make him at least pass his courses. In the afternoon, the classroom is given a new lease on life by special, musically gifted students attending the music school which is temporarily housed here. Noisy contraptions pounce like locusts upon the silent spaces of thought. And throughout the day, the school is inundated by lasting values, by knowledge and music. These music pupils come in every size, shape, and form, even high school graduates and university students! They are all concerted in their efforts to produce sounds, alone or in groups.

SHE snaps her teeth more and more fiercely at the air bubbles of an inner life, of which the others have no inkling. At the core of her being, she is as beautiful as something ethereal, and this core has concentrated in her mind all by itself. The others do not see this beauty. SHE thinks she is beautiful and gives herself a fashion-model face, all in her mind. Her mother would order her to stop. She can change these faces at will; sometimes they are blondes, sometimes brunettes—gentlemen prefer either. And she goes along with such preferences, because she'd like those gentlemen to like her. She is everything but beautiful. She's talented—lovely to listen to, but not lovely to look at. She is homely, and that's what her mother keeps telling her, so the child won't think she's beautiful. Mother threatens her in the meanest way: The only way she'll ever captivate anybody is with HER knowledge and HER ability. Mother threatens to kill the child if she ever so much as sees her with a man. Mother keeps her eyes peeled, she checks, hunts, calculates, concludes, punishes.

SHE is swathed in her daily duties like an Egyptian mummy, but no one is dying to look at her. For three long years, she tenaciously longs for her first pair of high-heeled shoes. She never forgoes and forgets. She needs tenacity for her wish.

Until she gets her wish and her shoes, she can apply her tenacity to Bach's solo sonatas, because Mother craftily promises her the shoes in exchange for mastering the Bach. She'll never get the shoes. She can buy them herself someday when she earns her own money. The shoes are constantly held out to her as bait. In this way, Mother keeps luring another bit and yet another bit of Hindemith out of the child. Mother loves the child more than the child could ever love the shoes.

SHE is superior to everyone else. Her mother puts her high above them. SHE leaves the others far behind and far below.

HER innocent wishes change over the years into a destructive greed, a desire to annihilate. If others have something, then she wants it too. If she can't have it, she'll destroy it. She begins stealing things. In the garret studio, where drawing classes are held, things vanish: armies of watercolors, pencils, brushes, rulers. A pair of plastic sunglasses with iridescent lenses (a stylish innovation!) also vanishes. She is so scared that she throws her loot, which will never do her any good, into the first garbage can, so it won't be found in her possession. Mother seeks and always finds any evidence of a secretly purchased chocolate bar or ice-cream cone for which she secretly saved her trolley money.

Instead of the sunglasses, she'd much rather have the new gray-flannel ensemble that one of the girls is wearing. But it's hard to steal clothes if the wearer wears them all the time. To make up for it, SHE does some masterful sleuthing and finds out that the ensemble was earned by child prostitution. SHE shadows the wearer's gray silhouette for days on end; the music conservatory and the Bristol Bar—together with middle-aged businessmen, so lonely—are in the same district. The schoolmate, only sweet sixteen, is reported for her misdemeanor (law and order!). SHE tells her mother which ensemble she wants and where she can earn the money herself. The words flow over her lips in feigned childhood innocence, so her mother can delight in the child's blissful ignorance and praise her for it. Mother instantly attaches the spurs to her hunting boots. Snorting and foaming, tossing her head, she stomps off to the school and gets the culprit kicked out but good! The gray ensemble leaves with its wearer; it is now out of sight, but not out of the mind that it haunted for such a long time, cutting bloody furrows and fissures. The ensemble wearer is punished by becoming a salesgirl in a cosmetics store. She will have to suffer through the rest of her life without the benefit of general education. She will never be what she could have been.

Meanwhile, SHE is rewarded for reporting the delinquent so promptly. SHE is permitted to make an extravagant schoolbag out of cheap leather remnants. In this way, Mother makes sure SHE does something useful with her leisure, which she really doesn't have. It takes HER a long time to complete the schoolbag. But now, something has been created that no one else can or would call her own. SHE is the only one to have such an extraordinary bag, and she actually has the nerve to carry it outdoors!

The future men and present music pupils with whom she performs chamber music and is forced to play in orchestras arouse an ache in her, a yearning, which has always seemed to lurk in her. That is why she flaunts tremendous pride, but what is she so proud of? Mother begs and beseeches her never to forget anything, for she will never forgive herself. SHE cannot overlook the tiniest mistakes; they sting and stab her for months on end. Often she stubbornly broods about what she might have done, but it's too late now! The small would-be orchestra is conducted personally by the violin teacher. The first violin embodies absolute power here. She wants to side with the powerful, so they'll pull her up. She has always sided with power, even since she first laid eyes on her mother. During breaks, the young man, on whom the other violins orient themselves like the wind on a weather vane, reads important books for his upcoming degree examination. He says that soon life will become serious for him, by which he means that he will begin attending the university. He is making plans and courageously talking about them. Sometimes, he absentmindedly gazes through HER in order to repeat a perhaps mathematical, perhaps cosmopolitan formula. He can never catch her eye since she has been majestically eyeing the ceiling for a long time now. She does not see the person in him, she sees only the musician; she does not look at him, and he is to realize that he means nothing to her. But on the inside, she almost burns up. Her wick burns brighter than a thousand suns, focusing on the rancid rat known as her genital. One day, in order to make the young man look at her, she violently shuts the lid of her wooden violin case, slams it on her left hand, which she needs for fingering. The pain makes her scream. Maybe he'll cast an eye at her. Maybe he'll act gallant toward her. But no, he would like to join the army, just to get it over with. He would like to teach natural science, German, and music in a high school. Of the three, music is the only subject he has already mastered to any extent. In order to have him recognize her as a woman and register her as "female" in his mental notebook, she plays the piano for him alone during breaks. She is very skillful on the keyboard, but he judges her purely by her terrible ungainliness in daily practical life—the clumsiness with which she cannot trample into his heart.

She makes up her mind: She will not entrust the utmost and ultimate edge of her being, the very last bit of herself, to anyone! She wants to keep everything and, if possible, add to it. You are what you have. SHE piles up steep mountains, her knowledge and abilities form a smooth, snowy peak. Only the most courageous skier will reach the top. The young man can slip on her slopes at any time, he can slide through a crack in the ice, plunge into a bottomless pit. SHE has given someone the key to her precious heart, to her finely polished icicle mind; so she can take the key back at any time.

SHE waits impatiently for her value as a future star to rise on the stock exchange of life. She waits silently, more and more silently, for someone to choose her, and she will then promptly choose him. He will be an exceptional man, musically gifted, but not conceited. However, this man has already made his choice: He'll be majoring in English or German. His pride is justified.

Outside, something beckons, but she deliberately refuses to take part, so she can boast about not taking part. She desires medals, badges for successful completion of nonparticipation, so she won't have to be measured, weighed. A clumsily swimming animal with porous webs between its dull claws, she paddles along in fits and starts through the warm maternal discharges. Her head looms out anxiously. Just where is the shore, where has it vanished to? It's so difficult to scramble up to the foggy shore, she has slid back down the smooth embankment far too often.

She yearns for a man who knows a lot and can play the violin. Once she bags him, he'll caress her. That mountain goat, ready to flee, is already clambering through the detritus, but he doesn't have the strength to track down her femininity, which lies buried in the debris. He is of the opinion that a woman is a woman. Then he makes a little joke about the female sex, which is known for its fickleness: oh, women! Whenever he cues HER to play, he looks at her without really perceiving her. He does not decide against HER, he simply decides without HER.

SHE would never get into a situation in which she might appear weak, much less inferior. That is why she stays where she is. She only goes through the familiar stages of learning and obeying, she never looks for new areas. The gears squeal in the press that squeezes the blood out from under her fingernails. Learning requires her to be sensible: No pain, no gain, she's told. Her mother demands obedience. If you take a risk, you perish. That advice comes from Mother too. When SHE's home alone, she cuts herself, slicing off her nose to spite other people's faces. She always waits and waits for the moment when she can cut herself unobserved. No sooner does the sound of the closing door die down than she takes out her little talisman, the paternal all-purpose razor. SHE peels the blade out of its Sunday coat of five layers of virginal plastic. She is very skilled in the use of blades; after all, she has to shave her father, shave that soft paternal cheek under the completely empty paternal brow, which is now undimmed by any thought, unwrinkled by any will. This blade is destined for HER flesh. This thin, elegant foil of bluish steel, pliable, elastic. SHE sits down in front of the magnifying side of the shaving mirror; spreading her legs, she makes a cut, magnifying the aperture that is the doorway into her body. She knows from experience that such a razor cut doesn't hurt, for her arms, hands, and legs have often served as guinea pigs. Her hobby is cutting her own body.

Like the mouth cavity, this opening cannot exactly be called beautiful, but it is necessary. She is entirely at her own mercy, which is still better than being at someone else's mercy. It's still in her hands, and a hand has feelings too. She knows precisely how often and how deep. The opening is caught in the retaining screw of the mirror, an opportunity for cutting is seized. Quick, before someone comes. With little information about anatomy and with even less luck, she applies the cold steel to and into her body, where she believes there ought to be a hole. The aperture gapes, terrified by the change, and blood pours out. This blood is not an unusual sight, but presence doesn't make the heart grow fonder. As usual, there is no pain. SHE, however, cuts the wrong place, separating what the Good Lord and Mother Nature have brought together in unusual unity. Man must not sunder, and revenge is quick. She feels nothing. For an instant, the two flesh halves, sliced apart, stare at each other, taken aback at this sudden gap, which wasn't there before. They've shared joy and sorrow for many years, and now they're being separated! In the mirror, the two halves also look at themselves, laterally inverted, so that neither knows which half it is. Then the blood shoots out resolutely. The drops ooze, run, blend with their comrades, turning into a red trickle, then a soothingly steady red stream when the individual trickles unite. The blood prevents HER from seeing what she has sliced open. It was her own body, but it is dreadfully alien to her. She hadn't realized that one cannot control the path of the cut, unlike a cut in a dress, where you can roll a tiny wheel along the individual dotted, broken, or alternately dotted and broken lines, thus maintaining control. First SHE'll have to stop the bleeding. She's scared. Her nether region and her fear are two allies of hers, they usually appear together. If one of these two friends drops into her head without knocking, then she can rest assured: The other cannot be far behind. Mother can check whether or not SHE keeps her hands outside the covers at night; but if Mother wanted to gain control of HER fear, she would have to pry her child's skull open and personally scrape out the fear.

In order to stem the flow of blood, SHE pulls out the popular cellulose package whose merits are known to and appreciated by every woman, especially in sports and for any kind of movement. The package quickly replaces the golden cardboard crown worn by the little girl when she is sent as a princess to a children's costume party. SHE, however, never went to a children's party, she never got to know the crown. The queen's crown suddenly slips into her panties, and the woman knows her place in life. The thing that once shone forth on the head in childlike pride has now landed where the female wood has to wait for an ax. The princess is grown up now, and this is a matter of opinion on which opinions diverge. One man wants a nicely veneered, not-too-showy piece of furniture; the second wants a complete set in genuine Caucasian walnut. But the third man, alas, only wants to pile up huge heaps of firewood. Yet he, too, can excel: he can arrange his woodpile functionally and efficiently to save space. More fuel can fit into a neat cellar than one in which the wood is dumped helter-skelter. One fire burns longer than the other, because there is more wood.

❑

Right outside her building door, Erika K. was expected by the wide-open world, which insisted on accompanying her. The more Erika pushed the world away, the pushier the world became. A violent spring storm whirled her along. It swept under her flaring skirt, and then, crestfallen, let it drop. The air, leaden with exhaust fumes, banged and bashed her, clawing her lungs. Objects rattled and crashed against a wall.

In small shops, the modern mothers, dressed colorfully and taking their job seriously, bend over a ware, flinch behind the wall of the wind. The children are kept on long leashes while the young women, applying knowledge they have gleaned from gourmet magazines, test innocent eggplants and other exotic foods. Poor quality makes these women cringe, as if an adder were rearing its ugly head out of the zucchini. At this time of day, no healthy man is out in the street, he has no business being here. Around the entrances to their stores, the green-grocers have piled up crates of colorful vitamin-sources in all stages of rot and decay. An obvious connoisseur, the woman grubs around in these heaps. She braces herself against the storm. A repulsive inspector, she taps everything, checking freshness and hardness. Any vestiges of pesticidal ammunition on surfaces provoke dismay in the educated young mother. Here, on this bunch of grapes, you can see a fungus-green coat, probably poisonous; the grapes were crudely sprayed while still on the vine. Going over to the storekeeper's wife, who wears a dark-blue apron, the disgusted customer shows her the grapes as proof that once again chemistry has conquered nature, and that the seed of cancer could be planted in the young mother's child. A recent poll has demonstrated beyond the shadow of any doubt that people realize you have to test food for its poisons; in fact, more people know that than the name of Austria's poisonous old chancellor. Even the middle-aged housewife cares about the quality of the soil in which the potato was grown. This customer, unfortunately, is at greater risk because of her age. And now the lurking risk has drastically increased. Ultimately, she buys oranges; after all, you can peel them, thus palpably reducing the ecological damage. This housewife has tried to draw attention with her knowledge of poison, but it doesn't help, for Erika has already walked past her, ignoring her. This evening, the woman's husband will also ignore her; he will read tomorrow's paper today, having bought it on the way home, so he can be ahead of his time. Nor will their children appreciate the lovingly prepared lunch: They are already grown and don't even live at home anymore. They got married long ago and are now eagerly buying their own poisonous produce. Someday, they will stand at this woman's grave, weeping halfheartedly, and time will then be reaching for them. They won't have to worry about their mother anymore, and *their* children will already have to worry about them.

Such are Erika's thoughts.

On her way to school, Erika compulsively sees people and food dying everywhere; she very seldom sees that something is growing and thriving—at most in the city hall park or in the Volksgarten, the vast park where roses and tulips are pushing up and fleshing out. But their joy is premature, because they already contain the time of withering. Such are Erika's thoughts. And everything confirms them. Only art, she reflects, can survive longer. Art is cultivated by Erika, pruned, tied back, weeded, and finally harvested. But who can tell how many things have already been disparaged and dispatched with no justification. Every day, a piece of music, a short story, or a poem dies because its existence is no longer justified in our time. And things that were once considered immortal have become mortal again, no one knows them anymore. Even though they deserve to survive. In Erika's piano class, children are already hacking away at Mozart and Haydn, the advanced pupils are riding roughshod over Brahms and Schumann, covering the forest soil of keyboard literature with their slug slime.

Erika K. resolutely plunges into the spring storm, hoping to arrive safe and sound at the other end. She has to cross this open square in front of city hall. A dog next to her likewise senses the first breath of spring. Erika despises anything pertaining to bodies, animals; they are constant handicaps on her straight and narrow path. She may not be as handicapped as a cripple, but her freedom of movement is limited, after all. You see, most people move lovingly toward another person, a partner, a mate. That's all they ever hanker for. If a female colleague at the conservatory takes Erika's arm, Erika shies away from her presumptuousness. No one is allowed to lean on Erika. Only the featherweight of art may settle on Erika, but it is always in danger of floating off at the slightest puff of air and settling somewhere else. Erika squeezes her arm so hard against her ribs that her colleague's arm, unable to break in between Erika and Erika's arm, sinks back in discouragement. Such a person is usually called unapproachable. And no one approaches her. People take detours. They would rather wait, endure a delay, so long as they don't have to make any contact with Erika. Some people vociferously attract attention; Erika doesn't. Some people wave; Erika doesn't. It takes all sorts. Some people hop up and down, yodel, shout. These people know what they want. Erika doesn't.

Two female students or trainees approach her, giggling loudly, huddling arm in arm, sticking their heads together like two plastic beads. They cling together, like apples. They will probably dissolve their togetherness the moment either girl's boyfriend approaches. They will instantly tear themselves out of their warm, friendly embrace in order to aim their suckers at him and burrow under his skin like antitank mines. Later on, vexation will explode with a bang, and the wife will leave her husband in order to develop a talent that has been lying fallow.

People can barely make it alone, they have to move in packs, as if each single person weren't already a strain on the earth's surface. Such are the thoughts of Erika, a loner. Nocturnal slugs, shapeless, spineless, mindless! Never touched or overwhelmed by any magic, by the spell of music. They stick to one another with their skins, which are never agitated by a puff of air.

Erika cleans herself by patting herself. With soft whipping strokes, she runs her hands over her skirt and jacket. It was so stormy and gusty outside that the dust must have settled in her clothes. Erika sidesteps passersby before they even come within eyeshot.

It was on one of those wickedly flickering spring days that the Kohut ladies delivered the feebleminded and completely disoriented father to the sanitarium in Lower Austria. That was before the public madhouse Am Steinhof (known far and wide from somber ballads) welcomed him and invited him to remain. As long as he liked! Who could ask for anything more!

Their family sausage dealer, a famous self-made slaughterer, offered to transport the patient in his gray VW van (which normally contains dangling halves of calf carcasses). Papa traveled through the spring landscape, breathing the fresh air. He was accompanied by his baggage, each piece neatly monogrammed, each sock bearing a clearly embroidered K. A painstaking handiwork that he had long been unable to admire or even appreciate, even though he benefited from this manual skill. After all, the initial would prevent an equally dotty Herr Novotny or Herr Vytvar from misusing Papa's socks, albeit with no malicious intent. Their names would have different initials—but what about that senile Herr Keller, who made in his bed? Well, he lived in a different room, as Erika and her mother were delighted to learn.

They started off; they would get there soon. They'd arrive any moment! They drove past Rudolfshöhe and the Feuerstein, past Vienna Woods Lake and Mount Kaiserbrunnen, past Mount Jochgraben and Mount Kohlreit, which they used to climb with Father in the old days, which weren't good. They would almost pass Mount Buch if they didn't have to turn off first. Snow White herself was surely waiting beyond the mountains, in delicate splendor, laughing joyously because someone new had entered her domain—a huge two-family house belonging to a rural family with tax-evasive income. This mansion had been remodeled for the humane purpose of housing humans with unsound minds and sound finances. In this way, the building served not two families, but many, many patients, offering them refuge and protection from themselves and from others. The inmates could choose between taking a walk or practicing a handicraft. Either choice was supervised. In the workshop,

there were harmful scraps; and on walks, there were dangers
(escape, injuries, animal bites); plus good country air, gratis.
Anyone could breathe it, as much as he liked and needed. Each
inmate paid a nice tidy sum through his legal guardian, in order
to be accepted and remain acceptable, which required many
extra gratuities, depending on the seriousness of the case and
the untidiness of the patient. The women were lodged on the
third story and in the garret, the men on the second story and
in the side wing, which had officially renounced its former
identity as an add-on garage, because it had turned into a real
little cottage with running cold water and a leaky roof. The
sanitarium cars were not expected to get moldy or mildewed,
so they stood outdoors. In the kitchen, someone sometimes
relaxed in between special sales and extra-special sales; he sat
there, reading with the help of a flashlight. The ex-garage was
built large enough to hold an Opel Cadet; an Opel Commodore
would get stuck in the door, unable to advance or retreat. The
area was enclosed by a good, strong wire fence as far as the
eye could see. After all, the family couldn't just take a patient
back after going to so much trouble to bring him here and
paying such an enormous amount of money for the privilege.
The administrators had made so much off their guests that they
had probably bought an idiot-proof chalet somewhere else. And
they would probably live there alone in order to recover from
all their charity work.

Father, going blind, but safely guided, goes toward his future
home after leaving his hereditary home. He has been assigned
a nice room, it is waiting for him. Someone else had to die a
lingering death before a new patient could be accepted. And
this new patient will someday have to make room for someone
else. Mentally damaged people need more room than the normal sort, they can't be put off with excuses, and they need at
least as much space to run around in as a medium-sized sheep

dog. The house declares: We are always fully occupied and we
could even increase the number of beds! However, the individual inmate, who usually has to remain lying down, because
he makes less dirt that way and is thereby stored in a space-
efficient manner, is exchangeable. Unfortunately, the house
cannot suddenly double its price; otherwise it would do so.
Anyone who lies here is stuck here—and he pays through the
nose, so the administrators can profit. And anyone who lies
here remains here, because that's what his family wants. If
worst comes to worst, he can only get worse, and wind up in
a Bedlam!

The room is neatly subdivided into single beds, each inmate
has his own little bed, and these little beds are small, so that
more beds can be squeezed in. Between the beds, a foot of space
is left free, so the inmate can, if necessary, get up and relieve
himself, something he cannot do in his bed, otherwise he would
require intensive care. He would cost more than his presence
is worth and he would be transferred to a more terrible place.
Often, someone has good reason to ask who has lain in his bed,
eaten from his plate, or rummaged in his chest. These dwarfs!
When the lunch gong rings (they've been hungering and han-
kering for it), the dwarfs form disorderly packs, trudging and
jostling toward the refectory, where their Snow White tenderly
waits for each of them. She loves every last one and hugs every
last one—this long-forgotten femininity with skin as white as
snow and hair as black as ebony. But here there's only a gigantic
canteen table coated with acid-proof, scratch-resistant, washable
plastic, for these pigs don't know how to behave at a meal. And
the dishes are made of plastic so that no idiot will beat himself
or anyone else, and there are no knives or forks, only spoons,
don't you know. If meat were served, which it's not, it would
be cut up in advance. They shove their own flesh against one

another, pressing, pushing, pinching, in order to defend their tiny dwarf places.

Father doesn't understand why he's here, for he has never been at home here. Many things are forbidden, and the rest are not appreciated. Anything he does is wrong, but he's used to that with his wife. He's not supposed to hold anything or even budge; he's supposed to fight his restlessness and lie still—that stalwart stroller. He's not supposed to bring in any dirt or carry off any sanitarium property. The outside and the inside should not be confused, each belongs in its place; clothes must be changed or added to for the outside, even though the man in the next bed has stolen them in order to nip Father's plan in the bud. Nevertheless, Father instantly tries to get away when they put him to bed, but he is promptly apprehended and forced to remain. How else would the family get rid of their troublemaker, who disrupts their comfort; and how else would the administrators get hold of his money? One family requires his absence, the other his presence. One lives from his coming, the other from his going and never coming again. So long, it's been good to know you. But all good things come to an end. When the two ladies drive off, Father, supported by an involuntary helper in a white smock, is supposed to wave at them. But instead of waving his hand, he holds it unreasonably in front of his eyes and begs the man not to beat him. This casts a harsh light on the departing vestige of the family, for Papa was never beaten, absolutely never. How could he say such a thing? This question is directed at the good, still air. The air doesn't answer. The sausage-maker drives faster than before; he has been relieved of a dangerous person. Today is Sunday, and he wants to get his children to the soccer field. It's his day of rest. Carefully picking his words, he tries to console the ladies. He condoles with them, pickily choosing his

words. Businessmen are well versed in the language of picking
and choosing. The butcher speaks as if discussing a choice between filet mignon and rump steak. He uses his normal professional lingo, even though today is Sunday, the day for the
language of leisure. The store is closed. But a good butcher
never stops working. The K. ladies spew out a torrent of innards. The expert finds that these innards are suitable, at best,
for cat food. The ladies babble: This action was regrettable, but
necessary—indeed quite overdue! And it was so difficult for
them to finally make up their minds! They overdo it. The
butcher's suppliers usually underbid one another. But this
butcher has fixed prices and he knows what he's asking for
what. An oxtail costs this, a ham that, a steak even more. The
ladies can save their torrent of breath. They should be more
generous when purchasing sausages and smoked meats; now
they owe the butcher, who doesn't take a Sunday drive for
nothing. Only death is free, and even death costs you your
life. And everything has an end, only a sausage has two ends,
as the helpful businessman points out, bursting into loud laughter. The K. ladies agree somewhat mournfully because they
are losing a member of their family; but they know what is
proper for customers of many years' standing. The butcher,
who considers them part of the solid core of his clientele, is
encouraged: "You can't give birth to an animal, but you can
give it a quick death." He has become quite earnest, this man
with the bloody occupation. The K. ladies agree with his last
statement, too. But he should keep his eyes on the road. Otherwise his statement will come horribly true before they even
realize what's happening. The streets are filled with inexperienced weekend drivers. The butcher replies that driving is second nature to him, it's in his blood. The K. ladies have nothing
to respond with except their own flesh and blood, and they
have no intention of losing either. After all, they have just

lodged some very precious flesh and blood in an overcrowded dormitory, for which they spent precious money. The butcher shouldn't believe that it was easy for them. A piece of them went along and remained in the home. Which piece, the butcher asks.

Soon the ladies enter their slightly emptier apartment. In this cavern, which closes protectively, they now have more room for their hobbies. The apartment doesn't welcome just anyone, only people who belong here!

A new squall—the supernaturally huge, soft hand of a giant—arose and pressed Fräulein Kohut against an optician's display window, which was chock full of glittering glasses. Mammoth eyeglasses containing violet lenses hung broadly over the store, trembling under the lashes of the gusts, a danger to passersby. Then all at once, the air grew very still, as if catching its breath and being frightened in the process. At this very moment, Mother must be cozily burrowing into their kitchen, frying something in fat for the evening, when it will be served cold. Afterward, some needlework will be waiting for her, a white lace doily.

In the sky, there are clouds with hard, rosy outlines. They don't seem to know where they're heading, so they race headlong, now here, now there. Erika always knows several days in advance what will be awaiting her several days hence; she'll be serving art at the conservatory. If not, then she'll be doing something else with music, that bloodsucker, which Erika serves to herself in various states and conditions: canned or freshly roasted, as gruel or as a gourmet delight, on her own or in charge of other people.

Several blocks away from the conservatory, Erika begins searching and sniffing around, as is her wont. An experienced hound, she picks up the scent. Will she catch a student without an assignment, with too much time on his hands, leading his

own private life? Erika wants to enter, she wants to squeeze
her way into these vast domains, which, although beyond her
supervision, nevertheless stretch out far and wide, divided into
farms. Bloody mountains, meadows of life, into which she has
to clamp her teeth. The teacher has every right to do so because
a teacher acts *in loco parentis*. She absolutely has to know what
is going on in other lives. No sooner has a student retreated
from her, no sooner has he poured himself into his portable
leisure container, where he believes he is not observed, than
K. is there, trembling, ready to join him secretly, without being
asked. She leaps around corners, she pops up unexpectedly from
corridors, she materializes in elevators—an energy-charged ge-
nie swirling up from a bottle. In order to expand her taste in
music and force it on her students, she occasionally attends
concerts. She weighs one interpreter against the other, anni-
hilating the students with her yardstick, to which only the
greatest musicians can measure up. She pursues, always out
of the eyeshot of students, but always within her own eyeshot;
she observes herself in the display windows, watches herself
hot on the trail. Most people would call her a good observer.
But Erika herself is not most people. She is one of those people
who lead and guide most people. Sucked into the vacuum of
the absolute inertia of her body, she shoots out of the bottle
when it opens, and she is then flung into a previously selected
or unexpected alien existence. No one can prove that her spying
is deliberate. And yet suspicions seem to develop against her
in various places. She pops up at a time when one doesn't care
to have witnesses. Every new hairdo sported by a female student triggers thirty minutes of violent discussion at home. Erika
then accuses her mother of always spitefully keeping her in
the house, so she won't go somewhere and experience something. After all, she, the daughter, is long overdue for a new
hairdo. But Mother, who doesn't dare do what she'd like to

do, sticks to Erika infectiously, like a burr or a leech. Mother is sucking the marrow from Erika's bones. What Erika knows from her secret observations, Mama knows; and what Erika is in reality, a genius—why, no one knows that better than her mama, who knows the child inside and out. Seek and you shall find the repulsive things you secretly hope to find.

Outside the Metro Film Theater, Erika has been finding hidden treasures for three merry spring days, ever since they changed the program; for the student, obsessed with himself and his mental obscenities, buried his distrust long ago. His senses are concentrated on new focal points: film stills. The movie house is featuring a soft-core porno flick, even though children pass by closely on the way to their music. One of the students standing outside the theater judges every photograph by the acts it depicts. Another is more interested in the beauty of the women. A third student stubbornly yearns for what is not visible: the insides of female bodies. Two future young men are engaged in a fruitful argument about the size of the female breasts. Then all at once, hurled by the squall, the piano teacher explodes in their midst—like a hand grenade. Her face has assumed a quietly punitive, slightly pitying look. One would never believe that she and the women in the photos belong to one and the same sex, namely the beautiful sex. Indeed, a less sophisticated person might even conclude, just from her outer appearance, that the piano teacher belongs to an entirely different subcategory of the human species. However, a photo does not show the inner life; so any comparisons would be unfair to Fräulein Kohut, whose inner life is actually in blossom and in sap. Without saying a word, she walks on. No ideas are exchanged, but the student knows that he has once again not practiced enough because his mind was on something other than the piano.

In glass showcases, men and women keep their noses to one

another's grindstones; they are hooked into everlasting lust—
an arduous ballet. Their work makes them sweat. The man is
working on various parts of the woman's flesh, and he can
publicly display the fruit of his labor: when the juice shoots
out and drops on her body. In real life, a man must usually
support and feed a woman; he is judged by his ability to do
so. And here too, he offers the woman warm food, which his
innards have cooked on his front burner. The woman moans—
figuratively. But one can almost see the shriek. She is delighted
with the gift, she is delighted with the giver, and her screams
continue. The photos are silent, of course, but a sound track is
waiting inside the theater, where the woman will shriek out
her gratitude for the man's effort once the spectator has bought
his ticket.

The student, who has been caught unawares, strides behind
Professor Kohut, maintaining a respectful distance. He rebukes
himself for injuring her female pride by gawking at naked
women. Maybe she considers herself a woman and feels lethally
wounded. Next time, his inner clock should tick loudly when
the teacher comes stalking up. Later, in piano class, the teacher
will deliberately avoid looking at the student, that leper of lust.
By the time they get to Bach, right after the scales and finger
exercises, the student's insecurity spreads out and takes the
upper hand. This intricate musical texture can endure only the
secure hand of the master pianist, who draws the reins gently.
The main theme was messed up, the other voices were too
importunate, and the whole piece was anything but transparent.
An oil-smeared car window. Erika jeers at the student's Bach.
It is a muddy creek, faltering over obstacles like small rocks
and mounds, stumbling along in its dirty bed. Erika now explains Bach's work in greater detail. Its passion is a cyclopean
structure. It is also a well-tempered foxhole with regard to the
other contrapuntal business for keyboard instruments. Delib-

erately trying to humiliate the student, Erika praises Bach's
work to the skies. She claims that Bach rebuilds gothic cathe-
drals whenever his music is played. Erika feels the tingling
between her legs, something felt only by those chosen by and
for art when they talk about art. And she lies, saying that the
Faustian yearning for God produced both the Cathedral of
Strasbourg and the introductory chorus of the *St. Matthew
Passion*. Then she tells her student: That was not exactly a
cathedral he was playing. Erika can't help pointing out that
God also created woman. She adds the stale male joke that he
did it because he had nothing better to do. But then she negates
her little joke by asking the student in all seriousness whether
he knows how one should look at the photo of a woman. Respectfully, for his mom, who carried him and gave birth to
him, was a woman, too; no less and no more. The student
makes several promises that his professor demands. Erika returns the favor by explaining that Bach's mastery is the triumph
of craft in his extremely diverse contrapuntal forms and tech-
niques. Erika knows all about craft: If practice alone counted,
she would have won by points or even by a knockout! But, she
triumphs, Bach is more, he is a commitment to God; and the
latest edition of the *Encyclopedia of Music*, Vol. I, even trumps
Erika by crowing that Bach's works are a commitment to the
special Nordic man struggling for God's grace.

The student resolves never again to be caught in front of
the photograph of a naked woman. Erika's fingers twitch like
the claws of a well-trained falcon. When she teaches, she breaks
one will after another. Yet deep inside, she feels an intense
desire to obey. That's why she's got her mother at home. But
the old woman keeps getting older and older. What will happen
when she falls apart and becomes a dismal creature in need of
care herself, when she has to obey Erika? Erika pines for difficult
tasks, which she then carries out badly. She has to be punished

for that. This young man, who is covered with his own blood, is not a worthy opponent; why, he was already defeated by Bach's miraculous music. Imagine his defeat when he has to play the role of a living human being! He won't even have the courage to pound away; he's much too embarrassed by all the notes he's fluffed. A single phrase from her, a casual glance— and he falls to his knees, ashamed, making all kinds of resolutions, which he will never be able to carry out. Anyone who could get her to obey a command (there must be a commander aside from her mother, who cuts glowing furrows into Erika's will) could get *anything* and *everything* from Erika. Erika needs to lean against a hard wall that won't give. Something pulls at her, tugs at her elbow, weighs down the hem of her skirt: a small lead ball, a tiny concentrated weight. She has no idea what damage it could do, once released from its chain. This fierce dog, baring its teeth as it strides up and down the bars, the fur bristling on the back of its neck, is always exactly one centimeter away from its victim, with a dark growling in its throat, a red light in its pupils.

She is waiting for that one command! For that steaming yellow hole in the wide mass of snow, a tiny cup of piss. The urine is still warm; and soon the hole will freeze into a thin yellow pipe in the mountain, a signal for the skier, the coaster, the hiker, revealing that human presence became a brief threat here and then moved on.

She knows about the form of the sonata and the structure of the fugue. That's her job, she's a teacher. And yet, her paws ardently grope toward ultimate obedience. The final snowy hills, the heights—landmarks in the wasteland—gradually pull apart, becoming plains, smoothing out in the distance, turning into icy, mirrorlike surfaces, untrodden, untouched. Other people become champion skiers; first prize in the men's division, first prize in the women's division, and always first prize in the Alpine Combined!

No hair stirs on Erika, no sleeve flutters on Erika, no speck of dust rests on Erika. An icy wind has arisen, and she glides across the field, a figure skater in a skimpy dress and white skates. The smoothest surface of all stretches from one horizon to the other and even farther! Whirring across the ice! The organizers have misplaced the cassette, so this time there will be no musical medleys, and the unaccompanied buzzing of the steel runners will turn more and more into a deadly metallic scraping, a brief flashing, an unintelligible Morse code on the edge of time. Gathering speed, the skater is compressed into herself by a gigantic fist: concentrated kinetic energy, hurtling out at exactly the right split second into a microscopically precise double axis, whirling around, landing right on the dot. The impact jolts her through and through, charging her with at least double her own body weight, and she forces that weight into the unyielding ice. Her motion cuts into the diamond-hard mirror, and into the delicate network of her ligaments, straining her bones to the utmost. And now she squats in a sit spin! Under that same momentum! The ice ballerina becomes a cylindrical tube, an oil drill. Air whooshes away, powdered ice screeches in flight, clouds of breath scurry off, a howling and sawing resound. But the surface is indestructible, it shows no trace of damage! The whirl slows down, we can make out the graceful figure again, the unclear, light-blue blur of her skirt begins to sway down, carefully arranging itself in pleats. A final curtsy to the audience on the right, one to the audience on the left, and the skater then skates away, waving with one hand, brandishing flowers in the other. But the audience remains invisible. Perhaps the ice maiden only assumes it exists because she has heard the applause. She skates away in quick spurts, growing tiny in the distance. Nothing is calmer now than the place where the hem of the light-blue skirt rests on the firm, pink panty-hose thighs, slapping, hopping, waving, swinging, the center of all rest and relaxation: this short skirt, these velvety soft flares and pleats, this snug leotard with its embroidered neckline.

❑

Mother sits in the kitchen: a percolator, dripping her orders about. Then, once her daughter's left, she turns on the TV to watch the morning programs. She is calm, for she knows where her daughter is going. What should we watch today? A program on Albrecht Dürer or a talk show?

After the trials and tribulations of the day, the daughter screams at her mother: She should finally let her lead her own life. She's old enough, the daughter yells. Mother's daily reply is that Mother knows best because she never stops being a mother.

However, this "life of her own," which the daughter longs for, will culminate in a zenith of total obedience, until a tiny, narrow alley opens up, with just enough room for one person to be waved through. The policeman signals: All clear. Smooth, carefully polished walls right and left, high walls with no apertures or corridors, no niches or hollows, only this one narrow alley, through which she must squeeze in order to reach the other end. Somewhere, she doesn't know where, a winter landscape is waiting, stretching far into the distance, a landscape with no path, with no castle to offer refuge. Or else nothing is waiting but a room without a door, a furnished cabinet containing an old-fashioned washstand with a pitcher and a towel, and the landlord's footfalls keep coming nearer and nearer, but never arrive because there is no door here. In this endless vastness or in this cramped, doorless narrowness, the frightened animal will confront a larger animal or merely the small wash-stand on wheels, which simply stands there to be used, and that's all.

Erika keeps exerting self-control until she feels no more drive within her. She puts her body out of commission because no panther leaps at her to grab her body. She waits, lapsing into silence. She assigns difficult tasks to her body, increasing the difficulties by laying hidden traps wherever she likes. She swears that anyone, even a primitive man, can pursue "the drive" if he is not afraid to bag it out in the open.

Erika K. corrects the Bach, mends and patches it. Her student stares down at his entangled hands. She gazes through him, but sees only a wall that bears Schumann's death mask. For a fleeting instant, she needs to grab the student's hair and smash his head against the inside of the piano until the bloody bowels of strings and wires screech and spurt. The Bösendorfer will not emit another peep. This desire flits nimbly through the teacher and evaporates without consequences.

The student promises to do better, no matter how long it takes. Erika hopes so and asks for the Beethoven. The student shamelessly strives for praise, although he is not as addicted to it as Herr Klemmer, whose hinges usually creak under the strain of his zealousness.

Meanwhile, in the glass cases of the Metro, pink flesh waits unhindered in various shapes, sizes, and price ranges. The flesh runs wild, runs riot, because Erika cannot stand guard there at this time. The admission prices are standardized, front rows are cheaper than back rows even though you're closer up front and you have a better view into the bodies. Extra-long blood-red fingernails bore into one woman; a sharp object—a riding crop—bores into another. This object makes an imprint in her flesh, showing the viewer who's boss and who's not, and the viewer too feels he's boss. Erika can feel the crop boring. It emphatically assigns her a seat on the audience side. One woman's face is twisted in joy, for only her expression can tell the man how much pleasure he is giving her and how much pleasure has been wasted. Another woman's face on the screen is twisted in pain, for she has just been whipped, albeit lightly. The woman cannot demonstrate her pleasure in her face. The man is entirely dependent on clues and hints. He reads the pleasure in her face. The woman jerks around to avoid offering a good target. Her eyes are shut, her head is thrown back. If her eyes aren't shut, then perhaps they're twisted back. They seldom look at the man. That is why he has to strain himself: Her facial expression won't improve the results or help him make points. The woman is so absorbed in her pleasure that she doesn't see the man. She doesn't see the forest for the trees. She gazes only into herself. The man, a trained mechanic, works on the woman, a damaged car. In porno flicks, people work harder than in movies about the workaday world.

Erika is geared to watching people who work hard because they want results. In this respect, the normally large difference between music and sexual pleasure is quite tiny. Erika is less interested in seeing nature. She never goes to the forest area, where other artists are renovating farmhouses. She never climbs mountains. She never dives into lakes. She never lies on beaches. She never whizzes over snow. The man greedily hoards orgasms until finally, bathed in sweat, he remains lying where he first started out. On the other hand, he has greatly increased his account balance for the day. Erika saw this flick long, long ago in a working-class district, where she is unknown (only the cashier knows her by now and addresses her as "ma'am"). In fact, she saw it twice. She won't go again, for she prefers a stronger diet when it comes to pornos. These gracefully formed exemplars of the human species in this downtown movie house act without pain and without any possibility

of pain. They are solid rubber. Pain itself is merely a consequence of the desire for pleasure, the desire to destroy, to
annihilate; in its supreme form, pain is a variety of pleasure.
Erika would gladly cross the border to her own murder. Fucking
in a slum contains more hope for shaping pain, decorating pain.
These shabby, frazzled amateur actors work a lot harder, and
they're a lot more grateful for the chance to appear in a real
movie. They are defective. Their skin has spots, pimples, scars,
wrinkles, scabs, cellulite, fat. Poorly dyed hair. Sweat. Dirty
feet. In aesthetically demanding films at luxuriously uphol-
stered cinemas, you mostly see the surfaces of men and women.
Both genders are squeezed into nylon body stockings dirt-
repellent durable, acid-proof, heat-resistant. Furthermore, at a
cheap porno house, the man smashes into the woman with
more blatant lust. The woman doesn't talk, although she may
squeal, "More! More!" That exhausts the dialogue, but not
the man, not by any stretch of the imagination. For he greedily
wants to concentrate his climaxes, adding as many as possible.

Here, in the soft-core porno, everything is reduced to outer
appearances. They are not enough for Erika, who's such a picky,
choosy woman. They are not enough, because Erika, absorbed
in these ensnarled people, would like to get at the bottom of
this business, which is supposed to be so hard on the senses
that everyone wants to do it or at least watch it. Entering the
inside of the body won't offer a complete explanation, and it
allows a certain measure of skepticism. After all, you can't slice
open a human being just to get every last bit out of him. In a
cheap flick, you can get a deeper look into the woman. But you
can't advance as far into the man. However, no one sees the
light at the end of the tunnel. Even if you cut the woman open,
you'd see only bowels and innards. The man, standing actively
in life, grows outward physically. Eventually, he produces the
awaited result, or else he doesn't. But if he does, everyone can

look at it, and the producer is delighted with his valuable native product.

The man must often feel (Erika thinks) that the woman must be hiding something crucial in that chaos of her organs. It is those concealments that induce Erika to look at ever newer, ever deeper, ever more prohibited things. She is always on the lookout for a new and incredible insight. Never has her body— even in her standard pose, legs apart in front of the shaving mirror—revealed its silent secrets, even to its owner! And thus the bodies on the screen conceal everything from the man who would like to peruse the selection of females on the open market, the women he doesn't know; and from Erika, the unrevealing viewer.

Erika's student is demeaned and thereby chastised. Loosely crossing her legs, Erika sneers at his half-baked Beethoven interpretation. She need say no more; he's about to cry.

She doesn't even consider it advisable to play the passage in question. He will get no more from his piano teacher today. If he doesn't notice his mistakes himself, then she can't help him.

Does the former wild beast and present-day circus animal love its tamer? Perhaps, but this is not obligatory. Each urgently needs the other. With the help of tricks and feats, each can hog the limelight amid the oompah-oompah of the band and puff himself up like a bullfrog. Each requires the other as a fixed point in the blinding chaos. The animal has to know where up is and where down is. Otherwise it will suddenly find itself upside down. Without its trainer, the animal would plummet helplessly in free fall or drift around in space, biting up, clawing up, eating up any objects that crossed its path. But if the animal has a trainer, there's always someone to tell it whether something is edible. Sometimes the edibles are pre-chewed for the animal or served in pieces. The animal doesn't have to endure the hardships of hunting for its own food. Or finding adventures in the jungle. For in the jungle, the leopard knows what's good for it and grabs the prey, whether it's an antelope or a careless white hunter. Now, during the day, the animal leads a life of introspection, reflecting about the tricks it has to perform in the evening. It will then leap through burning hoops, clamber onto stools, crackingly enclose a head in its jaws without mangling it, do dance steps to a given beat, alone or with other animals, whose throats it would rip if it encountered them in the wild, unless it had to scurry away from them, if it could. The animal wears foppish disguises on its head or back. Some animals have even been known to sport a leather mantle while riding horses! And the animal's master, his tamer, cracks his whip! Praising or punishing, it all depends. According to what the animal deserves. But not even the most daring tamer would ever dream of sending a leopard or lioness out with a violin case. A bear on a bike is as far as the human imagination can stretch.

THE LAST BIT of daylight crumbles like leftover cake in clumsy fingers. Evening is coming, and there are fewer and fewer students in the daily chain. There are more and more intervals, during which the teacher goes to the bathroom and covertly nibbles on a sandwich, which she then carefully rewraps. In the evening, the adults, who have to work hard all day, come to her in order to practice music. The students who want to be professional musicians, mainly as teachers of the discipline in which they are now students, come during the day because they have nothing else but music. They want to master music as thoroughly and completely as possible in order to get their degrees. They generally listen to their colleagues play and then they sharply criticize them together with Professor Kohut. They are unabashed about correcting other people's mistakes, of which they themselves are guilty. They listen frequently, but they can neither feel nor emulate. After the last student, the chain runs backward all night, until nine in the morning, when, filled with fresh candidates, it advances again. The gears click, the pistons bang, the fingers move in and out. Sounds are emitted.

Herr Klemmer has sat through three South Koreans and is now cautiously inching toward his teacher. She mustn't notice, but suddenly he will be inside her. And just a short time ago, he pursued her at a distance. The Koreans have only a sketchy grasp of German and are therefore supplied with judgments, prejudices, and rebukes in English. Herr Klemmer speaks to Fräulein Kohut in the international language of the heart. The Far Easterners play the accompaniment for him; in their tried-and-true equanimity, they are insensitive to the vibrations between the well-tempered teacher and the student who wants the absolute.

Erika, using a foreign language, talks about the sins against the spirit of Schubert: The Koreans should feel, they should not stolidly imitate a recording by Alfred Brendel. For Brendel will always play a good deal better in his style! Unbidden, unsolicited, Klemmer voices his opinion about the soul of a musical work, that soul being very difficult to drive out of it. Yet some people manage to do so! They should stay home if they can't feel. Klemmer, the honor student, jeeringly points out that the South Korean will not find a soul in the corner of the room. Klemmer calms down slowly and, quoting Nietzsche, with whom he identifies, says he is not happy enough, not healthy enough for all Romantic music (including Beethoven). Klemmer begs his teacher to glean his unhappiness and un-healthiness from his marvelous playing. What we need is a music that makes us forget our sufferings. Animal life (!) should feel deified. People want to dance, triumph. Light, rollicking rhythms, tender, golden harmonies, no more and no less. Such are the wishes of the philosopher whose anger is provoked by so little; and Walter Klemmer concurs. When do you actually live, Erika? the student asks, pointing out that there is enough time left in the evening to live if one takes the time. Half the time belongs to Walter Klemmer; the other half is for her to dispose of. But she always has to stay with her mother. The two women scream at each other. Klemmer talks about life as if it were a cluster of golden muscatel grapes, which a housewife arranges in a bowl for a guest, so that he can also eat with his eyes. The guest hesitantly takes a grape, then another, until all that's left is a stem, plucked bald, and a freely improvised pile of seeds underneath.

Random touches threaten this woman, whose mind and art are appreciated. They may threaten her hair, her shoulder under the loose sweater. The teacher's chair is moved forward. The screwdriver plunges deep, scraping out the final bit of content from *Der Wiener Liederfürst*, which today is heard only on the keyboard. The Korean gawks at his sheet music, which he bought at home, in Korea. These many black dots signify a completely foreign culture, with which he can show off back home.

Klemmer has taken up the banner of sensuality; he has even encountered sensuality in music! The teacher, that female mind-killer, recommends a solid technique. The Korean's left hand cannot yet keep up with his right hand. There's a special finger exercise for that problem. She moves his left hand back to his right hand, but teaches the former to be independent of the latter. His hands are always fighting each other, just as Klemmer, a know-it-all, is constantly arguing with other people. The Korean is dismissed for the day.

Erika Kohut feels a human body behind her, and it gives her the creeps. He shouldn't get so close as to graze her. He goes somewhere behind her and then goes back. This movement demonstrates his aimlessness. As he goes back, he finally emerges in the corner of her eye, wickedly jerking his head like a pigeon, insidiously holding his young face in the luminous cone emitted by the lamp, which burns brightest here. Erika feels dry and small. The outer shell hovers weightlessly around her compressed centrosphere. Her body is no longer flesh, and something closes in on her, likewise turning into an object. A cylindrical metal tube. A very simple apparatus, applied in order to be thrust in. And the image of this object (Klemmer) is glowingly projected into Erika's visceral cavity and cast, upside down, on her interior wall. Here the image stands sharp, on its head; and at this very moment, when it has turned into a body for her, a body that can be touched with hands, it has also turned completely abstract, losing its flesh. The very instant that both have become physical for each other, they have broken off any reciprocal human relations. There are no parliamentarians who could be sent with letters, messages, missives. No longer does one body grab the other; instead, each becomes a means for the other, a state of being different, which each would like to penetrate painfully. And the deeper one goes, the more intensely the flesh rots, becoming light as a feather and flying away from these two mutually alien and hostile continents, which crash into each other and then collapse together, turning into a rattling thing with a few canvas tatters that dissolve at the slightest touch, disintegrating into dust.

Klemmer's face is as smooth as a mirror. Erika's face is starting to get marked by its later decay. The skin creases, the eyelids arch weakly like heated paper, the delicate texture under the eyes crinkles bluishly. The two sharp notches that run from the nostrils can never be ironed out again. The surface of the face has become too large, and this process will continue for years and years, until the flesh under the skin shrivels and vanishes, and the skin nestles snugly against the skull, which it can no longer keep warm. Single white threads in the hair, fed by stagnant saps, multiply incessantly, until they form ugly nests, which hatch nothing, enclose nothing, nurture nothing; and Erika, too, has never enclosed anything warmly, not even her own body. But she would like to be enclosed. He should lust for her, he should pursue her, he should lie at her feet, he should be haunted by her, there should be no escape for him. Erika can seldom be seen in public. And her mother, too, usually keeps out of the public eye. They remain inside their four walls, and they don't like visitors tracking them down. In this way, the two women save on personal wear and tear. Of course, when they do make a very rare public appearance, no one offers them very much.

Erika's decay knocks with scurrying fingers. Indistinct physical ailments, vascular deficiencies in the legs, tweaks of rheumatism, twinges of arthritis spread through the body. (These diseases seldom bother children. They never used to assault Erika.) Klemmer, a live brochure for the health benefits of white-water canoeing, scrutinizes his teacher as if he wanted to wrap her up and take her along, or perhaps eat her up, right there in the store. Maybe he's the last man who'll ever desire me, Erika thinks furiously, and soon I'll be dead, only another thirty-five years, Erika thinks angrily. Jump on the train, because once I'm dead, I won't hear, smell, or taste anything ever again! Her claws scratch at the keys. Her feet scrape pointlessly, embarrassedly; she touches herself vaguely, picks at herself; the man makes the woman nervous, robbing her of her mainstay, music.

Mother waits at home. She looks at the kitchen clock, the relentless pendulum that will tick her daughter into the apartment no sooner than thirty minutes from now. Mother, who has nothing else to acquire, would rather wait here. What if Erika came home earlier than expected because a lesson was canceled? Then Mother wouldn't have waited. But Erika is impaled on her piano stool, even as she is drawn to the door.

The powerful magnet of domestic silence, interlaced with the sound of the TV (that center of absolute rest and inertia), is turning into physical pain inside her. Klemmer should just shove off! Why does he keep talking and talking here, while the water keeps boiling at home until the kitchen ceiling turns moldy?

The tip of Klemmer's shoe nervously ruins the inlaid floor as he blows out the small, superimportant realities of keyboard technique like smoke rings into the air. Meanwhile, the woman longs to go home. Klemmer asks what constitutes sound, and then answers his own question: the touch, the approach. His mouth discharges a torrent of words: that shadowy, intangible remnant made up of sound, color, light. No, no, the things on your list do not constitute music as I know it, chirps Erika, the cricket, who wants to get back to her warm hearth. You're wrong, that and that alone is music, the young man erupts. For me, the criteria of art are the imponderables, the immeasurables. Klemmer's dictum contradicts the teacher. Erika closes the piano lid, pushes objects around. The man has chanced upon Schubert on some mental shelf, and he instantly exploits his find. The more Schubert's spirit dissolves in smoke, scent, color, thought, the more indescribable his value. His value grows to gigantic proportions, beyond understanding. Shadow is far superior to substance, states Klemmer. Why, reality is probably one of the greatest errors in the world. Hence, lies go before truth, the man concludes from his own words. The unreal comes before the real. And that enhances the quality of art.

The domestic delight of dinner, inadvertently delayed, is a black hole for the star known as Erika. She knows that her mother's embrace will completely devour and digest her, yet she is magically drawn to it. Carmine settles on her cheekbones, consolidating its position. Klemmer should clam up and clamber away. Erika doesn't want to remember even a speck of dust on his shoes. She yearns for a long, intimate embrace, so that, once the embrace is over, this marvelous woman can regally push him away. Klemmer has never felt less inclined to leave her. After all, he has to tell her that he can love Beethoven's sonatas only as of Opus 101. Because, he blabbers on, that's when they really become soft, flow into one another; the individual movements become flat, washing out at the edges, they don't clash with one another. That's what Klemmer comes up with. He squeezes in the final remnant of these ideas, then ties up the end of the sausage, so the insides won't burst out.

To change the subject, Professor, I must tell you—and I shall explain it in greater detail—that a human being attains his supreme value only when he lets go of reality and enters the realm of the senses, which should apply to you, too. And also to Beethoven and Schubert, my favorite masters, with whom I feel personally involved. I don't know precisely how. But I feel—and it also applies to me—that we despise reality and regard both art and the senses as our sole reality. It's over for Beethoven and Schubert. But I, Klemmer, am in the ascendant. He accuses Erika Kohut of lacking all that. He tells her that she clings to superficial things while a man abstracts and separates essentials from nonessentials. Klemmer, a student, has given an impudent answer. He has dared to do so.

In Erika's mind there is only one source of light, illuminating everything as bright as day, especially the sign that says: Exit. The comfy TV easy chair spreads its arms wide, the lead-in for the evening news plays softly, the anchorman stirs soberly above his tie. The side table sports an exemplary wealth of colorful bowls containing goodies and gumdrops, of which the two ladies partake, alternately or simultaneously. An empty bowl is promptly refilled; this is Never-Never Land, where nothing ends and nothing begins.

Erika pushes things from one end of the music studio to the other and then back again. She looks pointedly at the clock, she emits an invisible signal from her lofty mast, showing how tired she is after her hard day's work, during which art was dilettantishly abused in order to satisfy parental ambitions.

Klemmer stands there, gazing at her.

Erika doesn't want a silence to develop, so she utters a platitude. Art is platitudinous for Erika because she lives off art. How much easier it is for the artist, says the woman, to hurl feelings or passions out of himself. When an artist resorts to dramatic devices, which you so greatly esteem, Klemmer, he is simply utilizing bogus methods while neglecting authentic ones. She talks to prevent the eruption of silence. I, as a teacher, favor undramatic art—Schumann, for instance. Drama is always easier! Feelings and passions are always merely a substitute, a surrogate for spirituality. The teacher yearns for an earthquake, for a roaring, raging tempest to pounce upon her. That wild Klemmer is so angry that he almost drills his head into the wall. The clarinet class next door, which he, the owner of a second instrument, has been frequenting twice a week, would certainly be astonished if Klemmer's angry head suddenly emerged from the wall, next to Beethoven's death mask. Oh, that Erika, that Erika. She doesn't sense that he is actually talking about her, and naturally about himself as well! He is connecting Erika and himself in a sensual context, ejecting the spirit, that enemy of the senses, that primal foe of the flesh. She thinks he is referring to Schubert, but he really means himself, just as he always means himself whenever he speaks.

He suddenly ventures to adopt a familiar tone with Erika; using a formal tone, she advises him to remain objective! Her mouth puckers, willy-nilly, into a wrinkly rosette; she cannot control it. She controls what the mouth says, but she cannot control the way it presents itself to the outside world. She gets goosebumps all over.

Klemmer is frightened; blissfully grunting, he wallows in the warm tub of his words and thoughts. He pounces upon the piano, enjoying himself. In a tempo that exceeds the speed limit, he plays a longer phrase that he happened to learn by heart. He wants to demonstrate something with the phrase; he wonders what. Erika Kohut is happy about this slight diversion; she throws herself against the student, in order to stop the express train before it really gets going. You're playing much too fast and also much too loud, Herr Klemmer, and you're merely proving that the absence of the spiritual in an interpretation can cause terrible lacunae.

The man catapults backward into a chair. He stands, steaming, like a racehorse that has brought home a lot of victories. In order to be rewarded for victories and to prevent defeats, he demands expensive treatment and tender loving care, at the very least like a silver service for twelve.

Erika wants to go home. Erika wants to go home. Erika wants to go home. She offers some good advice: Simply walk around Vienna and breathe deeply. Then play Schubert, but this time correctly!

I'm leaving, too. Walter Klemmer violently assembles his compact stack of scores and makes an exit like a stage star, except that not too many people are watching. Still, a star and an audience in one person, he also plays the spectators. And he offers a bonus of thunderous applause.

Outside, Klemmer's blond hair flutters behind him as he dashes into the men's room, where he gulps down a pint of water straight from the faucet. However, the liquid can't wreak much havoc inside his water-weathered body. He then splashes his face, splashes his head: Billows of mountain springwater,

flowing cleanly from the headwaters, end on Klemmer's face
and head. I always drag beautiful things through the mud, he
says to himself. Vienna's famous but now venomous water is
wasted. Klemmer scrubs his hands with energy that he cannot
use elsewhere. He keeps tapping green liquid soap from the
dispenser, over and over again. He sprays and gargles. He keeps
repeating his ablutions. He waves his hands around, wetting
his hair. His mouth emits artificial sounds, which are arty, but
meaningless. Because he's got love trouble. He snaps his fingers
and cracks his joints. Using the tip of one shoe, he maltreats
the wall under the small, blind window to the courtyard, but
he can't release what's locked inside him. A few drops do spurt
out, but the rest of the contents remains in its container, slowly
growing rancid because it can't reach the female port-of-call.
Yes, indeed, no doubt about it: Walter Klemmer is truly in
love. Not for the first time, to be sure, and certainly not for
the last time. His love, however, is unrequited. His feelings
are unreturned. This turns his stomach, and he proves his
disgust by hawking up mucus and noisily placing it in the sink.
Klemmer's love placenta. He closes the faucet so tight that his
successor will assuredly not get it open, unless he's a pianist,
too, and has steel wrists and fingers. Since Klemmer doesn't
rinse the sink, his clams linger at the drain hole. Anyone who
takes a close look will see them distinctly.

At that very second, a deathly pale student (piano or something of the sort) comes dashing in, straight from his examination. Plunging into one of the stalls, he throws up into the
commode. It is like a natural disaster. An earthquake seems to
be raging inside his body; many things seem to have collapsed
inside him, including any hope of getting his degree all that
soon. This examinee had to hold back his agitation because the
head of the school was present at the exam. Now the agitation
forcefully demands its rights—right into the toilet bowl. The

student messed up the chromatic étude. He began in double time, which no human being can endure, including Chopin. Klemmer scorns the closed stall door, behind which his fellow musician is now struggling with the runs. Any pianist who is so powerfully dominated by his body cannot possibly add anything crucial to his performance. He probably sees music only as a handicraft, and he takes it unnecessarily hard whenever one of his ten tools fails him. Klemmer has already progressed beyond this stage; he heeds only the inner truth of a piece. For instance, he feels there is nothing more to say about the sforzandos in Beethoven's piano sonatas; one has to feel them, one has to suggest them to the listeners rather than play them. Klemmer could spend hours lecturing on the spiritual profit to be gained from a musical piece, whose surplus value is within reach, but can be grasped only by the most courageous. The important thing is what the composer says, what he feels, and not the mere structure of the piece.

Klemmer lifts his music case high and, emphasizing his thesis, smashes it down on the porcelain sink several times, in order to squeeze out his last few drops of energy—on the off chance that he's got any left. Yet, as Klemmer notices, he is already drained. He has lavished all his strength on that woman, he says, quoting a famous novel. He's done everything he could, as far as she's concerned. I pass, says Klemmer. He offered her his very best part, all of him. He even repeatedly interpreted himself. Now all he wants is to spend a weekend of white-water canoeing in order to find himself again. Perhaps Erika Kohut is far too withered to understand him. She understands only parts of him, not the grand total.

The student who failed because of the chromatic étude trudges out of his stall and to the mirror. Somewhat comforted by his shimmering reflection, he gives his hair an artistic sweep, the finishing touch, to make up for the failure of his hands.

Walter Klemmer is comforted by the thought that his teacher never made it as a concert artist. Then, audible for miles around, he spits on the floor, getting rid of the last inner foam that his temper has produced. His fellow pianist glares reproachfully at the spit, because he is accustomed to order. Art and order, the relatives that refuse to relate. Klemmer passionately grabs dozens of paper towels from their dispenser, crushes them up into a ball, and tosses them at the wastebasket, missing it by a gnat's eyelash. The flunker looks askance at this action. He is dismayed once again, this time by the waste of property belonging to the City of Vienna. His mother and father own a mom-and-pop store, and he will have to return to his petty-bourgeois family if he can't pass the exam next time around. His parents will then stop supporting him. He will have to switch from art to business, which will, no doubt, be mentioned when he goes a-courting. And his wife and children will have to suffer the consequences of that truth. Thus business and pleasure will remain intact. At the mere thought of this, his frost-red sausage fingers, which have to help out in the store, convulse into raptorial claws.

Walter Klemmer sensibly places his heart in his head and mentally reviews the women he has already possessed and remaindered. He gave them detailed explanations for dispensing with them. He didn't hold back; he wanted to make sure they understood (no pain, no gain). If a man feels like it, he can walk out without a word. The woman's antennae flicker nervously in the air; after all, a woman is an emotional creature. She is not dominated by reason, as you can tell from the way she plays the piano. A woman usually won't do more than hint at her ability; she's quite content to go no further. Klemmer, on the other hand, always likes to go all the way.

Walter Klemmer is well aware that he wants to take on his teacher. He resolutely wishes to conquer her. Klemmer, like

an elephant, tramples two white tiles underfoot at the mere
thought that his love might go unrequited. A few seconds from
now, he will zoom, like the Arlberg Express from the tunnel
of the same name, into an icy winter landscape dominated by
reason. And this landscape is so cold partly because Erika Kohut
has not lit a light in it. Klemmer advises that woman to give
some serious thought to her meager possibilities. A young man
is simply bursting at the seams for her. At the moment, they
share a mental foundation. But if that foundation is suddenly
pulled out from under their feet, Klemmer will have to paddle
his own canoe.

His footfalls echo through the deserted corridor of the conservatory. He bounces emphatically down the stairs, like a
rubber ball, from step to step, slowly finding his good mood,
which was patiently waiting for him. No sound comes from
behind Kohut's door. Sometimes, when her teaching day is
over, she plays a little, because her piano at home is a lot worse.
He's already found that out. He briefly gropes for the doorknob
in order to feel something that the teacher touches day after
day; but the door remains cold and mute. It doesn't budge even
one millimeter, because it's locked. The lessons are over. She's
already halfway home to her senile mother, with whom she
huddles in their nest, forever exchanging punches. Yet they
can't part company, not even on vacation, which they spend at
a Styrian resort, squabbling and bickering. And it's been like
that for decades already! It's a pathological situation for a sensitive woman, who, if viewed mathematically from all sides,
isn't all that old. Such are Walter Klemmer's positive thoughts
about his beloved in his wait-and-see position, as he starts off
to his parents, with whom he lives.

He asked them to prepare an extra-hearty dinner. For one
thing, he has to refill the energy tanks that he drained because
of his teacher; for another, he wants to work out tomorrow,

set off at the crack of dawn. The sport doesn't matter, but he'll probably go to his canoeing club. He has a very personal urge to work out until he drops, inhaling completely unused air, rather than air that thousands of other people have already breathed in and out. An air in which Klemmer doesn't have to suck in the vapors of engines and the cheap food of average people. He'd like to take in something freshly produced by Alpine trees with the help of chlorophyll. He'll go to the darkest and most deserted part of Styria. There he'll lower his boat into the water, near an old weir. A harsh orange splotch because of his helmet, life jacket, and spray cover, he'll shoot along between two forests, careening now here, now there, but always in the same direction: forward, following the course of the torrent. You have to do your best to avoid rocks. Don't turn turtle! And keep speeding! Some buddy, another paddler, will be in hot pursuit behind him, but he won't catch up, much less shoot ahead of Klemmer. Friendship in sports ends where the other guy threatens to surpass you. A buddy is someone who measures his own strength against his buddy's lesser strength and increases his own lead. Toward this end, Walter Klemmer carefully picks out a less experienced paddler far in advance. When it comes to working out or playing out, Klemmer is not a good loser. That's why he's so annoyed about Erika Kohut. When he gets knocked down in a drag-out discussion, he doesn't throw in the towel. He angrily throws something in the opponent's face: a heap of pellets, the kind regurgitated by carnivorous birds—a pack of bones, indigestible hair, pebbles, raw grass. Then he gazes absently, mentally reviewing all the things he could have said, but, alas, didn't; and finally, he leaves the ring in a foul temper.

Now, out in the street, he reaches into his back pocket and pulls out his love for Fräulein Kohut. Since he happens to be alone and has no one to beat at sports, he climbs up this love (an invisible rope ladder), reaching a height that is both physical and spiritual.

Taking resilient broad jumps, he races up Johannesgasse, then hangs a left at Kärntnerstrasse and dashes over to the Ring. Trolley cars winding along like dinosaurs in front of the Opera form a natural barrier that is difficult to surmount. So Klemmer, albeit a daredevil, has to take the escalator into the bowels of the Opera underpass.

A short while ago, the figure of Erika Kohut slipped out of a building entrance. She sees the young man racing by, and, like a lioness, she hits the trail and follows his track. Her foray is unseen, unheard, and therefore nonexistent. She couldn't know that he would spend so much time in the bathroom, but she waited. Waited. He has to pass here today. That is, unless he headed in the other direction, which, however, is not his direction. Erika is always waiting somewhere, patiently. She observes from a place where no one would suspect her presence. She neatly trims the frazzled edges of nearby objects that explode, detonate, or simply lie still, and she takes them home. Then, alone or with Mother, she turns them over and over, combing their seams, looking for crumbs, dirt, or torn-off bits to analyze. The refuse of other people's lives or deaths, if possible before their lives are taken to the cleaners. There's so much to seek and to find. For Erika, these chips and snips are the true gist. The K. ladies, alone or together, eagerly bend over their home operating table and hold candle flames to material leftovers in order to determine whether these fibers are pure vegetable or pure animal, mixed bags or pure art. The smell and consistency of the charred remains identify them unerringly, and the bewildered investigator can then decide what use to make of them.

Mother and child put their heads together. They are inseparable, virtually one person. And those alien remains, unmoored from their original anchorage, probably lie before them, not touching them, not threatening them, yet gravid with the misdeeds of other people, which is why they must be scrutinized. These remains cannot get away; nor can the students normally get away from the jurisdiction of their piano teacher, who catches them everywhere, whenever they leave the seething waters of piano practice.

Klemmer lopes along in front of Erika. He charges forward single-mindedly, avoiding detours. Erika eludes everyone and everything, but if a nimble person eludes her, she sets off after him, dogging his heels: her savior, to whom she is drawn as if to a giant magnet.

Erika Kohut hurries through the streets after him. Klemmer, burning with rage over things unfulfilled and anger about things undesired, doesn't suspect that love, no less, is dashing after him, and at the same speed, to boot. Erika distrusts young girls; she tries to gauge their clothing and physical dimensions, hoping to ridicule them. What fun she and Mother will have, laughing at these creatures! Those girls harmlessly cross the harmless student's path; and yet they could seep into Klemmer like the singing of sirens, dazzling him, making him follow them. She checks to see how long he looks at a woman, and she then neatly erases that look. A young man who plays the piano can have high standards, which no woman will fulfill. He had better not choose any woman, although many women would choose him.

The two of them wind and weave through the streets of Vienna, the man trying to cool off, the woman heating up with jealousy.

Erika snugly pulls in her flesh, that impenetrable cloak; any touch would be unendurable. She is locked into herself. Yet she is drawn to her student. He is the head of the comet, she the tail. Today, she forgets about adding to her wardrobe. But she will remember to wear something different at her next lesson; she will dress so elegantly now that it's spring. Mother, at home, doesn't want to wait any longer, and the sausages she is cooking don't like to wait either. A roast would be too chewy by now, inedible. Once Erika does show up, Mother will be so offended that she will use a housewife's trick to make the sausages burst and maliciously soak up water, so they'll taste bland and dull. That will be warning enough. But Erika suspects nothing.

She runs after Klemmer, and Klemmer runs along in front of her. They virtually dovetail. Smoothly and smartly. Erika follows in Klemmer's footsteps. Naturally, Erika isn't quite capable of punishing the boutique windows by ignoring them altogether. She checks them out from the corner of her eye. She has never investigated the clothing in this district, even though she is always searching for new and splendid attire. She desperately needs a new concert dress, but she doesn't glimpse any here. She'd be better off buying one downtown. Merry carnival coils and confetti have descended upon the first spring models and the last winter specials. And there are glitzy things that would look like elegant evening wear only at night. A feather boa, pointedly casual, is draped over two cunningly arranged champagne glasses filled with artificial fluid. A pair of high-heeled genuine Italian sandals are likewise strewn with glittering confetti. A middle-aged woman stands at the boutique window, totally absorbed. Her feet wouldn't even fit into size-twelve camel's-hair slippers; they're too swollen, she's been standing in front of stale, stagnant things all her life. Erika glances at a diabolically crimson chiffon frock with ruffles on the sleeves and neckline. Learning is better than looking. She likes this, she doesn't like that (after all, she's not that old yet).

Erika Kohut follows Walter Klemmer, who, without looking back, enters the doorway of a middle-class town house. His

parents are waiting for him in their second-floor apartment.
Erika Kohut doesn't go in after him. She doesn't live that far
away; her home is in the same area. She knows from the school
records that Klemmer lives in her neighborhood. Perhaps one
of them is made for the other, and the other will realize it after
a great deal of storm and strife.

The sausages won't have to wait much longer. Erika is already coming to them. She knows that Walter Klemmer has
stopped nowhere, he has gone straight home. So she can give
up her supervisory task for today. But something has happened
to her, and she takes along the result, takes it home to lock it
up in a cabinet, so Mother won't find it.

People are enjoying themselves at the Prater. The little people at the amusement park, the lecherous people on the meadows; each group in its own way. At the carnival, the parents,
who have filled their bellies and their children with wine or
beer, with dumplings or roast pork, stick the kids on multicolored plastic ponies, elephants, dragons, automobiles; and the
tots, spinning into orbit, chuck up everything they have choked
down. They are roundly slapped because the food at the restaurant cost a pretty penny, and we can't afford such treats
every day. The parents keep their meals down, for their stomachs are hard, and their hands are fast when they rain down
upon their offspring. This makes the kids move faster. However, if Mom and Pop have drunk too much, they may not be
able to afford the rocking roller coaster.

In order to test their mettle and flaunt their get-up-and-go,
the younger generation head for the electronic pleasures of the
penultimate chip generation. These vehicles have names taken
from space travel. Infinitely variable, they zoom through the
air with the greatest of ease, wobbling, yet steered with pains-

taking precision, and perhaps exchanging up for down. The cosmic ferry is an elevator consisting of two gigantic hulls of colorful metal. And indeed, you need courage to take your pleasure here. These rides are for teenagers who have been toughened by life but bear no responsibilities as yet, not even for their bodies. They can endure up when it's down and down when it's up. Meanwhile, back on earth, men are trying to impress their girlfriends by shooting for kewpie dolls. They take their prizes home; and years later, the frustrated wives can see how valuable they used to be to their boyfriends.

Things are more discordant in the wide green yonder of the wilder parts of the Prater. One area is ruled by flimflam. Big, beautiful, or viciously fast cars discharge passengers who are dressed for horseback riding. Sometimes they go without a basic necessity, the horse, so they can afford the costume to strut around in. Secretaries go broke here, because they also have to maintain elegant wardrobes at work. Bookkeepers work their butts off in order to place those same butts on some horse for one hour every Saturday afternoon. They work overtime to get out from under. Department heads and company managers are more relaxed about the whole business, because they can afford the pleasure, but don't have to. Anyone can tell who they are anyway, and they can start thinking about their golf game.

There are probably more attractive riding areas, but nowhere else can one be gaped at and gawked at by so many innocent families with innocent children and dogs on leashes: Look at the horsie! say the children; and they'd like to ride the horsie themselves. If they nag too loudly, they get slapped. We can't afford it. Instead, the little boy or little girl is planted on the rocking and rolling plastic horse on the merry-go-round, where he or she can keep whining and wailing. This is a good lesson for the children: they learn that most expensive originals have cheap imitations. Unfortunately, a child remembers only the original and hates his parents.

There are also places in the Prater where horses race their asses off. They have to push themselves; their drivers can only do so much. The ground is strewn with empty cans, betting tickets, and other refuse that Nature cannot digest. She can just about handle the delicate tissues; the paper used to be a natural product, but it will be quite a while before it becomes one again. Paper plates, an inedible crop, cover the trampled earth. Four-legged lean machines, cunningly fed and marvelously muscular, zoom along under their blankets, faithfully guided. All they have to worry about is what tactic to win with in the third race; their jockeys or drivers will let them know in time, before they get a chance to lose.

When the light of day goes out, and the night comes out with lamps and work or with guns and brass knuckles, it is accompanied by people who have lost out on life, mostly women. And, very seldom, very young men; for when these young men grow older, they will be worth less to their johns than to older women. Who, young or old, are, of course, worth nothing to the homosexuals. The whores hustle and the hustlers whore through the Prater.

Every Viennese, starting in infancy, is warned never to come anywhere near this area in the dark: boys to the left, girls to the right. You can find a lot of elderly women here, at the edge of their profession and at the end of their lives. Often one finds only their shot-up remains, dumped out of speeding cars. The police usually come up with nothing, for the culprit has long since returned to the orderly silence he emerged from. It could have been the pimp, but he's got an alibi. This is where the hiking mattress was invented and first used. If you don't have an apartment, a room, a one-night cheap hotel, or a car, then you have to have a transportable bed, which keeps you warm

and on which you can land softly when you're floored by lust.
Here, Vienna, in its boundless malice aforethought, puts forth
its most beautiful flowers when a nimble Yugoslav or a quick
locksmith, trying to get a freebie, dashes by, pursued by the
foul-mouthed professional who has been cheated of her just
reward. But there's nothing the locksmith yearns for more than
an extra wall, so that he and his girlfriend can conceal the
raunchiness of their private lives. Books, a stereo system with
speakers and albums, a TV, a radio, a butterfly collection, an
aquarium, hobby implements and instruments, and goodness
knows or doesn't know what else can be shielded from prying
eyes and stored safely. A visitor can see only the dark-stained
rosewood partition; he doesn't see the chaos on the other side.
He may—and should—see the small home bar with its colorful
liqueurs and the angrily glittering, endlessly polished glasses
that are judiciously matched to those hues and shades. The
glasses are carefully maintained during the early years of marriage. Later on, they get smashed by the children, or else the
wife forgets to polish them because the husband always comes
home so late after drinking outside somewhere. The mirrored
bar slowly develops a coat of dust.

The Yugoslav and the Turk have a congenital hatred of
women. The Viennese locksmith hates a woman only if she's
unclean or wastes money on makeup. This money can be spent
on something more useful, more durable. He doesn't have to
pay for something as short-lived as hairspray; after all, when
she's with him, the woman will experience a pleasure she won't
find with other men. Simply by living his own life, he has
created his own sperm, arduously and tediously. Once he's
dead, he won't be able to produce any juice or tap any sap, to
the great regret of various females. Often the locksmith can't
go to other women because he's known in the neighborhood
and pitilessly observed. But if he's faced with an acute financial

crisis, say, overdue installments, he'll risk getting beaten up or something even worse. His longing for variety in vaginas is not always consistent with his pecuniary desires and possibilities.

Now, he's looking for a woman who doesn't look as if any other man would think of protecting her. She'll be very grateful to him, for the locksmith is a chunky hunk of a guy. He's chosen a typical loner in the realm of the senses, a crone. A Bohunk or a Turk often can't risk it because the women often won't let him get anywhere near them. At least no nearer than a stone's throw. If a woman does take one on, she can't ask for very much money, because her work isn't worth very much anymore. The Turk, who is not worth as much to his employer as the sum on his paycheck, is disgusted by his sexual partner. He refuses to slip on a condom, for the female is the pig, not the male. And yet, like the locksmith, the Turk is attracted to a fact that cannot be shrugged off, however disagreeable it may be: the female. Turkish men don't like women; they never suffer their company willingly. But since women are a fact, what can you do with them? What's the first thing that crosses a man's mind?

The locksmith will treat his fiancée decently for at least one week. He describes her as clean and hardworking. He tells his friends that he's never embarrassed to be seen with her, and that's saying a lot. He can take her to any nightspot; undemanding as she is, she asks little of him. She gets even less and scarcely notices. She's a lot younger than he. She comes from a disorderly home and therefore appreciates an orderly one. He has something to offer her.

You can't talk about the Turk's private life, for it doesn't exist. He works. And after work, he must be stored somewhere, to be protected against the elements; but no one knows where. Evidently in the streetcar, for which he doesn't buy a ticket.

To the non-Turkish world around him he is a cardboard figure, the kind you aim at in a shooting gallery. In case he's needed for work, he is pulled out and set in motion; someone shoots at him, and, whether hit or not, he vanishes at the other side of the gallery, then revolves invisibly (no one sees him, but there's probably nothing worth seeing). He moves along behind the papier-mâché background, ending up at the starting point. He then reenters the scenery (the artificial cross on the mountain peak, the artificial edelweiss, the artificial gentian), where Viennesse coziness, rearmed, is already waiting for him. The marksman has been stirred up by his wife in her Sunday best, by the local tabloid, and by his teenage son, who would like to outshoot Dad and is only waiting for him to miss. The hit will be rewarded with a small kewpie doll. There are other prizes: Aaron's rod and goldenrod. But whatever the prize, it is geared toward the woman, who waits for the victorious shooter and is always his greatest prize. She knows he is making his effort only for her sake, and if he fails, then he is angry only for her sake. Either way, she'll have to stew in his juice. A deadly argument can develop if the man can't stand the thought of having shot and missed. The woman only makes matters worse if she tries to comfort him. She has to pay for it when he lunges straight into the main course, screwing her with no appetizer to whet her appetite. He gets roaring drunk, and if she refuses to take his cock tonight, he'll beat up on her like there's no tomorrow. The police car arrives, the siren screams, the officers jump out and ask the woman why she's shouting. She should at least let her neighbors sleep if she can't sleep herself. Then they give her the address of the women's shelter.

❏

Erika, a small skiff hunting for prey, weaves loosely through the area, which stretches across the entire green portion of the

Prater. This has recently become her new happy hunting ground. She is widening her scope, because she is long since overly familiar with the wild game in her own neighborhood. Coming here requires courage. Erika wears solid shoes, so that if push comes to shove—that is, if someone finds her out— she can escape into the bushes; into dog turds; into empty, phallus-shaped plastic bottles containing the liquid remnants of venomously dyed kiddie lemonade (each flavor touted on TV by a different species of singing animal); into piles of greasy paper once used for mysterious purposes; into paper plates smeared with mustard; into filled rubbers still vaguely maintaining their former cock shape. Erika, nervously anticipating, tries to scent prey. She draws air in and blows it out again.

The Praterstern, that large square where she gets out of the trolley, isn't dangerous. Granted, a couple of horny men mingle with harmless pedestrians and strollers; but even the elegant lady can visit the Praterstern informally, although the area isn't all that fashionable. All sorts of mysterious things can happen here. For instance, if the foreigners standing around by themselves are not hawking newspapers, they might reach into their plastic briefcases and pull out a man's sport shirt with fancy pockets (straight from the factory), stylish women's dresses (straight from the factory), children's toys (straight from the factory), albeit slightly damaged, boxes of cigars (straight from the factory), small electrical and electronic parts (straight from the factory or a burglary), transistor radios or record players (straight from the factory or a burglary), cartons of cigarettes (from goodness knows where). And the vendors peddle them, calling discreetly. Despite her simple clothing, Erika looks as if her extra-large shoulder bag had been specially made, or at least specially brought here, to take in and conceal from public eyes a tiny factory-fresh tape deck of uncertain nationality and working order, in brand-new plastic wrapping. But along with lots of necessities, her bag contains the most important thing of all: a good spyglass. Erika looks fully solvent: Her shoes are genuine leather and sensibly soled; her coat neither shrieks nor conceals itself beyond recognition, it calmly and expensively drapes its wearer, proudly carrying its world-famous, albeit unseen British label. This coat can be worn for a lifetime if it doesn't get on your nerves first. Mother urged Erika to buy it, for she advocates as little change as possible in life.

Now, Fräulein Kohut sidesteps an impudently groping Yugoslav, who tries to force a defective coffee maker on her, as well as his further accompaniment. He only has to pack up. Pointedly turning her head, Erika climbs over some invisible hurdle and strikes off toward the Prater meadows, where a person can quickly get lost. But Erika has no intention of losing herself, she intends to win. And, assuming she did get lost, her mother, whose assets Erika has been increasing since birth, would instantly get into gear. The whole country would hunt for her, with press, radio, and TV. Something is sucking Erika into this landscape, and this isn't the first time. She's come here several times before, she knows her way. The people thin out. The throng unravels at its edges, individual members scurry apart like ants, each of whom has taken on a specific task in their state. One hour later, the ant will proudly present a smidgen of fruit or carrion.

Clusters, groups, islands form at the trolley stops in order to charge somewhere in unison. Darkness has fallen quickly, just as Erika calculated, and the lights of human presence are also going out. On the other hand, more and more figures are clogging around the artificial lights. The only people here, on the periphery, are here for professional reasons. Or else they pursue their hobby, fucking, or perhaps fucking over the people they've fucked with, mugging and killing them. Some people just watch calmly. A tiny number pointedly expose themselves near the entrance to the Tunnel of Fun.

A final straggling child, bristling with belated ski equipment, stumbles toward a final light in a trolley shelter. The child is harried by parental voices, inwardly audible, warning him not to be alone in the Prater at night. And they list cases of skis that were bought at a winter close-out and could only be used next season—but violently changed hands. The child struggled far too long for these skis to lose them now. Arduously handicapped, he hobbles past Fräulein Kohut, almost grazing her, surprised at this lonesome lady who provides a living contrast to everything his parents tell him.

Erika, drawn by the darkness, strides into the meadows, which calmly spread out here, interrupted by bushes, woods, and streamlets. The meadows simply loll about, and they have names. Erika's goal is Jesuits' Meadow. That's still quite a ways off. First, the amusement park. Distant lights flash off and dash away. Shots ring out, voices roar victoriously. Adolescents scream with their battle implements in the video arcades, or else they shake machines, which rattle all the more noisily, chattering, clattering, hurling bolts of lightning. Erika resolutely turns her back on this commotion even before she lets it get to her. The lights grope toward her, find nothing to hold on to, run their fidgety fingers over her kerchief, slide off, draw a regretful trail of color down her coat, and then fall on the ground behind her, to die in the dirt. Tiny explosions tug away at Erika, but they too have to let Erika by without banging a hole into her. They repel her rather than attract her. The gigantic Ferris wheel made up of sparse lights dominates everything else. But it has its rival in the far more harshly lit roller coaster, where tiny, screechy cars zoom by, carrying shrill daredevils who, terrified by the power of technology, cling desperately to one another. The men have flimsy excuses to cling to the women. This is nothing for Erika. If there's one thing she doesn't want, it's being clung to. At the peak of the Haunted Ride, an illuminated ghost greets the world. He won't catch any fish with his bait, at most some fourteen-year-old girl with her first boyfriend, the two of them, like kittens, playing with the horror of the world before they themselves become part of that horror.

Row houses, one-family houses, the final rear guard of the day; the people who live there have to listen to the distant rumpus all day long and deep into the night. Truck drivers from Eastern Bloc countries, tanking up with a final spurt of the big world. A pair of sandals for the wife at home; the sandals emerge from a plastic bag, and the customer has to check whether they are up to Free World standards. Barking of dogs. Amorous flickers from a TV screen. Outside a porno movie, a man shouts that you've never seen anything like what you can see here, just walk right in. No sooner has darkness broken in than the world seems to consist largely of male participants. The appropriate female portion waits patiently beyond the final cone of light, hoping to earn something from whatever the porno flick has left of the man. The man goes into the movie alone; after the movie, he needs a woman, who beckons eternally both out here and in there. He can't do everything alone. Unfortunately, he has to pay twice: once for the flick, once for the fuck.

Erika forges ahead. Deserted meadows open their sucking maws. It's a long, long way into the landscape and, beyond the landscape, to foreign lands. To the Danube, to the Lobau petroleum harbor, the Freudenau harbor. The Albern grain harbor. The meadow forests around Albern harbor. Then Potter's Field and the Commercial Wharf. Prater Quai, where the ships dock and then sail on. And beyond the Danube, the gigantic floodplain, which ecology-minded youth is fighting for; sandy shoreland, meadows, alders, undergrowth. Licking waves. But Erika doesn't have to walk that far, the distance is too great. Only the well-equipped hiker can make it, and only if he rests and has a snack. Now Erika has soft meadowland underfoot, and she strides ahead. She walks and walks. Small, frozen islands, lace doilies of snow, yellow and brown grass still frozen from the winter. Erika places foot after foot, as steady as a metronome. If one foot steps into a pile of dog turds, the other foot instantly realizes it and avoids the long-lasting stench. The first foot is then wiped off in the grass. The lights slowly retreat behind Erika. The darkness opens its gates: Come right in! Fräulein Kohut knows from experience that around here prostitutes let themselves be seen taking on and carrying out their assignments. Erika's handbag contains a roll stuffed with minced pork sausage. Her favorite food, even though condemned as unhealthy by her mother. A tiny flashlight in case of emergency, a blank-cartridge pistol in case of extreme emergency (as small as a finger joint!), a pint of chocolate milk to quench her thirst after the minced pork sausage, lots of tissues just in case, not much money but certainly enough for a cab, no ID card, not even in case of emergency. And the binoculars. Inherited from Father, who, when still possessed of a lucid mind, used them to spot birds and mountains even at night.

Mother, who believes that Erika has gone to a private chamber-music recital, has loudly boasted to her daughter that she allows her to go so that Erika can have a private life rather than constantly berating her mother for not letting her out of her clutches. Within one hour at the very latest, Mother will start ringing up Erika's home-recital colleague, and the colleague will serve up an intricate excuse. Erika's colleague believes that Erika is involved in some kind of romance and that she, the colleague, is in on it.

The soil is black. The sky is only a tad brighter, just barely bright enough to reveal where earth is and where sky is. Frail silhouettes of trees loom on the horizon. Erika practices caution. She moves silently, as light as a feather. She is soft and weightless. She is very nearly invisible. She almost vanishes into thin air. She is all eyes and ears. The binoculars are the extensions of her eyes. She avoids the paths taken by other wanderers. She seeks the spots where other wanderers take their pleasures—always in twosomes. After all, she's done nothing wrong, nothing that would make others shrink away from her. Using the binoculars, she scours the area for couples, from whom others shrink. She cannot investigate the ground under her shoes; she switches into blind. She relies entirely on her ears—a professional habit. Sometimes she trips, almost stumbles, but on she forges in the correct direction. She walks and walks and walks. Garbage nestles into the profiles of her shoes, smoothing them out. But she keeps walking across the meadow.

Then she reaches it. Blazing like a huge campfire, the shrieks of an amorous couple flare up from the bottom of the meadow. At last: the homeland of the peepers. The sight is so close that Erika doesn't need her binoculars. The special night glass. Like a house looming up from a homeland, the couple is fucking itself out of the beautiful meadow ground and into Erika's eyeballs. A man emitting foreign yelps screws his way into a woman. The woman doesn't yowl, she issues almost morose, sotto-voce directions and commands, which the man may not comprehend. Jubilating in Turkish or some other rare language, he ignores the woman's shrieks. The woman growls deep in her throat like a dog ready to leap; she's trying to tell her john to shut up. But the Turk soughs and sighs like the spring wind, only louder. He emits long-drawn-out yelps, offering Erika a good orientation point, so she can sneak up closer, even though she is already quite close. The same bushes that provide refuge for the loving couple supply sufficient camouflage for Erika. The Turk or Turklike foreigner seems to be having a good time. So is the woman, as we hear. Except that she's applying the brakes. She's telling him where to go. It's hard to say whether he's obeying; he wants to follow his own orders, and so there's a good chance that he may occasionally collide with the woman's wishes. Erika is a witness. The man doesn't do what the woman says, he does what he wants. The woman seems to be gradually losing her cool because the man won't give her the right of way, as is appropriate. If she says, "Slow down," he steps on the gas; and vice versa. Maybe she's no professional, just your standard drunken woman getting laid. Maybe she won't get anything for her trouble. Erika hunkers down. She makes herself comfortable. Even if she were stamping around in nailed shoes, the couple wouldn't hear her; they're yelling much too loud, or at least one of them is. Erika isn't always this lucky with her peeping. Now the woman says something to the man. She tells him to hold it for a moment. Erika can't tell whether the man pays any attention. He emits a relatively short sentence in his language. The woman berates him, but her ranting is incomprehensible. Just wait, understand? Wait! Me no wait. Erika makes out what's happening. He smashes into the woman as if he wanted to break the world's record for soling a pair of shoes or welding a car body. The woman is shaken by the thrusts—down to her foundation walls. Shriller than the occasion warrants, she spews spite: Slower! Not so hard, please! Evidently, she's switched to pleading. Bottom line: zero again. The Turk has unbelievable energy and is in a frightful hurry. He increases his gear ratio in order to make as many thrusts as possible within the time unit and perhaps even the monetary unit. The woman resigns: She will never come to a good end. She vituperates: Isn't he done yet, or is he gonna keep on till next Tuesday? The man expels breathless

Turkish fanfares from his innermost depths. He fires on both
sides. Language and emotion seem to be drawing together in
him. He screeches in German: *Frau! Frau!* The Frau tries one
last time: Slower! Erika, in her hiding place, puts two and two
together: This is no Prater hooker; a prostitute would rev him
up rather than slam on his brakes. She'd have to collect as
many Johns as possible in as short a time as possible, in contrast
to the man, who feels the exact opposite. He wants to get as
much as possible for as long as possible. Someday he may not
be able to do anything anymore, and then he'll only have his
memories.

The opposite sex always wants the exact opposite.

Erika is but a puff, she scarcely breathes, but her eyes gape.
These eyes sniff, the way a deer sniffs with its nose. These are
highly sensitive organs, they turn as nimbly as weathervanes.
Erika does what she does so she won't be left out. She goes
first here, then there. She's in control of where she wants to
be, and where not. She doesn't want to take part, but nothing
should take place without her. When it comes to music, Erika
sometimes performs; at other times, she looks and listens.
That's how her time passes. Erika jumps aboard and then jumps
off, as if time were an old-fashioned trolley without pneumatic
doors. In modern streetcars, once you're aboard, you have to
stay inside. Until the next stop.

The man drives nails into an endless board. Sweating like a
pig, he holds the woman in an iron grip so she won't get away.
He covers her with spit as if he wanted to eat up his prey. The
woman has stopped talking, she only moans, infected by the
man's eagerness. She whimpers a series of meaningless falsetto
words. She whistles like an Alpine marmot when it smells an
enemy. She anchors her hands deep in her partner's back, so
he won't get away. So she can't be shaken off so easily, and,
once the duty's done, she can be remembered with affection or

a quip. The man works: piecework. He raises his limit high. This is his first chance with a native Austrian in a long time, and he's taking advantage of his chance with hectic activity. Above the couple, the treetops get the creeps. The nocturnal sky seems to be alive under the wind. The Turk obviously can't hold back as long as he thought he could. His throat disgorges something that doesn't even sound like Turkish anymore. This is the homestretch, and the woman spurs him on: Giddyap!

The effect on the spectator is devastating. Her hands itch to take an active part; but if she's not allowed, she'll hold back. She waits for a resolute prohibition. She needs to act within a solid framework, she needs to be stretched on it. The twosome, without realizing it, is turned into a threesome. Suddenly, certain organs labor in the spectator, and she can't control them: they work double-time or even faster. Strong pressure on her bladder, an irksome disturbance that overcomes her whenever she gets excited. Always at the most inappropriate moment, even though there are miles of terrain here, waiting to wipe away every last trace of this natural urge and its bottom line. The lady and the Turk are acting out an activity for her. Erika involuntarily reacts, making the twigs rustle. Did she desire the rustling or didn't she? The urge, squeezing out from inside, gets worse and worse. The spectator has to ease her squatting position in order to propitiate this itching, twitching urge. It's truly urgent. Who knows how long it can be contained? She mustn't give in to it now, no matter what. A loud swishing and rustling. Erika herself doesn't know whether she deliberately helped the branch along, which would be rather silly. She bumped into the branch, and the branch wreaks nasty, noisy vengeance.

The Turk, a child of nature, is rooted more solidly here, with the grass, the flowers, and the trees, than with the machine that he normally tends. He breaks off whatever he's doing. He breaks with the woman first. The woman doesn't realize it right away, she keeps yelping for another second or two, even though the Turkish guest has gone into neutral. He now remains motionless, which is fine and dandy. He's finished—what a coincidence—and he's resting. He's tired. He listens to the wind. The woman now listens, too, but only after the Bosporus dweller hisses at her to stop screaming. He bellows a terse question, or is it an order? The woman tries halfheartedly to soothe him; perhaps she wants something more from her love neighbor. The Turk doesn't understand her. Perhaps he has to hit her for pleading in descant: Stay here. Or something similar that Erika didn't quite catch. She was distracted, for she fled some thirty feet when the shaking, jerking Turk was still utterly devoted to the woman. Luckily, the woman didn't notice it, and now the Turk belongs to himself once again. And he's all man. The woman nags him for money or love. She sobs and cries loudly. The man from the Golden Horn barks at her, then unplugs himself from her and from his wireless communication with her. During her retreat, Erika sounded like a herd of Cape buffaloes at the approach of a lioness. Perhaps her noise was deliberate, or unconsciously deliberate, which boils down to the same thing.

The Turk bounces up and down on his feet and is about to spurt off—but tumbles down; his pants and his white, shimmering shorts blaze around his knees in the darkness. Unleashing a flood of curses, he yanks up his clothes and gesticulates ominously. His hands make an earnest threat to the left and one to the right—toward the nearby bushes, where Fräulein Kohut is bating her breath, pulling everything in, and biting into one of her ten small piano hammers.

The Turk is sack-hopping now between cloth paths. He misses one path, then the other. He doesn't take time for basic necessities. The spectator observes all this, and a thought flashes

through her mind: Some people don't think, they just act, no
matter what. The Turk belongs to this group. The frustrated
lower portion of the loving couple shrieks at him: It was probably just a dog or a rat that wanted to gorge itself on the
condoms. There's a lot of yummy garbage around here. Her
honeybunch should come back to her. He should please not
leave her alone. The foreigner's pretty, curly head pays no
attention. It rises to its normal level—he seems to be a relatively
large Turk. At last his pants are up. He breaks into the undergrowth. Luckily, perhaps intentionally, he stomps in the
wrong direction, toward the denser section of bushes. Erika,
not giving it much thought, has chosen a sparser area, where
he wouldn't suspect her of hiding. His woman croons and
swoons for him from afar. She's getting it together again.
Stuffing something between her thighs, she vigorously wipes
herself. Then she tosses away some crumpled tissues. She
curses in a newly devised gruesome scale that seems to be her
natural vocal range. She shouts and shouts. Erika shudders.
The man bleats terse replies at his woman as he seeks and
seeks. He keeps groping along from the same place to the next
place, which is once again the same place. Then he stereotyp-
ically returns to the first place. Maybe he's scared and doesn't
really want to find the peeper. For he merely keeps wandering
from the one birch to the bushes, and then from the bushes to
the one birch. He never goes over to the other bushes. The
woman's voice, rising a fire-engine fourth, shrieks that nobody's there anyway. Come back, she demands. The man
doesn't want to. He tells her in German to shut her trap. The
woman now prophylactically wedges a second heap of tissues
between her thighs, just in case anything is still left inside.
She hoists up her panties. Then she smoothes her skirt. Focusing on her open blouse, she pulls her coat out from underneath her body. She built herself a little nest, just like a woman.

She didn't want to soil her skirt, but now her coat is smeared and squashed. The Turk shouts something new: C'mon! The Turk's girlfriend rebels, insisting on a quick retreat. Now Erika sees her in her full glory. The woman's no spring chicken, but for a Turk she's still a downy chick. She cautiously stays in the background, handicapped by all those tissues in her panties. They're so easily lost! Sexually, she didn't get her money's worth, and now she wants to make sure she doesn't get killed in the bargain. Next time, she'll make sure she can enjoy herself in peace and quiet until the end. The woman visibly becomes an Austrian, and the Turk turns back into the Turk he always was. The woman commands respect, the Turk automatically watches out for enemies and adversaries.

Erika doesn't allow a single leaf to whirr or whisper on her body. She remains still and dead, like a rotten branch that has broken off the tree and is uselessly perishing in the grass.

The woman threatens to walk out on the guest worker. The guest worker wants to make a nasty retort, but changes his mind and just keeps searching mutely. He has to put up a bold front to keep the respect of the woman, who has abruptly reawakened into an Austrian. Encouraged by the fact that nothing is stirring, he moves in an ever-widening circle, thereby becoming more ominous for Fräulein Kohut. His woman gives him one last warning and picks her handbag off the ground. She arranges the last things in and of themselves. She buttons, she tucks, she shakes something out. She starts walking back slowly, in the direction of the restaurants, gazing at her Turkish friend one last time, but quickening her step. She howls some unintelligible nastiness by way of farewell.

The Turk shilly-shallies. Once this woman's gone, he might not find a replacement for weeks on end. The woman shouts: She can find another jerk like him very easily. The Turk stands and jerks his head, once toward the woman, once toward the

invisible bushman. The Turk is unsure of himself, he wavers
between one instinct and the other; both instincts have often
brought him misery. He barks—a dog who doesn't know which
prey to follow.

Erika Kohut can't stand it anymore. Her need is stronger.
She gingerly lets down her panties and pisses on the ground.
A warm stream patters down between her thighs to the meadow
ground. It ripples upon the soft mattress of twigs, foliage,
refuse, filth, and humus. She still doesn't know whether she
wants to be discovered or not. Rigidly furrowing her brow, she
simply lets the stream run out. She grows emptier and emptier
on the inside, and the ground soaks up the fluid. She ponders
nothing—no cause and no consequence. She relaxes her muscles, and the initial patter turns into a gentle, steady running.
She has stretched the image of the upright, motionless foreigner
in the micrometer spindles of her pupils, fixing it there while
urinating vigorously upon the earth. She is ready for either
solution, they're both fine with her. She leaves it to fate, in
the form of chance, whether the Turk is good-natured or not.
She carefully holds her plaid skirt together over her bent knees
to keep it from getting wet. It's not the skirt's fault. The itching
finally stops; soon she'll be able to turn off the faucet.

The Turk still looms statuesque in the meadow. His companion, however, is hurrying away, shrilly yelling across the
vast meadow. Now and then she looks back and makes a dirty
gesture that's known worldwide. She thus overcomes a language barrier.

The man is drawn now here, now there. A tame animal
between two masters. He can't tell what the swishing and whis-
pering mean, he didn't notice any water around here. But
there's one thing he knows for sure: The companion of his
senses is slipping away from him.

At this point, Erika Kohut is certain he will manage to take the two giant steps separating him from her; at this point, Erika Kohut shakes out the last few drops while awaiting a human hammer to thud down upon her from the sky: this mockup of a man, fashioned out of a thick oak board by a skillful carpenter, will crush Erika like an insect. But then he about-faces and, while constantly looking around, walks hesitantly, then more rapidly and resolutely, pursuing the prey he pulled down at the outset of this merry evening. A bird in the hand. After all, you can't tell whether a bird in the bush will measure up to your demands. The Turk flees from the uncertainty that has so often reared its painful head for him in this country. He dogs the woman's heels. He has to hurry, for she has dwindled into a distant dot. And soon he too becomes but a flyspeck on the horizon.

She's gone, he's gone too, and in the darkness, heaven and earth again hold hands, the hands that loosened for a moment.

Erika Kohut's one hand has been playing the keyboard of reason, the other the keyboard of passion. First, passion had its say; now, reason has its way, quickly driving Erika home through dark avenues. However, others have reaped the fruits of passion in Erika's place. The teacher observed them and graded them on her curve. She very nearly became involved in one of these passions, and only barely escaped detection.

Erika dashes along rows of trees that are endangered by many varieties of mistletoe. Many branches have had to bid farewell to their boles, and they bite the dust. Erika scurries away from her observation post in order to settle in her nest. She betrays no outward signs of inner disturbance. But a whirlwind sweeps up in her the instant she sees young men with young bodies strolling along the edge of the Prater, for she is practically old enough to be their mother! Everything that occurred before this age is irrevocably gone and can never come again. But who knows what lies ahead? Given the lofty achievements of modern medicine, a woman can perform her female functions even when she reaches a ripe old age. Erika pulls up her panties. This isolates her from contact. Even chance contact. But in her bruised interior, the tempest rages over her succulent pastures.

She knows exactly where the taxis are; she gets into the one at the head of the line. Nothing is left of the vast Prater meadows aside from a wee bit of dampness on her shoes and between her legs. A slightly sour odor rises from under her skirt, but the cabby probably doesn't notice, his deodorant covers everything. He doesn't want to force his hack sweat on his fares, and he doesn't have to perceive the grossness of his passengers. The cab is warm and dry; the heater operates silently, struggling against the cool night. Outside, the lights race past: the endless dark chunks of slums in numb, lightless sleep; the bridge across the Danube Canal; small, unfriendly, debt-ridden bars, from which drunks come tumbling, only to jump up and start punching one another; old women in kerchiefs, walking their dogs one last time for the day, hoping that just once they'll run into a lonely old man, a widower with a dog. Erika flashes by—a rubber mouse on a string, with a gigantic cat playfully leaping after it.

A pack of mopeds. Girls in skin-tight jeans with would-be punk hairdos. However, their hair doesn't quite manage to stand on end, it keeps falling. Grease alone won't do the trick. The hair keeps collapsing despondently on the scalp. And the girls hop on behind the moped pilots and zoom away.

A lecture hall releases a crowd of knowledge-seekers, who throng and jostle around the lecturer. They'd like to find out more about the Milky Way even though they've heard everything that can be said about it. Erika recalls that she once lectured here on Franz Liszt and his misunderstood work. She spoke in loosely crocheted air stitches. And two or three times, she lectured in a regular knit-two/purl-two on Beethoven's early sonatas. She explained that Beethoven's sonatas, whether late or, as in this case, early, show so much variety that one has to ask oneself the fundamental question of what the much-vilified word "sonata" really means. Perhaps Beethoven applied the word to entities that are not even sonatas in the strict sense of the term. One has to perceive new laws in this highly dramatic musical form. Often in the sonata, feeling eludes form. In Beethoven, that is not the case, for here the two go hand in hand; feeling makes form aware of a hole in the ground and vice versa.

The night is growing brighter: The center of Vienna is approaching. Light is used more generously here, so that tourists can easily find their way home. The opera is over for the night. This generally means that it is already so late that Frau Kohut, senior, will rage and roar in her domestic precinct, where she does not go to bed until her daughter has come home safe and sound. Mother will scream in jealous rage, she will create a dreadful scene. It will take Mother a long time to make up with Erika. The daughter will have to court her with a dozen highly specialized services. Tonight has finally made it clear that Mother gives her all, while the child won't even give up one second of her leisure! How can Mother fall asleep knowing she'll wake up the instant her daughter climbs into her half of the double bed? Looking daggers at the clock, Mother stalks through the apartment like a wolf. She pauses in her daughter's room, which has neither its own bed nor its own key. She opens the closet and angrily throws senselessly purchased clothing through the air, an action contrasting with the delicate materials and recommended handling. Tomorrow morning, before leaving for the conservatory, her daughter will have to put everything away. For Mother, these clothes are evidence

of egotism and obstinacy. And the child's selfishness is made
even more evident by the late hour. It's already past midnight,
and Mother is still all alone. It's outrageous! After the movie
on TV, there's no one for her to talk to. The movie is followed
by a late-night talk show. She doesn't want to watch because
she'd doze off, which she mustn't do before her child is
scrunched up into a shapeless wet blob. Mother wants to stay
wide awake. She digs her teeth into an old concert gown, which,
in its pleats, still hopes that someday it will belong to an international piano star. They once saved up for it, Mother and
crazy Father, pinching and scraping, gritting their teeth. Now,
Mother's nasty teeth bite into the gown. At the time, Erika,
that vain hussy, would rather have died than perform in a white
blouse and taffeta skirt like the others. Mother and Erika figured
it would be a good investment if the pianist looked nice. So
much for that. Mother tramples the gown under her slippers,
which are as clean as the floor and therefore unable to violate
the gown. Besides, her soles are soft. Ultimately, the gown just
looks a bit crumpled. So, grabbing some kitchen shears, Mother
charges onto the field of dishonor to put the finishing touches
on this creation by a squinting tenement seamstress, who hadn't
looked into a fashion journal for at least ten years when she
got to work on the gown. Mother doesn't improve on it. The
frock might cut a better figure if Erika had the guts to wear
this innovative striped creation with air between the narrow
ribbons of material. Mother slashes her own dreams along with
the dress. Why make Mother's dreams come true if Erika can't
even take care of her own dreams? Erika doesn't dare follow
her own dreams through, she always just stupidly gazes up at
them. Mother resolutely slashes away at the neckline trimming
and the graceful puff sleeves, which Erika rebelled against.
Mother then slices away remnants of the gathered skirt on the
top. She toils. First she had to scrimp and scrape to pay for the

dress. She pinched pennies from the housekeeping money. And now she has the drudgery of destroying it. The various parts lie before her; they ought to go into a meat grinder, which she doesn't have. The child still hasn't come home. Soon the phase of fear will replace the state of fury. It's hard not to worry. Terrible things can happen to a woman at night, where she doesn't belong. Mother calls up the police. They know nothing, they haven't even heard rumors. The police explain to Mother that if anything happened she'd be the first to know. Since no one has heard anything about anyone fitting Erika's age and height, there is nothing to report. Besides, no body has been unearthed. Nevertheless, Mother rings up one or two hospitals, and they don't know anything either. They explain that such calls are completely useless, ma'am. But perhaps at this very moment, gory packages containing pieces of her daughter are being dumped into garbage cans all around the city. Mother will then be all alone, destined for an old-age home, where she can never be all alone! On the other hand, no one will sleep with her in a double bed, as is her wont.

It is now ten minutes later than before, and there is no grinding in the lock, no friendly telephone buzzing that says: Please come to the hospital immediately. There is no daughter who says: Mama, I'll be home in fifteen minutes, I was delayed unexpectedly. The alleged chamber-music hostess doesn't answer the phone, even after thirty rings.

The maternal puma steals from the bedroom, where the bed is made and ready. She stalks into the living room, where the TV, switched on again, fades out with the national anthem. It is accompanied by the red-white-red Austrian flag billowing in the wind, a sign that day is done. It wasn't worth turning on the TV, for Mother knows the national anthem by heart. She transposes two knickknacks. She shifts the big crystal bowl from one spot to another. There is wax fruit in the bowl. She polishes the fruit with a soft white cloth. The daughter, a connoisseur of art, calls the fruit horrible. Mother negates this harsh judgment; it is still *her* apartment and *her* daughter. Someday, when Mother is dead, everything will change of its own accord. In the bedroom, the arrangement is meticulously checked yet again. A corner of the bedcover is carefully folded back, to form an equilateral triangle. The sheet is as stiff as an upswept hairdo. On the pillow lies a bedtime chocolate in the form of a tinfoil-coated horseshoe, left over from New Year's Eve. This surprise is removed, for sweets are only for the sweet. On the night table, next to the night-table lamp, the book that the daughter is reading. Inside it, a bookmark from a hand-painted childhood. Next to it, a filled glass of water for nocturnal thirst (the removal of the candy is punishment enough). Erika's kindhearted mother refills the glass with tap water for the nth time, to keep the water cold and fresh, so no bubbles will rise, indicating staleness and flatness. On her own side of the bed, Mother is somewhat more casual about these precautions. However, she is considerate enough to remove her dentures from her mouth early in the morning in order to clean them. Then in they go again, right away! If Erika has a wish at night, it is promptly satisfied if at all possible. This applies only to external wishes. Erika should keep her internal wishes to herself—doesn't she have a nice, warm home? After lengthy deliberation, Mother places a large green apple next to the bedtime book to widen the selection. Like a mother cat who drags her kittens around because she doesn't trust their peace and quiet, Mother carries the slashed dress from one place to another. And then finally to a third, where it can be seen glittering. The daughter should instantly see the destruction for which she is ultimately to blame. But it should not be too conspicuous. Eventually, Frau Kohut spreads the vestiges of the gown over the TV couch, very carefully, as though Erika were to slip into this creation for a piano recital. Mother has to make sure that the gown keeps body and soul together. She arranges the sleeve tatters in various ways. Her lawful devastation is virtually presented on a silver platter.

Mother briefly suspects that Herr Klemmer, from that long-past home recital, is forcing his way between mother and child. That young man is very nice, but he can't replace a mother. A mother comes in a unique model, and Erika's got the original. If Erika did get together with Herr Klemmer, it will have been the last time. They are approaching the deadline for the down payment on the newly built apartment. Every day, Mother forges a new plan, then rejects it, which is why her daughter will have to sleep in the same bed with her, even in the new apartment. Mother should also forge Erika right now, while the iron is still hot. And not yet hot for that Walter Klemmer. Mother's reasons: various dangers such as fire, theft, burglary, leaky pipes, Mother's heart attacks (blood pressure!), nocturnal anxieties of a general and specific nature. Every day, Mother refurnishes Erika's room in the new condo, and always more cunningly than the day before. But there'll be no bed for her daughter—forget it! A comfortable easy chair will be the sole concession.

Mother lies down, then instantly gets up again. She is already wearing her nightgown and robe. She traipses from wall to wall, pushing away decorative objects and taking their places. She looks at all the clocks in the apartment and compares them with one another. The child is going to get it, she'll pay for this.

Okay, here we are, the child's arriving, the lock is clearly clicking, the key grinds briefly, then the gates open up to the gray and gruesome land of mother love. Erika enters. She squints like a drunken moth in the bright hall light. All the lights are switched on as if for a party. However, the time of the eucharist went by, unused, hours ago. Softly, but crimson with rage, Mother sprints out of her abode, accidentally knocking something over, almost knocking Erika over (that phase of the struggle won't come till later). Mother soundlessly strikes out at her child, and the child strikes back ⸱   ⸱ a brief reaction time. Erika's shoe soles give off an animal smell, indicating at least decay. Because of the neighbors, who have to get up early in the morning, the two women keep their wrestling silent. The outcome is uncertain. In the end, the daughter may allow her mother to win out of sheer respect. Mother, worried about her child's ten little musical hammers, may allow the child to win. Actually, the child is stronger because she is younger. Besides, Mother used up all her strength fighting with her husband. However, the child has not yet learned how to exploit her strength fully against her mother. Mother smacks away at the loosened hairdo of the late-season fruit of her womb. The silk kerchief adorned with horseheads flutters up, settling, as if deliberately, on a hall lamp, toning it down, damping it— the proper lighting for moodier performances. The daughter is at a disadvantage, her shoes are slippery from all the shit, clay, and grass. She slips on the mat. Her body crashes on the floor, which is barely softened by the red sisal runner. A noisy development. Mother hisses at Erika: Quiet! (The neighbors!) Erika gives tit for tat, reminding Mother about the neighbors: Quiet! They scratch each other's faces. The daughter shrieks like a falcon pouncing on its prey. As for quiet, Erika says the neighbors can complain all they like tomorrow, Mother's the one who'll have to put up with it. Mother howls, then instantly chokes back her howl. It is followed by a half-voiceless, half-vocal gasping and whimpering, sobbing and simpering. Mother starts pressing the "pity" button, and, since the fight is still undecided, she resorts to such unfair devices as her age and her imminent death. She mumbles these arguments, a sobbing chain of poor excuses for not winning today. Her laments hit home. Erika doesn't want Mother wearing herself out in this struggle. She says Mother started. Mother says Erika started. It's taken at least a month off Mother's life. Erika scratches and bites only halfheartedly. Mother takes her advantage and rips out a handful of Erika's forelock, some of the hair that Erika is proud of because it curls down in such a pretty twirl. Erika lets out a falsetto shriek, which frightens Mother so intensely that she stops. Tomorrow, Erika will have to wear a Band-Aid on her scalp. Or else she'll have to keep on her kerchief, *quasi una fantasia*, when she teaches. The two women sit on the crumpled runner, facing each other under the shaded glow of the lamp, loudly breathing in and out. After several gulps of air, the daughter asks whether this was necessary. Like a loving wife who has just received dreadful news from abroad, Erika presses her right hand convulsively against her throat, where an artery hops and twitches. Mother, a retired Niobe, sits next to the hall bureau, which sports all kinds of things with vague functions and unexplained uses. Mother answers without finding words. She says that it would not have been necessary if Erika had only come home on time. Then they aim silence at each other. Their senses are heightened. They have been polished into inconceivably thin blades by rotating whetstones. Mother's nightgown has slipped down during the fight, showing that, despite everything, she is still first and foremost a woman. Her embarrassed daughter recommends that Mother cover herself. Ashamed, Mother obeys. Erika gets up, saying she's thirsty. Mother hurries to satisfy this modest wish. She's afraid that Erika, out of sheer defiance, will buy

herself a new dress tomorrow. Mother gets some cider from
the refrigerator, a special weekend sale, for she seldom lugs the
heavy bottles home from the supermarket. She normally buys
concentrated raspberry syrup, which lasts a lot longer for the
same amount of effort. The concentrate, diluted with water,
can be stretched out for weeks. Mother says she's finally going
to die, the flesh is willing and the heart is weak. The daughter
tells her not to exaggerate. She is already numbed by those
constant threats of dying. Mother wants to cry, which would
make her the winner by a knockout in the third round—or, at
worst, by default. Erika warns Mother not to cry so late at
night. Erika wants to drink the juice, then go straight to bed.
Mother should do the same, albeit on her side of the bed. She
should not talk to Erika anymore! Erika is not going to be so
quick to forgive her for assaulting a blameless homecomer, a
chamber musician. Erika doesn't want to shower because the
pipes can be heard throughout the building. She lies down, as
is, next to her mother. Today, one or two of her fuses shorted,
but Erika returned home all the same. Since the fuses were
meant for rarely used devices, Erika doesn't notice they're out.
She lies down and falls asleep right after saying good night, to
which there is no response. Mother lies awake for a long time,
secretly wondering how her daughter could fall asleep right
away, with no sign of regret. Erika should have noticed that
Mother paid no attention to her good night. On a normal
evening, both of them would lie motionless for about ten minutes, stewing in their own juice. Then the inevitable reconcil-
iation would take place with a long, quiet heart-to-heart talk,
sealed by a good-night kiss. But today, Erika simply fled into
sleep, whisked off by dreams that Mother will never know about
because she never hears about them the next day. Mother tells
herself to practice utmost caution during the next few days and

weeks, even months. These thoughts keep her awake for hours on end, until the gray dawn.

❑

When discussing Bach's six *Brandenburg* concertos, the artistically aware person usually states, among other things, that when these masterpieces were composed, the stars were dancing in the heavens. God and his dwelling place are always involved whenever these people talk about Bach. Erika has taken over the piano part for one of her students, whose nose was bleeding and who had to go lie down. The student rests on a gym mat. Flutes and violins complete the ensemble, lending a rarity value to the concertos. After all, the makeup of the players is always extremely varied. And so are the instruments. Once, a group even used two recorders!

In Erika's wake, Walter Klemmer has begun a new and serious offensive. He has cordoned off a corner of the gymnasium and settled down. This is his own auditorium, where he listens to the chamber orchestra rehearsing. He pretends to be absorbed in his score, but he is actually staring only at Erika. Not a single one of her movements at the keyboard escapes his notice, not because he wants to learn from them, but because he'd like to unnerve the pianist—a typical male trick. He gazes at the teacher, passively but provokingly. He wants to be one big masculine challenge, something that only the strongest woman and artist can take on. Erika asks him whether he would like to play the piano part himself. He says no, he wouldn't, and he inserts a meaningful pause between the two phrases, charging the pause with something ineffable. He reacts with significant silence to Erika's claim that practice makes perfect. Klemmer says hello to a female acquaintance, kissing her hand—a deliberately playful gesture.

Then he laughs with a second girl about some nonsense or other.

Erika feels the spiritual vacuum emanating from such girls. A man soon gets bored with them. A pretty face is used up very quickly.

Klemmer, the tragic hero, who is far too young for this role (while Erika is actually too old to be an innocent victim of his attentions), runs his finger correctly along the mute notes in the score. Everyone can tell instantly that Klemmer is a musical victim, not a musical parasite. Klemmer is a performer, who is prevented from playing by unfortunate circumstances. He briefly places his arm around a third girl's shoulder. She is wearing a miniskirt, which is back in fashion. She seems un-burdened by any thoughts. Erika thinks: If Klemmer wants to sink that low, then let him. But I won't accompany him. Her skin crinkles jealously, like fine crepe paper. Her eyes hurt because she can catch everything only out of their extreme corners. She simply mustn't turn toward Klemmer. He mustn't notice her attention no matter what. He jokes with the third girl. The girl writhes under volleys of laughter. She shows her legs almost up to where they end and run into the body. The girl is showered with sunlight. Constant canoeing has painted a healthy color in Klemmer's cheeks. His head flows into the girl's head. His blond hair lights up together with the girl's long hair. When he goes canoeing, Klemmer protects his head with a helmet. He tells the girl a joke, and his eyes flash blue, like taillights. He can sense Erika's presence constantly. His eyes do not signal a brake maneuver. Why, Klemmer, no doubt, is in the middle of a new advance. Wind, water, rocks, and waves have warmly recommended that the discouraged paddler should keep going. He was about to give up, he was about to pick younger garden flowers than Erika. However, there are signs that his secret beloved will waver and soften. If only he

could get her into a canoe just once. It doesn't have to be a
paddle boat, which must be so hard to handle. It can be a
motionless boat. There, on a lake, on a river—that would be
Klemmer's element, his most intrinsic one—he could exert sure
control over her, because he feels at home in water. He could
conduct and coordinate Erika's hectic movements. Here, on the
keyboard, on the trail of notes, Erika is in *her* element, and
the conductor conducts (an exiled Hungarian, who, in a thick
accent, foams his rage at the flock of students).

Since Klemmer diagnoses his attachment to Erika as affection, he again decides not to give up. He sits hard, assiduously
digging his back legs in. She very nearly got away; or else,
discouraged, he would have given up. That would have been
terribly wrong. She now strikes him as physically more dis-
tinctive, more accessible than last year: picking at the keys,
sending nervous side glances at the student, who won't go, and
who also won't come and talk about the pyre blazing inside
him. As for a musical analysis of the performance, he again
doesn't seem all there. But he *is* here. Is he here for her sake?
She plays hard to get, but lets Klemmer know that he is the
only one she's noticed here, from the very start. Aside from
Klemmer, the only thing that exists for Erika, the music tamer,
is music. A connoisseur, Klemmer does not believe what he
thinks he sees in Erika's face: rejection. He alone is worthy of
opening the gate to the pasture, ignoring the No Trespassing
sign. Erika shakes the pearl strand of a trill out of her white
blouse cuffs; she is loaded with nervous haste. Perhaps the
haste is caused by the newly arrived spring, which announced
itself long ago with denser bird traffic and inconsiderate drivers
everywhere (in winter they spared their cars so as not to damage
the piston rods; but now they shoot out, together with the first
snowdrops, and, somewhat rusty at the wheel, they cause
dreadful accidents). Erika plays the simple piano part mechan-

ically. Her thoughts drift far afield, to a study trip with student Klemmer. Just the two of them: a small hotel room and love.

Then a truck loads up all her thoughts and dumps them out again in the small room for two. Shortly before the day ends, Erika's thoughts have to be back in the small hamper that her mother has lovingly lined with pillows and freshly covered, so that youth can snuggle in with old age.

Herr Nemeth taps his baton again. The violins weren't mellow enough for him. Once again from the fifth measure, please. Now the nose bleeder returns, fortified, and requests her place at the piano as well as her rights as a soloist, a privilege she has arduously won against all the competition. She is a favorite pupil of Professor Kohut because she too has a mother who adopted an ambition as her own child.

The girl takes Erika's place. Walter Klemmer winks encouragingly at the girl and checks to see what Erika thinks of his wink. Before Herr Nemeth can even pick up his baton, Erika whooshes out of the room. Klemmer, profoundly grateful to her and renowned far and wide as a fast starter in both art and love, gets into gear: he wants to sniff the trail. But the conductor's glare pushes Klemmer, the spectator, back into his seat. The student has to decide whether he wants in or out. Once he decides, he'll have to abide by his decision.

The string section heaves its right arms into the bows and scrapes away mightily. The piano trots proudly into the arena, twists its hips, prances loosely, performs an exquisite feat from the *haute école*—a trick that is not in the score; devised through long nights, and now illuminated in pink, it struts gracefully around the semicircular curve. Herr Klemmer has to stay seated and wait until the next time the conductor breaks off. This time, the maestro wants to make it to the end or bust, assuming that no one busts out. But not to worry: these music makers are adults. The children's orchestra and the singing-school groups, a variegated jigsaw of all the existing vocal schools, already rehearsed at four o'clock: a composition by the recorder teacher, with vocal solos by the singing-school teachers gathered from all the music-school branches. A bold opus, alternating between even and odd beats, that turned some of the kids into bedwetters.

The future pros are indulging themselves musically, here and now. Tomorrow's members of the Lower Austrian Orchestra, the provincial opera houses, and the Austrian Radio Network Symphony Orchestra. Even the Philharmonic, in case a male relative of the student is already playing in it.

Klemmer sits and broods about Bach, but like a brood hen that is somewhat neglecting her egg. Will Erika come back again soon? Or is she washing her hands? He doesn't know his way around here. But he can't help exchanging winks with pretty students. He wants to live up to his reputation as a womanizer. Today the rehearsal had to take refuge in this surrogate space. All the large rooms in the Conservatory are needed for an urgent full-scale rehearsal of the opera class: an ambitious suicide mission, Mozart's *Figaro*. An elementary school has lent out its gymnasium for the Bach rehearsal. The gym apparatuses have retreated up against the walls; physical culture has yielded to high culture for once. The school, located in Schubert's old neighborhood, houses the local music school on its top floors, but this space is far too small for a rehearsal.

Today, the students of this musical subsidiary are permitted to attend the rehearsal of the famous Conservatory Orchestra. Few of the students avail themselves of the privilege. It is meant to facilitate their choice of a future career. They can see that hands can not only ride roughshod but also caress delicately. Their vocational goals—carpenter or university professor—

vanish into the distance. The students sit raptly on chairs and exercise mats, lending their ears. None of them has parents who would expect their child to study carpentry.

On the other hand, the child should not assume that a musician's life is a piece of cake. The child has to sacrifice his or her leisure to constant practice. For quite a while now, Walter Klemmer has been depressed by the unfamiliar school surroundings; he again feels like a child in front of Erika. Their pupil/teacher relationship is solidly cemented, their lover relationship seems further away than ever. Klemmer doesn't even dare use his elbows to jostle his way to the exit. Erika fled, closing the door without waiting for him. The ensemble fiddles, scrapes, grumbles, and bangs the keys. The performers strain hard, because one always strains hard in front of ignorant listeners—they still appreciate worshipful faces and concentrated expressions. Thus the orchestra takes its playing more seriously than normal. The wall of sound closes up in front of Klemmer; he doesn't dare try to break through, he's too worried about his career. He doesn't want Herr Nemeth to reject him as soloist for the big final concert of the semester. Klemmer's been nominated. A Mozart recital.

Walter Klemmer spends his time in this gymnasium measuring female dimensions, squaring the curves off against one another, which isn't too difficult for a technician. Meanwhile, his piano teacher is irresolutely rummaging through the dressing room. Today, the room is crammed with instrument cases, covers, coats, caps, scarves, and gloves. The wind players keep their heads warm, the pianists and string players their hands— it all depends on which part of the body conjures up the sounds. Countless pairs of shoes are standing about, because you can enter a gymnasium only in sneakers. Some people forgot their sneakers, and so they sit around in socks or stockings, catching cold.

From far away, the thunder of a noisy Bach cataract reaches the ears of Erika the piano player. She is standing on a floor that prepares people for average athletic achievements. She doesn't know what she's doing or why she scooted out of the rehearsal room. Did Klemmer drive her out? It's unbearable, the way he tossed about those young girls on the rummage counter in the gourmet-food department. If asked, he would excuse himself by saying he has a connoisseur's appreciation of female beauty in every age and category. It is an insult to the teacher, who took the trouble to flee a feeling.

Music has often comforted Erika in times of distress. But today, the music grinds into sensitive nerve endings exposed by the man named Klemmer. Erika has landed in a dusty, unheated restaurant. She wants to rejoin the others, but she can't leave, she's stopped by a muscle-bound waiter, who advises the gracious lady to make up her mind, the kitchen is closing. Vegetable or liver-dumpling soup? Feelings are always ridiculous, especially when unauthorized people get their hands on them. Erika strides through the smelly room, a bizarre spindle-shanked bird in the zoo of secret needs. She forces herself to walk very slowly, hoping someone will come and stop her. Or hoping someone will keep her from carrying out the misdeed she is planning and for which she will have to endure horrible consequences: a tunnel bristling with sharp, scary apparatuses and utter darkness through which she will have to dash quickly. No shimmer of light at the other end. And where is the light switch for the niches in which the emergency personnel are concealed?

All she knows is that at the other end she'll find the arena, lit white-hot, where further feats of dressage and demonstrations of accomplishment await her. An amphitheater of ascending stone benches, releasing a shower upon her: peanut shells, popcorn bags, soda bottles with bent straws, rolls of toilet paper. This would be her real audience. From the gymnasium comes Herr Nemeth's hazy shriek. He's yelling at the students to play louder: Forte! More sound!

The sink is made of porcelain and veined with cracks. There's a mirror above it. Under the mirror, a glass shelf rests on metal brackets. A tumbler stands on the shelf. The tumbler wasn't placed there cautiously or caringly; the person was heedless about a lifeless object. The tumbler stands where it stands. An isolated drop of water is still dangling from the bottom of the tumbler, relaxing before it evaporates. Some student probably took a drink from the tumbler. Erika combs through the pockets of coats and jackets, looking for a handkerchief, which she soon finds. A product of the flu and head-cold season. Erika takes hold of the tumbler in the handkerchief, bedding the glass in the cloth. The glass, with innumerable fingerprints left by clumsy juvenile hands, is all wrapped up. Erika places the cloaked tumbler on the floor and smashes her heel into it. The glass, muffled, splinters. The injured tumbler is then stamped on several times more, until it is turned into a splintery but not shapeless gruel. The splinters mustn't be too small! They should be nice and sharp! Erika picks up the handkerchief with its jagged contents and carefully lets the splinters slide into a coat pocket. The cheap, thin glass has left very sharp, nasty fragments. Its whirring whimper of pain was deadened by the cloth.

Erika clearly recognized the coat both because of the fashionably loud color and because of the newly stylish mini-shortness. At the start of the rehearsal, this girl distinguished herself by trying to come on to Walter Klemmer, who towers head and shoulders above her. Erika would like to find out how the girl can give herself airs with a slashed hand. Her face will twist into an ugly grimace in which no one will recognize her former youth and beauty. Erika's spirit will prevail over the assets of the flesh.

Erika had to skip miniskirt phase no. 1, at her mother's request. Mother had packed her command for a low hem in a warning: The mini style was unbecoming for Erika. All the other girls had shortened and rehemmed their skirts, dresses, and coats. Or else they bought them short and sweet. The wheel of time, bristling with naked female legs like candles, rolled on; but Erika, at Mother's orders, skipped ahead, leaped across time. She had to explain to everyone, whether or not they wanted to hear: It doesn't really suit me and I don't really like it! And she jumped across space and time. Shot from the maternal catapult. From way up high, she applied the most rigorous criteria, developed through nights of musing and mulling, to judge thighs exposed till goodness knew where and even farther! She handed out individual marks to legs revealing all levels of panty hose or summery nakedness—which was even worse. Erika would then say to whoever was there: If I were her, I just wouldn't have the gall! Erika offered detailed descriptions of why so few girls had the figures to get away with it. Then she betook herself beyond time and its fads, sticking to "timeless knee-length," as the fashion journals put it. And thus, more rapidly than other women, she became a victim of the relentless ring of knives on the wheel of time. She believes that one should not kowtow to fashion: instead, fashion should kowtow to what looks good on you and what doesn't.

That flutist, made up like a clown, has heated up her Walter Klemmer with thighs that can be seen far and wide. Erika knows that the girl is a much-envied student of fashion design. As Erika Kohut slips a deliberately smashed tumbler into the girl's coat pocket, it crosses her mind that she would not care to relive her own youth at any price. She is glad that she's as old as she is; she managed, just in time, to replace youth with experience.

No one has come in as yet, but the risk was great. Everyone in the gym vies with the music. Merriment, or what Bach meant by it, fills every nook and cranny and clambers up the ladders. The finale is not too far away. Hurrying and scurrying, Erika opens the door and returns self-effacingly. She rubs her hands as if she had just washed them, and she huddles silently in a corner. Needless to say, Erika, being a teacher, can open doors even though Bach is still bubbling. Herr Klemmer registers her return with a glow in his naturally gleaming eyes. Erika ignores him. He tries to greet his teacher like a child greeting the Easter bunny. Hunting for colored eggs is more fun than finding them; and that's how Walter Klemmer feels about this woman. For a man, the hunt is a greater pleasure than the inevitable union. The only question is: When? Klemmer is still concerned about that damned age difference. However, he is a man, and that easily makes up for the ten years Erika has over him. Furthermore, female value decreases with increasing years and increasing intelligence. The technician in Klemmer computes all these data, and the bottom line of his calculations reveals that Erika still has a wee bit of time before wandering into the tomb. Walter Klemmer is less abashed when he perceives the creases in Erika's face and body. He is more abashed when she explains something on the keyboard to him. But ultimately, the only things that count are creases, wrinkles, cellulite, gray hair, bags under the eyes, large pores, artificial teeth, glasses, and loss of the figure.

Luckily, Erika has not gone home early as she often does. She likes taking French leave. She never emits a word of warning, not even a wave of her hand. All at once, she's gone, far and away. On days when she deliberately runs out on him, Klemmer plays *Die Winterreise* on a record player over and over, humming along softly. The next day, he tells his teacher

that only Schubert's saddest song cycle can soothe the mood I
was in yesterday, all because of you, Erika. Something in me
trembled with Schubert, who, when he wrote "Loneliness,"
must have trembled just as I did yesterday. We suffered in the
same rhythm, so to speak, Schubert and your humble servant.
I may be minor and trivial compared with Schubert. But on
evenings like yesterday, I come off better than usual in com-
parison with him. Normally, I'm rather superficial. Do you
see, I own up to it honestly, Erika.

Erika orders Klemmer not to look at her like that. But Klemmer is as open as ever about his desires. The two of them are
wrapped up like twin pupae in a cocoon. Their hulls, delicate
as cobwebs, are made of ambition, ambition, ambition, and
ambition, resting weightless, fragile, on the two skeletons of
their bodily wishes and dreams. It is these wishes that make
each person real to the other. It is the wish to penetrate thoroughly and be penetrated thoroughly that makes them Klem-
mer-person and Kohut-person. Two pieces of meat in the well-
cooled window of a tenement butcher, the rosiness of the cut
surface turned toward the public. After long deliberation, the
housewife asks for a pound of this and then two pounds of
that. The two pieces are wrapped in parchment that is imperme-
able to fat. The customer places them unhygienically in a shop-
ping bag lined with plastic that is never cleaned. And the two
chunks of meat, the fillet and the pork cutlet, snuggle together,
one dark red, the other pale pink.

In me you see the barrier on which your will shall break,
for you will never get across me, Herr Klemmer! And Klemmer
contradicts her sharply, setting his own limits and standards.

Meanwhile, a chaos of trampling feet and grabbing hands
has broken out in the locker room. Voices yammer that they
can't find this or that, which they left here or there. Others
squawk that someone owes them money. A violin case crashes

crackingly under the foot of a young man, who didn't buy the case; otherwise he'd be more careful with it, as his parents have pleaded. Two American girls twitter in falsetto about an overall musical impression that was impeded by something, they can't put their finger on it, maybe it was the acoustics. But they did hear some interference.

Then a shriek slices the air in half, and a slashed, bloody hand is pulled out of a coat pocket. The blood drips on the new coat. It leaves deep stains. The girl to whom the hand belongs screams in terror and blubbers in pain, after a moment of shock in which she feels nothing. The flutist's shredded tool, which will have to be sewn up, the hand that presses and releases keys, has shards and shivers stuck in it. The adolescent gapes aghast at her dripping hand. Mascara and eye shadow, in carefully nuanced harmony, are already running down her cheeks. The public is dumbstruck, then it cataracts toward the center with double strength, like iron filings when a magnetic field is switched on. Clinging to the victim doesn't help them much. It doesn't make them perpetrators, they do not enter a mysterious relationship with the victim. They are sent packing. Herr Nemeth picks up the baton of authority and demands a physician. Three model students rush off to the telephone. The others remain spectators, unaware that this incident was brought about by certain yearnings that were manifested so disagreeably. They just can't understand who could *do* such a thing. They would never be capable of something so awful.

A helpful group concentrates into a hard core that will soon spit itself out. No one moves away, everyone wants to have a close look.

The victim has to sit down, she feels sick. Maybe that'll put an end to her awful flutiness.

Erika pretends that she's feeling sick from being so close to blood.

Something happens that's humanly possible only after an injury. A few people telephone because others are telephoning too. Lots of people yell at everyone else to pipe down, few people actually do pipe down. They jostle into one another's lines of vision. They accuse completely innocent people. They act contrary to calls for order. They prove utterly indifferent to renewed entreaties to keep quiet, keep back, keep away from this terrible incident. Two or three students are already opposing the most primitive rules of decency. From various corners, to which the better-bred and the indifferent have retreated, one hears questions about who the culprit might be. Someone speculates that the girl inflicted the injury upon herself in order to attract attention. A second one vehemently protests and circulates the rumor that the deed was done by a jealous boyfriend. A third party says that the motive *was* probably jealousy, but a jealous girl's.

An unfairly accused boy blows up. An unfairly accused girl begins to blubber. A group of students resist measures dictated by reason. Someone emphatically rebuffs a rebuke, the way he sees politicians do it on TV. Herr Nemeth asks for quiet, which is soon disrupted by an ambulance siren.

Erika Kohut observes everything carefully and then leaves. Walter Klemmer observes Erika Kohut like a freshly hatched chick that recognizes its food source; he then almost dogs her heels as she leaves.

◻

The steps of the staircase, hollowed by angry footfalls of children, bounce away under Erika's sneakers, vanishing underfoot. Erika gyrates aloft. Meanwhile, makeshift councils have formed in the gym, conjecturing and speculating. And recommending. They focus on possible hiding areas and form chains to beat through these fields with noisemakers. This tangle of people will not dissolve all that soon. Eventually it *will* disintegrate, bit by bit, because the young musicians have to get home. But now they throng around the misfortune, which, fortunately, has not struck them. Still, one or two people believe they'll be next. Erika hurries up the stairs. Everyone who sees her flee thinks she feels sick—her musical universe knows no injuries. But, she has only been seized with her old familiar urge to pass water at the untimeliest moments. She feels a downward tug between her legs; that's why she has to run upward. She looks for a toilet on the top floor, because no one would surprise the teacher there during a banal physical chore.

She yanks open a door at random; she doesn't know her way around. But she's had experience with toilet doors, since she is often forced to track them down in impossible places. In unfamiliar buildings or offices. The door looks so worn that its very appearance pleads its case. This must be the door to one of the facilities in this school. Its case is backed by the stench of children's urine.

The faculty toilets can be unlocked only with special keys; these facilities have exquisite hygienic gadgets plus special state-of-the-art equipment. Erika has the unmusical feeling that she is about to burst. All she wants to do is pour herself out in a long, hot stream. This urge often overcomes her at the more awkward moment of a concert, when the pianist is playing pianissimo as well as working the soft pedal.

Erika fulminates inaudibly against that wretched habit of many pianists who are of the opinion—an opinion they advocate publicly—that the soft pedal is to be employed only for pianissimo passages. Yet Beethoven's personal instructions speak loud and clear in favor of the soft pedal. Thus, Erika's logic chats with her expertise, both of which hobnob with Beethoven. Erika secretly regrets that she could not fully savor her crime against the unsuspecting student.

She is now in the front room of the latrine and can only feel astonishment at the rich imagination of a school architect or interior decorator. To the right, a dwarf door leads to the boys' pissoir. The stench is pestilential. An easily accessible enamel gutter runs along the floor next to the oily wall. The drain contains a neat arrangement of waste pipes, some of them clogged. Here the little men hiss out their yellow streams into the toilets or else paint patterns on the wall. Their handwriting is on the wall.

Things that do not belong here are also stuck in the gutter: scraps of paper, banana peels, orange rinds, even a notebook. Erika pulls open the window and notices an artistic frieze on the facing wall, somewhat off to the side. The exterior decoration, from Erika's bird's-eye view, shows something like a seated naked man and a seated naked woman. The woman's arm is around a small dressed girl, who is doing some kind of work with her hands. The man is peering up with obvious goodwill at a dressed son, who is vigilantly holding an open compass and seems to be solving scientific problems. Erika recognizes a stony admonition of Social Democratic educational policies in the frieze, and she makes sure not to lean too far out the window, so she won't fall. Erika prefers closing the window, even though the stench has been only spurred on by the opening. Erika cannot waste her time looking at art, she must forge ahead.

The little schoolgirls relieve themselves behind a false front, something like a stage set. The set depicts, not very convincingly, something like a row of stalls. As at a beach. Countless holes of the most diverse shapes and sizes are bored into the wooden partitions. Erika wonders what they were bored with. These walls are brutally sawed off at the level of the teacher's shoulders. Her head looms out. An elementary-school pupil can just conceal herself behind this screen, but not a full-grown faculty member. The pupils have to peek through the holes to gain a side view of the toilet bowl and the user. If Erika stands up behind the wall, her head towers over it like a giraffe munching away at a high branch. One reason for these partitions may be that an adult can always check what the child is taking such a long time to do behind the door or whether she has locked herself in.

Erika hurriedly settles on the grimy bowl after pushing up the concomitant seat. Others before her have had the same flash of wisdom, so the bowl is probably covered with bacilli. Something is floating in the bowl, but Erika hasn't looked, she's in too much of a hurry. In her state, she'd even squat over a snakepit. But there has to be a closable door! If she can't bolt herself in, then she can't drop anything at any price. The bolt functions, releasing a sluice in Erika. Erika, heaving a sigh of relief, pushes the small lever so that a red segment on the other side indicates: Occupied.

Someone opens a door and comes in. He is not intimidated by these surroundings. The approaching footsteps are unmistakably masculine, and, as it turns out, they belong to Walter Klemmer, who dashed after Erika a few minutes ago. Klemmer gropes along from one loathsomeness to the next, which is unavoidable if he wants to track down his beloved. She's been rejecting him for months, even though she must know what a Casanova Klemmer is. He wishes she would finally free herself of her inhibitions. She ought to discard her teacher personality and turn herself into an object that she can then offer to him. He'll take care of everything. Klemmer is now a concordat made up of bureaucracy and lust. A lust that knows no limits, or if it does know them, does not respect them. Such is Klemmer's assignment for his teacher. Walter Klemmer shakes off a hull named inhibition, a hull named timidity, and a hull named restraint. Erika can flee no farther; behind her there is nothing but massive brickwork. He'll make her forget everything but him; she'll be seeing stars. He'll throw away the instruction brochure; no one else will be able to utilize Erika in this way. The time has come: So much for Erika's vagueness and dimness. She will no longer be hedged in like Sleeping Beauty. She should be a free person, presenting herself to Klemmer, who is fully informed about her secret desires.

That is why Klemmer now asks: "Erika, are you there?" There is no answer, only a diminishing splash resounds from a stall, an increasingly decreasing noise. A half-suppressed throat-clearing. It indicates the direction. No answer is offered Klemmer—which could be interpreted as scorn. He was able to identify precisely whose throat was cleared. You're not going to repeat that answer to a man, says Klemmer, talking into a forest of stalls. Erika is a teacher, but also a child. Klemmer may be a student, but he is the adult here. He has realized that he, not the teacher, is setting the standard. Klemmer applies this newly acquired qualification by looking for something to climb up on. Quick-witted, he finds a dirty tin pail on which a rag is drying. Klemmer shakes off the rag, transports the pail to the stall in question, turns the pail upside down, gets up on it, and reaches across the partition, behind which the final drops have dripped. Only a deathly hush emerges. The woman behind the partition puts down her skirt, so Klemmer won't see her at a disadvantage. Klemmer's upper portion appears over the door and leans forward defiantly. Erika's face is beet-red. She is silent. From up there, Klemmer, a long-stemmed flower capable of doing anything, unbolts the door. Klemmer pulls the teacher out because he loves her, and she is probably in fullest agreement. She will grant him the concession immediately. These two lead performers intend to put on a love scene, completely private, no extras, no walk-ons, only one lead under the leaden heaviness of the other lead.

In accordance with the occasion, Erika instantly gives herself up as a person. A present wrapped in slightly dusty tissue paper, on a white tablecloth. As long as the guest is present, his present is lovingly turned and twisted; but as soon as he leaves, the present is shoved aside, heedlessly and confusedly, and everyone hurries to supper. The present cannot go away by itself, but for a while it is comforted by the fact that it is not alone. Plates and cups clatter, silverware scrapes on porcelain. But then the package notices that these noises are produced by a cassette player on the table. Applause and the clinking of glasses—everything on tape! Someone comes and takes the package. Erika can relax in this new security: She is being taken care of. She waits for instructions or orders. She has been studying for years—not toward her concert, but toward this day.

Klemmer has the option of putting her back unused in order to punish her. It's up to him, he can utilize her or not. He can even toss her around mischievously. But he can also polish her and place her in a showcase. Maybe he'll never wash her, but just keep pouring fluids into her; and her edge would be sticky and greasy from all the mouth prints. A day-old coat of sugar on the bottom.

Walter Klemmer pulls Erika out of the toilet stall. He yanks her. For openers, he presses a long kiss on her mouth; it was long overdue. He gnaws on her lips, his tongue plumbs her depths. After endlessly ruinous use, his tongue pulls back and then pronounces Erika's name several times. He puts a lot of work into this piece known as Erika. He reaches under her skirt, knowing that this means he is going places. He goes even farther, he feels that passion has permission. Passion has carte blanche. He burrows around in Erika's innards as if he wanted to take them out, prepare them in a new way. He reaches a limit and discovers that his hand can't get much farther. Now he pants as if he has run a great distance in order to reach this goal. He must at least offer this woman his exertion. He is unable to force his entire hand inside her, but maybe he can manage one or two fingers. No sooner said than done. Feeling his index finger slip in deeper than deep, he jubilantly transcends himself and bites Erika all over, promiscuously. He covers her with spit. His other hand holds her tight, but it doesn't need to, for the woman is staying put anyway. He wonders whether his other hand should raunch around under her sweater, but the V-neck isn't enough of a décolleté. And then there's that stupid white blouse underneath. Now he angrily tweaks and squeezes Erika's abdomen twice as hard. He is punishing her for letting him dangle until he almost gave up—which would have been too bad for her. He hears a pained whimper from Erika. He promptly subsides; he doesn't want to harm her wantonly before she really gets going. Klemmer has an illuminating flash: Maybe he can get into the sweater and the blouse by going under the waistband, i.e., from the opposite direction. First he has to pull the sweater and the blouse out of the skirt. He spits harder because he's trying so hard. He keeps barking Erika's name (which she knows anyway) into her mouth. But no matter how much he yells into this chasm, there's no echo. Erika stands and rests in Klemmer. She's ashamed of the situation he's involved her in. Her shame is pleasant. It fuels Klemmer, who whimperingly whets himself on Erika. He kneels without letting go. He wildly hoists himself up Erika only to take the elevator down again, albeit stopping at lovely places. He kisses himself fast to Erika. She stands on the floor like a much-used flute that has to deny itself, because otherwise it could not endure the many dilettantish lips that keep wanting to take it in. She would like this student to be absolutely free and leave whenever he likes. She makes it a point of honor to stand still where he has stood her up. He will find her there again, faithful to the very millimeter, when he feels like working her again. She starts drawing something out of herself, from that bottomless vessel of her self, which will no longer be empty for the student. Let's hope he catches invisible signals. Klemmer applies the full hardness of his sex in order to throw her back on the floor. His landing will be soft, hers hard. He demands the ultimate from Erika. Because they both know that someone could come in at any moment. Walter Klemmer shouts something completely new about his love into her ear.

In an illuminating cadre, two hands appear in front of Erika. From two different directions, they make their way toward her. They are amazed at what has so unexpectedly fallen into them. The owner of the hands is stronger than the teacher. That's why she keeps using the often misused word "Wait!" He doesn't want to wait. He explains why not. He sobs lustfully. But he also weeps, because he is overwhelmed by how easy the whole thing is. Erika has cooperated like a good girl.

Erika holds Walter Klemmer at arm's length. She pulls out his dick, which he has already slated for deployment. It only needs the finishing touch, for it is already prepared. Relieved that Erika has taken over this difficult task, Klemmer tries to push his teacher down all the way. Now Erika has to resist him with her entire weight so she can remain upright. She holds Klemmer's genital at arm's length while he fumbles about randomly in her vagina. She lets him know that if he doesn't stop, she'll leave. She softly repeats her threat several times, because her suddenly superior will has a hard time getting through to him and his rutting fury. His mind seems fogbound with angry intentions. He hesitates. Wondering whether he's misunderstood something. Neither in the history of music nor anywhere else is the suitor simply barred from events. This woman has not a spark of submission. Erika starts kneading the red root between her fingers. She demands a privilege, but refuses to grant it to the man. He must go no further with her. Klemmer's pure reason commands him not to let her shake him off. After all, he is the horseman and she the horse! She'll stop masturbating his cock if he doesn't stop grazing down her lower body. It finally occurs to him that it's more fun feeling than making others feel. So he obeys. After a few more unsuccessful attempts, his hand sinks away from Erika for good. Incredulous, he gazes at his organ, which seems detached from him as it huffs and puffs up in Erika's hands. Erika orders him to look at *her*, not at the size his penis has reached. He is not to measure or compare with others, his measure is his alone. Whether large or small, it's enough for her. This is unpleasant for him. He has nothing to do, and she works on him. It would make more sense the other way around, and that's how it goes in class. Erika holds him far away. A yawning abyss, made up of seven inches of dick, plus Erika's arm, and ten years difference in age, gapes open between their bodies. Vice is basically the love of failure. And Erika has always been trained for success, although she has never managed to achieve it.

Klemmer wants to get to Erika through a work/study program, reaching her intimately. He calls her name several times. His hands paddle through the air, venturing once again into forbidden territory: Perhaps she'll open her black festival mount to him after all. He predicts that she, indeed both of them, could have a lot more pleasure, and he declares he is ready for it. His penis twitches in bluish bloating. It bangs around in the air. Klemmer is now forced to be more interested in his wormy extension than in Erika as a whole. Erika orders Klemmer to keep silent and not to stir no matter what. Otherwise she'll leave. The student straddles the air in front of the teacher and still sees no light at the end of the tunnel. Bewildered, he gives in as if he were following directions for Schumann's *Carnaval* or the Prokofiev sonata he is practicing. He keeps his hands helplessly near his fly; he can't think of any other place to put them. His silhouette is distorted by his penis, which presents itself forward like a well-behaved boy—this protuberance, which throbs about, trying to strike aerial roots. It is growing dark outside. Luckily Erika is near the light switch, which she operates. She examines the color and makeup of Klemmer's cock. She inserts her fingernails under his foreskin and orders him not to let out a peep, whether in joy or in pain. The student freezes in a somewhat stifling position in order to draw the thing out. He squeezes his thighs together and tenses the muscles of his buttocks into steely hardness.

It just shouldn't stop now, please! Klemmer is gradually getting to enjoy the situation as well as the feeling in his body. In lieu of amorous activity, he speaks amorous words, until she orders him to keep silent. For the last time, the teacher commands the pupil to say nothing—in regard to the matter at hand or anything else. Has she made herself clear?! Klemmer wails because she is handling the full length of his lovely love organ. She deliberately hurts him. A hole opens, leading into Klemmer and fed by various conduits. The hole breathes into itself, asking about the time of the explosion. The time seems ripe, for Klemmer cries out the usual warning that he can't hold back. He asserts that he is doing everything he can to hold back and that his efforts are to no avail. Erika digs her teeth into the crown of his dick, the crown doesn't lose any points, but the owner shrieks nonetheless. He is told to shut up. So he whispers like a spectator in a theater: It's coming, now, now! Erika removes the tool from her mouth and instructs its owner: In the future she is going to make a list of all the things he can do to her. My wishes will be jotted down and made available to you at any time. For such is man in all his contradictions. Like an open book. Klemmer has something to look forward to!

Klemmer doesn't catch her drift. Whimpering, he begs her not to stop for God's sake, he's about to discharge his volcanic load. He holds out his little machine gun, trigger-happy, so she can shoot it. But Erika says she's doesn't want to touch it anymore—not for all the tea in China. Klemmer bends over, pulling his torso down almost to his knees. In this position, he reels through the front room of the toilet. He is illuminated by the merciless light of a round white lamp. He pleads with Erika, but she refuses. He touches himself in order to complete Erika's handiwork. He explains to his teacher why it is irresponsible, indeed unhealthy, to treat a man so disrespectfully when he's in such a state. Erika replies: Hands off, otherwise you'll never see me again in such a situation or a similar one, Herr Klemmer. The student depicts the notorious painfulness of blue balls. He won't even be able to walk home. Then take a cab, Erika advises calmly. She quickly washes her hands in the sink. She swallows some water. Klemmer stealthily tries to play with himself (the score doesn't exist). But a sharp shout holds him back. He should simply stand in front of the teacher until she commands otherwise. She would like to study his physical transformation. He can rest assured that she won't touch him. Herr Klemmer begs, trembling and whimpering. He suffers from the abrupt break of relations, even though these relations were not mutual. He vehemently reproaches Erika. He goes into meticulous detail about every single phase of suffering between his head and his toes. Meanwhile, his dick shrinks in slow motion. Klemmer is anything but a born follower. He is the sort of man who has to ask why, and so he finally starts reviling his teacher. He loses all control because the man in him is being abused. After playing and working out, the man must be polished clean and reinserted into the case. Erika talks back: Just shut up! Her tone keeps him shut.

While growing limp, he stands a few feet away from her. After allowing ourselves a short breather, Klemmer wants to list all the things a woman shouldn't do to such a man. Erika's behavior initiates a long chain of prohibitions. He wants to review the reasons. She tells him to keep quiet. It is her final demand. Klemmer does not go mute, he promises retaliation. Erika K. walks to the door and takes silent leave. He has not obeyed her even though she gave him several chances. Now he will never experience what he could carry out with her, what judgment, what sentence, if she allowed it. She squeezes the doorknob, but Klemmer begs her to stay.

He'll keep still, word of honor. Erika opens the toilet door all the way. Klemmer is framed inside the aperture—not a very valuable painting. Any passerby would see his exposed dick without being prepared for such a sight. Erika leaves the door open in order to torment Klemmer. Of course, she can't afford to be seen here either. She boldly takes a chance. The stairs end right next to the toilet door. Erika runs her fingers one final time across the shaft of Klemmer's penis, which draws new hope. But it is once again cold-shouldered. Klemmer trembles like leaves in the wind. He has given up resisting, he exposes himself freely and does nothing about it. This is perfect therapy for a viewer. Erika has already fulfilled her obligation, gotten through her crash course without a single mistake.

The teacher is rooted calmly to the floor. She absolutely refuses to touch his love organ. The love hurricane is raging only feebly now. Klemmer says nothing more about mutual sensation. He diminishes painfully. Erika already finds him ridiculously small. He endures it. From now on, she will keep a sharp eye on his professional and leisure activities. If necessary, she will prohibit all canoeing for just a silly mistake.

She will leaf through him as if he were a boring book. She
may even put him aside soon. Klemmer may wrap up his oar
only when she allows him to. A stealthy attempt to stow it
away and zipper up his fly is blocked by Erika. Klemmer is
getting impudent, he senses the end is nigh. He predicts that
he won't be able to walk for three days. He describes his anxieties about this, because for Klemmer the athlete, walking is
basic training without weapons. Erika tells him that he will
receive instructions. Written or oral or by telephone. Erika
allows him to pack away his asparagus. In an instinctive movement, Klemmer turns away from Erika in order to do so. But
ultimately he has to do everything in full view. While she
watches him. He's glad just to stir again. He indulges in a few
seconds of exercise, a little shadow-boxing. So he's suffered no
ill effects. He runs back and forth through the latrine. And the
looser and more flexible he appears, the more rigid and more
convulsive his teacher seems to become. She has, alas, retreated
fully into her snail shell. Klemmer has to liven her up by
playfully patting her cheeks, slapping her on the back of her
neck. He tells her to lighten up, laugh a little, beautiful lady!
Laugh and the world laughs with you! And now out into the
fresh air, which, to be honest, is what he missed most during
those past few long minutes. At Klemmer's age you forget a
trauma faster than at Erika's.

Klemmer swoops out into the corridor and completes a
thirty-meter sprint. Breathing violently, he zooms past Erika,
back and forth. Laughing loudly, he gives vent to his confusion.
He thunderously blows his nose. He swears that next time
things will be a lot better for us! Practice makes a woman
perfect. Klemmer's laughter booms through the corridor. He
leaps down the stairs, taking each curve by a hair's breadth.
It's almost frightening. Erika hears the heavy school door slam
below.

Klemmer seems to have left the building.
Erika Kohut slowly walks down the stairs to the main floor.

◻

During Walter Klemmer's lesson, Erika Kohut, who no
longer understands herself because a certain feeling is starting
to control her, senselessly loses her temper. No sooner had she
touched him than the student obviously became negligent about
practicing. Now Klemmer is making mistakes on the keyboard,
he falters, with his nonbeloved in back of him. He doesn't even
know what key he's in! He modulates senselessly in the air.
He keeps getting farther and farther away from A major, where
he belongs. Erika Kohut feels an ominous avalanche of jagged
refuse rolling toward her. For Klemmer, this refuse is delightful—the beloved weight of the woman, bearing down upon
him. His musical desires, which do not keep pace with his
abilities, are diverted. Erika, scarcely moving her lips, warns
him that he is sinning against Schubert. To remedy this griev-
ance and to rouse the woman's enthusiasm, Klemmer thinks
about the mountains and valleys of Austria, about the charms
galore that this country allegedly possesses. Schubert, that
homebody, sensed it even if he didn't investigate it. Klemmer
then recommences the great A major sonata by the Biedermeier
bourgeois who was head and shoulders above his time. Klemmer plays the piece in the spirit—or rather spirited unspir-
itualness—of a German dance by the same master. He soon
breaks off because his teacher derides him: He's probably never
seen a very steep cliff, a very deep chasm, a raging creek smash-
ing through a gulch, or Neusiedler Lake in all its majesty. Such
violent contrasts are expressed by Schubert, especially in this
unique sonata, and not some dreary province in the mild afternoon light of five-o'clock tea, which is more akin to Smetana's
Moldau landscape. And it's not for her, Erika Kohut, the con-

queror of musical obstacles. It's for the audience listening to
Sunday-morning concerts on the Austrian Radio Network.

Klemmer blusters: If anyone knows what a raging creek is
like, then it's Walter Klemmer, whereas his teacher always
huddles in dark rooms, next to her mother's old age, and her
mother does nothing but peer into the distance through a TV
screen. Her mother doesn't care whether she's above the ground
or six feet under. Erika Kohut remembers Schubert's expression
marks, and she is stirred up. Her water seethes and rages. These
marks range from screams and whispers, not from loud speech
to soft speech! Anarchy is not your forte, Klemmer. The athlete
is too strongly rooted in convention.

Walter Klemmer wishes he could kiss her on the throat. He's
never done it, but he's often heard about it. Erika wishes the
student would kiss her on the throat, but she doesn't give him
the cue. She feels surrender rising inside her; and in her mind,
surrender collides with old and new hatred, especially of women
who have lived less life than she and are therefore younger.
Erika's surrender does not resemble her surrender to her
mother in any way. Her hatred resembles her usual normal
hatred in every way.

In order to cloak these feelings, the woman hectically contradicts everything she has always publicly advocated about
music. She says: In the interpretation of any piece of music,
there is a certain point at which precision ends and the impre-
cision of personal creativity begins. The interpreter no longer
serves, he demands! He demands the ultimate from the composer. Perhaps it is not too late for Erika to get a new lease on
life. It can't hurt to advocate new theses. Erika says with subtle
irony that Klemmer has now reached a level of ability, a level
on which he would have the right to place his heart and soul
next to his ability. The woman instantly slaps the student's
face by saying she has no right to tacitly assume he has any

ability. She was mistaken, she adds, although as a teacher she should have known better. Klemmer should go paddle his own canoe, but he should steer clear of Schubert's spirit if he encounters it in the forest. Hideous Schubert. The student is reviled as handsome and young, while Erika adds yet another disk on each side of her hate-loaded dumbbell. She arduously manages to heave the dumbbell up to her chest. Trapped as you are in your flashy mediocrity of good looks, you don't recognize an abyss even when you tumble into it, says Erika to Klemmer. You never take a risk! You step across puddles so you won't get your shoes wet. When you turn upside down while canoeing—I do understand this much—you instantly turn yourself right side up. You're even scared of the water, that unique submission, in which your head's been dunked! It's so obvious you'd rather dabble in the shallows. You scoot around crags gingerly—gingerly for you!—before you really notice them.

Erika shrilly struggles for breath. Klemmer wrings his hands in order to prevent his beloved—who is not yet his beloved—from taking this path. Do not block the way to me forever, he tells her for her own good. And he seems strangely fortified, emerging from the athletic struggle as if from a war between the sexes. An aging woman writhes and wriggles on the ground, the foam of fury on her chin. This woman can peer into music the way one peers into the wrong side of a telescope, making music look very distant and very tiny. You can't slam on her brakes when she feels she has to say something that is inspired by this music. Then she talks a blue streak. Erika feels eaten up by the injustice: Nobody loved that fat little boozer Franz Schubert. When she looks at Klemmer, she very keenly feels that incompatibility: between Schubert and women. A dark chapter in the porno mag of art. Schubert did not live up to the popular image of the genius, either as a creator or as a virtuoso. Klemmer is a crowd-pleaser. The crowd creates images and is not satisfied until it encounters its images in the wild. Schubert didn't even own a piano—how well off you are by contrast, Herr Klemmer! How unfair that Klemmer lives but doesn't practice enough, while Schubert is dead. Erika Kohut insults a man from whom she nevertheless desires love. She unwisely thrashes away at him, nasty words booming under the membrane of her palate, on the hide of her tongue. At night, her face swells shut while Mother snores next to her, not suspecting a thing. In the morning, Erika peers into a mirror, but can't see her eyes because of the fall of the folds. She gapes and gawks at her reflection, but the image doesn't improve. Man and woman once again face each other, paralyzed in a struggle.

In Erika's briefcase, a letter to the student rustles among the music scores. She will hand him the letter after scornfully telling him the score. Her angry nausea is still rising up the column of her body in regular cramps. Klemmer disgorges a freshly stuffed thought-sausage through his teeth: Schubert may have been highly talented, since he managed to get on without a teacher comparable to a Leopold Mozart, but Schubert was definitely no genius. Klemmer hands his teacher the thought-sausage on a paper plate, with a dab of mustard. A man who dies that early can't be a genius! I'll never see twenty again, and I still know so little, I keep realizing it again every single day, says Klemmer. So how much could Franz Schubert have known at the age of thirty! That enigmatic, enticing little schoolmaster's child from Vienna! Women killed him with syphilis.

Women will drive you to the grave, the young man moodily jokes, scherzando; then he talks a little about the moodiness of the female. Women waver in one direction, then another, and you can't glimpse any pattern in their wavering. Erika tells

Klemmer he doesn't have the foggiest inkling of tragedy. She tells him he's a good-looking young man. His teacher tosses him a thighbone, and he crunches it with his healthy teeth. She has told him he doesn't have a clue about the way Schubert places accents. Beware of mannerisms: That is Erika Kohut's opinion. The student goes with the flow at a brisk pace.

It's not always appropriate to be so generous with instrumental signals—say, brasses—in Schubert's piano works. However, before you, Klemmer, learn it all by heart, you ought to beware of wrong notes and too much pedaling. As well as too little! Don't hold every note as long as the score tells you to; on the other hand, not every note is marked the way it ought to sound.

For a bonus, Erika shows him a special exercise for the left hand, which he needs. She wants to calm her own nerves. She wants her own left hand to atone for what the man forces her to suffer. Klemmer does not wish to calm his passions by way of piano technique; he seeks the struggle of bodies and pain, a struggle that does not stop with Erika Kohut. Klemmer is convinced that ultimately his art will profit, once he has endured the struggle, icy and victorious. When they go their separate ways after the final bell, the distribution of points will be as follows: He'll have more, Erika less. And he's already looking forward to it. Erika will be one year older, he will be one year ahead of everyone else in his development. Klemmer digs his claws into the topic of Schubert. He bickers: His teacher has suddenly and confusingly spun around 180 degrees. She is expressing as her own opinion something that he has always advocated. Namely, that the imponderable, the unnamable, the ineffable, the unplayable, the unassailable, the incomprehensible are more important than any tangibles: technique, technique, and more technique. Have I caught you napping, Frau Professor?

Erika feels boiling hot because he has spoken of the incomprehensible, by which he can only mean his love for her. She feels bright, warm, luminous. The sun of amorous passion, which she has not, unfortunately, felt all the while, is now shining again. He stills feels for her, the very same feeling he felt yesterday and the day before yesterday! Obviously Klemmer loves and respects her ineffably, as he tenderly told her. Erika lowers her eyes for a split second and murmurs meaningfully that she only meant that Schubert likes to express orchestral effects purely on the keyboard. One must be able to recognize and play these effects and the instruments they symbolize. But as she said before, without mannerisms. Erika offers friendly female solace: Don't worry, you'll get it!

Teacher and student face each other, woman and man. Between them: heat, an insurmountable wall. The wall prevents them from climbing across and sucking out the other's blood. Teacher and student are seething with love and a comprehensible desire for more love.

Meanwhile, under their feet, they can feel the seething gruel of culture, which never finishes cooking; they assimilate it in small bites, their daily diet, without which they could not exist. The gruel throws off iridescent gas bubbles.

Erika Kohut is in the dreary, callous skin of her years. No one can or wants to remove it. This skin cannot be worn out. So many things have been missed out on, especially Erika's youth, including the eighteenth year of her life, which Austrians call "sweet eighteen." It lasts for only one year, and then it's gone. Now others are enjoying this famous eighteenth year in lieu of Erika. Today, Erika is more than twice as old as an eighteen-year-old girl! Erika keeps checking the figure, but the gap between her and the eighteen-year-old will never lessen—although, granted, it will never widen either. The repugnance that Erika feels toward any girl of that age increases the gap unnecessarily. At night, Erika sweatily turns on the spit of anger over the blazing fire: maternal love. She is regularly basted with the pungent gravy of musical art. Nothing alters this immovable difference: old/young. Nor can anything be altered in the notation of music by dead masters. What you see is what you get. Erika has been harnessed in this notation system since earliest childhood. Those five lines have been controlling her ever since she first began to think. She musn't think of anything but those five black lines. This grid system, together with her mother, has hamstrung her in an untearable net of directions, directives, precise commandments, like a rosy ham on a butcher's hook. This provides security, and security creates fear of uncertainty. Erika is afraid that everything will remain as it is, and she is afraid that someday something could change. She struggles for air, experiencing something like an asthma attack—then she doesn't know what to do with all this air. Her throat rattles, she can't drive a peep out of it. Klemmer is terrified down to the very foundations of his indestructible health. He asks what's wrong with his beloved. Should I get you a glass of water? he asks carefully. He is so amorously attentive—this representative of the firm of Knight Errant & Co. The teacher coughs convulsively. She coughs herself free from something far worse than a tickle in her throat. She cannot express her feelings vocally, only pianistically.

Reaching into her briefcase, Erika produces a letter that is hermetically sealed for safety's sake. She hands it to Klemmer, just as she has pictured it at home a thousand times. The letter indicates the progress a certain kind of love should take. Erika has written down everything she does not wish to say out loud. Klemmer thinks that this is something ineffably wonderful that can only be written down, and he shines bright like the moon on mountain peaks. How terribly he missed this sort of thing! Today, he, Klemmer, by dint of steady labor on his feelings and their expressive potential, is finally in the fortunate position of being able to say aloud anything at any time! Indeed, he has learned that he makes a fine, fresh impression on everyone when he pushes ahead in order to be the first to say something out loud. Don't be shy, it won't help. As far as he's concerned, he would, if necessary, shout out his love. Luckily, it is not necessary, because no one is supposed to hear it. Klemmer leans back in his movie seat, munching his popcorn and delighting in his image on the screen, where, larger than life, the delicate theme of a young man and an aging woman is being played out. Also starring a ridiculous old mother, who wants all of Europe, England, and America to be fascinated by the sweet sounds that her child has been producing for so many years. The mother expressly wants her child to stay tied to the maternal apron strings rather than to stew in the juice of sensual love and passion. Feelings cook faster in a pressure cooker, and more of the vitamins are preserved. That good advice is Klemmer's response to the mother. Within six months at the latest, he will have greedily guzzled Erika up and can then turn to the next delight.

Klemmer showers kisses upon Erika's hand, which gives him the letter. He says: Thank you, Erika. He wants to devote the entire weekend to this woman. Horrified that Klemmer wishes to break into her closed sacrosanct weekend, she rejects the idea. She improvises an excuse for why it won't work this weekend or probably next weekend or the one after that. We can always talk on the telephone, the woman lies impudently. Current flows through her in both directions. Klemmer meaningfully crackles the mysterious letter; he announces the thesis that Erika can't mean it as nastily as she thoughtlessly babbles. The dictate of the hour is: Don't string the man along.

Erika shouldn't forget that, given her age, every year of Klemmer's life is equal to three years of hers. Erika should

jump at the chance, seize the day, Klemmer advises her kindly.
Crumpling the letter in one sweaty hand, he hesitantly holds
his other hand out, feeling the teacher like a chicken that he
might wish to buy. But he has to check whether the price is
right, whether it's commensurate with the age of the hen.
Klemmer doesn't know how to tell whether a soup chicken or
a roaster is old or young. But he can see it in his teacher, very
precisely. He's got eyes in his head, he can tell she's no spring
chicken, though she is relatively well preserved. You might
almost call her crisp, if it weren't for that somewhat mellow
look in her eyes. And then the never-waning charm of her
being his teacher! It inspires him to turn her into a pupil at
least once a week. Erika eludes the student. She pulls away
from him, and is so embarrassed that she wipes her nose for a
long time. Klemmer depicts nature before her eyes. He describes it just as he got to know it and love it. Soon he and
Erika will indulge and delight in nature. The two of them will
go to where the forest is densest, they will settle down on moss
cushions and have a picnic. There no one will see the young
athlete and artist (who has already appeared in several competitions) rolling around with a decrepit old woman (who would
have to avoid competing with younger women). Klemmer has
a hunch that the most exciting aspect of their future relationship
will be its secrecy.

Erika has grown mute, her eyes do not gape, her heart does
not swell. Klemmer feels it's time for his thorough retrospective
correction of everything his teacher just said about Franz
Schubert. He will barge his way into the discussion. Lovingly
he rectifies Erika's image of Schubert, placing it and himself in
the best light. He will win more and more debates. That is
what he forecasts to his beloved. One reason he loves this
woman is her wealth of experience with the overall repertoire
of music. But in the long run, her experience cannot hide the

fact that he knows a lot more about everything. This realization gives him supreme pleasure. He raises a finger to underscore his opinion when Erika tries to disagree. He is the insolent victor, and the woman has taken refuge behind the piano to escape his kisses. Words will falter eventually, and feelings win out by sheer persistence and vehemence.

Erika boasts that she knows no feelings. If ever she has to acknowledge a feeling, she will not let it dominate her intelligence. She inserts the second piano between her and Klemmer. He calls his beloved superior cowardly. Someone who loves someone like Klemmer has to appear before the whole world and proclaim it loudly. Of course, Klemmer doesn't want it to get around the conservatory, because he normally grazes on younger pastures. And love is fun only when you can be envied for having a beloved. In this case, later marriage is out of the question. Luckily Erika has her mother, who won't allow her to marry. Klemmer drifts along on his own head waters; he is never in over his head. When it comes to water, he's in his element. He shreds a final opinion that Erika has about Schubert's sonatas. Erika coughs and, in her embarrassment, she swings back and forth on hinges that Klemmer, limber and nimble, has never noticed on other people. She buckles at the most impossible places; and Klemmer, surprised, feels his gorge rising slightly, but is unable to integrate his nausea into the scope of his feelings. You could say that it fits. But one shouldn't spread out like that. Erika cracks her knuckles, which is beneficial to neither her playing nor her health. She stubbornly peers into remote corners, although Klemmer orders her to look at him, freely and openly, not tensely and stealthily. After all, no one's watching.

Encouraged by the dreadful sight, Walter Klemmer investigates: May I ask something unheard-of from you, something you've never done? And then he instantly demands this test

of love. For her first step into a new love life, she is to do
something incomprehensible, namely come with him and cancel
her lesson with her last student this evening. Of course, Erika
should, by way of precaution, plead illness or a headache, so
the student won't get suspicious and tell tales out of school.
Erika balks at this easy task: she is a wild mustang that has
finally managed to smash the stable door with its hooves, but
nevertheless remains inside because it has changed its mind.
Klemmer tells his beloved how others have shaken off the yoke
of contracts and common laws. He cites Wagner's *Ring* as one
of the countless examples. He hands Erika art as an example
of everything and nothing. One need only hunt through art—
that pitfall lined with scythes and sickles mounted in
concrete—and one will find examples enough of anarchistic
behavior. Mozart, that examplar of *everything*, who, for example, shakes off the yoke of the prince bishop. If that ubiq-
uitously popular Mozart—whom neither of us particularly
appreciates—could do it, then we can manage it too, Erika.
How often have we agreed that neither the creator nor the
performer can endure rigidity. The artist prefers to avoid the
bitter pressures applied by truth or by rules. I'm amazed—
please don't be offended—that you've been able to endure having your mother around all these years. Either you're simply
not an artist, or else you do not feel that a yoke is a yoke even
when you're choking in it. Klemmer, now taking a familiar
tone with his teacher, is glad her mother is looming up as a
buffer, a scapegoat, between them. Her mother will make sure
he doesn't suffocate under this elderly woman!

Mother provides incessant topics of conversation—as a
thicket, a hindrance for all kinds of fulfillments. On the other
hand, she holds her daughter fast in one place, so her daughter
cannot follow Klemmer everywhere. How can we meet regularly for our irregularities, without anyone finding out, Erika?

Klemmer relishes the idea of a secret room for the two of them, furnished with an old record player and records he's got duplicates of. After all, he knows Erika's taste in music; it's duplicated too, because he's got exactly the same taste in music! He's got duplicates of a few Chopin LPs and an album of some eccentric pieces by Paderewski, who was overshadowed by Chopin—unjustly, according to Klemmer and to Erika, who gave him the record, which he had already bought for himself.

Klemmer is bursting to read the letter. If you can't say something out loud, then you ought to write it down. If you can't stand something, then don't do it. I am so much looking forward to reading and understanding your letter of 4/24, dear Erika. And if I deliberately misunderstand your letter—something I am also looking forward to—then we'll kiss and make up again after the fight. Klemmer promptly starts talking about himself, about himself, and about himself. She's written him this long letter, so he's got the right to let it all hang out. He'll have to spend some time reading the letter, and he can already use that time now, for talking, so Erika won't get the upper hand in their relationship. Klemmer explains to Erika that two extremes are struggling within him: sports (competitively) and art (regularly).

As the student's hands move toward the letter, Erika orders him not to touch it. Klemmer, clamp yourself down to researching Schubert, Erika puns, taking Klemmer's precious name in vain.

Klemmer rears up. For a whole second, he toys with the idea of yelling out the secret about him and his teacher, shouting it out in the face of the world. It happened in a toilet! But since the deed did not work out to his greater glory, he holds his tongue. Later on, he can twist the facts, informing posterity that he won the fight. Klemmer suspects that if he were forced to choose between the woman, art, and sports, he would not

choose art or sports. He still conceals these foolish things from
the woman. He now senses what it means to introduce the
uncertainty factor of someone else's self into his own intricate
game. After all, sports involve certain risks too; for example,
your form can vary considerably on any given day. This woman
is so old, and yet she still doesn't know what she wants. I'm
so young, but I always know what I like.

The letter is scrunched up in Klemmer's shirt pocket. Klemmer's fingers twitch. He can't stand it anymore, and so he,
fickle hedonist that he is, decides to read the letter in peace, in
some peaceful spot out in the country. And he'll take notes
right away. For an answer that might be longer than the letter.
Maybe in the castle garden? He'll seat himself in the Palm
House Café and order a cappuccino and an apple strudel. The
two diverging elements, art and Erika, will increase the charm
of the letter ad infinitum. Between them, Klemmer, the referee,
who always rings the gong to indicate who's won the round:
Nature outside or Erika inside him. Klemmer blows hot, then
cold.

No sooner has Klemmer disappeared from the piano classroom, no sooner has the next pupil, a girl, begun the bumpy
contrary motion of her scale, than the teacher tells her we'll
have to stop for today, alas, because I've got an awful headache.
The pupil soars aloft like a lark and flies away.

Erika squirms because of her unrequited and disquieting fears
and anxieties. She is now suspended from the infusion tube of
Klemmer's good graces. Can he really climb over high fences
and wade through raging torrents? Is he prepared to risk anything for his love? Erika doesn't know whether she can rely on
Klemmer's constant protests that he has never shied away from
any risk—the bigger, the better. This is the first time in all
these years that Erika has dismissed a pupil untaught. Mother
always warns Erika about precipitous paths. If Mother is not

beckoning with the ladder of success, which goes upward, then
she depicts the horror of the primrose path, which leads downward. Better the peak of art than the slough of sex. Contrary
to the popular notion of his wantonness, the artist, Mother
believes, must forget about sex. If he can't, then he's a mere
mortal; but he shouldn't be a mere mortal. He should be divine!
Unfortunately, biographies of artists, which are the most important things about artists, teem all too often with the sexual
ruses and abuses of their protagonists. They inveigle the reader
into thinking that the cucumber bed of pure harmony grows
upon the compost heap of sex.

Whenever they fight, Mother reproaches the child for having
once stumbled artistically. But once doesn't count—you'll see.

Erika dashes home from the conservatory.

Rot between her legs, an unfeeling soft mass. Decay, putrescent lumps of organic material. No spring breezes awaken
anything. It is a dull pile of petty wishes and mediocre desires,
afraid of coming true. Her two chosen mates will encompass
her like crab claws: Mother and Klemmer. Erika can't have
both, and she can't have just one, because then she would miss
the other dreadfully. She can tell her mother not to let Klemmer
in if the doorbell rings. Mother will be delighted to comply. Is
this why Erika has always led such a quiet life—for this
wretched disquiet? Let's hope he doesn't come tonight. He can
come tomorrow, but not tonight, because Erika wants to catch
an old Lubitsch film. Mother and daughter have been looking
forward to it since last Friday when the TV schedule came out.
The program listings are awaited more longingly by the Kohut
family than True Love, which is not supposed to show up at
all!

Erika took a step by writing a letter. Mother had no say in
the matter; indeed, Mother mustn't even find out about this
step forward, toward the feeding trough of the forbidden. Erika

has always confessed every infringement to that maternal eye, the eye of the law, which then claimed it knew about each one anyway.

Striding along, Erika hates that porous, rancid fruit that marks the bottom of her abdomen. Only art promises endless sweetness. Soon the decay will progress, encroaching upon larger parts of her body. Then she will die in torment. Dismayed, Erika pictures herself as a numb hole, six feet of space, disintegrating in the earth. The hole that she despised and neglected has now taken full possession of her. She is nothing. And there is nothing left for her.

Erika doesn't realize that Walter Klemmer is dashing along behind her. He pulled himself together after an initial, powerful urge. He decided not to open the letter for now; he wants to have a serious talk with a warm, live Erika before he reads her lifeless letter. This living woman is dearer to him than a dead scrap of paper for which trees had to die. I can read the letter later on, at home, in peace and quiet, Klemmer thinks, preferring to keep his eye on the ball. The ball rolls, hops, jumps along, stopping at traffic lights, leaving reflections in store windows. This woman is not going to tell him when to read letters and when to make a personal advance. The woman isn't used to the role of quarry, she doesn't look around. Yet she's got to be taught that she is the prey and man the hunter. Start teaching her right now, there's no time like the present. It never occurs to Erika that her superior willpower might someday not dictate everything, even though she is constantly dictated to by her mother. However, this situation has become so much a part of Erika that she no longer notices. Trust is fine, but control is better.

A delightful home beckons with its entrance. Warm light beams embrace the teacher. Erika surfaces as a swift dot of light on Mother's radar screen. She flutters along—a butterfly, an insect, on the pin of the stronger creature. Erika will not want to find out how Klemmer reacted to her letter, for she will not pick up her receiver. She will immediately tell her mother to tell the man that she is not home. Erika actually believes she can tell Mother something that Mother has not already told Erika. Mother wishes Erika good luck for taking the step of closing herself off on the outside and confiding only in her. Mother lies obsessively, with an internal fire that belies her age: My daughter is not at home. I do not know when she will return. Do come again. Thank you. At such moments, the daughter belongs to her more completely than ever. To Mother and no one else. For everyone else, the child is absent.

The man, completely buried by the refuse of Erika's thoughts, follows the object of his feelings. Once, the biggest and most modern movie theater in Vienna stood right here, on Josefstädterstrasse; but now it's been replaced by a bank. Erika sometimes went to the movies here with her mama to celebrate some holiday or other. But usually, in order to economize, the women went to a small, cheap neighborhood house. To economize even more, they left Father at home. In this way, he could also save the final vestige of his mind, which he didn't want to waste at the movies. Erika never turns around. Her senses feel nothing; they do not even feel the nearby beloved. Yet all her thoughts are focused on one point, the beloved, growing gigantically: Walter Klemmer.

So they hurry along, one after the other. The piano teacher, Erika Kohut, is driven along by something behind her back; it is a man, who pulls the angel or the devil out of her. It's all in her hands now: She can teach the man tender consideration. Erika begins to lift a tiny corner of sensual power and everything that this power can imply; but Klemmer, so fully in possession of all his senses, is behind her, and she doesn't even notice him. On the way home, she has not bought a new foreign fashion journal or a gown depicted inside it or a dress copied from a gown depicted inside it. She has not so much as glanced at the brand-new spring models in the shop windows. In her confusion over the male ardor she has kindled, she's got only one glance left. And she devoted that glance, casually and absentmindedly, to the front page of tomorrow's newspaper: today's photo, looking slightly the worse for wear, of a bank robber—a wedding picture of the adorable criminal. Evidently, he had someone snap his portrait, for the last time, at his respectable wedding. Now, everyone knows him only because he got married. Erika imagines Klemmer as a bridegroom and herself as a bride and Mother as the mother of the bride, who will live with them. But Erika does not see the student, whom she thinks about incessantly and who is pursuing her.

Mother knows that her child can show up in half an hour at the earliest, if circumstances are favorable; yet she already waits for Erika yearningly. Mother doesn't know that a lesson has been canceled; yet she awaits her punctual daughter, who always arrives home. Erika's will shall be the lamb that nestles down with the lion of maternal will. This gesture of humility will prevent the maternal will from shredding the soft, unformed filial will and munching on its bloody limbs. Suddenly, the door to the building is yanked open. Darkness shoots out. The staircase, that heavenly ladder to the evening news and subsequent programs, stretches upward. A mild, gentle glow wafts down from the second floor after Erika switches on the stair light. The apartment door is not opened; today no footsteps are recognized, because the daughter is not expected for another half hour. Mother is still absorbed in the final preparations, which will have their crowning glory in a meatloaf.

For half an hour now, Walter Klemmer has been viewing his teacher only from behind. This may not be Erika's favorite side, but he could identify it among a thousand others! He knows women, knows them from all sides, inside and out. He sees the soft, slightly squooshy pillow of her behind, which rests upon solid leg columns. He thinks about how he will handle this body; he, the expert, is not so easily put off by malfunctions. An anticipatory joy, mingling with horror, takes hold of Klemmer. Erika is still striding along peacefully, but soon she'll howl in pleasure! He, Klemmer, will produce that pleasure all by himself. Her body is still harmlessly occupied with various gearshifts; soon Klemmer will make it shift into overdrive! Klemmer doesn't truly desire this woman, she doesn't actually attract him; and he doesn't know whether his lack of desire is due to her age. But Klemmer is single-minded, he is thoroughly focused on exposing her pure flesh. So far, he knows her only in one function: that of teacher. Now he'll squeeze another function out of her, he'll see whether he can get anywhere with the other function: that of lover. If not, then too bad. He resolutely wants to tear off the meticulously accumulated strata of modish and sometimes outmoded convictions and those hulls and shells held together by a feeble sense of form, those colorful disguises of rags and skins that stick to her. She doesn't have a clue, but soon she will. She'll learn how a woman ought to decorate herself: nicely, but, above all, practically, so as not to interfere with her movements. He, Klemmer, does not wish so much to possess Erika as to unwrap this package of skin and bones, which is carefully dolled up in a patchwork of fabrics and colors! He'll scrunch the paper up and throw it away. This woman, inaccessible for such a long time in her colorful skirts and scarves—Klemmer wants to make her accessible to himself before she crosses over into decay. Why does she buy that stuff, anyway? She could find clothes that are attractive, practical, and not even expensive! That's what he'll tell her, while she tells him how to handle a suspension in Bach. Klemmer wants the flesh to appear before him, no matter how much effort is required. He simply wants to possess what's *underneath*. Once he strips away this woman's husk, then Erika the human being will come to the fore, with all her failings, the person he's been interested in for so long. Such are Klemmer's thoughts. Each of her textile layers is always harder and more washed-out than the next. And Klemmer only wants the best from Erika, only that small, innermost kernel, which may taste good: He wants to use *the body*. Use it for his own benefit. If necessary by force. He knows her mind sufficiently. Yes, indeed, in case of doubt, Klemmer always listens only to his own body, which is never wrong, and which speaks in the language of the body. In addicts or invalids, the body may often fail to tell the truth because of weakness and misuse. But Klemmer's body is healthy, thank you very much. Knock on wood! During a workout, Klemmer's body always tells him when it's had enough or when there's still something left in the reserve tank. Until he's given his all. Afterward, Klemmer simply feels wonderful! It's indescribable! That's how Walter Klemmer joyously describes his state. He wants to realize his own flesh at last under the humbled eyes of his teacher. He's been waiting far too long. Months have worn by, and he's been holding out long enough to stake his claim. The signs were interpreted correctly. Recently, Erika has conspicuously adorned herself for Klemmer's sake: chains, cuffs, belts, cordings, high-heeled pumps, kerchiefs, scents, removable fur collars, and a new plastic armband that rubs against the keyboard. This woman has made herself attractive for *one* man. However, this man wants to smash all the feeble, unhealthy ornaments, shake the woman's final vestige of originality out of the wrappings. He wants to have everything! But without really desiring her. These adornments make Klemmer, who is straight as an arrow, lose his irrational temper. After all, Nature doesn't get all gussied up when it starts mating.

Only a few birds, mostly male, have enticing plumage, but that's part of their normal appearance.

Klemmer, tooling along after his future beloved, still believes that his naked rage is aimed purely at her meticulous, albeit clumsily applied, grooming. This finery, this frippery, which Klemmer feels disfigures her, must be discarded at once! For his sake! He will make it clear to Erika that, it anything, precise cleanliness is the only embellishment he can accept in a pleasant, not unappealing face. Erika makes herself ridiculous, which is something she doesn't need. Two showers a day, that's what personal grooming means to Klemmer, and it's enough. Klemmer demands a clean coiffure because unwashed hair is anathema to him. Lately, Erika has been bridling herself like a circus horse. She's been plundering her long-unused clothing reserves in order to look even more appealing to the student. This *has* to knock him for a loop, and this too! Everyone, everywhere, gapes and gawks at her for gilding the lily and reaching too deep into her makeup kit. She's going through changes. She not only produces clothes from her rich treasure trove, she also buys pounds and pounds of matching accessories: belts, bags, shoes, gloves, fashionable adornments. She wants to fascinate the man, she captivates his evil desires. She should have let the sleeping tiger sleep on so he won't eat her up. That's Klemmer's advice to her in regard to his own worthy self. Erika tramples about like a drunken figurine, in boots and spurs, in harness and armor, spruced up and smartened up. Why didn't she break her closets open earlier in order to speed up this complicated love affair? More and more splendors burst out! She has finally dared to break into her silky, colorful reserves, and she looks forward to unabashed glances of courtship, which she does not receive. She fails to notice the unabashed mockery from people who have known Erika for such a long time and are giving serious thought to the changes in her appearance.

Erika looks ridiculous, but she's solid, well developed. Every salesman knows: packaging is everything! Ten layers, protective and alluring, one on top of the other. And all fitting together if possible! No minor achievement. Mother scolds Erika, who has bought a new, cowboyish hat for her suit; the hat's got a band and tiny strap for mooring the hat under her chin so it won't be carried off by a puff of air. Mother laments noisily about the expenditure and her suspicions about her child's ultrafashionable ways, which are, no doubt, carefully aimed: to hurt Mother and to catch men. If it's a specific man, then he'll get to know Mother all right! And from her least pleasant side. Mother pokes fun at a tasteful combination. She envenoms hulls and hides, cloaks and covers, which the daughter thoughtfully dons; Mother poisons them with the pale venom of her scorn. Her derision is such that the daughter is bound to realize that her mockery is due to jealousy.

Behind this splendidly caparisoned creature, which cannot find its like in nature, Walter Klemmer, the creature's natural enemy, dashes along. His goal is to break the teacher of her unnatural clothing habit as soon as possible. Jeans and T-shirts are enough for Klemmer, no matter how high his standards. The building entrance indicates a gloomy interior—in which a rare plant grew, despite everything, unnoticed, for a long time. All the colors that manage to blossom outside die here. Halfway up the stairs to the next landing, a furious Klemmer catches up with Erika. Ineluctably. There's no garage, no coach house, no parking lot.

Man and woman meet, but not by chance. And the invisible third party, in the guise of maternal supervision, is upstairs, waiting for her cue. Erika advises the student to get away from here. She is majestic. The student resists, although he wouldn't care to run into Mother. He demands that the two of them go somewhere, so they can finally be alone and talk. He wants to have a conversation! Erika panics, she stamps and kicks; the man wants to invade her seclusion. Mother is intimately beckoning with her dinner for two—what will she say? The meal is scheduled for mother and child alone.

Klemmer makes a grab for Erika, who tests him to see whether he has read the letter. Have you read my letter, Herr Klemmer? Why do we need letters? Klemmer interrogates the beloved woman, who heaves a sigh of relief because he hasn't read the letter. On the other hand, she's afraid he won't go along with the demands she has voiced in her letter. Even before the fighting begins, the two amorously interlocked people misunderstand what each wants from the other. The misunderstandings solidify into granite. They are not mistaken about Mother, who is going to take drastic measures and send away the superfluous part (Klemmer) immediately. She will keep the part that constitutes her entire property, her heart's delight (Erika). The woman, indecisive, flinches now in one direction, now in the other. Klemmer understands her; he is proud to be the cause of this indecisiveness. He will help Erika give birth to decisions. He would like to remove the cowboy hat from the head of his prey. What ingratitude toward this hat, which, like a friendly signpost, always loomed up in the tumult: a morning star for the Three Magi, a hat that no one passes without paying it the homage of derision. People notice this hat, and they are annoyed even if they don't always blame their annoyance on the hat, which triggers the annoyance in the first place.

There are only the two of us here on the stairs, and we're playing with fire, Klemmer cautions the woman. He warns her not to keep teasing his desire and then playing hard to get. Erika stares at the man, who should go because he has to stay. Under her gift wrapping, the woman blossoms darkly. This blossom is not made for the raw climate of lust, it is not meant for a long sojourn in the staircase, for the plant needs light, sunshine. The most suitable place for her is next to Mother, in front of the TV. Erika looms obscenely from under her new hat, which is then removed. Hers is the unhealthily reddened face of a creature that has found its master. Klemmer feels incapable of desiring this woman, but for some time now he has wanted to penetrate her. Whatever it may cost him—words of love at least. Erika loves the young man and is waiting for him to redeem her. She reveals no sign of love, so she won't have to endure defeat. Erika would like to show weakness, but determine the form of her submission herself. She has written everything down. She wants to be simply sucked up by the man until she is no longer present. Her cowboy hat has to cover both untouchability and passionate touching. The woman wants to soften petrifications that are many years old, and if she is devoured by the man, that's fine with her. She wants to lose herself completely in this man, but without his noticing it. Do you realize we're alone in the world? she voicelessly asks the man. Mother is waiting upstairs. She's going to open the door any moment. The door is not yet opened because Mother does not yet expect her daughter.

Mother doesn't sense that her child is yanking at her fetters, because she won't see or sense the child yanking at her fetters for another half hour. Erika and Klemmer are busy trying to fathom who loves whom more and is therefore the weaker. Erika cites her age, pretending that she's the one who loves less because she has loved too often. Hence, Klemmer is the one who loves more. On the other hand, Erika has to be loved more. Klemmer has cornered Erika, she's got only one loophole, and it leads straight into the hornets' nest on the second landing; they can already see the appropriate door. The old hornet is buzzing around inside with pots and pans. She can be heard and seen, a silhouette, through the lighted kitchen window that faces the hallway.

Klemmer issues an order. Erika obeys. She seems to be deliberately racing toward her own destruction; it is her final, her friendliest destination. Erika gives up her will. Her mother has always possessed Erika's will, and now Erika hands it, like a runner's staff, to Walter Klemmer. She leans back, waiting to hear his decision. But, though giving up her freedom, she stipulates one condition: Erika Kohut is using her love to make this boy her master. The more power he attains over her, the more he will become Erika's pliant creature. Klemmer will be her slave completely when, say, they go strolling in the mountains. Yet Klemmer will think of himself as Erika's master. That is the goal of Erika's love. That is the only way that love won't be consumed prematurely. He has to be convinced: This woman has put herself entirely in my hands. And yet *he* will become Erika's property. That's the way she pictures it. Things can go awry only if Klemmer reads the letter and disapproves. Out of disgust, embarrassment, fear—it all depends on which feeling gets the upper hand. After all, we're only human and therefore imperfect. Erika comforts the male face confronting her; she wants to kiss that face, which grows softer, almost melting under her teacher eyes. Sometimes we really do fail, and I almost believe that this inevitable failure is our ultimate goal, concludes Erika. Instead of kissing, she rings the doorbell. Behind the door, Mother's face, in a mixture of expectation and annoyance, wondering who can dare be bothering her, almost instantly flowers—and then withers when she realizes her daugher has an attachment. The attachment promptly indicates its destination: here, c/o Kohut, sr. and jr. We've just arrived. Mother is rigid. She has been brutally yanked out from under her dreamy quilt, and now she's standing in her nightgown, facing a gigantic mob of howling people. Using her well-rehearsed eye language, Mother asks Erika what this young man is doing here. Mother's eyes demand that this young man leave immediately. After all, he's neither the plumber nor the meter reader. Erika replies that she has to discuss something with the student; it would be best if the two of them went to her room. Mother points out that her daughter has no room of her own, because what Erika in her megalomania refers to as *her* room actually belongs to her mother. As long as this apartment is mine, we'll decide everything together, and Mother then puts the decision into words. Erika Kohut advises her mother not to follow her and the student into the room, otherwise there'll be trouble! The ladies screech at each other. Klemmer exults, Mother balks. Mother relents, almost voicelessly pointing out how little food there is, only enough for two light eaters, but not for two light eaters and a voracious one. Klemmer begs off: No thanks. I've already eaten. Mother loses her cool; she simply stands on the ground of unpleasant facts and she gazes. Anyone could now carry Mother away. A puff of wind could topple this feisty, crusty lady, who usually shakes her fist at any squall and resists any downpour, with the help of sensible clothing. Mother stands there, and her layers peel away.

The procession consisting of the daughter and the strange man, whom Mother knows only casually but lastingly, moves past the old woman and into the daughter's room. Erika murmurs something by way of goodbye, which doesn't alter the fact that this is goodbye for Mother. She is not dismissing the student who has invaded this home. It is obviously a plot to weaken the holy name of Mother. That is why Mother murmurs a prayer to Jesus; the prayer is heard by no one, including the addressee. The door closes relentlessly.

Mother hasn't a clue as to what is about to happen between the two people in Erika's room; but she can easily find out because, thanks to wise maternal precaution, the door cannot be locked. Mother inaudibly tiptoes toward the child's room in order to hear what instrument is being played. Not a piano, for the piano stands resplendent in the parlor. Mother believed that her daughter was innocence personified; and now, suddenly, someone is paying to rent her child. Mother will indignantly reject such a fee. She can do without such income. This boy will probably pay with fleeting, misty amorousness, something that won't last.

As Mother reaches for the doorknob, she clearly hears a heavy object being yanked from its place—probably Grandmother's bureau, which is stuffed with replacement parts and new accessories for Erika's newly bought, albeit superfluous clothing. The bureau is violently detached from its location of many years' standing and dragged across the floor. Outside her daughter's door, which is being deliberately blockaded before her very eyes, stands a disappointed mother. She manages to marshal some final vestige of strength in order to bang senselessly on the door. She uses the tip of her right foot, which is covered by a camel's-hair slipper that is much too soft for kicking. Mother feels pain in her toes; but the pain doesn't sink in because she is much too agitated. Food begins to give off a stench in the kitchen. No hand takes pity and stirs it. Mother is not even considered worthy of formal address. No explanations have been offered her, even though this is Mother's home too, and even though she keeps a beautiful home for her daughter. In fact, this is even more Mother's home than Erika's, because Mother almost never goes out. The apartment does not belong to the child alone; Mother is still alive and intends to go on kicking. This very evening, when the unpleasant visit is over, Mother will tell her daughter, purely for show, that she intends to move out. To the old-age home. If Erika then probes a little, she'll find that Mother isn't really serious, for where should she go? In the guise of a shift of power and a changing of the guard, disagreeable insights invade

Mother's disagreeable mind. Going into the kitchen, she throws
half-cooked food around. Her action is one of fury rather than
despair. Sooner or later, old age must hand over the staff.
Mother spots the poisonous seeds of conflict in her daughter,
but the conflict will pass once the child recalls how much she
owes her mother. When Mother reached Erika's present age,
she no longer planned to abdicate. She imagined she would
hold out until death do them part. Until the big gong clanged.
Perhaps she won't outlive her child; but as long as she lives,
she'll stay in charge. Her daughter is past the age at which
unpleasant surprises from a man can be expected. But now he's
here, the man, whom, one would have thought, the daughter
had expelled from her mind. Mother talked the child out of
thinking about him, and now he resurfaces, unscathed, brand-
new—and in their very own home!

Out of breath, Mother sinks into a kitchen chair, surrounded
by the ruins of the meal. No lesser person than she must now
pick everything up. At least it'll take her mind off her problems.
Tonight, when they're watching TV, she'll give Erika the silent
treatment. And if Mother does break the silence, she'll tell
Erika that everything Mother does is motivated by Love.
Mother will declare her love for Erika, which should excuse
any possible mistakes that Mother might make. Mother will
cite God and other superiors, who also uphold Love, but never
the egotistical love that is budding in this young man. To punish
her daughter, Mother will not waste a single word on the movie.
There will be no customary exchange of ideas tonight, because
Mother has decided to omit it. Tonight, the daughter will have
to accede to Mother's wishes. The daughter can't talk to herself.

Mother goes into the living room without food and switches
on the everlasting lure of the color TV, turning the volume up
extra loud so her sulking daughter will regret choosing the
more vapid of two pleasures. Mother seeks desperately, and

she eventually finds some comfort: After all, the daughter has brought the man here, rather than going somewhere else with him. Mother is afraid that the flesh is now speaking behind the closed door. She is also afraid that the young man is after money. Mother can imagine that someone might want money even if he cleverly disguises his intention by pretending to want the daughter. He can have anything he likes, but not money. Such is the decision of the family's minister of finances, who is going to change the computer code for the bankbook tomorrow. It will no longer be: ERIKA. The girl is going to be terribly embarrassed when she goes to the bank tomorrow and tries to give the young man her savings.

Mother is terrified that her daughter, behind the door, is listening only to her body, which may now be blossoming under someone's touch. Mother turns the volume up so high that the neighbors are sure to complain. The apartment quakes under the blaring fanfare of the Last Judgment, announcing the evening news. Any moment now, the neighbors will be banging with broomsticks or knocking at the door to lodge a personal complaint. Serves Erika right, for she will be named as the reason for the acoustic transgression, and from now on she won't be able to look any of the neighbors in the eye.

Not a peep comes from the daughter's room, where cells unhealthily run riot. Not a bird shriek, not a toad croak, not a thundering. No matter how hard Mother might try, she couldn't possibly hear her daughter now, even if the daughter screamed. Mother lowers the volume of the TV, which is raging over bad news; Mother wants to hear what's happening in her daughter's room. She still hears nothing, because the bureau also muffles noise, not just deeds and steps. Mother turns off the sound, but nothing stirs beyond the door. Mother turns up the volume, in order to camouflage her action: She tiptoes to the door in order to eavesdrop. What kind of sounds will

Mother catch: pleasure, pain, or both? Mother puts her ear to
the door. Too bad she doesn't own a stethoscope. Luckily
they're only talking. But what are they talking about? Are they
talking about Mother? Mother has lost all interest in watching
TV, even though she always tells her daughter that there's
nothing like TV at the end of a long, hard day. The daughter
does the work, but the mother can always watch TV with her.
For Mother, togetherness with her daughter is the spice of TV
watching. But now the spice has been cooked away, and the
TV is insipid. Mother's lost her taste for it.

Mother goes over to the poison cabinet in the parlor. She
drinks a liqueur, then several more. The liqueur makes her feel
weary and heavy. She lies down on the sofa and drinks some
more. Behind the door, something is proliferating like a cancer
that keeps growing even after its owner has long since died.
Mother keeps drinking.

❑

Walter Klemmer readily yields to his wish to pounce on
Erika now that the preparatory work is done and the door is
closed. No one can get in, and also no one can get out without
his express manual assistance. The bureau is blocking the door
with the help of his strength; the woman is with him, and the
bureau protects them both against the outside. Klemmer paints
a Utopian partnership with Erika, spiced with loving emotions.
How beautiful love can be when enjoyed with the right *Thou*.
Erika indicates that she wants to be loved only after trials and
tribulations. She spins herself into the cocoon of her status as
an object and locks out her feelings. She convulsively holds the
bureau of her shame, the chest of her malaise, in front of her,
and Klemmer is to shove this furniture aside violently in order
to get to Erika. She only wants to be an instrument on which
she will teach him to play. He should be free, and she in fetters.

But Erika will choose the fetters herself. She makes up her mind to become an object, a tool; Klemmer will have to make up his mind to use this object. Erika forces Klemmer to read the letter; she mentally begs him to transcend the contents of the letter once he has read it. If only because what he feels is truly love and not just a flimsy mirage shining on the meadows. Erika will withdraw entirely from Klemmer if he refuses to expect violence from her. But she will always be happy about his affection, which excludes violence against the creature of his choice. He can take on Erika only under the condition of violence. He is to love Erika to the point of self-surrender; she will then love him to the point of self-denial. They will continually hand each other notarized evidence of their affection and devotion. Erika waits for Klemmer to abjure violence for the sake of love. Erika will refuse for the sake of love, and she will demand that he do to her what she has detailed in the letter, whereby she ardently hopes that she will be spared what is required in the letter.

Klemmer gazes at Erika in love and veneration as if someone were gazing at him gazing at Erika in love and veneration. The invisible spectator peers over Klemmer's shoulder. She commends herself into Klemmer's hands, hoping for redemption through absolute trust. She desires obedience from herself and commands from Klemmer in order to complete her obedience. She laughs: It takes two! Klemmer joins in the laughter. Then he says we don't need an exchange of letters, a simple exchange of kisses would be enough. Klemmer assures his future beloved that she can tell him anything, anything, she doesn't have to bother writing it down. The woman who learned to play the piano should be ashamed of herself, honestly! A nice appearance can replace sex appeal that's been killed off by knowledge. Klemmer finally wants to storm the sky of love and not wait for traffic signals that are set down in writing. He's got the

letter here, why doesn't he open it? Erika tugs away at her
freedom and her willpower, which can finally hand in their
resignations; the man doesn't understand her sacrifice. She
feels a numb spell emanating from this lack of willpower; the
enchantment excites her violently. Klemmer gaily jokes: I'm
starting to lose my desire. He threatens: this soft, fleshy, oh-
so-passive body, this mobility narrowly focused on the piano,
will not arouse any great longing in him if such obstructions
pile up. Now that we're alone, let's get the show on the road!
There's no going back and there's no mercy. Taking many
circuitous routes, he has finally managed to arrive here. He
eats up his portion and wants more, he shovels up some of the
trimmings. Klemmer vehemently shoves away the letter, telling Erika that she has to be forced to enjoy her good fortune.
He describes the happiness she will enjoy with him, his assets
and merits, and also imperfections—as opposed to the dead
paper. After all, Klemmer is alive! And she'll soon feel how
alive, considering how alive *she* is! Walter Klemmer hints ominously at how quickly some men get fed up with some women.
A woman simply has to serve herself with great variety. Erika,
one step ahead of him, is already well informed. That is why
she pushes the letter at Klemmer, the letter that explains how
one can lengthen the hem of the relationship under certain
circumstances. Erika speaks: Yes, but first the letter. Klemmer
has no choice but to take it; otherwise he'd have to drop it on
the ground, thus insulting the woman. He showers Erika with
vehement kisses, delighted that she has finally become sensible
and amorously cooperative. In exchange, she will receive ineffable amorous favors, all from him, Klemmer. Erika orders him:
Read the letter. Klemmer reluctantly releases Erika from his
open hand and starts tearing the envelope open. He peruses
the letter in amazement, even reading some parts aloud. If
what the letter says is true, things will go badly for him, but

even worse for this woman, which he can guarantee. However hard he now tries, he can no longer see her as a human being; you've got to wear gloves to touch something like that. Erika produces an old shoebox and unpacks what she has saved up inside it. She wavers: Let him decide, she would like to be made utterly immobile. She would like to cede all responsibility to external aids. She wants to entrust herself to someone else, but on *her* terms. She challenges him!

Klemmer explains that it often takes courage to reject a challenge and opt for the norm. Klemmer is the norm. Klemmer reads and wonders who this woman thinks she is. He racks his brain: Is she serious? *He* is very serious; he has learned to be serious in wild waters, where one often faces grave dangers and overcomes them.

Erika asks Herr Klemmer to come closer while she will be dressed only in a black nylon slip and stockings! She'd like that. Her most haunting wish—the adored Herr Klemmer reads—is for you to punish me. She would like Klemmer as a punishment. And in such a way that he ties her up with the ropes I've collected, and also the leather straps and even the chains! Hogtie her, bind her up as thoroughly as he can—solidly, intensely, artfully, cruelly, tormentingly, cunningly. He should bore his knees into her abdomen, if you'll be so kind.

Klemmer has a good, hard laugh. What a joke—she wants him to smash his fists in her stomach and sit down so hard on her that she'll lie there like a plank, unable to stir in his cruel, sweet bonds. Klemmer snorts because she can't be serious, it's all make-believe. Erika is showing a different side of herself, thereby chaining the man to her all the more securely. She's looking for entertainment, anything goes. For example, her letter says, I will writhe like a worm in your cruel bonds, in which you will have me lie for hours on end, and you'll keep me in all sorts of different positions, hitting or kicking me, even whipping me! Erika's letter says she wants to be dimmed out under him, snuffed out. Her well-rooted displays of obedience require greater degrees of intensity! And a mother is not everything, even though you usually have only one. She is and remains primarily a mother, but a man wants even greater achievements. Klemmer asks her just what she means, anyway. He wants to know who she is. He has the impression that she's not even ashamed of herself.

Klemmer would like to get out of this apartment, which has become a trap. He didn't realize what he was letting himself in for. He was hoping for something better. The paddler is investigating unsafe waters. He won't quite admit to himself what he's maneuvered himself into. And he'll never admit it to others. He's afraid: What does this woman want from me? Did he get it right: By becoming her master, he can never become her master? So long as she dictates what he should do to her, some final remnant of Erika will remain unfathomable. How easily a lover imagines he has advanced into the deepest regions, where no secret is left to reveal. Erika believes she's still got a choice at her age, whereas he is so much younger and therefore has first choice and is the first to be chosen. Erika demands in writing that he take her on as his slave and assign her things to do. He thinks to himself: If that's all it is . . . But he will never punish her, the generous young man, it would be too hard for him. There's a certain point that he never exceeds in his cherished habits. You have to know your limits, and the limits begin where pain is felt. Not that he wouldn't have the nerve. He just doesn't want to. Her letter says she will always apply to him in writing or by telephone, never personally. She doesn't even have the nerve to say it out loud! Not when peering into his blue eyes.

Klemmer finds it all so funny that he slaps his thighs: She

wants to give *him* orders! And he's supposed to obey her on
the spot. She goes on to say that you should describe what
you're going to do to me. And threaten me loudly in case I
refuse. Let me know what I'll be in for if I don't obey. Everything has to be depicted in loving detail. Levels of intensity
should also be described very precisely. Klemmer again mocks
the silent woman: Who does she think she is! His mockery
tacitly implies that she is nothing or not much. He talks about
a farther limit, which he alone knows, because he drove in the
boundary marker: This border starts at the very place where
I'm supposed to do something against my will. Herr Klemmer
jokes about the seriousness of the situation. He reads, but only
for fun. He reads aloud, but only for his own amusement: No
one could endure the things she desires, without dying sooner
or later. This inventory of pain. I'm supposed to treat you as
a mere object. During our piano lessons, I'm not to let anyone
notice anything. Klemmer asks her whether she's gone absolutely crazy. If she believes no one's going to notice anything,
then she's wrong. Dead wrong.

Erika doesn't speak; she writes that her dull-minded herd of
piano students may ask for explanations, but they won't receive
any. Klemmer objects that Erika is grossly underestimating her
students. He doesn't want to make a total fool of himself in
front of people who are a lot less intelligent than he. That is
not what I expected of our relationship, Erika. In the letter,
which he cannot take seriously no matter how hard he tries,
he reads that he is to ignore any request coming from her. If
I ask you to loosen the rope, darling, then I may be able to
free myself should you go along with my request. That's why
you must pay no attention to my pleading, that's very important! On the contrary: If I plead, act as if you're going to go
along with it. But actually, you have to tighten the ropes, pull
them in, draw the belt in at least two or three notches—the

tighter the better. There'll be old nylons lying around. Just stuff them into my mouth as deep as you can and gag me so cunningly that I can't emit the slightest peep.

Klemmer says no, the whole business should stop. He asks Erika whether she wants a slap in the face. Erika does not give herself permission to speak. Klemmer threatens that if he keeps reading, it'll only be because he's interested in her as a clinical case. He says: A woman like you doesn't need this stuff. After all, she's not ugly. She has no visible bodily defects, aside from age. Her teeth are real.

This paragraph says: Use a rubber hose—I'll show you how—to stuff the gag so tightly into my mouth that I can't stick out my tongue. The hose is ready! Please use a blouse to increase my pleasure: tie up my face so skillfully and thoroughly that I can't get it off. And let me waste away in this torturous position for hours on end, so I can't do anything. I'll be stuck with myself and in myself. And what about my reward? Klemmer jokes. He asks because he doesn't enjoy other people's torments. The athletic torment he takes upon himself is a different matter: He's the only one who suffers it. A session in the sauna after the coldest mountain waters. I can do that to myself, and I should explain to you what I mean by an extreme condition.

Mock me and call me a "stupid slave" and even worse names, Erika asks in the letter. Please tell me loudly what you're about to do to me, and describe the degrees of intensification—without, however, getting any crueler. Talk about things, but don't do more than hint at them. Threaten me, but don't go any further. Klemmer thinks about how far he has gone on his mountain streams, but he has never come across such a woman! He won't seek new shores with her: smelly old sewer, he calls her joylessly, albeit mentally. He mocks and maligns her, albeit to himself. He stares at this woman, who wants to be swept away by bliss, and he asks himself: Who can understand the female sex anyway? All she thinks about is herself. The man discovers that she's going to kiss my feet in gratitude. The letter pulls no punches. It proposes secret things between them, things that will not be noticed by the outside world. Lessons offer a fertile soil for stealth and secrecy, as well as for shining in public. Klemmer realizes that the letter drools on in this tone ad infinitum. He can only regard it as a curiosity. I'd really like to get out of here: That's his ultimate destination. He's held back by curiosity; he wonders how far a person can go if he's ready to grab at the stars! Klemmer, the fixed star, has been illuminating her for some time now. The universe of music is vast, the woman only has to grab something; but she resigns herself to less! Klemmer has an itch to kick her.

Erika looks at the man. She was once a child, she will never be a child again.

Klemmer jokes about the injustice of undeserved strokes. The woman wants to earn these strokes purely by her presence; that's not much. Erika thinks about the old escalators in the department stores of her childhood. Klemmer quips that my hand might take a swipe at you now and then, I won't dispute it, but too much never does much good. Let's not take intimacy too far. No overexuberance. She's probing him about love even a blind man could see that. It's only a test of how far he would go with her in regard to love. She's fathoming him about Everlasting Fidelity, she wants assurances right away before we even get started. Just like a woman. She seems to be sounding him out, trying to determine how solidly she can build on his devotion and how solidly he can knock on the wall of her submission. Absolute, if anything: her ability to submit. Abilities become knowledge.

Klemmer is of the opinion that in this stage of the game a man can promise a woman everything, but doesn't have to keep anything. If the white-hot iron of passion is forged too timidly, it quickly cools off. Strike while it's hot. The man rationalizes a decline of interest in an exemplar of female architecture. Overwork wipes a man out. He is devoured by the need to be alone.

Reading the letter, Klemmer infers that this woman wants to be devoured by him. Thanks but no thanks; Klemmer isn't very hungry. He rationalizes his rejection: I do unto others as I would have them do unto me. He wouldn't want to be tied and gagged. I love you so much, says Klemmer, I could never hurt you, not even if you wanted me to hurt you. After all, a person wants to do only what he himself wants. Klemmer is not going to follow the letter; that much is certain.

From beyond the door, the muffled thunder of the TV, in which a male is threatening a female. Today's soap installment cuts painfully into Erika's mind, which is open and receptive to it. Inside its own four walls, her mind unfolds splendidly, because it is not threatened by anything that smacks of competition. Maternal presence is inflicted on this mind only in regard to unsurpassable keyboard abilities. Mother says: Erika is the best. That is the lasso she uses to rope her daughter.

Klemmer reads a written sentence that allows him to establish punishments for Erika as he sees fit. He asks, Why didn't you write the punishment down? And his question bounces off the battleship Erika. Klemmer is told it was only a suggestion. She offers to buy a chain with two locks that I definitely can't unlock. Please don't worry about my mother. Mother, however, is worried about Erika and bangs on the door. They scarcely notice because of the bureau, which patiently holds out its hump. Mother barks, the TV buzzes. The screen locks in tiny figures that one controls by arbitrarily switching them on and off. Big real life is pitted against tiny TV life, and real life wins because it has full control over the image. Life adjusts to television, and television is copied from life.

Figures with venomously swollen hair-dryer coiffures gape fearfully at one another's faces. But only the figures outside the screen can see anything. The others peer out of the screen, assuming nothing and perceiving nothing.

Erika expands her suggestions: We have to get a lock or some kind of device for this door! You can leave that to me, darling. I'd like you to turn me into a package that is completely at your mercy.

Klemmer nervously licks his lips in the face of control and power. Miniature worlds, like those on TV, open up to him. There's barely room to put your foot down. This tiny figure stamps about in his brain. The woman before him shrinks down to a miniature. You can throw her like a ball without catching her. You can squeeze the air out of her. She deliberately belittles herself even though she doesn't have to. For he does acknowledge her talents. She does not want to be superior because she won't find anyone who can feel superior to her. Erika wants to buy accessories until we have an entire torture kit. We can then play *à deux* on this private organ. But no organ sound is to reach the outside world. Erika is concerned that the other students might notice something. Outside the door, Mother sobs softly and furiously. And in the TV set, an unobserved woman sobs almost voicelessly because the volume was lowered. Mother is able, and also quite willing, to make this woman from the TV family sob so loudly that the apartment will quake. If she, Erika's own mother, can't interfere, then the permanent-wave intimacy of that female Texan will do a fine job of disrupting. All you have to do is manipulate the remote control.

Erika is presumptuous: She wants to be naughty so she can

be punished on the spot. She will fail to do something. Mother will not find out, but Erika will screw up. Please don't worry about my mother at all. Walter Klemmer could certainly manage not to worry about Mother, but Mother can't help trumpeting out her worries by means of the TV din. Your mother's awfully annoying, the man whines. Erika suggests he get Erika a kind of apron made of solid black plastic or nylon and cut holes in it so One Can Glimpse the Sexual Organs. Klemmer asks where one can find such an apron without stealing it or making it. So she's only offering the man peepshow peeps, he jeers, that's how sophisticated she is. Did she learn that from TV? You never see everything, only peeks and glimpses, each one a world unto itself. The director supplies the peek, and your head supplies the rest. Erika hates people who watch TV without thinking. You can profit from everything as long as you open your mind. The TV set supplies ready-made data, your mind manufactures the external coverings. The TV set arbitrarily changes facts and spins out plots. It rips apart lovers and binds together things that the writer keeps separate. The mind twists and turns as it sees fit.

Erika wants Walter Klemmer to perform some torture on her. Klemmer does not wish to perform any torture on Erika. He says that's not what we worked out, Erika. Erika asks him to please tie all the cords and ropes so tight that you yourself could barely unravel them. Don't spare me in any way. On the contrary, give it your all! And do it everywhere. What do you know about my strength, Walter Klemmer rhetorically asks this woman, who has never seen him paddle. She underestimates the limits of his strength. She hasn't the foggiest notion what he could do to her. That was why she wrote him: Do you know you can intensify the effect by first soaking the ropes in water for a very long time? Please do it whenever I

feel like it, and please enjoy it thoroughly. Someday—I'll indicate the day in a letter—surprise me with ropes that have
been thoroughly soaked; they shrink as they dry. Punish
offenses!

Klemmer tries to describe just how Erika, who is silent, is
transgressing a simple rule of propriety with her silence. Erika
remains silent, but does not hang her head. She feels she's on
the right track, and she wants him to take good care of all the
keys to the locks he will use to lock her up! Don't lose anything.
Don't worry about my mother. Just ask her for the substitute
keys—and there are lots of them! Lock me in with my mother,
from the outside! I expect you'll have to leave for some urgent
reason, and it's my most fervent desire that you leave me tied
up, bound up, roped up, together with my mother. Except that
I'll be behind the door of this room. She won't be able to get
to me. And leave me like that until the next day. Don't worry
about my mother, leave her to me. Take along all the keys to
the rooms and the apartment. Don't leave a single key here!

Klemmer again asks what do I get out of it? Klemmer laughs.
Mother scratches. The TV screeches. The door is shut. Erika
is still. Mother laughs. Klemmer scratches. The door screeches.
The TV is off. Erika is.

To keep me from whimpering in pain, please stuff nylons
and panty hose into my mouth, gag me with pleasure. Tie the
gag skillfully to my mouth with a rubber hose (you can buy
it in any hardware store) and more nylons—so skillfully that
I can't possibly remove it. And please wear a small black bikini,
which reveals more than it conceals. I won't breathe a word!

Address me as a human being and say: You'll see what a
nice package I'll make out of you, you'll see how fine you'll
feel after my treatment. Flatter me, tell me the gag fits so well
that I'll have to stay gagged for at least five or six hours, not

a minute less. Use a solid rope to tie up my ankles as solidly as my wrists, and please hogtie me even though I won't allow it.

We'll try it out. I'll explain to you each time how I want you to do it, just as you've done it in the past. Can you possibly gag me and tie me up like a column and then stand me up in front of you? I'll thank you from the bottom of my heart. Use a leather strap to tie my arms as tightly to my body as you can. Eventually I should be unable to stand up straight.

Walter Klemmer asks: Really? And then supplies his own answer: Really now! He nestles against the woman, but she is not his mother, and she shows she isn't by not enclosing the man in her arms like a son. She keeps her hands at her side, clear and calm. The young man asks for a tender emotion and moves tenderly close to her. He requests a loving reaction, which only a complete monster could refuse him after such a shock. Erika Kohut encloses only herself, nobody else. Please, please, comes monotonously from the student; the teacher does not thank him politely. She reacts as if she were rebuffing him, allowing him to graze upon her, but refusing to give him her red lips. Reading isn't like the real thing, the man curses hideously. The woman offers the letter again. Klemmer attacks her: That's all you've got to offer. How dare you! One can't always be a taker. Klemmer volunteers to show her a universe that she doesn't know yet! Erika doesn't give and Erika doesn't take.

But in her letter she threatens to disobey. In case you witness a transgression on my part (she advises Walter Klemmer), please hit me, with the back of your hand too, slap my face when we're alone. Ask me why I don't complain to my mother or hit you back. In any case, tell me these things so I can feel my helplessness properly. Treat me just as I've told you to in writing. A high point, which I don't dare think about now, is that you'll mount me like a horseman, challenged by my hard work. Please sit down on my face with all your weight and crush my head between your thighs so solidly that I can't move. Describe how much time we have to do it and assure me that we've got enough time! Threaten to leave me in that position for hours and hours if I don't carry out your assignments properly. You can let me pine away for hours with my face under you! Do it until I turn black. My letter demands blissful things from you. You can easily guess the greater delights that I wish for. I don't dare write them down. The letter shouldn't get into the wrong hands. Slap me hard, over and over. Ignore my protests. Ignore my cries. Ignore my begging. As for Mother: Pay no attention to her!

Outside, the TV is cooing softly. Mother starts drinking in earnest. This is the diversion she has been seeking. Families are eating everywhere. You can wipe out the little people on TV anytime, just by pressing a button. Their destiny would then be fulfilled without closer inspection, but Mother just doesn't have the heart. Risking a glance or two, she watches. Tomorrow, if her daughter wishes, she can bring her up to date on tonight's installment, so Erika won't have to gape and gawk at the next bitter installment. Klemmer regards himself as standing outside desire and objectively considering the perspective of this female body. But he is moved imperceptibly. The glue of lust smears up his diverse attitudes, and the bureaucratic solutions that Erika prescribes offer him the guidelines to act in accordance with his pleasures.

Klemmer, willing or not, is affected by the woman's wishes. He is still an outsider, only reading her wishes. But soon he will be won over by pleasure!

Erika desires one thing: that desire make her body desirable.

She wants to be certain of this. The more he reads, the more she wants to have it over with. Darkness is gathering. No light is switched on. The streetlight is still adequate.

Does she really mean what it says here: that she's supposed to stick her tongue in his behind when he mounts her? Klemmer is skeptical about what he reads, he blames it on the poor lighting. A woman who plays Chopin so marvelously can't possibly mean that. Yet that is precisely what the woman desires, because she has never done anything but play Chopin and Brahms. Now she pleads for rape, which she pictures more as a steady announcement of rape. When I can't stir or budge, please talk to me about rape, nothing could save me from it. But please, always talk about more than you actually do! Tell me in advance that I'll be beside myself with bliss when you treat me brutally but thoroughly. The twins Brutality and Thoroughness are hard to raise, and they scream whenever someone tries to separate them. Like Hansel and Gretel when Hansel is in the witch's oven. The letter asks Klemmer to be sure that Erika will be beside herself with bliss if Klemmer just follows every point of the letter. He should blissfully keep slapping her, hard and steadily. Thank you very much in advance! Please don't hurt me; that's what's written illegibly between the lines.

The woman wants to choke on Klemmer's stone-hard dick when she is so thoroughly tied up that she can't move at all. The letter is the fruit of Erika's years of silent reflection. She now hopes that love will prevent anything from occurring. She will insist on it, but an amorous reply will make up for his refusal. Love excuses and forgives, that's what Erika thinks. That's also the reason why he should shoot in her mouth, if you please, until her tongue almost breaks off and she may have to throw up. She imagines in writing, and only in writing, that eventually he should even piss on her. Although at first

I may resist, so far as your rope allows me to. Just keep doing it, often and generously, until I no longer resist.

A tinkle on the keyboard, played by the mother because the child's fingering was incorrect. Unerring memories pop up from the inexhaustible box of Erika's brain. Meanwhile, Mother drinks a liqueur, and then another liqueur in a contrasting color. Mother tries to arrange her limbs, but has a hard time finding them. She begins her preparations for going to bed. It is time, and late.

Klemmer has finished reading the letter. He does not honor Erika by addressing her directly, for this woman is unworthy of such gifts. Klemmer finds a welcome accomplice in his body, which reacts unintentionally. The woman has made contact with him in writing, but a simple touch would have scored a lot more points. She deliberately refused to take the path of tender female touching. Yet she seems to be in basic agreement with his lust. He reaches for her, she doesn't reach for him. That cools him off. He therefore replies silently to the woman's letter. He remains silent until Erika suggests an answer. She asks him to mark her words, but not show them. Just follow your secret heart. Klemmer shakes his head. Erika points out that he normally obeys hunger and thirst. Erika says he's got her telephone number, he can call her up. Think it over in peace and quiet. Klemmer's silence has no musical termination or suspension. His hands and feet sweat; so does his back. Long minutes have worn by. The woman, who has awaited an emotional reaction, is disappointed, for he merely asks for the twentieth time whether she's serious, or is this just a bad joke? Klemmer is an image of time-delayed calm about to explode! He looks like people obsessed with possessing—just before their fulfillment. Erika tries to figure out where his love has gone. Are you angry with me? I hope not. Erika attempts a timid preemptive blow: It doesn't have to happen now. Tomorrow is another day, *mañana* is good enough for me. In any case, the predestined cords and ropes are in the shoebox today. There's a nice assortment. She forestalls an objection, saying she could easily buy more. You can have chains custom-made. Erika utters several sentences that go with the color of her willpower. She speaks as if she were teaching. Klemmer does not speak because only the teacher speaks during class. Erika demands: Speak now!

Klemmer smiles and jokingly replies that they can discuss it! He wonders whether she's gone totally overboard. He pokes her: Has sex driven her completely out of her mind?

For the first time, Erika is afraid that Klemmer will hit her before they even get started. She hastily apologizes for the banal diction of the letter; she tries to create a relaxed atmosphere. Without disgust, and in a good mood, Erika says that ultimately the basis of love is utterly banal.

Could you always come to my apartment? You can let me waste away here in your sweet, cruel chains from Friday evening to Sunday evening, if you dare. I would like to waste away as long as possible in your chains, I've been longing for them for such a long time.

Klemmer doesn't waste many words: Maybe. A short time later, he's quite serious when he says: Absolutely not! Erika wants him to kiss her ardently, not hit her. She says that the act of love can straighten out a lot of things that seem hopeless. Say something loving to me and forget about the letter, she asks inaudibly. Erika hopes that her savior is here, and she also hopes for discretion and secrecy. Erika is dreadfully afraid of being hit. She therefore hits on an idea: We can keep writing letters to each other. We won't even have to spend money on postage. She boasts that their correspondence can become even raunchier than this letter. It was only a beginning, and a start has been made. May I write another letter? Maybe it'll be better. The woman longs for him to kiss her intensely, not hit her. He can kiss her painfully so long as he doesn't hit her. Klemmer replies that it doesn't matter. He says please and thank you. His voice is almost toneless.

Erika knows that tone from her mother. I hope Klemmer won't hit me, she thinks fearfully. She stresses that he can do anything to her. Anything, she stresses, so long as it hurts, for there is hardly anything I don't desire. Klemmer should forgive her for not, she thinks, writing beautifully. I hope he doesn't hit me unexpectedly, the woman thinks. She reveals to the man that she has been longing to be hit for many years now. She assumes she has finally found the master she has been longing for.

Erika is so scared that she talks about something else. Klemmer replies: Thank you. Erika allows Klemmer to pick out her clothes from now on. In case of transgressions on her part, he can take drastic measures regarding her wardrobe. Erika pulls open the closet door and shows a selection. She takes a few items out or displays a few things on their hangers. She hopes he'll see what an elegant wardrobe she has; she offers him a colorful view. If there's something you especially like, I can buy it just for you. Money's no object. Money's an object for my mother, but it's nothing for me. You don't have to worry about my mother. What's your favorite color, Walter? My letter was no joke; she cringes before his hand. You're not angry, are you? If I asked you to write me a few personal lines, would you do it? Write me what you think about my letter, how you feel about it.

Klemmer says goodbye. Erika cringes, hoping his hand will come down lovingly, not destructively. I'll have a lock installed tomorrow. Erika will then offer Klemmer the only key to her door. Just think how nice that will be. Klemmer is silent about the suggestion. Erika is pining for affection. She hopes he'll react in a friendly way when she offers him access to her at any time. No matter when. Klemmer shows no reaction beyond breathing.

Erika swears she will do everything she has written in her letter. She emphasizes: What I've written isn't carved in stone! And better late than never. Klemmer switches on the light. He doesn't speak and he doesn't beat her. Erika tries to find out whether she can send him her desires again. Will you allow me to keep writing to you, please? Klemmer says nothing that would elicit an answer.

Walter Klemmer answers: We'll have to wait and see. He raises his voice over Erika, an obscure standard value, who is dying of terror. He tentatively hurls a four-letter word at her, but at least he doesn't hit her. He calls Erika names, adding the adjective "old." Erika knows she has to be prepared for such reactions, and she shields her face with her arms. She drops her arms: If he's going to hit now, then go right ahead. Klemmer says he wouldn't touch her with a ten-foot pole. He swears he felt love before, but now it's over. He is not going to go looking for her. He's disgusted with her. She dares suggest such things! Erika buries her face in her knees, the way air passengers get into a fetal position when the plane is about to crash. They want to forestall death. She wants to forestall Klemmer's blows, which she will probably survive. He won't hit her because, as he puts it, he doesn't want to dirty his hands on her. He throws the letter at the woman, trying to get her face. But he only gets the back of her bent head. He lets the letter snow down on Erika. Klemmer jeers at the woman: Lovers don't need to write letters. A written pretext is necessary only if lovers have to deceive each other.

Erika sits solidly on her couch. Her feet lie parallel in their new shoes. Hopelessly, she waits for something like an amorous advance from Klemmer. She senses irrevocably that love is about to disappear! She hopes his love hasn't disappeared. As long as he's here, there's hope. She hopes for at least passionate kisses, if you please. Klemmer answers her question: No thanks. Instead of torturing her, she wants him to practice love with her according to Austrian standards. If he let go with her passionately she would jab him with her words: Either my way or no way. She expects the inexperienced student to court her with his lips and hands. She'll show him how. She'll show him, all right.

They sit facing each other. Salvation through love is nigh, but the rock sealing the tomb is too heavy. Klemmer's no angel, and women are no angels either. Roll away the rock. Erika is harsh toward Walter Klemmer when it comes to her wishes, which she has written down for him. She has no wishes other than those in the letter. Why waste words? Klemmer asks. At least, he's not beating her.

He embraces the unfeeling bureau with all the strength he can muster and pushes it millimeter by millimeter, without Erika's help. He pushes it until a tiny air sluice appears, so he can open the door. We have nothing more to say to each other, Klemmer doesn't say. He leaves without saying goodbye and slams the apartment door behind him. He's gone.

❑

Mother, in her half of the bed, is snoring away, under the influence of unwonted alcohol, which is meant only for guests who never come. Many years ago, in this very same bed, desire led to sacred motherhood; and desire was terminated as soon as that goal was achieved. A single ejaculation killed desire and created a space for the daughter. Father killed two birds with one stone. And killed himself with the same stroke. Because of his internal indolence and weak mind, he was unable to follow through on the consequences of his ejaculation. Now Erika slides into her own half of the bed, and Father is six feet under. Tonight, Erika hasn't washed or cleaned herself in any way. She smells of her own sweat, like an animal in a cage, where the odor of sweat and the vapor of the wild gather and cannot withdraw, for the cage is too small. If one animal wants to turn around, the other has to squeeze up against the wall. Covered with sweat, Erika settles down next to her mother and lies there, sleepless. After two hours of stewing in her own juice, neither sleeping nor thinking, Erika suddenly feels her mother waking up. The thought of her child must have aroused her, for the child has not moved. Mother recalls what the liqueur helped her to flee. She jerks around, silvery bright, gleaming without sunlight. Glaring at the child, she issues a grave accusation, coupled with a dangerous threat and the utopia of bodily injury. Next come taluses of unanswered questions, in no special order as to priority or urgency. Erika remains silent, so Mother turns away, insulted. She interprets her feeling of insult as disgust at her daughter. Yet she turns back to her daughter and reemits an acoustic version of her threats, only louder. Erika is still gritting her teeth; Mother curses and nags. Her wild accusations drive her into a state beyond self-control. Mother gives in to the alcohol, which is still raging in her blood. The egg liqueur has an insidious effect. And so does the chocolate liqueur.

Erika mounts a halfhearted love attack, for Mother is already picturing far-reaching consequences for their future life together. Mother is horrified at the worst consequences—for instance, a separate bed for Erika!

Erika is carried away by her own amorous overture. She throws herself upon Mother, showering her with kisses. She kisses Mother in a way in which she has not even thought of kissing her for years. She clutches Mother's shoulders, and Mother angrily waves her fists, not striking anyone. Erika

kisses Mother between her shoulders, but doesn't always hit
her target, for Mother keeps jerking her head toward the side
that's not being kissed. In the semidarkness, Mother's face is
merely a bright splotch surrounded by dyed blond hair, which
helps orientation. Erika promiscuously kisses this bright spot.
She is flesh of this flesh! A crumb of this maternal cake! Erika
keeps pressing her wet mouth into Mother's face, holding her
in steely arms so Mother can't resist. Erika lies halfway, then
three-quarters upon Mother, because Mother is starting to flail
her arms seriously, trying to thrash Erika. With hectic thrusts
of the head, Mother's mouth tries to avoid Erika's puckered
mouth. Mother wildly tosses her head around, trying to escape
the kisses. It's like a lovers' struggle, and the goal isn't orgasm,
but Mother per se, the person known as Mother. And this
Mother resolutely puts up a fight. It's no use, Erika is stronger.
She winds around Mother like ivy around an old house, but
this Mother is definitely not a cozy old house. Erika sucks and
gnaws on this big body as if she wanted to crawl back in and
hide inside it. Erika confesses her love to her mother and
Mother gasps out the opposite, namely that she too loves her
child, but her child should stop immediately! Now! Mother
cannot defend herself against this tempest of emotions, but she
feels flattered. She suddenly feels courted. It is a premise of
love that we feel validated because someone else makes us a
top priority. Erika sinks her teeth into Mother. Mother begins
to beat Erika away. The more Erika kisses, the more Mother
thrashes away at her: first of all, to protect herself, and sec-
ondly, to ward off the child, who seems to have lost control
even though she's cold sober. Mother yells "Stop!" in various
keys. Mother resolutely orders her to halt! Erika's kisses keep
dashing over Mother. Erika hits Mother demandingly, though
lightly, because Mother's reaction is not desirable. Erika hits
Mother wantingly, but not wantonly. Mother takes it the

wrong way; she threatens and hollers. Mother and child have exchanged roles, for a mother is usually the one who does the hitting; from up there, she's got the best overview of the child. Mother feels she has to defend herself against her offspring's parasexual attacks; she slaps out blindly.

The daughter pulls Mother's hands down and kisses Mother's throat. Erika's intention is cryptosexual; she is a strange and unpracticed lover. Mother, who has likewise never enjoyed any higher education in love, employs the wrong technique: She tramples everything around her. This wears hardest on her old flesh. It is treated purely as flesh, not as Mother. Erika's teeth graze down her mother's flesh. She kisses and kisses Mother wildly. Mother calls her daughter's actions disgusting. Erika's lost all control. It's no use—Mother hasn't been kissed like this for decades, and there's more to come! For the kisses keep on, until, after an endless drumroll of kisses, the daughter collapses in exhaustion, half lying on her mother. The child weeps over the mother's face, and the mother bulldozes the child off her. She asks whether the child has gone crazy. When no answer follows and none is expected, Mother orders Erika to go to sleep immediately, for tomorrow is another day! She cites professional duties that lie waiting. The daughter agrees: It's time to sleep. Like a blind mole, the daughter reaches toward Mother's body, but Mother shovels Erika's hands away. For a brief moment, Erika managed to see her mother's sparse pubic hair, which closes off the fat belly. The sight was unusual. Mother has always rigorously kept this pubic hair under lock and key. During the struggle, the daughter deliberately shoved around in her mother's nightgown, so she could finally see this pubic hair which she has always known was there. Unfortunately, the light was very poor. Erika cunningly uncovered her mother so she could see everything, simply everything. Mother's protests fell on deaf ears. Erika is stronger than her slightly work-worn mother, at least from a purely physical point of view. The daughter now hurls what she has seen into her mother's face. Mother remains silent, as if nothing happened.

The two women fall asleep, cheek by jowl. Not much left of the night. Soon the day will herald itself with unpleasant brightness and irksome bird calls.

❏

Walter Klemmer is astonished at this woman, for she dares to do what others merely promise. After a breather and some deliberation, he is reluctantly impressed by the limits she pushes against in an attempt to expand them. The elbow room of her pleasure is expanded. Klemmer is impressed. Other woman have only a jungle gym and one or two swings in their playground—a dusty area covered with cracked concrete. But this woman has an entire soccer field with tennis courts and a cinder track—all for the happy user! Erika has known her limits for years; Mother drove in the stakes. But Erika is not afraid to pull those stakes out, as Klemmer acknowledges, and to hammer new ones in. Klemmer is proud that she is making this effort with him of all men. His insight comes to him after long reflection. He is young and ready for something new. He is healthy, and ready for disease. He is open to anything and everything, no matter where it comes from. He is broad-minded and willing to slam open yet another door. He might even lean out the window, indeed far enough to nearly lose his balance. He'd be standing on tiptoe! He deliberately takes a risk, and enjoys the risk because *he* is the one taking it. He has always been a blank page waiting for the ink of an unknown printer; and no one will ever have read the likes of this. He'll be marked for life! Afterward he won't be the same person, he will *be* more and *have* more.

If necessary, he will inflict cruelties upon this woman. Such are his thoughts. He will accept her conditions without qualms and dictate his own: greater cruelty. He knows exactly what will happen after he steers clear of her for a few days in order to see whether emotion will survive the inhuman stress test of reason. His mental steel is sagging, but it hasn't broken under the weight of promises made by the woman. She will place herself in his hands. He is proud of the trials he will undergo. Why, he may very nearly kill her!

Nevertheless, the student is glad to maintain a distance of several days. Better to play hard to get than give someone your little finger. He's been waiting a couple of days, to see what this woman, whose turn it is to get loved, will fetch in her mouth. A dead hare, a partridge. Or just an old shoe. Showing his independence, he arbitrarily stops his lessons. He hopes this will make the woman shamelessly try to waylay him. Then he'll say no and wait for her next move. Meanwhile, the young man prefers keeping to himself. The wolf knows no better friend before he meets the goat.

As for Erika, she learned how to do without years ago. Now she wants to change thoroughly. The much-used press of her lust crushes her wishes. The sap runs red. She keeps looking at the door, waiting for the student. All the other students come, but not Klemmer. He remains AWOL.

Klemmer is addicted to learning. He begins many things and completes few, including Japanese martial arts, languages, travel, painting. For some time now the education addict has been attending the clarinet class next door in order to gain some groundwork, which he will eventually apply to the saxophone for jazz and improvisation. He has been avoiding only the piano and its mistress. After learning the basics in a number of fields, Klemmer usually opts out. He lacks perseverance. But now he'd like to become a high-achievement lover—the woman is practically challenging him to do so. But then again, he com-

plains (when he has the time) that the corset of classical music
training is much too tight for him. He likes to enjoy a view
that's not marred by any limits. He senses a vast landscape,
he suspects there are fields he has never seen, and, of course,
that no one else before him has seen. He lifts up corners of
cloths and, terrified, drops them; only to raise them again: Did
his eyes deceive him? He can scarcely believe them. Kohut
keeps trying to bar him from those fields and meadows, yet in
private she keeps beckoning with them. The student feels the
suck of the limitless. During lessons, the woman is relentless.
She can hear the slightest detail, the tiniest particular, from
far away. But in real life, she wants to be forced to beg. On
the keyboard, she wraps him around her little finger, in an
elastic bandage of finger exercises, trill drills, the Czerny *School
of Velocity*. It will be a slap in her face when the clarinet releases
him from the constrictions of counterpoint. How thrillingly
he'll be able to improvise someday on the soprano sax! Klemmer practices the clarinet. He resolutely opens new musical
horizons and plans to start out in a student jazz band—he knows
the members personally. But once he outgrows them, he'll start
his own group. He'll make his own music, according to his own
dictates. He's already got a name for it, but he's keeping it
secret for the moment. These musical plans will fit in well with
his distinct urge for freedom. He's already registered for the
jazz class. He wants to study arranging. First, he wants to
adjust, conform. But at the right time, he'll break out of for-
mation, like a wellspring, with a breathtaking solo. His willpower isn't easily classified; his desires and abilities aren't easily
pigeonholed in the box containing the score. His elbows row
cheerily alongside his body, his breath rolls merrily into the
tube, his mind is a blank. He's happy. He's training himself
in intonation and changing reeds. Wonderful progress is visible
way down the road. That's what his clarinet teacher says, and

the teacher is happy to have such a student, who's got such a good background from Professor Kohut and whom the clarinet teacher can hopefully steal from her, in order to bask in the student's light at the annual school concert.

Wearing a refined hiking outfit, a woman who is not immediately recognized approaches the door of the clarinet class and waits. She wants to come here, and that's why she's here. Erika Kohut is all dolled up for the occasion, as usual.

Didn't Klemmer promise her nature, nature fresh as a daisy, and doesn't he know best where nature is to be found? The student comes through the door with a small black instrument case. He is startled. Stammering and stuttering, she proposes a walk along the river. Right now! Her outfit indicates what she is planning. The reason for my coming here, she says: to go across the river and into the trees. This properly outfitted woman triggers a landslide of achievement, thundering, unappetizing moraines. Goal-oriented efforts are to be demonstrated at an uninviting mountain station; banana peels and apple cores on the floor, vomit in the corner, and all the devaluated documents, those dirty scraps of paper in the nooks and crannies, those torn railroad tickets are never swept into the garbage.

Erika, as Klemmer will notice, is sporting new clothes; her clothing matches the occasion, and the occasion matches her clothing. Her clothes, as usual, seem to be the most important thing for her. A woman generally needs adornment for her image, and the forest alone has never adorned any woman. On the contrary, a woman should decorate a forest with her presence; in this way, she resembles an animal observed through the hunter's binoculars. Erika has purchased solid hiking boots and soaked them in fat, so they won't rot in the damp. Wearing these boots, she can easily walk for miles, if they want. She's sporting a sporty checkered blouse, a loden jacket, knickerbockers, and red woolen knee stockings. She's even got a small knapsack containing gourmet treats! She doesn't have a rope, because she doesn't go to extremes. And even if she did go to extremes, she wouldn't use a net or a rope. She wouldn't even take along a waist anchor when braving the wilderness of physical wallowing, in which one is dependent entirely on oneself and one's mate.

Erika is planning to dole herself out to the man in tidbits. He mustn't overeat, he should always be ravenous for her. That's what she pictures when she's alone with Mother. She is thrifty with herself, she spends herself very reluctantly, and only after indulging in all sorts of pros and cons. She makes the most of her pounds of flesh. She will take the small change of her modern body and avariciously count it out on the table for Klemmer, so he'll think she's spending twice as much as she really is. After impudently thrusting ahead with her letter, she has gone backward from her forwardness, which wasn't such an easy thing to do. She's stuck in the piggybank of her body, in that bluish tumor that she carries around all the time, bursting at the seams. For instance, this hiking outfit: She had to lay a lot of money on the line in the backpacking shop. She buys quality, but beauty is more important to her. Her wishes are far-reaching. Klemmer inspects the woman in peace and quiet—a source of strength. His eyes stroll leisurely across imitation peasant buttons and a small silver watch chain (likewise an imitation) such as hunters wear; studded with stag's teeth, it runs down Erika's belly. Erika whimpers at him: She's been promised a hike today, and she's come to put in her claim. He asks why exactly here, now, today? She says: Don't you remember, you said *today*? Silently, she holds out the coupons of his heedless promises. He expressly promised, and today's the day. He was the one who suggested: today. The student shouldn't think a teacher forgets anything. Klemmer says this isn't the right place or the right time. Erika instantly offers more distant places and better times. Soon, the couple will no longer require circuitous routes through forests and across lakes. But today, the sight of treetops and mountain peaks might increase the man's desire.

Walter Klemmer reflects. He decides he doesn't have to go too far in order to try out something new. Given his profound scientific interests, he offers—Erika will be amazed—to do it right on the spot! Why go far afield? Besides, this way he can still make his judo club by three o'clock! However, love means never having to say you're joking. If she's serious, then that's fine and dandy with him. So far he's been loving and friendly, but, as he will prove, he can also be brutal. As desired. Instead of replying in due form, Erika Kohut drags the student into the cleaning staff's cabinet, which, as she knows, is always unlocked. Let him show his true grit. The woman exerts the driving force. Let him show what he's never learned. Detergents emit sharp, biting smells, cleaning utensils are piled up. For openers, Erika begs forgiveness; she didn't dare write to the young man. She expands this idea. She kneels before Klemmer and drills awkward kisses into his resisting belly. Her hiking knees, which have never genuflected to the higher art of love, are bathed in dust. The cleaning staff's cabinet is the dirtiest room. Brand-new soles shine in the dark. Student and teacher are each welded to his or her own little love planet, to ice floes, which are inhospitable continents, repelling one another and drifting apart. Klemmer is already embarrassed by her humility and terrified by demands that this humility feels it has the right to make, and make so vociferously because it is so inexperienced.

This humility yells louder than any uncurbed lust could yell. Klemmer answers: Please stand up immediately! He sees that she has dumped her pride overboard, and now makes it a point

of pride never to go overboard. If necessary, he'll tie himself
to the wheel. No sooner has it begun than the two of them
can no longer be united; yet they obstinately desire it. The
teacher's feelings, a warm upwind, waft aloft. Klemmer doesn't
want to, but he must, because it is asked of him. He squeezes
his knees together—an embarrassed schoolboy. The woman
races across his thighs and asks for forbearance and a forward
thrust. What a nice time we could have! Bits of her flesh crash
down on the floor. Erika Kohut makes a declaration of love,
which consists of nothing but boring demands, intricate contracts, and carefully worded guarantees. Klemmer does not give
love. He doesn't say "wow!" that quickly. You mustn't rush
things. Erika describes how far she'd like to go under various
circumstances, and the only thing Klemmer has in mind is a
leisurely stroll through the park. He asks: Not today, next
week! I'll have more time. When his requests fall on deaf ears,
he secretly begins to stroke himself, but his body remains lifeless. This woman drives him into a sucking space in which his
instrument is asked for but does not respond to questions.
Hysterically, he tugs, knocks, shakes. She hasn't noticed as yet.
She dashes toward him as a love avalanche. Sobbing, she takes
back some of the things she said; she promises better things.
How relaxed she is: at last! Klemmer works coldly on his nether
region; he twists his workpiece, beating it with iron tools. The
sparks fly. He is afraid of the piano teacher's inner worlds,
which haven't been ventilated for such a long time. They want
to devour him totally! Already, at the very start, Erika expects
everything he's got, and he hasn't even pulled out and displayed
so much as a tiny tip. She makes love motions as she pictures
them. And as she has seen others make. She emits signals of
clumsiness, which she confuses with signals of devotion, and
she receives signals of helplessness in exchange. He *must*,
therefore he *can't*. By way of excuse, he offers: Not with me!

Just remember! Erika starts tugging at his fly. She pulls out his shirt and rages as lovers are accustomed to doing. In Klemmer, nothing takes place that could prove anything. After a while, Erika, disappointedly clicking her soles, wanders up and down the room. She offers a completely furnished emotional world as a surrogate. She blames something or other on nervousness and overexcitement, and says how happy she is, nevertheless, about this extreme proof of love. Klemmer can't because he must. The *musts* emanate from this woman in magnetic waves. She is the *Must* per se. Erika squats down, a big hunk of clumsiness, doom awkwardly folding its bones together. She gyrates kisses into the student's crotch. The young man moans, as if her persistence were releasing something inside him. He groans the ultimate: That's no way to get me. You're not getting me. But in theory, he is ready and willing, anytime, to try out something new in love. In his helplessness, he finally throws Erika over and lightly strikes her neck with the edge of his hand. Her head obediently sinks forward and forgets its surroundings, which it can no longer see. All it can see is the floor. The woman easily forgets herself in love because too little of her is there to be remembered. Klemmer listens to the outside world and flinches. He shoves the woman's mouth upon his genital like an old glove. The glove is too big; his penis is drooping again after almost standing at attention. Nothing happens, and nothing happens in Klemmer, while the teacher's essence modestly wanes in the distance.

Klemmer wildly thrusts his penis into her mouth, but the proof he wants is wanting. His slack cock floats in her water: an unfeeling cork. Nevertheless, he clutches her hair, for his dick may grow after all. With half an ear, Klemmer listens to the sounds in the corridor, just in case the cleaning woman comes. Otherwise, he is entirely focused on his penis, waiting for it to stir. Tamed by love and taken down a peg or two, the teacher licks Klemmer's crotch: a cow and her newborn calf. She promises that it will work out and that they have endless time now that their passion can no longer be doubted. Just don't get nervous! Promises, emitted unclearly, drive the young man crazy: He hears the subliminal command as an intermediate tone. Doesn't the teacher, his superior, always order him to apply his fingers to the keyboard and his feet to the pedals in certain passages? Her knowledge of music places her above him, and, dissolving under him, she disgusts him more than he can say. She belittles herself in front of his dick, which stays little. Klemmer bangs and hammers into Erika, who feels her gorge rising; but his efforts remain useless. Talking with her mouth full, the woman offers loving comfort and points to the future. There will be future pleasures! No one sees her eyes; she does not issue orders, she is all hair, head, neck—unfathomable. A love robot that does not even respond to kicks. And all the student wants to do is whet his tool on the robot. Basically, his tool has nothing to do with the rest of his body. While love always encompasses the entire woman. The woman has the urge to spend all her love and say: Keep the change. Erika and Walter Klemmer say in unison: It's not working today. It's sure to work next time. For Erika, the most profound evidence of love is failure. Klemmer is furious about his incapacity; so he clutches the woman's hair, clutches it painfully, to keep her from escaping into her usual wishy-washiness. Well, she's here, so let's grab the opportunity and yank her hair hard, as agreed. Each of them, in agreement, yells something about love.

But the student's star is fading. His task does not help him grow. The labyrinth doesn't open up to him, no matter how hard he tugs and pulls the thread. No straight trail of pleasure appears amid unpruned trees and bushes. The woman rants about forests filled with the craziest fulfillments, but the only things she's familiar with are blackberries and mushrooms. Still, she claims she deserves the reward because she has waited for so long. The student works hard; a prize beckons. The prize is Erika's love, which the student now receives. Awkwardly rolling the little white worm between her palate and her tongue, she looks forward to her future pleasure as a sort of hiking path for beginners, a trail lined with neatly labeled plants. The hiker reads a label and is delighted to recognize a long familiar bush. He then sees the snake in the grass and is dismayed because the snake doesn't wear a label. The woman declares this inhospitable spot their trysting place. Here and now! The student wordlessly thrusts his dick into the soft cavern of her mouth, a toneless horn, in which he vaguely feels teeth that he advises her to conceal. In such a situation, the man fears teeth more than disease. He sweats and gasps, feigning performance. He expels words: He keeps thinking of her letter. How dumb! It's because of her letter that he can't perform love, but can only think about love. This woman has put up obstacles.

He excitedly tells her about the renowned and reliable size of his penis, which she has never duly appreciated. Usually it delights him, the way a new erector set delights a boy who's thirsty for knowledge. The size does not take shape. With the friendly eagerness of pleasure, the teacher, who has never known sexual pleasure, goes along with his detailed description. She goes along with him and looks forward to experiencing that and more, much more! Meanwhile, she tries to spit his dick out inconspicuously. But, ignoring their teacher/student relationship, the student Klemmer orders her to take it right back in. He doesn't give up that easily! She has to take the bitter medicine without sugar. His first terrors of impotence, which may be her fault, encircle Erika Kohut. Her young student keeps trying to enjoy sex thoughtlessly, which doesn't work. Inside the woman, who fills such chasms with all her being, the dark ship of fear grows and sets sail. Awakening from her madness, the woman begins to notice details in the tiny room. A low treetop beyond the window. A chestnut tree. The tastelessness of Klemmer's sourballs inside her oral cavity, as the man, moaning senselessly, presses his all into her face. Peering from the corner of her eye, Erika sees an almost imperceptible swaying of branches down below, as they start to get besieged by raindrops. Leaves are charged unduly and sink down. Next, an inaudible patter, then a downpour. A spring morning goes back on its early promise. Soundlessly, the fresh leaves bend under the attack of the drops. Celestial bullets hit branches. The man is still stuffing himself into the woman's mouth, clutching her hair and ears, while on the outside, natural forces rule with overwhelming power. She still wants, and he still can't. He remains small and loose instead of becoming solid and compact. The student screeches in rage, grinding his teeth, because he can't give his best today. He has little chance of discharging into her mouth, which is located in her better part, the upper region. Erika thinks nothing, she chokes, although she doesn't have much in her mouth. But it's enough for her. Her gorge rises, and she struggles for air. In lieu of sexual hardness the student now rubs his abdomen with its scratchy, wiry hair on her face, cursing his tool. Erika's gorge keeps rising. She violently pulls away and throws up into an old metal pail, which stands there, pleased to be available. It sounds as if someone is about to come in, but they are spared the bitter cup, the footsteps keep going. In between her vomiting, the teacher reassures the man: It's not as bad as it looks. She spews gall from her depths. She holds her hands convulsively on her stomach while, half fainting, she depicts later and greater joys. It wasn't all that much fun today, but soon Joy will burst from the starting gate. After catching her breath, she indefatigably offers far more intense, more honest feelings. She polishes them with a soft cloth and presents them boastfully. I've saved all this for you, Walter. Now it's time! She's even stopped throwing up. She tries to rinse her mouth with water, for which she is given a light slap. Furiously the man rages: Don't do that again. You've gotten me all mixed up. You couldn't wait until we reached my snowy peaks. You shouldn't wash your mouth out after you've tasted me. Erika tries to stammer a worn-out word of love, and he laughs in her face. Rain drums steadily. The panes are washed. The woman winds her arms around the man and rambles on. The man tells her she stinks! Does she realize she stinks? He repeats the sentence several times because it sounds so good, and he addresses her in the polite form: Do you realize you stink, Frau Erika? She doesn't understand and licks him again, weakly. But things aren't as they should be. Outside, clouds are darkening the world. Klemmer keeps repeating—senselessly, because he was understood the first time—that Erika stinks so horribly that the whole small room reeks of her, it's disgusting. She wrote him a letter, and now his reply is: He wants nothing from her, and besides, she stinks to high heaven. Klemmer pulls Erika's hair. She should leave town, so his young, fresh nostrils won't have to smell that peculiar, repulsive stench, that animal emanation of putrescence. Goddamnit, but you stink, piano teacher, you just can't imagine how bad you stink.

Erika glides down into the warmth, the body-warm brook of shame, a bath in which one submerges cautiously because the water is rather dirty. Things well up, gush up. Filthy whitecaps of shame, the dead rats of failure, scraps of paper, wooden scraps of ugliness, an old mattress caked with sperm stains. Things rise and rise. Higher and higher. Clucking, the woman climbs up the man until she reaches the relentless concrete crown of his head. His head utters monotonous sentences about even more stench, the cause of which, the student says, is his piano teacher.

Erika feels the gap between the domestic world and the void. She, Erika, supposedly stinks, as the student claims. He is ready to swear it. Erika is ready to go to her death. The student is ready to leave this room in which he has failed. Erika seeks a pain that will end in death. Klemmer closes the door to his trousers and wants to go to the exit. Erika, with breaking eyes, would like to watch him squeeze her throat shut. Her eyes will retain his image even as she rots. He stops telling her she stinks; she no longer exists for him. He wants to leave. Erika wants to feel his lethal hand come down upon her; and shame, a gigantic pillow, settles on her body.

They are walking along the corridor. Side by side. There is a gap between them. Klemmer softly affirms that it is so nice that her former stench isn't as strong in these more open spaces. In that tiny room, the stench was really unbearable! She can take his word for it. He heartily recommends that she leave town.

After a moment, teacher and student encounter the director in the corridor. Klemmer greets him humbly, as a student should. Erika exchanges greetings as colleagues do, because her superior does not make a point of his superiority. Not only that, but the director heartily greets Herr Klemmer as the soloist in the next annual concert. He also wishes him luck. Erika replies that she has not yet made up her mind about the soloist. This student is slipping, that much is certain. She still has to decide whether it should be him or someone else. She doesn't know yet. But she'll announce it in time. Klemmer stands there, wordless. He listens to his teacher talk. The director clicks his tongue over the terrible mistakes that Erika Kohut describes because Klemmer keeps making them over and

over again. Erika articulates unpleasant facts concerning the
student; she says them out loud so he won't accuse her of
talking behind his back. He's been lazy about practicing, she's
got proof. She's been forced to note that he has been applying
himself less and less, he seems less and less eager. He can't be
rewarded for such conduct! The director replies that she obviously knows the student better than he, the director, does,
and so, so long. I hope you do better, he tells student K.

The director has gone into his office.

Klemmer repeats that Erika stinks terribly, she ought to leave
town immediately. He could talk about other things concerning
her, but he doesn't want to make his mouth dirty. It's bad
enough that *she* stinks. He doesn't have to stink too! He's
going to wash out his mouth now, he can actually feel her
stench in his oral cavity. He can feel her disgusting teacher-
stench down in the pit of his stomach. She can't possibly realize
how nauseating her bodily vapors are, and it's a good thing she
can't imagine that she stinks like hell.

The two of them go off in separate directions without agreeing on a mutual keynote, without even agreeing on a mutual
key aside from Erika Kohut's nauseating stench.

Erika Kohut buckles down with zeal and circumspection. She
wanted to jump out of her skin, but couldn't. She feels pain
in many places. Little in her has been chosen. She's at sixes
and sevens. She once saw on TV that you can barricade a door
with other things besides a wardrobe. A detective story showed
her how. You shove the back of a chair under the doorknob.
She doesn't have to go to all that trouble, for Mother is asleep,
sweetly resting in peace as she has done more often in the past
few weeks. As she lies there, sweet alcohol evaporates through
her pores and polyps.

Erika reaches for her domestic treasure chest and goes through the rich contents. There are heaps of riches that Walter K. has not yet gotten to know because he prematurely destroyed their relationship with his ugly ranting and raving. Yet it was only just starting for her! She had finally gotten somewhere, and then he retreated into his shell. Erika picks out clothespins and, after hesitating, pins, a whole pile of pins from a plastic jar.

Shedding tears, Erika applies the greedy leeches of the cheery, colorful plastic clothespins to her body. To places that she can easily reach and that will be black and blue later on. Weeping, Erika nips and clips her flesh. She knocks the surface of her body off balance. She makes her skin miss a beat. She lards her fat with pins and needles. She peers at herself aghast and looks for free areas. If a blank spot shines in the register of her body, it is instantly tweaked by the greedy claws of a clothespin. The tense interstices become bristling pincushions. The woman is flabbergasted by her actions, which can have terrible consequences. She bawls and blubbers. She is all alone. She sticks needles into herself, pins with brightly colored plastic heads, each pin with its own head in its own color. Most of them tumble out again. Erika doesn't dare prick herself under her fingernails; it's too painful. Soon tiny blood bolsters appear on the meadow of her skin. The woman goes on crying. She is all alone. After a while, she stops and then stands in front of the mirror. Her image cuts into her brain with words of scorn and mockery. It is a colorful image. It would be a truly merry image if the causes were not so dismal. Erika is utterly alone. Mother is again sleeping the deep sleep induced by alcohol. If Erika, aided by the mirror, finds an unravaged place on her body, she grabs a clothespin or needle, while weeping and wailing. She drives the instruments hard, drives them into her body. Her tears flow down and she is all alone.

After a long time, Erika's hand removes the needles and clothespins and neatly places them back in their containers. Pain recedes, tears recede.

Erika Kohut goes to her mother so as to end her loneliness.

❑

It is evening again. The arterial roads fill up with traffic that races home unreasonably. Walter Klemmer, too, secretes a sticky thread of hectic activity in order to avoid leisure. He's not planning anything very exciting, but he keeps moving just the same. He's not straining himself all that much, but time whizzes around his urge to move. He's taking the trolley, then the subway, on a long, complicated trip, which he senses will end in the city park. But he still has to decide on a destination and on a route to that destination. He strolls energetically, delaying the start. He's killing time. He's willing to go, that much is certain. He will avenge himself unbelievably on the defenseless animals in the park. They've got flamingos and other exotic spawn, creatures that have never been seen here. And these creatures demand to be ripped apart. Walter Klemmer is an animal lover, but too much is too much, and an innocent party must be forced to believe him. The woman insulted him, so he injured her. The score has been evened, but a living creature must be sacrificed. An animal will have to die. Klemmer got the idea from the newspapers, which describe the bizarre habits of these unsuspecting exotics as well as attempts to harm and murder them.

The young man takes an escalator up into the open. The park is still and stiff, the hotel in front of it light and loud. No amorous couples are unnerved by Herr Klemmer, for he has come here not to gawk, but to commit brutalities without being seen. His unused drives are turning malevolent, all because of that woman. Klemmer wanders about, looking for a bird, but finding none. He goes off-limits, stepping on the lawn, pushing his way through foreign bushes; he is anything but considerate of them. He deliberately tramples neatly planted flowerbeds. His heels bend harbingers of spring. He offered something to that repulsive woman, but she didn't accept it. Now he has to live with the charge that he did not discharge. The load isn't all that heavy, but its consequences will prove devastating to animal life. Klemmer's drive could not punch a hole in its shell and shoot out. That finicky woman merely dug a few musical responses from his mind. She pulled the best out of him, checked it, and then chucked it away! Walter K. grinds pansies underfoot because he was so grossly frustrated in his courtship. It's not his fault he failed. If Erika continues along that road, she's going to suffer a lot more than she ever dreamed. Klemmer is scratched by the giant thorns of a bush; elastic branches bounce into his face when he violently breaks through because he has smelled water beyond the bushes. He is a wounded prey. The hunter, flouting all rules of sportsmanship, let it go after wounding it. The dilettantish hunter did not hit the heart. Hence, Klemmer is a potential danger for everybody, simply everybody!

A venomous love-dwarf, he wanders through this nocturnal scape of diurnal relaxation, seeking to vent his spleen on innocent animals. He looks for a stone to throw, but finds none. He picks up a short branch that has fallen from a tree, but the wood is soft and light. He offered his love to a woman, but she demanded cruelty from him. So he has to stoop to conquer, hoping to find a better weapon than rotten wood. Since he could not master his mistress, he now has to bend his back and tirelessly gather wood. This stick is so small, the flamingo will laugh in his face. It's no cudgel, just a dry little branch. Klemmer, who is inexperienced but would like to experience something new, cannot imagine where the birds go at night to escape their tormentors. Perhaps they've got their own little cabin! Klemmer does not care to be outdone by the vandals who have killed so many birds. He now smells water more keenly—his familiar element. There, according to the guidebooks, is where the pink prey lingers. Various things rustle in the wind. Bright trails wind in and out. Since he's advanced this far, Klemmer would even make do with a swan, a creatur   at is more easily replaced. This thought tells Klemmer how badly he needs an outlet for his boiling anger. If the birds are resting inactively on the water, he'll lure them over. If they're resting on the banks, he won't have to get wet.

Instead of birdcalls, only distant cars can be heard, humming in a steady stream. Out so late? The city noise pursues people all the way out here, where they seek relaxation, all the way out to these urban green zones, these lungs of Vienna. Klemmer, in the gray zone of his immense anger, is looking for someone who won't contradict him—in other words, someone who won't understand him. The bird may flee, but it won't talk back. Klemmer leaves his own nocturnal trail in the grass. He feels a rapport with the night prowlers who are also roaming about. Klemmer feels superior to other night people, who are wandering along, holding some lady's hands. He feels superior to them because his anger is a lot hotter than the fire of love. The young man has fled this far to escape women. Shrieks circle out from a small source of noise. They are as unmelodic as sounds produced by a bird's beak or a beginner on a musical instrument. There's the bird! Soon, vandalism will be reported, and Klemmer can get the newspaper hot off the press and show it to his obstructed beloved: He will have destroyed life. He can then likewise destroy his beloved's life. Threads of life can be cut. Frau Kohut made fun of his feelings. His love rained down upon her for months on end—but she didn't deserve it! His passion poured out on her from the cornucopia of his heart, and she stuffed that sweet rain right back into his horn. Now she'll get her just deserts in a gruesome act of annihilation.

All this time, time which Klemmer lavishes on tracking down a specific bird, the woman, who went to bed very early today, is sleeping away in her home. Unsuspectingly, she works her way through sleep as Klemmer works his way across the nocturnal meadows of the city. Klemmer seeks but does not find. He's following a different call, but cannot locate the caller. He is leery of advancing; he doesn't want to be felled by a wooden club. The streetcars, which, only a short while ago, were orienting him by jingling along the edge of the park, have taken a different name: Leading an underground existence, they cannot be heard. Klemmer cannot orient himself, he doesn't know where he's going. Perhaps he is heading deeper into the wilderness, where it's eat or be eaten. Instead of finding food, Klemmer himself would become prey! Klemmer is looking for a flamingo, and someone with a briefcase may be looking for a bullfinch. The man crashes through the bushes and into the open meadows. He looks left and right, waiting only for something trivial, a stroller like himself; and he makes fun of him in advance. He knows that a wanderer thinks about nothing but food and family, or about the external forms of the surrounding flora and fauna, which cause him great concern. After all, irreplaceable natural reserves are being diminished daily by pollution. The stroller will explain why Nature is dying, and Klemmer will make sure that a small part of Nature will go first as a good example. That is his threat into the darkness. Klemmer's one hand clings to his briefcase, his other hand clutches a cudgel. He can understand why a stroller has anxieties.

No matter how far he wanders, not a bird is to be seen. But eventually and unexpectedly, at the edge of abandoned hope, something does turn up: an entangled couple in an advanced stage of lust. The precise stage cannot be determined. Walter Klemmer almost steps on the woman and the man, who form a hybrid, a continually changing shape. His foot falls clumsily on an item of clothing, and his other foot almost stumbles into raging flesh that occupies another flesh in mad consumerism. Overhead, a huge, soughing tree, itself under ecological protection and therefore out of danger, solicitously camouflages the violent breathing. In his lust for the bird, Klemmer didn't watch where he was going. His hate discharges upon this flesh, which blossomed unexpectedly by the wayside, shamelessly crushing other blossoms because it wallowed—get this!—in a municipal flowerbed. The crushed flowers can be tossed away. Klemmer finds only a light stick with which to take an active part in the bodily struggle. Now we'll see whether he beats or is beaten. Here, a man can force himself into the universal joust of love as a laughing third party. Klemmer yells some nasty words. He yells from the bottom of his heart. He is heartened because the couple do not respond. A tool is swung. Hastily someone pulls things up and someone pulls things down. Order is restored in front of Klemmer. The two participants work silently and softly on themselves and their outer trappings. A few things are out of place, but they are quickly put right. A gentle drizzle falls. Original conditions are restored. Klemmer disagreeably explains the consequences of certain modes of behavior. He rhythmically beats the stick on his right thigh. He feels himself becoming indefatigably more powerful because no one contradicts him.

The couple's animal fear weighs on Klemmer and is better than fear emanating from a real animal. He can smell a demand for discipline. They're just waiting for it. That's why the park attracts them at night. Wide-open space stretches all around. The couple make themselves at home on this range by not retorting to Klemmer's quick, furious shrieks. Klemmer talks

about "pigs" and "sluts." The insights that inundate him when
he listens to music seem shopworn when he faces life and lust.
Musically, he knows what he's talking about. Here, he sees
what he always refuses to talk about: the banality of fleshliness.
The loving couple remain in the uncontoured shadow of the
tree. They are obviously going to submit humbly to whatever
comes: a denunciation or a quick blow. Rain falls harder. No
blow falls. The couple's senses focus on shelter and protection:
Is the blow about to fall? The attacker hesitates. The couple,
unnoticed, they hope, retreat backward into some cover. They
would like to stand up and dash away. Dash away! Both are
very young. Klemmer has just seen adolescents wallowing like
pigs. He wants to swing out his stick and hurl it into alien
yielding. But his weapon is still beating down on his own thigh.
He doesn't want to emerge from this night without prey. Standing here and generating fear, Klemmer achieves something he
can take to Erika, who's asleep now. He can also bring her a
puff of fresh air from distant plains, which she needs.

Klemmer swings freely through space: a freshly oiled door
hinge. If he swings forward, the lovers can expect pain. If he
swings back, he may open an escape hatch. The two children
flinch away until their backs come up against something solid,
which prevents their escape. Their spirits are willing, but their
flesh won't find the way unless they dash off to the side. Suddenly, the situation appeals to Klemmer. He goes through familiar muscle exercises. Standing, he checks one or two paddle
reflexes, though without water. This living image has substance, yet is easy to perceive. Two opponents facing him.
Manageable, and also cowardly, unwilling to fight. Will Klemmer seize this opportunity or let it pass unused? He is master
of the situation. He can express sympathy or act as the avenger
for disturbance of the park peace by corruptible youth. He can
also notify the authorities. But he has to decide quickly, for

the utter absence of other people makes escape so tempting. Klemmer's "Stop thief!" would be fruitless; he'd just stand uselessly in the landscape, and the land of his anger would retreat, his victims would be far away. The young couple notice very slight qualms in the man's voice. Perhaps an irresolution that Klemmer revealed overhastily, without realizing it himself. But it's a signal for the two children! He seems to have shifted imperceptibly from his standpoint of violence. They grab the opportunity. It won't knock again. Since he's not in water, Klemmer wonders: What should I do? The two children detour around a tree trunk and dash away. They are practically hurled by Klemmer's massive presence. Their soles thud dully on the meadow ground. Its lining, the earth, shines bright in certain places. They've forgotten some sort of jacket, or is it a short coat? A child's coat? Klemmer doesn't take off in hot pursuit. He'd rather trample the jacket. He doesn't look for a purse or wallet in its pockets. He doesn't look for an ID card. He doesn't look for valuables. He tramples the jacket underfoot, and makes himself at home in his trampling: a chained elephant, whose leg irons leave him only a few inches of free play, which he nonetheless knows how to exploit to the fullest. He tramples the jacket into the ground. He could cite no grounds for his trampling. Yet he gets angrier and angrier; the entire lawn is now his sworn enemy. Stubbornly and without inner calm, Walter Klemmer tramples the soft pillow underfoot, in his own peculiar rhythm. He tramples the jacket to pieces, slowly growing tired.

After leaving the park, Walter Klemmer walks through the streets for a while, aimlessly and shiftlessly. Lack of direction and light-footed energy carry him along while others sleep. A balloon of violence floats in his guts. The balloon never bumps into any wall of his body. Klemmer may feel disoriented, but his route seems to be oriented in a specific direction, toward a specific woman. Many things strike Klemmer as hostile, but he confronts no adversary, his goal is too precious: a very special lady with talent. He wavers between two or three women, then opts for this one. He will not sacrifice her for the sake of a fight. He therefore sidesteps violence, although he will not skirt it if he meets it head on.

He takes an escalator down into an almost empty passage. He buys a half-liquid ice at a small cart. He is handed the ice lovelessly and carelessly by a man disguised with a cap; the man doesn't realize how close his heedlessness brings him to getting beaten up. The man is not beaten. His cap suggests a sailor or a cook or both; the ageless face suggests fatigue. The ice is sucked up from the cup in two quick gulps by Klemmer's funnel-shaped mouth. Few people arrive, few people depart. Few remain seated in the glass house of the fast-food joint. The ice was lukewarm and insipid. Persistence nestles in Klemmer's comfortable calm. Its essence solidifies slowly; a tender effort takes shape in order to attack. All he cares about now is the end point of his trip; if he has any say in the matter, he'll reach his destination shortly. Not without rearing for a good fight, but he won't fight. Instead, Klemmer lopes through the streets toward a certain woman. She's probably waiting for him, she must be. And now, immodest in his wishes, uncompromising in his demands, he is going back to her. He has something to tell her, something that will be completely new to her; and he has a lot to say. He has a lot to dish out. Klemmer, a boomerang, is drawn to nothing but this woman, returning to her with new concepts of their common goal. Klemmer looks for the eye of his mental hurricane, where there is supposedly an absolute lull. He briefly wonders whether he ought to step into a coffee shop. I want to spend a few minutes with real people, he muses. This is no small desire in a man who would like to be a human being first and foremost, but is constantly prevented from being one. He does not look for a coffee shop. Dirty rags leave sticky traces on aluminum counters, under which colorfully glazed cakes and pastries, topped with whipped cream, wait in showcases. Stagnant drops, greasy smears on the planks of the sausage stands. No morning wind as yet; it will be sniffed like a wounded deer. Rhythm is intensified. Only one cab at the taxi stop, but it's hailed right away.

Klemmer has arrived at Erika's building. How keen the joy of arrival. Who would have thought! Anger resides in Klemmer. The man makes no attempt to announce himself by throwing stones, as a boy does at a girl's window. Student Klemmer has grown up overnight. He would never have guessed how quickly a fruit ripens. He does nothing to be let in. He looks up at various dark windows and silently gets his bearings. He looks up at a specific dark window, not knowing whether it's hers. He senses that the window belongs partly to Erika and partly to her mother. He assumes it is the conjugal bedroom. For the married couple: Erika and Mother. Klemmer cuts the lovingly tightened string to Erika and ties it to something new, in which Erika will play only a featured part, the role of means to the end. In the future, Klemmer will balance work and play. Soon he'll be done with school, then he'll have more time for his wet hobby. He won't desire any attention from this woman. He won't desire anything that hasn't been perfected. He will either attend to her or not, as he sees fit. A line of sweat digs into his right temple, quickly running down. His breath whistles. He ran for miles in rather warm weather. He does a breathing exercise that the athlete is familiar with. Klemmer notices he is shunning thoughts in order to avoid thinking about the unthinkable. Everything in his mind is quick and ephemeral. The impressions vary. The end is clear, the means are delineated.

Klemmer squeezes into the entranceway and unzips his jeans. He nestles into the maternal cavern, thinking about Frau Erika and jerking off. He is concealed from observers. Although distracted, he is concentratedly aware of his core, which has formed down below. He has a pleasant awareness of his body. He has the rhythm of youth. He is performing work in and of itself. He is the sole beneficiary. Throwing back his head, Klemmer masturbates up toward a dark window, not even knowing whether it's the right one. He is unmoved and relentless. His feelings are unstirred as he works on himself tenaciously. The window, unlit, stretches overhead like a landscape. He is stationed one story lower. Klemmer jerks vehemently; he has no intention of ever completing the job. He works the field of his body without joy or pleasure. He wishes to restore nothing and destroy nothing. He does not want to go up to that woman; but if someone opened the front door, he would go straight up to her. Wild horses couldn't stop him! Klemmer rubs himself so discreetly that anyone who saw him would open the door with no suspicion. He could stand here forever, as active as ever; he could also try to gain admission immediately. It's entirely up to him. Without resolving to wait for a late homecomer to unlock the door for him, Klemmer waits. Even if it takes all night. And if he has to wait until morning, when the first person emerges from the building—Klemmer tugs on his bloated cock and waits for the door to open.

Walter Klemmer stands in the entranceway, wondering how far he would go. He now has two lusts, hunger and thirst, both together. He gives in to his lust for the woman by rubbing himself. He experiences physically, and she should likewise experience physically, what it means to play games with him, games without aims. Palm off empty packages on him. Her

soft physical wrapping has to welcome him! He'll yank her out
of her lukewarm bed, away from her mother's side.

No one comes. No one unlocks the door and opens it wide.
In this changeable world, in which night has fallen, Klemmer
knows only the constant factor of his feelings. Eventually, he
goes to a phone booth. Aside from some decent baring, he has
remained calm and disciplined in the entranceway. Awaiting
late homecomers. To the outside world, he offered an image
of calm without anger. Inside him, his senses are rebelling.
The homecomers shouldn't see him like that, they shouldn't
get suspicious. He is touched by his own feelings. He is moved
by himself. Soon the woman will get off the high horse of Art
and join him in the river of Life. She will become part of hustle
and bustle and shame. Art is not a Trojan horse, Klemmer says
tonelessly to the woman upstairs, who seeks content only in
art. There's a phone booth not too far off. It is instantly used.
Klemmer despises the vandals who ripped the directories from
their moorings. Now some life might go unsaved because a
number is needed but not found.

Erika Kohut sleeps a fitful sleep of the just next to Mother,
who has often treated her unjustly, yet calmly dreams away.
Erika Kohut does not deserve such slumber; after all, someone
is fitfully roaming about because of her. With the well-known
ambition of her sex, she hopes, even in her dreams, for a happy
ending and ultimate enjoyment. She dreams about the man
taking her by storm. Please do so. Today she voluntarily went
without TV. Yet today of all days she could have seen her
favorite subject: foreign streets, into which she projects herself,
wallowing safe and sound. Mostly American landscapes, endless, because America practically knows no limits. She wishes
for the exaggerated attention and affection that TV people enjoy. Maybe I'll even go on a trip with that man, Erika muses
anxiously. But what will become of Mother? Not everyone can

exit at the right moment. Her body involuntarily reacts by
exuding moisture; it can't always be steered by its will. Mother
sleeps on, graciously unaware. The telephone rings. Who can
that be so late at night? Erika is startled. She knows right away
who that can be so late at night. An inner voice, to which she
is related, tells her. This voice is unjustly called love. The
woman is delighted by her victory and hopes for a loving cup.
She will put it next to her vases, giving it the place of honor
in her new apartment. She is completely liberated. Through
the dark room and hallway, she gropes her way to the telephone. The telephone shrieks. Love is the only reason why she
will deviate from her stipulations. She is looking forward to
deviating from them. What a relief. Mutuality in love is exceptional, after all. Usually, only one person loves, while the
other is busy running as fast as his feet can carry him. This
situation requires two people, and one is telephoning the other.
Isn't that great! How convenient. How marvelous.

The teacher has left a warm hollow in the bed, and it is
slowly cooling off. She has also left her mother, who is not yet
waking up. What an ungrateful child, to forget her tried-and-
true companion of so many years! The man on the telephone
demands that she unlock the front door immediately. Erika
clutches the receiver. She didn't expect his proximity. She actually expected the tenderest words, the announcement of nocturnal wishes and complete proximity very soon, perhaps
tomorrow afternoon at three, in a small café. Erika expected a
precise plan from the man in order to build a nest. They'll talk
about it tomorrow and during the next few days! They'll discuss
whether the relationship can be a joy forever; then they'll start
the relationship. The man enjoys and waits unwillingly; the
woman sets up whole blocks of buildings, because in her, everything is affected in its terrible and ominous totality. That disagreeable fact: woman and her feelings. This woman instantly

sets up complicated structures, similar to a wasps' nest, in order
to make herself at home inside. And Walter Klemmer generally
feels that once she's begun to build, he won't be able to get rid
of her. He's outside the front door again, waiting for it to open,
which would benefit Erika. It's now or never! Erika pedantically
weighs every last detail, then gets the keys. Mother sleeps on.
In her sleep, nothing shoots through the core of her brain,
because she already has her house and a daughter inside it. She
finds plans unnecessary. The daughter anticipates a reward for
long years of disciplined accomplishments. It was worth it. Very
few women wait for Mr. Right. Most women take the first and
worst Mr. Wrong. Erika chooses the very last one to come
along, and he is truly the best of the lot. There's no surpassing
him! The woman thinks—almost as if forced to—in terms of
numbers and equivalents. She imagines she is being rewarded
for loyal service in the realm of Art. If male willpower can
actually lead her away from her tried-and-true mother, then
her work has been a success. Fine with me. The student will
soon be getting his degree, she's got a job with a decent salary.
She decides for him that the age difference is trivial.

Erika opens the building door and trustingly puts herself in
the man's hands. She jokes that she is in his power. She swears
she would rather forget all about my stupid letter, but what's
done is done. She had a mishap, but she'll make up for it,
dearest. Why do we need letters? After all, we know everything
there is to know about each other. We reside in each other's
most intimate thoughts! And our thoughts nourish us constantly with their honey. Erika Kohut, who would not remind
the man of his body's failure for all the tea in China says:
Come right in! Walter Klemmer, who would rather act as if
his body had never failed him in the first place, enters the
building. Many things are made available to him, and he is

flattered by the selection. Some things he's simply going to take!

He says to Erika: Let's be clear about one thing. There's nothing worse than a woman who wants to rewrite Creation. A topic for humor magazines. Klemmer is material for a whole novel. He enjoys himself but never consumes himself. On the contrary, he enjoys his coldness, those ice cubes in his oral cavity. Acquiring property freely means being able to leave at any time. The property remains behind and waits. He will soon pass the phase represented by this woman; he could swear it. After all, she has rejected mutual feelings, an offer he originally meant sincerely. Now it's too late. Time for my conditions, K. proposes. He will not be laughed at a second time; K. assures her on his word of honor. He threateningly asks her who she thinks she is. This question is not improved by repeated use.

Walter Klemmer pushes the woman back into the apartment. A numb exchange of words results, because she won't put up with it. Sometimes she forestalls with words. During the exchange, she complains to the man that he has pushed her into her own apartment, where he is only a visitor. But then she discards a bad habit: constant nagging. I have a lot to learn, she says modestly. She even catches an excuse in her claws, and places the still-bleeding prey at his feet. She doesn't want to mess everything up right off the bat, she thinks. She regrets making so many mistakes, most of them right off the bat. The first step is always the hardest: Erika proves the importance of a true beginning. Mother now awakens slowly, hesitantly, because of the harsh exchange of words, as she is forced to realize. Mother's ambition is to rule. Who is talking here in the middle of the night, as loudly as in the daytime, and in my own apartment, with my own daughter? The man reacts with a threatening gesture. The two women are already laying the bricks for a counterattack against the lone man. Erika is slapped in the face before she even knows what's happening. Did you see that?! Yes, Erika did see that. The slap was dealt by Klemmer, and successfully! Astonished, she holds her cheek and fails to reply. Mother is dumbstruck. If anyone is going to slap Erika, it'll be Mother. A few seconds later, while Klemmer remains silent, Erika tells him to leave immediately. Mother backs her up and turns her back on them to demonstrate that she is disgusted by the entire spectacle. In triumph, Klemmer softly asks the daughter: This isn't how you pictured it originally, is it? Mother is astonished that the man will not vanish without an argument. She's not the least bit interested in what they're saying, she informs the air around her. No voice is raised in loud complaint. A second slap strikes Frau Erika's other cheek. This is no loving encounter of skin and skin. Erika keeps her whimpering down because of the neighbors. Mother perks up her ears. She is forced to realize that her daughter is being degraded into something like a piece of athletic gear. Mother indignantly points out that he is damaging someone else's property, namely hers! Mother concludes: Get out of here at once. And as fast as you can.

The man clutches this mother's daughter, as if appropriating a piece of equipment. Erika is still half numbed by sleep. She doesn't understand how it is possible that love can be requited so poorly—*her* love. We always expect rewards for our accomplishments. We believe that other people's accomplishments do not have to be rewarded. We hope to acquire those accomplishments more cheaply. Mother gets into gear; she wishes to involve the police. She is therefore shoved back violently into her room, where she crashes to the floor. Klemmer explains that he is not talking to her. It just won't sink in. Up till now, Mother always had the choice. Klemmer assures her we have time—all night, if necessary. Erika does not blossom upward anymore. Klemmer asks her whether this is what she imagined. Swelling up like a siren, she says no. Mother struggles into a seated position and threatens the student with something dreadful, in which Mother will play a decisive part. If worst comes to worst, she will get help from other people. That's what the aging saint swears. And he'll be sorry he's doing these things to a woman who should be treated with care, a woman who might also become a mother someday. He should think about *his* mother! Erika's mother feels sorry for his mother because she had to give birth to him. Meanwhile Erika's mother fights her way to the door, but there she is once again rudely shoved back. In order to shove her back, Walter Klemmer has to ignore Erika briefly. He then locks Mother's room, leaving Mother inside its narrow confines. The key to this bedroom is supposed to lock the daughter out whenever Mother finds such punishment desirable and necessary. In her initial shock, Mother thinks: Locked out! She scratches on the door. She whimpers and threatens. Klemmer grows stronger in the face of resistance. Woman spells danger for the competitive athlete before a difficult competition. Erika's and his wishes get all tangled up. Erika sobs: This isn't how I pictured it. She says what people say after a play: Is that all there is? On the one hand, Erika is inundated by her flesh; on the other hand, by a violence that developed out of unrequited love.

Erika expects him at least to say he's sorry, if not more. But no. She is glad Mother can't butt in. At last, Erika can deal privately with private things. Who thinks of Mother or mother love now, aside from a person who wants to produce a child? The man in Klemmer speaks out. Erika tries to ignite his willpower with a deliberate, if trivial, exposure. She pleads until the kindling blazes up and one can add a thicker log of desire. Her face is slapped yet again, although she says: Please, not my head! She hears something about her age, which is at least thirty-five, whether she likes it or not. She is slowly dimmed by his sexual repulsion. Her pupils cloud over more and more. The benefits of hatred are finally donated to Klemmer. He is enchanted. Reality clears up for him like an overcast day in late summer. He was not being true to his own self, that was why he camouflaged this wonderful hatred with love for such a long time. This camouflage appealed to him for a long time. But now he's sloughing it off.

The woman on the floor regards various things as passionate desire; his behavior would be halfway appropriate to passion alone. That's something Erika Kohut once heard. But that's enough, darling! Let's start with something better! She would like to see pain eliminated from the repertoire of love gestures. Now she's feeling it personally, physically, and she begs to return to the normal version of love. Let us approach the other with understanding. Walter Klemmer overcomes the woman violently, even though she says she's changed her mind. Please don't hit me. My ideal is shared feelings again. Erika revises her opinions too late. She expresses the opinion that she, as a woman, needs lots of warmth and affection. She holds her hand over her mouth, which is bleeding at one corner. It's an impossible ideal, the man replies. He's only waiting for the woman to retreat a bit; then he'll go after her. He is driven by a hunter's instinct. It's the instinct of the water athlete and engineer, warning him of depths and rocks. If the woman reaches out to him, he's gone! Erika pleads with Klemmer to show his good side. But Klemmer is getting to know freedom.

Walter Klemmer smashes his right fist, not too hard and not too soft, into Erika's belly. She tumbles back again after standing upright. Erika huddles over, pressing her hands into her abdomen. This is the stomach. The man managed to do it without straining himself. He is not at odds with himself. On the contrary, he has never been so intensely at one with himself. He jeers at her: Where are her cords and ropes? And where are her chains? I'm only executing your orders, madame. Now gags and straps can't help you, mocks Klemmer, who produces the effects of gags and straps without using such aids. Numbed by liqueur, Mother drums her fists on the door. She doesn't know what's happening to her, she doesn't know what to do. She is also nervous because she doesn't know what's happening to her daughter. A mother can see without seeing. She didn't oversee her child's freedom, and now someone else is heedlessly mishandling that freedom. From now on, I'll keep watch twice as carefully, Mother promises herself, hoping the young man will leave something still worth supervising. She finally twisted the child into shape, and now someone else is twisting her again. Mother is raging.

Meanwhile, Klemmer is laughing his head off at the flesh he has twisted: At your age, you'd better say good night! Erika weeps, citing the things they have experienced and suffered during lessons. She pleads: Don't you remember the differences between sonatas? He makes fun of men who put up with anything from women. That's not the kind of man *he* is. She's gone much too far. She's generally far gone—where are her whips and restraints now? Klemmer gives her a choice: either you or me. His solution is: me. But you're resurrected in my hatred, the man comforts her. Maltreating her head, which is poorly shielded by her arms, he tosses her a hard tidbit: If you weren't a victim, you couldn't become one! He asks her what's going to happen with her marvelous letter. No answers are necessary.

Mother, behind the bedroom door, expects the worst for her private one-person zoo. Erika, weeping, lists all the good things she's done for the student, her tireless efforts in training his musical taste and perfecting his musical abilities. Bawling, Erika mentions the benefits of her love—an extra assignment for the man and the student. She tries to gain control. Only naked power prevents her. The man is stronger. Erika foams and fumes: He can only control her with brute force. For which she is hit twice and thrice.

In Klemmer's hatred, the woman suddenly grows out freely like a tree. This tree is pruned and clipped and has to learn to take it. A hand numbly smacks a face. Behind the door, Mother doesn't know what's happening, but she is so agitated that she joins in the weeping. She wishes she could take one of her countless trips to the half-emptied liqueur cabinet. She cannot call for help: The telephone is in the hallway, unreachable.

Klemmer jeers at Erika about her age: A woman in her condition has nothing to expect from him in regard to love. He was only pretending, he never cared for her, it was just a scientific experiment. Klemmer thus denies his honorable needs. And where are your famous ropes now? He slices the air as if with a razor. She should stick to men her own age or older, he proposes, as he disposes of her. Klemmer strikes away at her aimlessly. His rage did not seek the opportunity to inflict evil or injustice. Quite the contrary. His rage was formed, gradually but thoroughly, by his falling in love. After a detailed investigation, Erika showed this man the appreciation of her love, and bang! What happens?

If he is to advance in love and emotion, he has to destroy the woman who actually laughed at him when she had the upper hand! She expected him to tie her, gag her, rape her, she demanded it, and now she's getting her just deserts. Just scream, Klemmer demands, just scream. The woman weeps loudly. Behind the door, the woman's mother weeps too. She doesn't even know why.

Erika, bleeding slightly, curls up like an embryo, and the work of destruction progresses. In Erika, the man sees many other women he wanted to get rid of. He snaps the words in

her face. He's still young. I have my whole life ahead of me.
Yes, now it's really gonna be great! After I graduate, I'm gonna
take a long vacation abroad. He holds out the bait, then yanks
it back: I'm going alone! No one can claim you're young, can
they, Erika? If he's young, she's old. If he's a man, she's a
woman. Walter Klemmer whimsically kicks her in the ribs as
she lies on the floor. He doses the violence out so carefully
that nothing breaks. He has always controlled his own body,
at least. Walter Klemmer steps across Erika, a threshold, out
into freedom. She brought this on by trying to control him
and his desires. This is what she gets.

He has a dark sense, a presentiment, about this woman. She
loudly disapproves of his hatred, but only because she has to
suffer from it physically. She yells and starts begging in disorderly words. Mother hears her yell and yells along in numb
fury. The man might not leave anything worth controlling in
the daughter. Furthermore, Mother is animated by animal fear
that something is happening to her child. She is driven to kick
against the door and threaten. But this door yields less than
her child's willpower did ages ago. Mother utters fears that
cannot be heard through the door. She shrieks horrible threats
about forced entry. She reminds her daughter of the prophesied
consequences of male love, but the daughter doesn't hear. The
daughter, weeping unrestrainedly, is kicked in the belly. Klemmer's actions pleasurably roll across female disapproval. Klemmer is delighted that he can ignore their disapproval. The man
wants to snuff out everything that Erika was, but it's not working. Erika keeps reminding him of what she used to be for him.
I beg you, she begs.

Behind the door, Mother expresses the fear that the child,
in fear of the man, will cringe and cower. Besides, her body
could be injured. Mother is worried about the old pod of her
own body. She implores God and His son. Since any loss would

be definitive, Mother is scared she may lose her daughter. Long
years of arduous training would be gone with the wind. The
training would be replaced by new feats with the man. Mother
will brew some tea once she can get out and someone wants
tea. She squeals something about revenge! About reporting
this to the authorities! Erika blubbers over a chasm of love.
The chasm points out that her written requests struck the man
as too frivolous. It tells her that his failure was too humiliating.
She's been going out in public thinking she was the best. But
once she was exposed to the public, her part in its life proved
very minor. And soon it will be too late.

Erika lies on the floor, the hallway runner sliding out beneath
her. She says please don't. Her letter doesn't deserve such
punishment. Klemmer is unleashed, but Erika is not leashed.
The man casually hits her and mordantly asks: Well, where's
your letter now? This is all you get. He boasts that he doesn't
have to tie her up, as she can see for herself. He asks her
whether the letter can help her now. While hitting her lightly,
Klemmer tells the woman that this is exactly what she wanted.
Erika tearfully protests that this isn't what she wanted, she
wanted something different. Well then you'll have to express
yourself more carefully next time, the man replies. Kicking
her, he demonstrates the simple equation: I am I. And I'm not
ashamed. I'm behind me one hundred percent. He threatens
the woman: She has to take him just as he is. I am as I am.
Erika's nose is broken; so is one of her ribs. She buries her
face in her hands, and Klemmer tells her, That's right, your
face isn't so great, is it? There are more attractive faces, says
the specialist, waiting for the woman to say there are also more
unattractive ones. Her nightgown has slid down, and Klemmer
thinks about raping her. But, to show his scorn for female sex
appeal, he says: First I have to drink a glass of water. He lets
Erika know that he is less attracted to her than a bear to a

hollow tree trunk in which the bees are still residing. Erika
caught his eye with musical accomplishments, not beauty. And
now she can simply wait a couple of minutes. I've solved the
problem in my own way; the engineering student is satisfied.
Mother curses. Erika thinks about escaping. She is used to
thinking, not acting. Always hermetically sealed, she has never
captured a prize.

In the kitchen, water runs for a long time. The man likes
his water cold. He is fully aware that his actions can have
consequences. He is a man, and he accepts the consequences.
The water has a slight taste of malaise. She'll have to suffer
the consequences too, he thinks more joyously. His piano lessons are obviously terminated. So he can really devote himself
to athletics. Nothing is agreeable to anyone here present. Nonetheless, something must be done. No one attempts reconcili-
ation. Klemmer listens, to hear whether the woman is willing
to assume at least part of the blame. You're at least partly to
blame, you've got to admit it, Klemmer admits to the woman.
You can't get someone all turned on and then turn everything
off. If a person feels too good, then you can't just close the
gate. Klemmer furiously kicks the door of a magic closet with
unknown contents. The door springs open, unexpectedly revealing a garbage can with a plastic liner. The shock wave makes
the topmost garbage come hippety-hopping out; various items
are distributed over the kitchen floor. Mainly bones. There is
burned meat in a pan. Klemmer involuntarily laughs. Outside,
his laughter hurts the woman. She suggests that we can talk
about everything, please. She is already publicly accepting part
of the blame. As long as he's here, there's hope. Please don't
go away.

She wants to get up but can't. She falls back. From behind
her barricade, which she didn't put up, Mother screams at her
daughter! What's happening to you? The daughter tells her

everything's all right. Everything's being taken care of. The daughter begs the man to let Mommy out. Crying "Mama," Erika crawls over to the door, and Mother calls Erika's name louder from behind the door. In the same breath, Mother utters a curse, as is her wont.

Klemmer has been fortified by cold water. He has been somewhat cooled off by cold water. Erika has almost reached Mother's door, but is then thrown back by the student. Again she begs him: Not on her head or her hands. Klemmer tells her he can't go out in this condition, he would only frighten the people he meets. It's all her fault that he's in such a state—just be a little nice to me, Erika. Please. He now rages across her, full speed ahead. He licks her face and asks for love. Who else but a loving woman can give him love more generously, and with fewer conditions? Asking for love, he opens himself by opening his fly. Asking for love and understanding, he resolutely penetrates the woman. He energetically demands his right to affection, a right that anyone can have, even the worst people. Klemmer, one of the worst, bores around inside Erika. He awaits a moan of pleasure from her. Erika feels nothing. Nothing comes. Nothing happens. It's either too late or too early. The woman openly avows that she seems to be the victim of deception, because she feels nothing. The core of this love is annihilation. She hopes that she loves him, Klemmer wishes that she loved him. Klemmer lightly hits Erika's face to evoke a moan. At heart, he doesn't care why she moans. Erika wishes for desire, but she desires nothing and feels nothing. She therefore begs the man to stop right away! Hitting her harder, with the palm of his hand, amid tiring requests for love, he turns his actions into a process of violence. An extreme mountain climbing. The woman does not submit cheerfully, but the man wants her to surrender voluntarily. He has no need to force a woman. He yells at her to receive him joyfully! He sees her unmoved face on which his presence leaves only one stamp: pain. Does that mean I might as well go? asks Klemmer, while beating her. He is performing his personal best for this woman, so he can finally get rid of his lust. Once and for all, as he threatens her. Erika whimpers, begging him to stop, because it hurts. Purely out of laziness or indolence, Klemmer cannot withdraw from the woman before he is done. He asks: Love me. He licks and beats her alternately. He is red with anger as he puts his head to hers. Mother wishes it were over. She bangs on the door like a machine gun. Ignoring the neighbors, she shoots rapid-fire. Klemmer increases his speed; he's moving very fast. He does not shoot over his target, he hits the bull's-eye. The champion has done it again.

He quickly cleans himself with a tissue, then throws the wet clump on the floor next to Erika. He advises her not to tell anyone. For her own good. He apologizes for his behavior. He explains his behavior by saying he just couldn't help it. Things like that happen to a guy. He makes some vague promise to Erika, who remains lying on the floor. I'm in a hurry: The man demands forgiveness in his way. I have to go now: The man offers the woman love and veneration in his way. If he had a single red rose, he would give it to Erika on the spot. He departs with a stock phrase: "Well, so long." He checks the hallway table, looking for the key to the front door. It's not such a good thing—two women so alone with each other. That's his advice for better living. He tugs at Erika's reins. She ought to think about the generation gap as objectively as possible! Klemmer suggests that Erika should circulate more, if not with him then on her own. He offers to escort her to functions to which he knows he'd never take her. He confesses: Well, that's it. Out of sheer curiosity, he asks her whether she'd ever try this sort of thing again with a man. He supplies himself with the only logical answer: No thanks. He reaches into the treasure trove of the past: Don't start anything you can't finish. And then he laughs. He has to laugh: You see, that's what happens. He advises her: Be careful! She ought to play a record now to calm down. This is a long goodbye, he's repeated it several times. He asks if anything's wrong, then answers his own question: Don't worry! By the time you get married, everything will be just fine and dandy. Drawing on popular wisdom, Klemmer peers into the future. He has to go home unkissed, but, on the other hand, did he ever kiss! He does not leave without remuneration. He has received his due. And the woman certainly got what was coming to her. What you see is what you get. That's Klemmer's reaction to Erika after Erika failed to respond physically to him.

He bounds down the steps, unlocks the front door, and throws the key back inside, on the floor. The tenants are left unprotected behind an unlocked door while Klemmer goes his own way. Ambling along, he decides he will glare impudently or arrogantly at any passersby. Today he will be a living provocation and burn his bridges behind him. He flips over on the parallel bar of self-assurance: The two women are not going to waste any words about what happened—for their own sakes. He weighs possible carrying costs and interest payments, but only briefly.

There are no more cars out, and if one were to come along, Klemmer's youthful reflexes would help him. You just resolutely jump aside. Young and quick, Klemmer can face anyone! He says: Tonight I could tear trees out with my bare hands! He is very glad that he feels a lot better now than before. He pisses powerfully against a tree. He deliberately allows only positive thoughts to pass through his brain: That is the entire secret of his success. You see, his brain is a one-way brain! You use and then you snuff. Klemmer doesn't want to drag any heavy weights around; that's his resolution. He walks in the middle of the street: a challenge.

❏

The new day finds Erika alone but covered with the bandages and poultices of maternal solicitude. Erika could have started this day with the man. She now meets the day ill prepared. No one appeals to the authorities to have Klemmer arrested. The weather, however, is beautiful. Mother remains unusually silent. Now and then, she tosses a well-meant ball, but never gets it into the basket, which she has hung much too high, all because of her daughter. For years, she kept hanging the hoop a bit higher and a bit higher still. Now you can barely see it.

Mother announces that her daughter should circulate more, get to know new places and new faces. At her age, it's high time. Mother calculates for her tongue-tied child: It's not good for you to stay with an old lady like me all the time, you're so young and exuberant. Given Erika's lack of knowledge about people, which she has just demonstrated, Erika has missed the mark for the second time this year. Mother discusses what is good for Erika. The fact that Erika realizes it too is the first step toward self-knowledge. There are other men, Mother anxiously comforts her about the nebulous future. Erika remains silent, not unamiably so. Mother is afraid that Erika is thinking now, and she expresses her fear. A person who doesn't speak could easily be thinking. Mother demands that Erika reveal her thoughts, rather than let them eat into her. If Erika thinks anything, she has to tell Mother, to keep her informed. Mother is scared of silence. Is her daughter vindictive? Will she dare talk back?

The sun rises over dusty wastes. Red washes the building fronts. Trees have covered themselves with green. They decide to become decorative. Plants set buds in order to put in their two cents. People move around in all this. Speech bubbles out of their mouths.

A lot of things hurt in Erika, and she moves cautiously, gingerly. Her bandages aren't always snug, but they've been put on lovingly. The morning could inspire Erika to find a reason why she has sealed herself off from everything all these years. In order to emerge grandly from behind the walls one day and surpass everyone else! Why not now? Today? Erika puts on an old dress in the outdated short style. The dress isn't as short as other dresses were back then. The dress is too tight; it doesn't close in back. It is completely outmoded. Mother doesn't like the dress either; it's too short and too tight for her taste. Erika is busting out all over.

Erika will walk through the streets, astonishing everyone; her sheer presence will suffice. Erika's Ministry of the Exterior wears an out-of-date dress, causing some people to look back in mockery.

To cheer her up, Mother suggests an outing—but you can't wear that outfit. Her daughter doesn't hear. Encouraged by her silence, Mother pulls out some hiking maps from old dusty drawers, in which Father used to dig and delve, tracing paths with his finger, looking for destinations, tracking down food stops. In the kitchen, the daughter sticks a sharp knife inside her handbag without being seen. Normally, the knife sees and tastes only dead animals. The daughter doesn't yet know whether she will commit murder or throw herself at the man's feet and kiss them. She will decide later whether to stab him. Or seriously and passionately plead with him. She does not listen to her mother, who is vividly describing routes.

The daughter waits for the man who should come to plead with her. She sits down quietly at the window and weighs departing against staying. First she opts for staying. I may go tomorrow, she decides. She looks down into the street. Then she leaves. The morning lectures are going to start soon at the Engineering School: Klemmer's department. She once asked him about it. Love points the way. Desire is its ignorant advisor.

Erika Kohut goes out, leaving Mother behind; Mother investigates Erika's reasons. For a long time now, Mother has been familiar with time as an extremely malevolent carnivorous plant; but isn't it too early in the day to expose oneself to it?

The child usually begins the day somewhat later; that's why the erosion of the day likewise sets in later.

Erika clutches the warm knife in her bag and walks through the streets, toward her goal. She offers an unfamiliar sight, as if made to flee people. People have no qualms about staring. They make remarks as they turn around. They are not ashamed of their opinion of this woman, they express their opinion. In her irresolute semi-miniskirt, Erika grows to her full height as she enters a hard competition with youth. Youth, visible everywhere, openly laughs at the teacher. Youth laughs at Erika because of her exterior. Erika laughs at youth because of its interior, which has no real substance. A male eye sends a signal to Erika: She shouldn't wear such a short dress. Her legs aren't all that great! The woman walks about, laughing. Her dress doesn't suit her legs and her legs don't suit her dress, as even a moderate critic would put it. Erika rises above herself and others. She anxiously wonders whether she can deal with the man. Youth mocks even downtown. Erika jeers back loudly. Anything they can do, she can do better. She's been doing it longer.

Erika crosses open squares in front of museums. Pigeons soar up. In the face of her resoluteness! Tourists gawk first at Empress Maria Theresa, then at Erika, then back at the empress. Wings rattle. Museum hours are posted. The streetcars on the Ring head toward traffic lights. Sunlight flickers through dust.

Young mothers begin their daily march behind the bars of the
Castle Garden. The first "Prohibited" signs are hurled down
on gravel walks. From their heights, the mothers drip venom.
Everywhere, two or more people now communicate. Colleagues
get together, friends get into arguments. Drivers dash energetically across the Opera Crossing because the pedestrians are
out of sight, remaining underground, where they have to bear
the brunt of any damage they themselves cause. Down there,
they cannot find scapegoats, i.e., drivers. People enter stores
after first evaluating them on the outside. A few people stroll
aimlessly. The office buildings on the Ring swallow up person
after person, people dealing in import/export. In the Aïda Café,
mothers discuss their daughters' sexual activities, finding them
dangerously premature. They praise their sons' commitment
to school and sports.

Erika Kohut clutches the aberration of a real knife in her
handbag. Is the knife going on a trip or is Erika going to eat
humble pie and beg for male forgiveness? She doesn't know as
yet; she will decide when she arrives. The odds are still on the
knife. Let it dance! The woman is heading toward the Secession
Gallery. A renowned artist is showing something after which
art can no longer be what it was. From here, Engineering, the
opposite pole of art, is already visible in the distance. Erika
only has to cross over and then through Ressel Park. Wind
wafts now and then. Voices of the youthful thirst for knowledge
accumulate here. Eyes graze Erika, who faces them. At last,
people are looking at me, Erika exults. For years upon years,
she avoided such gazes by remaining monoecious. But if something lasts and lasts, it eventually erupts. Erika does not confront the gazes unarmed—you dear little knife, you. Someone
laughs. Not everyone laughs so loud. Most people don't laugh.
They don't laugh because they see nothing but themselves.
They don't notice Erika.

Groups of young people coagulate in the flowing stream. They form vanguards and rear guards. Committed young men resolutely have experiences. They keep talking about them. Some want experiences with themselves, others experiences with others: to each his own.

On the facade of the Engineering School, the columns bear the metallic male heads of the institute's famous scientists, who invented bombs and defense systems.

A gigantic church, the Karlskirche, crouches like a toad in the midst of the bleak wasteland. Water bubbles up, self-assured and chatty. One walks purely on stone, except in Ressel Park, which is meant to be a green oasis. You can also take the subway, if you feel like it.

Erika Kohut discovers Walter Klemmer in a group of co[n]genial students at various stages of knowledge. They are laug[h]ing loudly together. But not at Erika, whom they do not e[ven] notice. Walter Klemmer loudly demonstrates that he is [...] playing hooky today. He has not had to rest longer afte[r...] night than after other nights. Erika counts three boy[s...] one girl, who likewise seems to be studying some k[ind of] engineering, thus constituting a technological inno[...] Walter Klemmer cheerfully puts his arm around her [shoul]ders. The girl laughs loud, briefly burying her blond[...] Klemmer's throat; his neck likewise has to carry [...] head. The girl laughs so hard she can barely sta[nd...] her body language communicates. The girl has [...] Klemmer. The others agree with him. Walter Kle[mmer] laughs and shakes his hair. Sun embraces him [...] circles him. Klemmer keeps laughing loudly, an[d...] join in at the tops of their lungs. What's so f[unny...] latecomer and then has to join in the laughte[r...] the bug. Something is described to him in splu[...] and now he finally knows what he's laugh[...]

outsplutters the others because he has to make up for lost laughing time.

Erika Kohut stands there, looking. She watches. It is broad daylight, and Erika watches. When the group has laughed its fill, it turns toward the Engineering School. As the students move, they keep bursting into hearty guffaws. They interrupt themselves with their own laughter.

Windows flash in the light. They do not open to this woman. They do not open to just anyone. There is no good person, although he is called for. Many would like to help, but do not. The woman twists her neck very far to the side and bares her teeth like a sick horse. No one puts a hand on her, no one takes anything from her. She feebly peers back over her shoulder. The knife should dig into her heart and twist around! The remainder of the necessary strength fails. Her eyes alight on nothing, and, with no burst of rage, fury, or passion, Erika Kohut stabs a place on her shoulder, which instantly shoots out blood. The wound is harmless, but dirt and pus must not get in. The world, unwounded, does not stand still. The young people must have vanished into the building for a long time. One building lies next to the other. The knife is placed back in the handbag. A gap yawns in Erika's shoulder; tender tissue has divided unresistingly. The steel has entered, and Erika exits. She places a hand on the wound. No one follows her. Many people come toward her, forking around her like water around a dead ship's hull. None of the terrible pains, expected at any second, begin. A car window blazes.

Erika's back, where the zipper is partly open, is warmed. Her back is warmed by the ever more powerful sun. Erika walks and walks. Her back warms up in the sun. Blood oozes out of her. People look up from the shoulder to the face. Some turn around. Not all. Erika knows the direction she has to take. She heads home, gradually quickening her step.

Also by Elfriede Jelinek and published by Serpent's Tail

Wonderful, Wonderful Times

Translated by Michael Hulse

'That's brutal violence on a defenceless person, and quite unnecessary, declares Sophie, and she pulls with an audible tearing sound at the hair of the man lying on an untidy heap on the ground. What's unnecessary is best of all, says Rainer, who wants to go on fighting. We agreed on that.'

It is the late 1950s. A man is out walking in a park in Vienna. He will be beaten up by four teenagers, not for his money, he has an average amount – nor for anything he might have done to them, but because arrogance is their way of reacting to the maggot-ridden corpse that is Austria where everyone has a closet to hide their Nazi histories, their sexual perversions and their hatred of the foreigner. Elfriede Jelinek, who wites like an angel of all that is tawdry, shows in *Wonderful, Wonderful Times* how actions of the present are determined by thoughts of the past.

'A dozen years after the collapse of the Third Reich, four adolescents commit a gratuitously violent assault and robbery in a Viennese park. So begins Jelinek's brilliant new novel, an unrelenting and horrifying exploration of postwar Austria' *Publishers Weekly*

'The writing is so strong, it reads as if it wasn't written down at all, but as if the author's demon spirit is entering first a boy and then a girl, a structure, a thing, a totality, to let it speak its horrible truth' *The Scotsman*

Lust

Translated by Michael Hulse

In a quaint Austrian ski resort, things are not quite what they seem.

Hermann, the manager of a paper mill, has decided that sexual gratification begins at home. Which means Gerti – his wife and property. Gerti is not asked how she feels about the use Hermann puts her to. She is a receptacle into which Hermann pours his juices, nastily, briefly, brutally.

The long-suffering and battered Gerti thinks she has found her saviour and love in Michael, a student who rescues her after a day of vigorous use by her husband. But Michael is on his way up the Austrian political ladder, and he is, after all, a man.

In Elfriede Jelinek's *mitteleuropa*, love is as distant from sex as the Alps are from the sea, and the everyday mechanics of husband, wife, and child, become a loveless horror. Both a condemnation of the myth of romantic love and an angry defence of women's sexuality, *Lust* is pornography for pessimists.

A bestseller throughout Europe, *Lust* conforms Elfriede Jelinek as the most challenging writer – female or male – in Europe today. It is a dark, dazzling performance.

'Extraordinarily well-written, with many brilliant turns of phrase, this remains in my mind, as the most disturbing European novel I have read this year' Robert Carver, *New Statesman*

Women as Lovers

Translated by Martin Chalmers

The setting is an idyllic Alpine village where a woman's
underwear factory nestles in the woods.

Two factory workers, Brigitte and Paula, dream and talk about
finding happiness, a comfortable home and a good man.
They realize that their quest will be as hard as work at the
factory.

Brigitte subordinates her feelings and goes for Heinz, a young,
plump, up-and-coming businessman. With Paula, feelings and
dreams become confused. She gets pregnant by Erich, the
forestry worker. He's handsome, so they marry.

Brigitte gets it right.

Paula gets it wrong.

Using the conventions and language of romantic fiction,
Elfriede Jelinek has written a moving tragedy whose power
lies in its refusal to take at face value its characters' dreams
and aspirations.